"JUST WHAT ARE YOU SUGGESTING?"

"I am thirty-two years of age, Miss Carewe. Unmarried. Excessively rich. And considered more than passably handsome."

I gaped at him. The utter arrogance of the man. Did he think I had such designs on him?

"I would sooner live out my life as a spinster than be forced to suffer your company one minute longer," I said.

"Be warned. If you use your wiles on me you will find yourself the loser."

With one quick pull, he brought me up against him. He cupped my chin with his hand and lifted my face to his. I gasped. He could not possibly mean to —

His mouth descended on mine. It was a hard kiss, not a lover's caress but a warning of what fate held for me if I dared cross him.

Also by Penelope Thomas

Master of Blackwood
*Passion's Child**
Thief of Hearts
The Secret

*written under the name P. J. Thomas

Available from
HarperPaperbacks

Harper
Monogram

Indiscretions

⊱ PENELOPE THOMAS ⊰

HarperPaperbacks
A Division of HarperCollinsPublishers

HarperPaperbacks   *A Division of* HarperCollins*Publishers*
10 East 53rd Street, New York, N.Y. 10022

Copyright © 1994 by P. J. Thomas
All rights reserved. No part of this book may be used or reproduced in any manner whatsoever without written permission of the publisher, except in the case of brief quotations embodied in critical articles and reviews. For information address HarperCollins*Publishers,*
10 East 53rd Street, New York, N.Y. 10022.

Cover illustration by Carla Dagwan

First printing: April 1994

Printed in the United States of America

HarperPaperbacks, HarperMonogram, and colophon are trademarks of HarperCollins*Publishers*

❖ 10 9 8 7 6 5 4 3 2 1

1

England, 1879

A door slammed. Glass panes rattled in their wooden casements, and a walking stick tapped a tightly controlled beat against wet flagstones. It was echoed by rapid steps that slapped through the forecourt of the neat brick row house and toward the street where I stood.

The hack I had hired had rolled off into the mizzling rain and malodorous London fog, leaving me alone on the curb. Forgetting the few pieces of luggage the cabbie had dropped at my feet, I turned and looked behind me. An iron gate had been set into the brick wall surrounding 21 Windemere Court, and I peered curiously through the bars.

A tall man, clad in top hat and calf-length dark overcoat, strode down the stone walkway. The brim of his hat and the headlong thrust of his approach hid his face from my gaze. But the waves of anger that emanated from him were as clear to me as the swirls of dark smoke pouring into the sky from an endless stretch of soot-stained chimneys.

My father, God rest his soul, would have viewed my perception as sheer foolishness. Typical of that feminine intuition claimed by women who resented their lack of power and influence. Women who insisted upon according themselves otherworldly abilities as compensation. Since he could expound tirelessly upon the subject, I had learned at a very young age to keep my observations to myself. In time, I had learned to dismiss them, although I had never truly rid myself of the occasional flash of insight.

But even my conservative and practical father would have had to agree that the gentleman I beheld was in a magnificent temper. One had only to note his heightened pace, the hissing, whiplike motion of his walking stick, and the spray splattering from pools of rainwater whenever his boots hit the stones.

It was a short distance from the front door of the row house to the gate, and I hastily stepped to one side to avoid being trampled. My move came none too soon. The hinges creaked a loud protest at the gentleman's rough handling and, scant seconds later, the gate clanged shut behind him.

Immediately upon reaching the street, he turned sharply to his left. Only then did he see me standing directly in his path. His eyes widened and he broke off in midstride, bringing himself to an abrupt and awkward halt. We avoided a collision by mere inches, and he teetered above me, the second button of his overcoat almost brushing the tip of my nose.

I lifted my chin and stared up into strong features and a pair of compelling gray eyes ringed by thick lashes. Had they not been glaring at me, I would have thought them striking. They were set beneath a pair of level, no-nonsense black brows that could only have belonged to a man who was both plain-speaking and honest. As for the rest of his countenance, it was well-balanced and pleasing. Even handsome.

But his brusque manner was not.

"Good Lord!" His fingers tightened on the brass knob of his walking stick. "Not another one?"

"I beg your pardon?"

"Do you, or do you not, intend to enter this establishment?"

"I cannot see how that is any of your business."

"Nor is it," he admitted, undeterred by the coolness of my response. "But I despise charlatans and dislike seeing fools robbed of their income, no matter how eagerly they invite others to steal from them."

Robbed? I was already startled by his assault. His last remarks seemed to be the ramblings of a drunkard or a madman. What harm could come to me in this quiet neighborhood—unless I was to suffer at his hands? Since I could smell no spirits upon his breath, I took a closer look at his face and wondered if I had been misled by his attractiveness and that even brow line. It had evoked a feeling of, if not complete trust, then certainly of mild confidence in his character—despite his foul mood.

He scowled down at me and I became horribly conscious of the sizable difference in our heights and weights. He was almost a foot taller than my quite reasonable five feet, five inches. And, whereas I was slender, he was both solidly and powerfully built. A man capable of single-handedly dealing with a gang of thugs and cracking the skull of a pickpocket for good measure. If he could not be quelled by my grand manner, then stronger steps would have been both useless and blatantly foolhardy. Unnerved, I took a step backward and found myself braced against the brick wall.

"Really, sir." An edge of fear sharpened my tone. "I haven't the faintest notion of what you are talking about. Kindly go on about your business and leave me in peace."

"It would serve you right if I did." He glanced impatiently across the street to where a carriage and driver waited, dark shapes blurred and softened by the fog. With a sad grunt, he turned back to me. "But I am not inclined to give up without a fight. I am talking about Mrs. Medcroft. You cannot mean to hover outside her gate and then pretend you do not know her."

The accusation was no less surprising than hearing the name of my benefactress spoken with such distaste. Briefly, I considered denying our association, slight as it was, purely in the hope of sending him on his way in the quickest possible fashion. That impulse was immediately countered by a sense of loyalty to the generous Mrs. Medcroft. And a glance at the man's expression told me that any attempt at prevarication would have been futile.

Furious, I lifted my chin and matched him glare for glare. "I do not recall making any such claim. But, again, I cannot see what business that is of yours."

"It may well be none. But as it happens, I am trying to do you a service."

"Then you could hardly have expected me to guess as much by your behavior."

"Why, of all the impertinent . . ." At a loss for an acceptable choice of words he broke off and studied my face, his expression an equal mix of annoyance and admiration. But he quickly recovered himself. "Does your family know you are here?"

My lip quivered. "My parents, sir, have been dead this month past, and I cannot rightly say what they do or do not know."

"Damn my soul. I should have guessed." A glow of comprehension lit his face, and I caught a brief glimpse of sympathy in his eyes.

But his statement was no less confusing than his earlier attack. All my mourning dresses were packed in my portmanteau, and I was wearing the only traveling suit I possessed. Since it had been made six months prior to my parents' demise, it had been fashionably cut and stitched from jade green serge. There was only my simple black bonnet to hint at my bereavement. Little enough reason for anyone to have guessed the truth. But even if my parents had not met with misfortune, this stranger's rude behavior was inexcusable. I delivered him a frosty stare that was all the colder for my earlier display of weakness.

He tipped his hat to me in the first show of good manners I had seen from him. "Please, forgive me. It was not my intention to cause you distress. Only to save you from making a serious error in judgment."

"There is nothing the matter with my judgment," I assured him. "And you, sir, have no business accosting young ladies on the street and demanding that they give an account of themselves."

"Of course, of course." He dropped his voice to a soothing level, speaking to me as though I were either a child or someone whose recent tragedy had relieved her of her senses. "But trust me, this is no place for you. You must accept their deaths, however difficult that might be."

"I am not in the habit of taking either advice or

comfort from strangers. Nor do I see what, if anything, this has to do with—"

"You are upset," he countered, smoothly disregarding my objections. "And deservedly so."

He lifted his head and frowned at the clouds and the falling rain. During our short conversation, the drizzle had become a steady downpour. Heavy droplets bounced off the brim of his hat, and I became aware of a small rivulet of water trickling from my bonnet and sliding beneath my collar. I shifted uncomfortably and his attention returned to me.

"Good heavens. You don't even have the sense to carry an umbrella. If you remain here you're certain to catch a chill, and that cannot possibly do you any good in your current frame of mind."

"I would already be dry and warm, save for this interruption."

"Anything less on my part would have been unthinkable. But let me make amends by driving you home. I have a carriage waiting." He moved to take my arm.

I stiffened and glared at him. Did he think me a fool? "I have no intention of going anywhere with you. Now, if you have not the courtesy to depart, then will you please step aside so that I might collect my luggage."

He glanced over his shoulder and, apparently for the first time, noticed the short row of bags sagging beside the curb. Immediately, his demeanor changed. All signs of sympathy and concern vanished, replaced by a menace that made me want to shrink against the brick wall for protection. Only pride held me in place, pride and an intuitive voice that warned me not to show either doubt or fear lest it be my undoing.

His gaze returned to me and he regarded me with hard eyes. "So I have misjudged the situation. You are not calling upon Mrs. Medcroft, but have come to live with her."

"I have."

"No doubt to assist her," he continued in a deceptively quiet voice.

"If that is what she requires."

"Then I will say to you what I have already said to her. If you think to take advantage of me, or any other member of my family, I will soon disabuse you of the notion. Do I make myself clear?"

"Nothing you have yet said is clear," I retorted, filled with the desire to slap him hard across the cheek. "You have harangued me quite enough, sir. If you do not desist I will be forced to call the constables."

His upper lip curled into a sneer. "Hardly the threat I would have expected. But I would not think of detaining you a moment longer. Clearly, *you* are in no danger. I only wish the same could be said of others who mistakenly come to this address in search of help."

With that last remark, he stepped around me and stalked off to the waiting carriage. I watched in disbelief until it had rolled down the street and turned the corner.

And what had all that been about?

With a shake of my head, I collected my luggage and shouldered my way through the gate. It swung shut behind me, nearly snagging the hem of my traveling skirt, and I trudged up the flagstone walk. The train journey from Bristol to London, following upon the funeral and repeated meetings with the solicitors, had been exhausting, and the stranger's attack had robbed me of the last of my energies. I could only be grateful the house stood less than ten feet back from the road. Another step would have finished me.

At the door I freed one of my hands and reached for the knocker—a leering brass devil balancing upon one foot. I lifted it and let it fall. The dull clap echoed through the interior of the house. Before the sounds had died away, the door swung open and a furious woman confronted me.

"How dare you—" She broke off upon seeing my face, which must have been a study in bewilderment.

She was a tall woman, topping me by a good six inches, and her hair was glossy black, a shade I would have thought darkened had it not been for the two silver wings that swept back from her temples. In stark contrast to her hair, her skin was pale and paper-thin. Faint lines creased about her eyes and across her upper lip, and I judged her to be in her late forties, several years older than my mother had been before her death.

"Mrs. Medcroft?" I asked.

She gasped. "Why, surely it isn't . . . but, of course, it must be. Hilary, my dear." Her voice deepened into pleasingly mellow tones. "Welcome to London." Even as she spoke, her gaze wandered over my shoulder, and she stared with red-rimmed eyes into the empty courtyard at my back.

I shifted the bag wedged beneath my arm. "I hope I haven't arrived at an inconvenient time."

Her gaze immediately returned to me and she smiled. "Not at all, my dear. There is no inconvenient time for Marion's daughter to call. It is just that . . . Never mind. Come in out of this damp air, and I will explain later."

She ushered me into a cramped foyer and insisted I set down my bags. "I'll have Chaitra take them

upstairs." Smiling pleasantly, she lifted a silver bell
from a carved teak stand and sent a tinkling wave
undulating through the house. "In the meantime, you
and I will have a talk. There's a fresh pot of tea in the
drawing room. Come along, dear. You look as though
you could use a cup."

Humming to herself, she turned and set off down
the hall. Her heels clicked upon the parquet flooring,
and the heavy scent of some exotic perfume wafted
along in her wake. Chaitra was nowhere to be seen,
but a faint crawling sensation ran down my spine and
told me we were not truly alone. The house had a
murky air, as though it were filled with an invisible
but dense fog. Even the simple act of drawing a
breath seemed unreasonably difficult.

Telling myself I was giving my imagination too free
a rein, I quashed the odd sensations before they took
a stronger hold. A few steps ahead of me, Mrs.
Medcroft stopped abruptly, and I barely recalled my
wandering attention in time to keep from bumping
into her.

"Here we are!" She spoke in a breathless and
excited voice—almost as though she had stumbled
onto some archaeological find—and opened a door.
A broad shaft of golden light poured into the hallway. It highlighted particles of floating dust and a
section of the lurid mauve paper that ran the length
of the wall.

I preceded her into the drawing room to discover
it was no less startling. It was filled with curios and
antiquities of all shapes and sizes, and I picked my
way through occasional tables covered in fringed
silk shawls and set with thin-necked cats, crystal
balls, and multiarmed Shivas. The scent, which I
had first supposed to be her perfume, permeated the

air, and thin lines of smoke issued from several incense braziers.

"Have a seat next to the Roman sofa," Mrs. Medcroft advised. "I like to lie there because it relaxes me, and relaxation is the key to conversing with the spirits. They do so dislike people who are tense and miserable."

"Yes, they would," I murmured inanely, and chose an ample wing chair that boasted only three satin cushions instead of the five or six allotted to its neighbors.

Mrs. Medcroft took a gilt-edged cup and saucer from a sideboard and poured me a cup of tea. "I usually save these for clients who want their tea leaves read," she confided. "But your coming to stay with me makes today a special occasion."

"Hardly to stay," I protested. "I would not think of imposing upon you for longer than a few weeks. By then, I am certain to have found myself a position as a governess or companion."

Her head lifted and she shot me an anxious glance. "I simply will not hear of such a thing. Your dear mother would never forgive me. I would be violating a sacred trust."

"Surely that is an exagger—"

"No." She raised her hand to stem my objection. "I will not hear of your leaving me. Had I been called to the far side of the veil so precipitously and left behind a child to mourn my passing, your mother would have done the same for me. The very notion that you might doubt my willingness to cherish and succor you as my own is abhorrent."

Good manners prevented me from laughing outright. Mrs. Medcroft's sense of the dramatic was unparalleled. I began to think I had found myself in the London equivalent of a gypsy encampment. All that was missing was the beribboned tambourines, and something told me I would only have to look in the nearest drawer to find them.

Nevertheless, her intent was kind and it was to that I responded. "It's not that I doubt your willingness to come to my aid," I hastened to assure her. "Indeed, I was very grateful for your unexpected invitation. After the creditors were paid, I was left with almost nothing. But I am nineteen, a grown woman, and capable of making my own way in this world."

"Nineteen." Her laughter welled up from deep within her. "My dear, you are a child. The world would devour you like a ravenous dog, as it devours all young women of youth and beauty who have no one to protect them. The things I could tell you." She sighed rapturously. "But I would not think to discuss the depravities of this world with someone of your innocence. Instead, I must ask you to put your faith in me and let me make decisions in your behalf."

I choked on the suggestion, and managed to turn the garbled sound into a polite cough. That, in itself, was dangerous. I did not doubt she would ply me with herbal concoctions if she even suspected I had been taken with a cold.

With a flourish, Mrs. Medcroft lifted the teacup and came and stood before me. "You shall be the child I never had. The daughter of my heart. And I will do everything within my power to make you happy."

Apparently, Mrs. Medcroft had known my mother well, although she and I had never met. I stared up at her and tried to fathom how the two of them had ever become close friends. Mother had been good-hearted, but she also had shown little patience to people who succumbed to what she thought theatrics. Perhaps when she was younger she had been more tolerant. That, or Mrs. Medcroft had once possessed a more serious turn of mind.

I took another look at my hostess, who was now wafting across the room with her hand on her brow, and decided it had to have been mother who had changed.

As for me, I was greatly entertained.

And there was plenty of time to make other arrangements when and if this situation proved untenable for either one of us.

"Are you quite certain I will not be a burden?" I asked.

"A burden? *Marion's* daughter? Never!"

Convinced the matter was settled, she fetched her own cup of tea, set it upon the occasional table that stood between us, and stretched out upon the sofa. Her gown, a blue-purple silk day dress with flowing, flounced train and knots of purple velvet ribbons at the sleeves, poured over the sides. She contemplated me from her position of repose.

"I can hardly believe it is you, sitting across from me. You are so much like your poor mama. At least, as I remember her. Goodness, there is so much to be said. I do not even know how your poor parents died. Had I not happened to see the notices in the newspaper, I should not have known at all. We had lost contact after her marriage."

"My father had been ill with a fever, and—"

"Forgive me, my dear." She waved my words aside. "But you will have to tell me another day. I fear I have not the strength to listen to your tragic news this afternoon." Her hand went to her forehead and she rubbed her temples as though they pained her.

"Do you have a headache?" I asked, remembering how upset she had been earlier.

She groaned. "It would be a wonder if I did not. You cannot know what I have suffered. The insult that has been shown my person. It is an outrage. A true outrage."

I suspected our definitions of outrages, true or otherwise, were somewhat at variance. I hazarded a guess. "It wouldn't, I suppose, have anything to do with the angry gentleman who left your home minutes before my arrival?"

Her hand went to her bosom. "What? Did you meet him? That dreadful creature. If he harmed you in any way—"

"He did not. Please do not distress yourself on my account. Although, certainly, I thought him rude in the extreme, and his suggestions infamous."

"What suggestions?"

"That I might somehow take advantage of him or members of his family."

She gasped. "Oh, my dear. What you have endured, and all because cruel, cruel fate has flung you onto my doorstep. It is bad enough that I must be humiliated and insulted by those disbelievers who seek to torment me at every turn. I am accustomed to *their* taunts and insults. It the price one pays for being different. For the powers that have been bestowed upon them by the spirits."

"The spirits?"

"Let me warn you, my dear." She leaned toward me confidentially. *"Never seek greatness. Greatness does not come without suffering. No one knows that better than I."*

Deciding it would be unwise to cough twice inside of one hour, I drowned my laughter beneath a gulp of hot tea, a mistake that resulted in a series of spluttering hiccups. When I had recovered, I said politely, "I gather you are a fortune-teller of sorts."

She stiffened. "Fortune-tellers are nothing but penny-a-pound charlatans that can be found at any county fair lightening the purses of bumpkins simple enough to believe their tales. *I* am a sensitive. I communicate with spirits. The tea leaf readings I sometimes do are merely a service to those women who would go elsewhere if I did not help them. Likely to be manipulated by those less scrupulous than I."

I supposed she had a point. "And the gentleman I encountered?" I asked. "What caused him to think the worst of both of us?"

"Mr. Llewelyn. The man is nothing short of a lunatic. You know yourself that you have done nothing to harm him, and yet he attacks you simply because he found you outside my door. I give you my solemn vow"—she held up her hand, palm outward— "I myself have done him no greater harm than you. Yet he abused me grievously."

She wafted her hand back and forth across her face. It had grown paler while she had been speaking of the difficult Mr. Llewelyn. Her efforts to fan herself seemed to give her no real relief, and her gaze wandered anxiously over the occasional table.

"Is everything all right?" I asked.

"Forgive me, my dear. But ever since I was a child, my health has been extremely fragile. That is the reason I am in such harmony with the spirit world. My physical energies are weaker than those of other people. I have some smelling salts somewhere. I keep them on hand for those moments when the spirits are particularly draining." She scanned the table again. "I cannot think where I left them."

I set down my cup and rose. "Perhaps they are on one of the other tables. I'll find them for you."

"Dear girl. It is so kind of you."

I made a hasty search of the drawing room and found a vial of smelling salts on the sideboard next to the tea pot. But by the time I had returned to the sofa with them, Mrs. Medcroft waved me away. "Just put them on the table, dear. The weakness is passing."

"Are you certain?" I asked, for her color looked no better than before.

"No, no. It is all right. Merely one of the many trials I endure." She slapped her cheeks lightly and a little of the blood returned.

Doubtfully, I took my seat but did not lift my gaze from her face until her shallow breathing deepened and the dullness faded from her eyes. Even then, I was not convinced she should not summon a doctor. At the suggestion, she managed a weak smile and took a sip of tea.

"There!" She set down the cup. "You see. I am as good as ever. These spells pass quickly, and the doctor would think me a hypochondriac if I summoned him every time I grew a little weak."

"Nevertheless, perhaps we should not discuss the matter since it seems to upset you."

"Nonsense. I refuse to be bullied or intimidated by men like Mr. Llewelyn. And what do you think I did to draw his wrath?" she demanded.

"I cannot begin to imagine."

Indeed, I dared not. The only possibilities that sprang to mind would, of a certainty, have offended her. I donned what I thought a grave expression and begged her to continue.

"It is because his sister sought me out for help. Help which clearly *he* cannot give her." Her hands fluttered as she talked. "Yesterday evening, she attended my Wednesday night séance. She was brought along by one of my regulars. Mrs. Pritchard is a sweet woman who has learned to trust in my powers and recommends me to any of her friends who she thinks may be in need of my services. Miss Llewelyn was much impressed with my abilities. Modesty prevents me from repeating her praise, but she went on for some while—you might say she waxed enthusiastic. I was terribly flattered."

"And was Mr. Llewelyn also in attendance?"

"Oh, not him. The man is a complete agnostic."

"And yet he came to hear of her interest."

"Nor does that come as a surprise. Before the evening concluded, his sister begged me to spend a fortnight at their house in Dorset. She is throwing a house party and would like to provide her guests with a more serious diversion than dances and bridge games. She herself has been interested in the here-after since the death of her mother when she was only ten."

"And Mr. Llewelyn does not approve?"

"So it would seem." Her hands fluttered in her lap. "Such a disagreeable man. He thinks, because of his wealth, he may insult people as he pleases with no fear of reprisal."

I remembered his rudeness and nodded with great feeling. Apparently, Mr. Llewelyn had supposed that the death of my parents had sent me in search of someone with Mrs. Medcroft's supposed talents. Or had, until I drew his attention to my baggage. It was only then he had demanded to know if I intended to assist her. And I, in all innocence, had admitted my willingness to help out as was required—although, at the time, I'd had no idea what that implied.

Still, whatever the man thought of spiritualists, he had no right to assault either of us in that fashion. It was, however, easy to appreciate his attitude. While I believed Mrs. Medcroft was honest and well-meaning—my mother would not have befriended her if she had been anything less—I doubted her abilities were anything but imaginary.

I relaxed and tried to get a sense of her beyond what I could gather with my eyes and ears. But I was disappointed. The murky air of the house seemed to have settled like a cloud around her head and shoulders, and it was like trying to read a book in a dense fog.

And that, I chided myself, is what comes of trying to exercise abilities that I do not truly possess.

Mrs. Medcroft released a long sigh and murmured, "I suppose we cannot possibly go to Dorset now. I simply haven't the strength to deal with the man. That poor woman. You have no idea how eagerly she begged me to visit her. I cannot begin to think what she will do without me. It really is most vexing."

For a moment, I was afraid distress would bring on another of her attacks, but any problem was forestalled by a soft knock. Both of us glanced up. The door to the drawing room slid open, revealing a small, dark woman of East Indian descent. Her sleek black hair hung over her left shoulder in a heavy braid, and she was swathed in a bright red cotton sari.

In a soft voice that was pleasantly melodic, she announced, "There's a Mrs. Broderick in the foyer."

"Not again? I've told her I can do nothing more for her. Did you tell her I had company?"

Chaitra nodded and her gaze wandered curiously from Mrs. Medcroft to me.

"This is Hilary Carewe. Marion's daughter. I told you she would be coming to stay with us."

The woman nodded and smiled shyly.

Mrs. Medcroft turned to me. "I'm afraid I must ask you to excuse me for a short while, my dear. It really is a nuisance, but I suppose it would be cruel to refuse to see the woman. Chaitra can show you to your room, and we can finish our conversation later."

Obediently, I rose and left the drawing room. In the foyer, the woman Chaitra had called Mrs. Broderick glanced at me and quickly retreated into the shadows. Before she slipped from view, I felt a strong sense of desperation emanating from her, mingled with what I felt certain was a concern over money. I had the strongest desire to reach out and reassure her.

But having seen her wish for privacy, I knew my intrusion would not be welcomed. Besides, it was ridiculous to act on a nebulous instinct after I had but recently tried to use my intuition and failed miserably. Instead, I dropped my gaze from my face to her hands. They were encased in fingerless net gloves, and she wore a single gold wedding band.

Chaitra paused at the bottom of the staircase that led from the foyer to the upper floor. "You'll find your room at the end of the hall, miss," she said. "I'll be up shortly to see that everything is all right."

Leaving her to attend to their caller, I climbed the stairs to the first-floor landing and made my way to the small bedroom intended for me. After the exotic ambience of the drawing room, the blue-striped wallpaper and unadorned furnishings seemed both plain and entirely respectable. Even the thick, smokelike atmosphere was pleasantly absent.

My baggage had been set beside a sturdy wardrobe, and my hatbox sat on the padded bench of a walnut dressing table. They gave a welcoming touch to otherwise unfamiliar surroundings. I sank onto the small armchair squeezed between the four-poster bed and the wall and tried to collect my thoughts.

Where had I found myself? Father would have been outraged by Mrs. Medcroft, given his distaste for anything that was not at once tangible and solid. Her theatrics, her talk of spirits and the other world, her apparent physical weakness, would have appalled him. As for Mama . . .

She, admittedly, had been cut from different cloth. There had been many occasions when, as a child, I had given voice to an insight that had discomfited everyone around me, and only she seemed to have any understanding of what had possessed me. But given father's shortness of temper on those occasions, she had never supported anything I said.

Privately, she had often cautioned me to silence. "Your father is a good man," she'd advised. "But he simply refuses to accept that things could exist in this world that do not have a solid rooting in physical reality. Please try to curb your impulse to speak out on matters about which you could know nothing."

Was that the reason she had lost touch with Mrs. Medcroft? Had Father disapproved of their association? Certainly, Mama had never mentioned having a dear friend in London to me. Her existence had come as a complete surprise.

My thoughts drifted back over my childhood. It had been straightforward and uncomplicated. Father had gone to the bank each weekday morning, impeccably dressed, his features set in what I came to regard as his honest-but-serious-and-efficient expression. Mama kissed him good-bye at the door, always upon the cheek. Privately, I imagined they must have been somewhat more intimate when they were alone in their private suite. But this was sheer speculation, since I was an only child and had been conceived a few short months after their wedding.

Still, they seemed happy in each other's company. And I was in theirs. The three of us spent many Sundays driving through the park, sitting in the back garden, or attending concerts together. I never noticed how rarely we entertained or were entertained by Father's business associates. Nor did I remark on my total lack of grandparents, aunts, uncles, or cousins. My parents always made certain that I received an excessive number of presents on my birthdays and at Christmas, and I was selfish enough, or self-contained enough, not to miss my relatives for other reasons.

Those few guests who did come to supper or Sunday tea consisted of the local vicar and his wife and our nearest neighbors. It was not until my father fell ill that I truly realized the extent of our isolation. There was no one to tend him but Mama and the servants, and she would not trust him to their care.

I had been packed off to the neighbors, since the doctors warned her that the illness could be contagious. Usually, my mother was indulgent and inclined to yield to my demands, but nothing I said would convince her to let me stay and assist her. I was, therefore, no help to her whatsoever. Despite the care I knew she gave Father, he succumbed to the fever within the week. By then, she, too, was seriously ill.

It was only a matter of days before she followed him, and I discovered how completely alone I was. A visit to my father's solicitors revealed that the happy life we had led together had eaten up all of his earnings. The house was leased, not owned. There were only the furnishings and a few personal possessions, and I was forced to sell off most of those to pay the servants their wages and satisfy our creditors.

In fact, I was penniless.

It was while I was contemplating the course of my future that a letter came. The postmark said London, but I did not recognize the handwriting or the return address. I tore open the envelope and learned, for the first time, of Mrs. Medcroft.

She had, she wrote, seen the notice of my parents' death in the newspapers and read that they were survived by a daughter. She referred to an old and deep friendship she had had with my dear mother when they were both young, and proffered her deepest sympathies. But it was the last paragraph that started my heart racing. In graceful, flowing script, she had written:

> I realize that you and I have never met, and perhaps this invitation will seem presumptuous, but it is my dearest wish that you and I become acquainted. If you can find it in your heart to indulge the whim of a foolish woman who loved your precious mother as deeply as she could have loved a sister, then I beg you to come to London and stay with me.

It was signed Mrs. Amelia Medcroft, and clipped to the single sheet was a train ticket. I scanned the letter several times and found my surprise only increased with each reading. Who was Mrs. Medcroft and why had I never heard of her? I had thought my life with my parents completely devoid of secrets. Now it appeared I was mistaken.

Father's solicitors knew no more than I. Nevertheless, they insisted that it was highly inadvisable to rush off to London and the home of a woman whose name and person were unfamiliar to me. I, however, had already made up my mind to accept.

Indeed, I had little choice. I could hardly live in a house with no servants and no money to put food on the table or coal in the fire. The vicar and his wife could not afford to take me in, although they had offered, and my neighbors had children of their own to support. I was determined that I should not be a burden to anyone. A short visit with my mother's old friend would give me a place to stay for the few weeks it would take me to find a position.

Nor was there any reason to mistrust her or suspect her of evil intentions. I possessed nothing of any value whatsoever.

Chaitra tapped on the open door, drawing me back to the present. Her slight figure hovered in the doorway. "Is there anything you need?" she asked in her melodic voice.

I smiled. "I cannot think of a thing. But thank you for carrying my bags upstairs."

"It was no trouble." She glanced around the room. "You will be comfortable in here."

It was a statement, not a question, and I looked at her curiously.

She stepped inside and closed the door behind her. "I suppose you didn't feel anything . . . different about the house," she asked, her voice even quieter than before.

"Only that it had a rather odd atmosphere."

Chaitra's eyebrows lifted and she regarded me

with greater interest. "It's the spirits. They come but they do not leave. I tell Mrs. Medcroft she should not welcome them into her home, but she laughs at me. You, too, must be careful, child. The spirits are aware of those who are aware of them. And they are not always good and helpful."

"And why is this room an exception?"

She smiled. "This one and my own I have protected." She opened the wardrobe and showed me a velvet pouch swinging from a hook on the inside of the door. "Do not remove this from your room, and the spirits will not trespass here."

The thought that a little bag, containing goodness-only-knew-what, could keep something as nebulous as spirits outside my door was hard to accept. But the atmosphere in here had felt fresher and, seeing her proud face, I could do nothing but thank her.

"Tell me, Chaitra," I asked, suddenly struck by a thought. "How long have you worked for Mrs. Medcroft?"

"More than fifteen years, miss."

I sighed and my excitement faded. "Then I suppose you did not know my mother?"

"No, miss. Although I have heard my mistress speak of her."

It was more than my mother had done. All she had told me of her past was that she had been orphaned as a child and raised by her grandmother—a strict, religious woman who had made her life intolerable. How did someone of her restrained background become friends with a spiritualist?

"I wonder how they met," I said aloud.

Faint lines creased Chaitra's brow. "Didn't you know, miss? She worked as Mrs. Medcroft's assistant for five years."

I gaped at her. My mother, assistant to a spiritualist? I could not credit the notion. A dozen questions rushed to the forefront of my mind, but none of them reached my lips. At that moment, there was a loud thump and the crash of shattering glass, arising from somewhere downstairs.

Chaitra flung open the bedroom door. Her long black braid slapping against her back, she hurried into the hallway. I came to my feet in a rush, meaning to follow, but was stopped by the sound of a woman's hysterical sobs flooding the foyer. A moment later, the front door slammed shut.

I ran to the windows in time to see Mrs. Broderick hastening down the flagstone path, her hands catching up her skirts so that she did not fall, the ties of her bonnet streaming out behind her.

2

I didn't linger at the window, but hurried downstairs to discover what had caused the commotion. I found Chaitra and Mrs. Medcroft in the drawing room, crouching before an overturned occasional table and picking up shards of broken crystal.

"Are you all right?" I asked, going immediately to help.

A silver wing of hair fell across Mrs. Medcroft's brow, and she wearily tucked the lock back into her chignon. "This day has been unrivaled—absolutely unrivaled—as a day of upsets. First, that dreadful Mr. Llewelyn, and now poor, foolish Mrs. Broderick. Whatever am I to do? I begin to wonder if I shall survive the day."

"You will be fine, mum," Chaitra assured her in a light tone.

"I would not be too certain," her mistress contended. "My nerves are not what they used to be, nor am I as young as I was. Not that I am old by any means," she hastened to add. "But I cannot say that I enjoy the same taste for excitement now that my twenties have gone."

"Along with your thirties," Chaitra contributed.

Mrs. Medcroft scowled at her. "Not yet. Not by a long shot."

"What on earth upset the woman?" I asked, in an attempt to make her forget her ruffled dignity. "If you don't mind my asking."

"Of course not, my dear. You are, after all, one of the family now and must be treated as such. I fear this sort of thing is inclined to happen now and again. People simply don't understand."

She rose to her feet, leaving the rest of the debris for Chaitra and me to collect, and busied herself brushing the creases out of her skirt. "I warn them when they come to me that just because I can communicate with spirits does not mean I can reach them whenever my clients wish. Often, contacting those who have recently passed over is a simple matter—for a period of a few weeks. But eventually they let go of this world and go on to the next. Thereafter, they are not always willing to be called back, even for their loved ones."

She released that rapturous sigh I had heard earlier. "The other side is a beautiful place. Full of flowers and birds singing. There are rivers and lakes and mountains whose lowest peaks outstrip this world's greatest ranges. We can hardly blame them for forgetting us."

Chaitra snorted, saving me the embarrassment of being caught at surrendering to my own irrepressible giggles. "Mrs. Broderick does not seem to agree with you," I said.

"Oh, that awful woman. If I were her husband, I would not come back to her either. She accuses me of failing her in her time of need. I, who was there for her when no one else could help. The sheer ingratitude of the creature." She turned to me, a heightened color in her cheeks. "Hilary. Never, never, *never* do as I have done and devote your life to others. There simply is no reward in being selfless."

With that announcement, she suggested I go back upstairs and rest. I would want to wash and change my dress before supper, and she was expecting a guest. I dropped the last piece of broken vase into the dustbin and allowed myself to be shooed from the room.

In one manner, at least, I agreed with Mrs. Medcroft. What a day it had been! Nothing in my quiet and proper upbringing had prepared me for a single day with this woman. The doubts that had sprung from my confrontation with Mr. Llewelyn and Mrs. Medcroft's exotic flair became a conviction with Mrs. Broderick's outburst. I seemed to have stepped into a lunatic asylum. And despite my hostess's obvious wish to take me into her home, I simply couldn't imagine remaining there.

Still, I hated to depart without having learned those things about my mother that I had never known. Now that she was lost to me forever, it was doubly important to capture any piece of her that remained. In the few weeks it would take for me to find a suitable position, I would be able to satisfy that desire. And, at some point over the next few days, I would find a tactful way to explain to Mrs. Medcroft that I thought myself unprepared for life beneath her sheltering wing.

Left to myself for an hour, I unpacked my clothes, shook out my black taffeta, and hung the rest of my dresses in the wardrobe. Then I set about washing my hands and face and restoring my chignon to some kind of order. At seven o'clock, I checked my appearance in the mirror, tucked a few wisps of my russet hair back into place, and went downstairs.

Mrs. Medcroft's words wafted from the drawing room. Her comments were interspersed with those of another person—a man, judging by the sounds of the low voice. I said a silent prayer that he was the guest she was expecting and not another client.

Upon reaching the drawing room doorway, I paused. In my absence, all had been set to rights. A warm fire crackled on the hearth and cast a orange-red glow across the painted and beaded curios, muting their garish colors and almost making them look tasteful. The atmosphere, too, was less oppressive, for the braziers had been covered and the incense extinguished, although the scent clung to the room.

Mrs. Medcroft had deserted the Roman sofa in favor of one of the wing chairs, and she had changed her purple dress for a watered silk in pale lavender. The color flattered her complexion. Either that, or the glow I saw in her face was due to her gentleman caller.

She looked up and caught me hovering there. "Hilary, my dear. Do come in. There's someone I'd like you to meet. One of my dearest friends—Mr. Quarmby."

The gentleman rose from one of the armchairs that faced away from the hall and turned to look at me. He was, I guessed, in his middle thirties and noticeably younger than Mrs. Medcroft. Younger and shorter, for he was not a fraction of an inch taller than I. His straight black hair had been parted on the side and brushed flat across the top of his head, and he boasted a narrow moustache. His eyes, too, were black, and the irises unnaturally small. They gave him a piercing look that seemed to bore into me, even though that might not have been his intent.

Unaware of my slight distaste for him, he smiled pleasantly and bowed stiffly at the waist in the manner of a European. Reluctantly, I stepped forward and gave him my hand. He brought it to his lips but, to my relief, it was no more than a gesture. He promptly released me.

"Mrs. Medcroft has been telling me all about you," he claimed.

I wondered what she could have said, since I had been allowed to tell her almost nothing about myself.

She, with a fluttering hand, beckoned for me to come and take the chair beside her. "I had intended to ask Mr. Quarmby to accompany us to the Llewelyn estate. But, of course, that is quite impossible under the circumstances."

"The man is guilty of the most monstrous behavior," he said, and I caught the hint of an accent that I hadn't immediately noticed. He gave Mrs. Medcroft an adoring look. "In all the years we have known each other, I have never known her to do anything but her best for the people who come to her. She has a reputation that rivals the Fox sisters."

"Oh, Mr. Quarmby." Mrs. Medcroft returned the adoring look. "Such flattery."

"It is deserved, dear lady. As well you know."

She tittered, and the color rose in her cheeks.

There seemed to be little I could add to their conversation. Both of them were completely enamored of each other, and, although I was glad to learn that Mrs. Medcroft had at least one admirer, I felt like an intruder on their happy twosome. I said nothing and tried to melt into the hill of cushions at my back.

"But enough of this silliness," Mrs. Medcroft protested. "I want the two of you to get to know one another. I will not be satisfied until my dearest friends come to love each other as deeply as I love them."

"There will be plenty of time for that." Mr. Quarmby turned to me and lightly stroked his moustache with his forefinger. "Mrs. Medcroft has spoken of nothing this last week save for your coming to London. It has been, 'When Marion's daughter this,' and 'When Marion's daughter that.' She has been as giddy as a schoolgirl."

I smiled politely, but was somewhat less impressed than I might have been. I had already seen that Mrs. Medcroft was easily excited. Rather than attempt to make some kind of response to his remark, I thought it wise to change the subject. "Chaitra told me that my mother used to work as your assistant," I said, hoping to learn more about their relationship.

She needed little prompting. "We spent five years together. It was at the height of my success. You cannot believe the demand there was for me. I was booked every evening and most afternoons. Someday I will show you my scrapbooks. Your mother accompanied me everywhere I went, and I would not have allowed anyone to exclude her. Oh, what a time that was."

"If only we had met then," Mr. Quarmby said. "Such memories we could have shared."

"Dear man." She beamed at him. "I wish it had been enough for Marion. It *was* enough until she met Mr. Carewe and fell in love." She leaned forward and covered my hand with hers. "Forgive me, my dear, but I never did approve their marriage. Do not mistake me. Your father was a good man. He would have been the ideal husband for another young lady. But he was all wrong for Marion."

"And yet they made a good marriage," I countered.

"No doubt. No doubt. Marion would never have let him see disappointment in her eyes. She was a sweet girl, truly generous with her affection. But he was such an unimaginative man, capable of believing in nothing beyond the ordinary, while Marion had developed a far greater vision of life during the years she spent with me. Without meaning to harm her, he would have stifled her, poor child."

I had to admit her view of my father was not entirely inaccurate. But in her assessment, she failed to credit him with his appreciation for art and the theater and his devotion to his family. Still, I could not help but wonder if Mama ever felt the sacrifices she made in his behalf were greater than the rewards.

"I suppose that is the reason the two of you lost touch," I murmured. "Father could not have approved of your friendship."

"Goodness me, no. Not to mention that I was a reminder of all those things he could not give her. The excitement. The celebrity. The chance to mix with the upper reaches of society. To be frank, my dear, he was jealous of the life she had shared with me and feared he would not be able to hold her for very long if I remained a part of her life."

"What a shame," Mr. Quarmby crooned. "To think that the two of you should have been torn apart forever."

Mrs. Medcroft pulled out her handkerchief and patted at her moist eyes. "I was hurt," she admitted. "But I did not take offense, for he insisted she sever ties with everyone she knew. It was sad, really. The poor man was infatuated with Marion and could not bear to share her with anyone."

"Sometimes it happens that way." Mr. Quarmby proprietarily fixed his black gaze on her.

It was true we had led an isolated existence, but it had never occurred to me to ask why. I began to wonder how well I had known my parents.

Or was Mrs. Medcroft being entirely honest?

Part of me wished to believe she'd lied, but there was too much in what she said that rang true. Nevertheless, I refused to accept her views without delving further into their relationship.

Mrs. Medcroft had failed to notice her friend's limpid look. All of her attention was for me. She leaned forward and squeezed my hand. "But now Marion's daughter has come to me and everything has been set right."

Once again, I managed a polite smile, but my questions tumbled through my mind.

Those questions were forestalled by a tap on the drawing room door. Chaitra entered immediately, but not—as I had supposed—to announce that supper was ready. Instead, her dusky complexion had a sickly, yellow cast, and there was a faint shine to her brow.

"Is it eight o'clock, already?" Mrs. Medcroft asked, seeing nothing amiss. "How quickly time passes when you are in pleasant company."

"There is none more pleasant," Mr. Quarmby agreed.

Chaitra's hands twisted together. "It's not that, mum," she mumbled, and glanced anxiously over her shoulder.

Mrs. Medcroft stiffened. "I hope you have not burnt the lamb. Not this evening of *all* evenings."

Her maid hesitated and glanced meaningfully over her shoulder again. Clearly, there was something she would rather have confided privately to her mistress.

I wondered if Mrs. Broderick had returned. Or worse—Mr. Llewelyn.

Mrs. Medcroft fluttered her hands impatiently. "Whatever is the matter with you? Out with it, this instant. I cannot be expected to read your mind."

Chaitra's hands dropped to her sides and she shrugged. "The constables are at the door, ma'am."

Mrs. Medcroft gave a little shriek. "The constables? My heavens, what has brought them here?" Her eyes appealed to Mr. Quarmby. "Do you think they could require my services?"

He rose to his feet. "What else could it be, dear lady? If you have no objection, I will go and speak with them myself. There is no need for you to be disturbed at this late hour."

"Dear, dear man. Where would I be without you?" She smiled at him and shamelessly fluttered her eyelashes.

Mr. Quarmby bowed and followed Chaitra out into the hallway. She closed the door behind them, thereby shutting off any snippets of conversation that might have wafted from the foyer—much to my disappointment. I was becoming increasingly uneasy about Mrs. Medcroft's professional practices, and dearly wished to discover what these new troubles might be.

"It is not the first time my help has been sought in criminal cases," she assured me, without waiting to be asked. "I was always particularly good in solving murders." She laughed deprecatingly. "Hardly a talent when you realize I had only to seek out the unfortunate deceased and ask them to direct us to their killers."

She sighed heavily. "But it has been many years since anyone requested my help. People have lost

their faith in these modern times. It's sad, but true."
She glanced at me. "But you will think me a silly old
woman who does nothing but make up stories."

"Not at all," I protested, although she had said
nothing less than the truth.

She waggled her finger at me. "No, no. I know
young people today. They require proof for everything." She frowned. "Now let me see. Where did I
put my scrapbooks? Chaitra would know, but we
won't bother her. Not with our supper in the balance."

She rose and twisted her head about to search the
room. "Not in the bookcase," she muttered to herself.
"The shelves were too short." Her gaze fell on a high-
backed desk. "Is that where I put them?"

She crossed the room and rummaged through the
drawers, lifting out boxes of stationery and envelopes
and tossing them aside. The stack at her side rose to
nearly two feet in height and wobbled precariously. I
wondered how much more she could add before the
whole pile collapsed and waited with amused anticipation for the crash.

"Here they are!" she exclaimed, startling me with
her cry. "I knew I had not lost them."

She pulled two enormous scrapbooks from the
bottom of the drawer and carted them across the
room to the card table that stood in the corner.
"Come and sit down over here and we can go through
them together."

I took one of the chairs that had been wedged up
against the table and watched while she turned the
pages. To my surprise, they were filled with newspaper clippings and embossed invitations. Some of the
articles dated back as far as 1852, and the most
recent were from 1858. Sandwiched in between the
pages were accounts of her successes, both in helping

with murder cases and in summoning restless spirits that haunted the houses of some very wealthy and notable families. Apparently, none of her claims had been exaggerated.

A yellowed photograph drew my gaze, and I gasped.

Mrs. Medcroft nodded. "I had forgotten about that. Yes, it was taken of your mother and me. As I recall it was the same evening we went to St. James's Palace. What an occasion that was."

I stared at the two images. A very young Mrs. Medcroft, dark and exotically attractive, sat in a large armchair. My mother stood at her side, her right hand resting on her employer's shoulder. She was beautiful, much more so than I remembered, although even as a child I had been secretly proud of my mother's looks.

Her thick hair had been swept up into a chignon, and her delicate eyebrows arched over luminous brown eyes. I had always envied her those eyes. My own were a blue-green—my father's eyes. I glanced at the date, written on the border in neat script. August, 1853. She would have been nineteen, and her youth was very obvious. There was a naïveté and purity about her that I thought endearing and, from her radiant expression, one could not assume that she was anything but completely happy.

Mrs. Medcroft pulled the photograph from the page. "You must take this for yourself. I don't suppose you have many of your mother when she was young, and it would please me to know you had this one."

"Thank you very much," I murmured, my throat tightening. "That's very kind of you."

"Nonsense." Her cheeks flushed with pleasure. She

closed the top scrapbook and thrust both of them toward me. "I'm sure you would like to have a longer look at them. You can take them to your room and return them when you are done."

"I would, indeed."

I had managed to read enough of the articles to realize that Mrs. Medcroft had been entirely honest in her recollections, but curiosity made me want to give the newspaper accounts a thorough study. My mother's name might have been mentioned on occasion and, even if it was not, I would certainly learn something about their life together.

I started to thank her again and was interrupted by Mr. Quarmby's return. He stepped in the room, and there was a grim set to his mouth. Mrs. Medcroft looked at him hopefully, but he shook his head.

"It is most distressing, dear lady. I have learned that Mrs. Broderick, the most contemptible of women, has made out a complaint against you."

"A complaint!" She came to her feet with a cry of dismay. "But I have not broken any laws."

"Indeed, you have not," he hastily assured her. "As the constables explained to that awful creature themselves. You did nothing but accept payment for services rendered."

"And she did not accuse me of trickery?"

"Not at all. Everyone in London knows you are genuinely sensitive. Any number of people would vouch for your honesty. It was more that she objected to the *cessation* of those services."

"Good Lord!" Mrs. Medcroft sank back into her chair. "The ingratitude of the woman. She should be thankful I did not charge her for what I could not produce."

"Indeed, she should," I agreed, coming to Mrs.

Medcroft's support. Had it not been for the scrap-books, my feelings might have been entirely different. But now my anger rose against the woman who had disrupted our evening and upset my hostess. And per-haps some of my ire was born of guilt for having myself taken her claims lightly.

Mr. Quarmby came to her side and patted her awkwardly on the shoulder. Despite the strain in the room, I couldn't help reflecting that he had very pudgy hands for someone of his slight stature. But Mrs. Medcroft seemed to take great comfort from his touch. The color returned to her face and she straightened in her chair.

"I gather that there is not going to be any trouble?"

He averted his gaze and swallowed.

She stared hard at him. "What are you not telling me, Mr. Quarmby?"

He cleared his throat. "It really is most awkward. But the constables requested . . . they thought . . . well, it seems they have little patience with spiritual-ists and have . . . have suggested that you might close your business."

"Close my business?"

"Or take it elsewhere," he finished, a miserable look in his black eyes.

"Did you tell them that the commissioner of police is a dear friend of mine?"

"He has been retired for some years, and the new commissioner is most unsympathetic."

Mrs. Medcroft dropped her head into her hands. "What am I to do?" she wailed.

"Now, now, dear lady. It will all blow over in a few weeks."

"But how am I to live in the meantime?" she demanded.

He brightened. "I have already considered the matter. You did, after all, receive an invitation to the Llewelyn estate."

She raised her head and stared at him. "You cannot think that I would be willing to go there. Not after his rudeness to me. And to my darling Hilary."

"I fear you may have no other choice. And whatever Mr. Llewelyn thinks of spiritualists, he cannot deny his sister the right to invite guests into her own home."

She took a deep breath and considered what he had said. After a long pause, she admitted, "You're quite right, of course. We will have to go. But I will not put one foot into that man's home unless both of you promise to accompany me."

"I would not hear of your going alone," Mr. Quarmby agreed. "You will need a protector at your side if you are to confront that awful man."

Although I hesitated, in the end I was compelled to say I would join them. Chaitra would also be going, and the London house would be shut up for several weeks. I could hardly insist that Mrs. Medcroft go without me and put her to greater inconvenience and expense than I had already done.

But nor could I say that I looked forward to another meeting with Mr. Llewelyn.

Perhaps because of my exhaustion, perhaps because of my uncertainty about what lay ahead, I lay awake long after I had gone to bed. It dismayed me that with all that had recently happened, my thoughts were dominated by the memory of the unpleasant and formidable Mr. Llewelyn.

His striking image had somehow fixed itself within

my mind, and I had only to shut my eyes to see him clearly. Tall, aristocratic in both manner and bearing, his good British breeding the one barrier that had protected me from his temper.

And a slim barrier it had been. I still felt bruised by our tumultuous encounter. Bruised and sorely wronged.

In all, he was a thoroughly unpleasant individual. Now that I had time to think, I was outraged by his accusations. Apparently, he knew little of Mrs. Medcroft and nothing at all of me. How dare he accuse two complete strangers of attempting to defraud him. If the choice had been mine, I would have deliberately snubbed him had chance brought us together a second time.

But as little as I wanted to see him again, I was soon to be a guest in his home.

I tried to imagine him in surroundings that were familiar and suited to him. A Tudor manor, perhaps. A place that would be formal, furnished in a manner that was restrained but entirely correct. A home with an atmosphere that was cold and overbearing, and entirely unsympathetic to those who passed through its doors or lived out their lives beneath its roof.

I felt a twinge of sympathy for his wife.

Or did he have one? He lived, after all, with his sister. But that did not necessarily rule out a wife. Someone timid and mouselike. Who crept unnoticed through the rooms of his manor house, a sorrowful look in her frightened face.

Or had he married someone as hard-hearted and judgmental as he himself? Someone with whom he would live in complete harmony. Drowsily, I imagined them denouncing their acquaintances over tea, condemning the human frailties of their friends between bites of hot scones and sips of steaming tea.

He was of an age to be married, appearing to be in his late twenties or early thirties. And he was wealthy, a fact that might have made his disposition seem pleasanter to some. And yet . . .

I was suddenly overwhelmed with the certainty that he was not.

And with that feeling came another sensation. As though I were standing on the edge of a precipice while rocks crumbled at my feet. Just as the ground gave way beneath me, I fell asleep.

At nineteen, one recuperates quickly, and by morning, my usual high spirits had returned. Although I found myself once again in the midst of packing my belongings, I was not daunted by the thought of a second journey following immediately upon the first.

Even my concern over the unpleasant reception we might anticipate had lessened. Surely, Miss Llewelyn would not permit her brother to abuse her invited guests. As for Mr. Llewelyn, he would not find me without words should he attempt a repeat of his first assault. Especially now that I knew Mrs. Medcroft to be all she professed to be.

I removed the last of my dresses from its hanger and started to close the wardrobe door. The silk charm bag swung back and forth on its hook, catching my eye, and I was struck by an overwhelming desire to include it in my suitcase. Of its own accord, my hand reached for the bag.

My fingers brushed the cord and I hesitated. Of all the nonsensical impulses. Magic was a trick of conjurers and sleight-of-hand artists; it was not to be taken seriously by any but the most gullible of individuals. Nor was it likely that spirits were given much of a welcome at the Llewelyn estate, where even the living need take their chances.

Besides, only the previous afternoon, I had given Chaitra my word that I would not remove her handiwork.

That recollection settled the matter. And, by then, the impulse had passed. I laughed at my foolishness and closed the wardrobe door.

It took us most of the afternoon to reach Dorset. At the station, either despite her brother's objections or because she was unaware of them, Miss Llewelyn's carriage was waiting for our party. We wound across barren heath-covered moors and rolling hills, finally pulling up outside high iron gates and a rambling stone wall that ran on in both directions as far as I could see.

While a gatekeeper hurried to admit us, I peered out of the carriage. My gaze fell on a brass plaque screwed into one of the stone gateposts.

Abbey House.

An odd name, I thought.

Iron hinges squeaked and the carriage rolled forward again, carrying us up a winding gravel driveway. It stretched a good mile from its start to its conclusion, but until I stepped down I was unable to appreciate the full magnificence of the Llewelyn estate.

Upon seeing the house, I understood the name. The stone edifice had the look of a medieval abbey, if one overlooked the odd attempts at modernization. It was two stories high, with arched Gothic windows set into thick stone walls. The windows were diamond-paned, and curved stone balconies projected from several of the upstairs rooms.

The double entry doors also rose to an arched peak and had been set in a battlemented tower that was a third again taller than the rest of the house. The tower had been set midway down the breadth of the abbey, and broke the house into two wings that ran east and west.

The whole had been erected in the middle of park-like grounds. Jade green lawns swept off in all directions, their smooth perfection broken only by well-tended rose beds and scattered trees. There were beech trees in profusion, and a long row of tall elms lined the driveway.

"Goodness, I had no idea," Mrs. Medcroft said, her usual exuberance quelled by awe.

Chaitra shook her head. "Just to polish the floors alone would take a fortnight."

"We could live here for a month," Mr. Quarmby declared, "and never once run into our host."

It was a cheering prospect.

We were given little time to contemplate our surroundings. One of the double doors in the tower swung open, and a woman stepped from the house to scowl at us. She wore a simple black taffeta dress, and her hair had been pulled back tightly from her face, making her eyes slant upward at the corners.

At first, I supposed her to be the housekeeper, but she looked too young to have the responsibility of such a huge household. At most, she was no older than Mr. Quarmby and, given the severity of her dress and hairstyle, she could have been much younger. Then, too, something in her handsome dark face reminded me of Mr. Llewelyn.

Not the kind of woman I would have expected to "wax enthusiastic" over the talents of a spiritualist. I glanced at Mrs. Medcroft's face to see if this was, indeed, our hostess. But she was staring blankly at the woman, no hint of recognition in her eyes.

Leaving our luggage to the auspices of the coachman, Mr. Quarmby took her by the arm and escorted her to the door. "Dear lady," he addressed the woman and made a slight bow. "Miss Llewelyn will be expecting us. If you would be so good as to admit us and inform her of our arrival."

"And who," she responded in a cold voice, "am I to say has arrived?"

He lifted his chin and, as though he were introducing royalty, announced, "Mrs. Medcroft and her party."

"That ridiculous spiritualist?" The woman's eyebrows rose incredulously.

Mrs. Medcroft stiffened beneath the insult. "And you would be?"

"Miss *Ursula* Llewelyn," the woman replied. "I believe my brother informed you that you were not welcome."

"Indeed, he did. But in good conscience, I could not ignore your sister's request."

"More likely you wanted to avail yourself of her hospitality. Well, you've done yourself no good in coming, for I won't admit you. You might as well turn around and go back home."

The three of us looked at each other in disbelief. To think we had come all that way only to be told to return. I doubted we would even be able to find a train leaving for London until the following morning. But what were we to do? We could hardly knock her down and storm the house.

Mr. Quarmby looked determined to do just that. His upper lip twitched and his black eyes glittered. Considering his short stature and the height and emphatic nature of his adversary, I would not have wagered a penny on his chances. To my great relief, he was forestalled by a cheerful voice that came from the far side of the door.

"For goodness' sake, what are you doing, Ursula?"

The woman glanced over her shoulder and scowled. "Showing more sense than you have done."

"Oh, bother. Now what has gotten you into a snit?"

The right half of the double door swung back and an attractive and cheerful young woman burst onto the steps. Pink silk skirts twirled about her, and the afternoon sunlight glanced across her golden hair and flooded her face with light. The instant she caught sight of us, she flashed a pleased smile.

"Mrs. Medcroft. You did come. I was horribly afraid that Edmund would scare you off. He can be most convincing when he chooses."

Mrs. Medcroft sniffed and searched for her handkerchief. "Yes, I have come—for all the good my charity has done me. I have disrupted my household and dragged my dearest friends this great distance, only to be turned away at the door as a charlatan."

The younger Miss Llewelyn turned on her sister. "Really, Ursula. Where on earth are your manners?"

"I'm doing no more than Edmund would do if he were here," Ursula retorted, crossing her arms across her chest defensively. "You know what he thinks about all this."

"Pooh! I don't give a whit for his opinions."

"You still shouldn't have invited them here against his wishes."

"And why not? It's my home, too. And my party. Or have you forgotten? Please, do come in, Mrs. Medcroft. And don't let Ursula's behavior upset you. No one pays her a bit of attention."

She jostled her sister to one side to let us pass, and signaled to the footman to bring our luggage. We filed through the gap she had made for us and found ourselves in a spacious foyer. The floor tiles were rose marble, and a sweeping mahogany staircase coiled upwards to a broad landing. Overhead, sunlight poured through a stained-glass dome, danced across the walls, and glittered off the polished tiles.

But despite the overwhelming brightness, a wave of cold air swept down from the landing and blew past me. It left a trail of prickles across my forearms. I shivered and glanced upward, but could see nothing wrong. Nothing but a draft, I told myself, although that was not at all what I really thought. Deliberately refusing to listen to any inner voices, I turned back to the rest of our small party.

Mrs. Medcroft was watching me with a curious look. "Is everything all right, dear?"

"Yes, fine," I mumbled.

Her gaze wandered up the stairs to the spot that had drawn my attention seconds earlier. After a brief moment, she shivered eloquently. "You were right to insist on my coming, Miss Llewelyn. Someone here is in desperate need of my help."

Ursula shut the front doors with a bang. "Utter nonsense! There are no spirits here."

Mrs. Medcroft held up her hand for silence. "Forgive me. I mean no offense, but I must contradict you. I am overcome by sadness. It is . . . it is a woman's sadness. Indeed, I am *drenched* in sorrow."

Everyone stared at her.

But that was not at all what I had felt.

When that cold draft had swept past me, I had been struck by a feeling of absolute evil.

3

Guided by a prim maid in black taffeta and a starched apron, we clattered up the stairs to the guest rooms. Mrs. Medcroft's buoyant mood carried her along at our head; I trailed behind, my feet as reluctant as my heart. On the landing, I glanced hastily around me. My gaze was drawn to an enormous walk-in fireplace that stood against the back wall. Demonic faces with slanted eyes and pointed chins had been carved in stone and set into columns on either end. They peered, sentient but unseeing, across the landing and down into the foyer. I suppressed a shudder and hurried after the maid.

The guest rooms lay in the east wing. Mine was the first door off the spacious landing. Across the corridor from me, Mrs. Medcroft and Chaitra shared a suite, their two small bedrooms standing either side of a gracious sitting room. Mr. Quarmby was separated from us by the full length of the long corridor, a distance of some fifty feet. After kissing Mrs.

Medcroft's hand, he left us to rest and change our clothes for supper.

"Goodness, what an enormous place," Mrs. Medcroft said again, idly examining one of the Dresden figurines on her mantelpiece.

I nodded. "They could set aside an entire wing for family ghosts with no fear of being disturbed."

"Really, Hilary. One should never be flippant about the dead. It offends them."

"Forgive me. I shall try to curb my tongue."

"There's a good girl. Now run along and have a nice nap. It's been a tiring day."

I kissed her on the cheek, said good-bye to Chaitra, who was hanging up Mrs. Medcroft's dresses in a massive wardrobe of carved teak, and went to the door.

"Hilary, dear?" Mrs. Medcroft called after me.

I turned back to her.

"Are you . . . are you quite certain something didn't upset you downstairs?"

I frowned and hesitated. It was difficult to put words to what I had felt, and anything I might have said sounded foolish. Nor had the odd sensation lasted longer than a second. I was beginning to wonder if I had felt anything at all.

"Hilary?" she asked.

I smiled. "It was nothing, really."

"Well, if you're certain," she said doubtfully.

I nodded.

"Run along then, dear. And . . . and if something should bother you, you will be certain to tell me?"

"Absolutely."

That seemed to satisfy her, and I left.

It was a short walk down the carpeted corridor to my bedroom, but at the door, I paused. The empty landing drew my gaze, and some inner compulsion urged me to examine that spot at the top of the stairs that had disturbed me. Although I told myself it was bad manners to wander about the house by myself, my legs seemed to have a will of their own.

I walked forward until I reached the banister. The polished mahogany was cool and slick beneath my fingers, but if I had anticipated a return of that feeling of dread, I was happily disappointed. All was quiet and peaceful.

I sighed loudly, only then realizing I had been holding my breath.

"Is that you, Fanny?" a baritone voice demanded.

Dismayed, I peered over the railing and into the foyer. Mr. Llewelyn stood on the bottom stair, his head thrown back in order to see who was there. His long legs were parted slightly to brace him, and his gray eyes were narrowed as a defense against the brightness streaming down the stained-glass dome above our heads.

He had but recently entered the manor. His hat rested lightly between his fingers, and he was still wearing his overcoat. With each intake of breath, his broad chest swelled and the buttons strained in their buttonholes. He was, I thought, like a magnificent stallion—virile, beautifully formed, but with a temper that was not to be trusted.

My assessment could not have been more apt. The instant he saw me, his handsome features hardened and the anger in his eyes was unmistakable. "So you have come in spite of my warning." He flung down his statement like a challenge.

"At your sister's insistence," I reminded him. "And I must also say you have misjudged Mrs. Medcroft. She only wishes to help."

"As do you, naturally."

"I see no reason why you should think otherwise. Certainly, you have been given no reason."

"I do not need to bite into sour fruit to know I do not like the taste. Nor need I be taken by frauds before I have the sense to guard my purse."

"Good heavens. What nonsense. You talk as though we were pickpockets."

"A fair analogy," he returned with irritating complacence. "Although I find more to admire in a common thief than I do in those reprehensible creatures who make a pretense of helping you with one hand while extricating your earnings with the other."

I bit back my rising temper. This was not an argument I would win by giving vent to my emotions. Nor did I need to give him any more excuse to release his. Instead, I smiled sweetly and attempted to wrestle my features into an expression that might have been deemed philosophical. "Thank goodness you are merely judgmental and not a judge. I could only pity the poor souls you would sentence to hang without being shown evidence of their guilt or allowing them speak a word in their defense."

"You do not seem to lack for words. Nor do you possess a ladylike reluctance to speak them."

"You leave me no choice. A better man with better manners would make no such demands on me. But when I find myself in your company, it is speak or be unjustly slandered."

"Ha! I doubt such a thing is possible."

"Nevertheless, your suspicions are unfounded. And, in that, I speak for Mrs. Medcroft as well as myself."

"Naturally, you would defend her. But do you suppose me foolish enough to believe you?"

"Certainly, you were foolish enough to have assumed the worst without giving either of us a chance to prove our good intent. But there is no need for you to accept my assessment of our characters. You will have plenty of opportunity to get to know us over the next few weeks."

"Of all the . . ." He glared at me. "You impertinent little—"

"Enough! May I remind you that I am a guest in your home and entitled to be treated with civility."

His mouth dropped, and I took advantage of his momentary loss of speech to make my escape. I stalked off down the corridor, holding my head high, all the while fervently praying that he would not follow. It was not until I had closed my bedroom door and pressed my weight against its length that I started shaking.

So much for our hopes of avoiding Mr. Llewelyn.

At eight, the three of us descended for dinner. Poor Chaitra was left to make her way alone to the servant's hall, and I did not envy her her difficult position. Not for an instant did I suppose the other servants would make her feel comfortable or welcome—household servants being inclined, as they were, to adopt their employers' attitudes. I wondered if we would fare much better.

We reached the foyer only to have our hostess hail us from the landing. Layers of pink chiffon shivered around her and draped tantalizingly over her upper arms in loops that left her shoulders bare. She waved at us with her painted fan, and several expensive rings winked at us from her fingers. "There you are. Do forgive me. I meant to fetch you before you left your rooms and take you downstairs myself, but it took me forever to fix my hair."

"That style looks very becoming, Miss Llewelyn," Mrs. Medcroft said.

"Goodness, you must call me Fanny. Everyone does." Face glowing, she rushed down the stairs with a dancer's grace. "'Miss Llewelyn' sounds horribly stiff and proper, and I fear everyone knows I am a silly, frivolous creature who doesn't deserve an ounce of respect. Not even from my dear brother and sister, who treat me like a child."

"That is very wrong of them," Mrs. Medcroft replied. "Anyone can see that you are a lovely young lady. High spirits should not be regarded as a lack of intelligence."

"You must tell that to Edmund and Ursula. They will not believe a word of it coming from me."

She led us down the hall and into a drawing room. Its magnificence brought an abrupt end to our conversation. The vaulted ceiling rose high above our heads, and an upstairs gallery ran along three sides of the room. This was supported from below by heavy wooden arches of dark oak. The fourth wall was broken up by two rows of bay windows, both the upper and lower being fitted with stained-glass panels.

It was only after I had absorbed something of my grand surroundings that I realized there were several other guests already seated on the velvet sofas. They had been chattering amiably with the two elder Llewelyns but, upon seeing us, they fell silent and stared with curious eyes.

Fanny pulled us into their midst. "We're all here save for Mrs. Pritchard. She won't arrive until tomorrow. But let me introduce you to the others. Ursula you already know, of course." She immediately dispensed with her grim-faced sister, and her gaze flickered to her brother, who was sitting stiffly in a railback chair. It was hard to tell which was straighter and more wooden, his back or the dark oak. Fanny dismissed him with a quick nod. "And Edmund does not deserve to be introduced. He has behaved abominably."

"I prefer to be addressed as Mr. Llewelyn, except by my friends," he said, his voice hard.

Mrs. Medcroft's chin jerked upward and her green eyes glittered. "And I, naturally, am *Mrs.* Medcroft."

Hastily, Fanny jostled her nearer the sofa. "Mr. and Mrs. Winthrop you will not have met. They are our nearest neighbors and have been friends of the family for eons. Oh, do call them Eglantine and Winnie. They won't mind, and I simply haven't the patience for formalities."

We nodded politely to Eglantine, a handsomely dressed but plain woman. Hazel eyes bulged in her long face, and her gray hair was plaited in a circlet at the crown of her head. From her age—she was in her late forties or early fifties—I guessed she had been a contemporary of the Llewelyns' parents rather than of Ursula or Fanny.

Eglantine stared dubiously at Mrs. Medcroft, her upper lip curling back over a row of prominent teeth. "You would be the medium about whom we have been hearing. I'm afraid you will find that Fanny has brought you here on a wild-goose chase. There are no ghosts at Abbey House, despite its long history."

"That's the absolute truth." Winnie, a man of moderate height with an oversized head and thick, tawny curls that gave him a leonine appearance, poised above his wife. "Edmund simply wouldn't allow it." His laughter boomed through the drawing room.

Winnie was a much younger man than his wife, a good ten years younger, I would have said. He was also attractive in a rakish fashion. His hair was silver at the temples, and his eyes were a fascinating sea green flecked with gold.

His glance fell upon me, and his eyes lightened several shades. "And you would be?" he asked.

Mrs. Medcroft placed her arm protectively about my shoulders. "This is Miss Hilary Carewe. She is the daughter of a dear friend of mine. The poor child has but recently lost both her parents, and I am the only friend she has left in the world."

"How unfortunate for her," Mr. Llewelyn commented from the corner.

His remark was deliberately vague, but Mrs. Medcroft chose to ignore the barb and nodded somberly.

Winnie gave my hand a firm and friendly shake and took several seconds longer than was necessary to release me. "Truly sorry, my dear. Truly sorry."

"Thank you," I murmured, and hastily stepped out of his reach.

My discomfort was due to more than his firm handshake and approving look. Eglantine Winthrop's gaze had not lifted from the two of us since he'd first shown an interest in me, and her left hand clenched the arm of the sofa. I hastily took shelter behind Mr. Quarmby.

He, obligingly, assumed my place. The electric lights from the wall sconces gleamed off his manicured and polished fingernails. "Manfred Quarmby. At your service," he said, with a quick bow to the group in general.

"And this is Dr. Kenneth Rhodes." Fanny drew our attention to the only guest she had not yet introduced and trailed proprietary fingers across his sleeve. "My fiancé."

I regarded him with interest. He was Ursula's age, and not at all the sort of man I would have expected to have captured Fanny's affection. He wasn't handsome, although he had nice features, and his particular shade of brown hair was, at best, ordinary. His blue eyes were kind, if somewhat serious, but they were hidden behind a pair of wire-rimmed spectacles and thick lenses that distorted their shape and size.

Nor could he have been considered personable. Instead, he was reserved and almost modest in his demeanor. Still, he seemed an intelligent and well-meaning gentleman, the kind of suitor who would have pleased the parents of any young lady, and I had to credit Fanny with having more sense than she pretended. She had impressed me as the sort of young woman who would attach herself to a more flamboyant—and less trustworthy—character.

His eyes downcast, Dr. Rhodes mumbled, "Pleased to meet you. Although I cannot say that I approve of Fanny's contacting her mother." He tucked his arm about her waist and absentmindedly patted her on the hip.

She wriggled impatiently within his embrace. "Really, Kenneth. You know how dearly I loved Mama and how desperately I miss her."

"What rubbish." Ursula glared at them both, disapproval written in the set of her mouth and her stiffly held shoulders. "You're too self-centered to miss anyone."

"As I recall, I am the only one here who bothers to put flowers on her grave," she retorted.

Dr. Rhodes gave her another pat, and his head

bobbed nervously. "That's true, Ursula. You must try to be fair."

"You are hardly one to talk to me about fair."

Mr. Llewelyn rose to his feet, immediately and effortlessly drawing all of our gazes to himself. Unquestionably, he had a commanding presence, an admission I begrudged making even though it was unspoken. To me, an authoritative presence denoted strong character, and nothing in his behavior toward us made me willing to credit him with good qualities of any kind.

He regarded his sisters with a coolness he might have shown to two strangers. "I think enough has been said on this subject. Am I mistaken?"

Fanny and Ursula looked at each other. Neither spoke, although I suspected there would be a great deal said between them when they were alone. I wondered what Fanny had done to incur her sister's animosity. Was it her familiarity with the doctor in front of their guests?

Or was it that she was engaged while her elder sister was without even a suitor? That seemed entirely possible, since Ursula, attractive though she might have been, seemed too unbending and short-tempered to inspire admiration in a man's heart.

Seeing no one was going to argue, Mr. Llewelyn turned his attention to us. "Since you are aware of my feelings, I will not reiterate them. Fanny may have her séances if she chooses, but only when I am in attendance. Is that understood?"

Mrs. Medcroft shrank beneath his gaze, but Mr. Quarmby did not hesitate. "Absolutely. An excellent idea. This dear lady will soon erase any doubts you might have." He patted her hand affectionately.

"But I am not certain the spirits—"

"Nonsense. I have every faith in your abilities."

"They do so dislike unbelievers," she explained. "And are often unwilling to be called into hostile company."

Winnie stretched out his legs and smiled lazily at his host. "Edmund, you will have to sit in a corner all by yourself and keep quiet. Otherwise you will spoil this for all of us."

His host bowed politely. "I would not think of ruining your entertainment. Shall we go into supper?"

It was not what I would have called a pleasant meal, and I was glad when it had ended. Only Fanny had seemed blissfully unaware of the tensions in the dining room. The rest of us had regarded each other warily from across our plates. Mrs. Medcroft drew the greatest number of looks—some of them scornful, some of them apprehensive—but I received more than my share.

Clearly, Mr. Llewelyn had not forgotten or forgiven me for my earlier remarks. If anything, I would have said he thought less of me than of Mrs. Medcroft —perhaps because she had been wise enough to accept his abuse without argument.

Winnie's attentions were no more welcome, but certainly more pleasant. More than once his jests were deliberately made for my benefit, and he often smiled at me and invited my comments and opinions. His wife's irritated glances did nothing to quell his exuberance, and before desert was served, I was also forced to endure her glares.

I was glad to leave the table. Mrs. Medcroft, her face pale, followed immediately and took my arm. She leaned heavily on me for support.

"Shall we adjoin to the parlor?" Fanny said, the color high in her cheeks. "I have had candles set out on the table, and there is more than enough room."

Mrs. Medcroft hesitated. "Surely, you cannot expect me to hold a séance tonight? It has been such a long day, and—"

"Oh, but you cannot refuse me. I have been waiting all week for you to come, and tomorrow Edmund expects to be in London all evening. Surely you could at least try."

"Of course, the dear lady will oblige," Mr. Quarmby agreed, accepting without regard for Mrs. Medcroft's objections. "Only let us retire for a few minutes to collect ourselves, and we will return to oblige you."

Fanny bestowed a glowing smile upon him. "Shall we say eleven o'clock, then? In the parlor?"

He bowed deeply.

Halfway up the stairs, Mrs. Medcroft turned to him. "Really, Mr. Quarmby. I wish you hadn't agreed. I don't feel at all up to this."

"Now, now, dear lady. You have a duty to the poor girl. Besides, it will be no easier another night. You must not let the rudeness of our host intimidate you."

"I suppose," she agreed. "But he really is a dreadful, dreadful man."

The French doors in my room let out onto a small, semicircular balcony. Glad for the few minutes alone, I opened them and stepped outside for a breath of air. It was a warm night, the kind of night in late spring that caresses you with the promise of the summer yet to come. The sky was clear, and stars sparkled from one end of the horizon to the other. I lifted my face to the night breeze and let its soft breath tickle across my cheeks.

Downstairs, the front door opened and shut,

disturbing my reverie. Light feet rushed down the stone steps and onto the driveway. They were immediately followed by a heavier, masculine tread. Both sets of footsteps came to a halt a short distance beyond my balcony.

"Really, Fanny." Mr. Llewelyn's words cut through the still night. "I just don't understand you."

"Go away, Edmund." There was a quick flash of pink silk in the moonlight. "I simply will not listen to another one of your lectures."

"If you would show a bit more sense, there would be no need for me to lecture you. And this goes beyond your usual pranks."

"Pooh! Who are you to tell me what I am and am not like?"

"I should think I know you as well as anyone."

"Apparently you do not."

A wave of anger drifted upward, like heat from a blazing fire. "You might at least tell me what put this ridiculous notion into your head," Mr. Llewelyn said, his voice tightly controlled.

"Not what," she taunted, "who. Sally Pritchard thought we needed to fill our hours with something other than Ursula's interminable bridge games. Why do you think she wanted to take me to Mrs. Medcroft's home?"

"And naturally you went."

"Sally is my dearest friend, after all. And life is deadly dull in Dorset. If you would let me visit her in London on occasion, I would not subject you to these little entertainments of mine."

He snorted. "And that's the real reason you've foisted these characters on us. To convince me to let you go off, unchaperoned, to London."

"Sally Pritchard is a perfectly acceptable chaperon."

"She's as flighty as you are. And a good deal less intelligent. Do not expect to earn my trust by acting foolishly."

There was an impatient rustle of silk and, without truly seeing, I sensed the quick toss of her head that set her ringlets bouncing on the back of her neck. "I did not act foolishly. I attended one of her séances and thought her . . . suitable."

"Suitable? She is a quack."

"Really, Edmund." Her tone changed and became coolly rational. "I, at least, have watched her work. What right have you to criticize my judgment?"

"Good Lord, Fanny. They are all quacks. I really gave you credit for a little more sense."

"Not another word, Edmund. You are being tiresome and I haven't the patience to put up with you." She left him standing there and dashed off across the lawns.

I had been standing near the stone rail, afraid to move lest they notice me and accuse me of eavesdropping. That had not been my intent, but their argument started too abruptly for me to make a discreet exit. I held my breath and hoped that Mr. Llewelyn would either follow his sister or return to the house.

Instead, he muttered something beneath his breath and turned on his heel. He was a tall black shadow against the night, indistinct only to my eyes. In my mind, he was forcibly and emphatically real. There was an energy about him, an aura that electrified the air. It was an intense energy that made prickles rise on my arms, and brought a warm flush to my cheeks. But despite its force, it was a wholly physical reaction, one that seared the flesh but left the heart untouched. I could not admire a man who had repeatedly, and without cause, insulted both my friends and me.

Some instinct made him glance upward, and he flinched. I could not see his eyes, any more than he could possibly have seen mine, but just as assuredly as though we were captured in bright sunlight, I knew our gazes met.

"Do you make a habit of eavesdropping?" he demanded.

I stiffened. "I was not eavesdropping. But if you insist upon carrying on an argument beneath my feet before I can politely withdraw, you must expect to be overheard."

"And what do you do with the information you gather?" he continued, ignoring everything I had said. "Advise your Mrs. Medcroft in order that she may give her spiritly rappings the sound of authenticity?"

"Of all the—I most certainly do not. Mrs. Medcroft needs no help from me."

"No doubt you mean she has done her research before she enters her victims' homes."

"How dare you suggest such a thing?" I gripped the rail tightly and bent over to stare at him. "You are the most obnoxious man I have ever met. If it were up to me, we would not remain another second beneath your roof."

"Ah! At last we are in accordance. For if it were up to *me*, your immediate departure would also be assured. Unfortunately, I must tolerate Fanny's whims, just as you must accede to those of your employer."

"Mrs. Medcroft is not my employer. She is my friend."

"Then you make a poor choice of friends."

He turned on his heel and stalked off, his broad

strides carrying him into the house before I could think of a suitable retort. Furious, I left the balcony and slammed the French doors behind me. Nothing would have pleased me more than to have caught his head between them. Instead, I did nothing worse than rattle the glass and start the curtains swaying.

My heart had only just stopped thudding against my ribs when Mrs. Medcroft summoned me for the séance. She appeared calmer, but her hands fluttered when she spoke, and Mr. Quarmby supported her arm. Behind them, apparently expected to join us, stood Chaitra.

It was Chaitra who guided us to the parlor, having learned something of the layout of the manor in the few hours we had been separated. She swept along in front of us, her heavy braid swaying down her back, her slippers whispering across the marble tiles.

"Are you certain you feel able?" I asked Mrs. Medcroft, not at all happy with her color.

"Dear child. I will do what I can and trust to the spirits not to fail me."

The parlor was a more intimate room than the drawing room. Ivory damask curtains draped the windows, and candles glowed across a circular rosewood table. This had been set round with nine straightback chairs. I wondered if no one had realized Chaitra would be joining us, then caught sight of Mr. Llewelyn's glowering face staring at us from a wing chair in the far corner. He, apparently, intended to take Winnie's advice and watch the proceedings from a distance.

Mrs. Medcroft stepped forward and ran her fingers across the polished wood surface. "This will please the spirits. They do prefer warm, rosy tones."

"Then we can expect good results," Fanny said from the doorway.

She shook her head. "One can never anticipate the behavior of spirits, my dear. And there are a great many other factors involved." She glanced meaningfully at her host.

Fanny laughed. "If Edmund keeps the spirits away, then we will exile him to his study."

"You will not," he declared, crossing his arms over his chest and settling back in his chair. I gave his dark face a quick glance and found myself doubting that all of us together could have budged him.

Mrs. Medcroft touched my arm, drawing my eyes back to the table in the center of the room. "Hilary, dear, I want you to sit on my right. Chaitra always has the place on my left, and Mr. Quarmby had better take the chair across from me. Everyone else may do as they please."

One by one, the other guests made their way into the parlor and took their seats. It surprised me to find that Ursula was joining us, given her outspoken disapproval.

Fanny wiggled on her chair, and her long fingernails tapped impatiently on the tabletop. Beside her, Dr. Rhodes watched her surreptitiously, his face clouded. His concern for her seemed to be professional, and I wondered if her health was as delicate as he seemed to think. She was unquestionably excitable, possibly even impressionable, but I would not have considered her dangerously high-strung.

Mrs. Medcroft looked around the table, and waited for the fragments of conversation to end. When absolute silence descended, she nodded and said, "If you would please clasp hands, we shall begin."

I gave her my left hand. Dr. Rhodes was to my

right. He had arrived in the parlor shortly after Fanny and, much to my relief, taken the seat between us. It forced Winnie to sit across the table from me and next to his wife. Our faces were pale circles in the gloom.

"Mr. Quarmby will ask the blessing," Mrs. Medcroft said in a somber voice. "One should never approach the spirits without first invoking God's protection for those of us who seek the truth. And on no account must you break the circle. Such an act could bring disastrous results."

"Do get on with it, Mr. Quarmby," Fanny urged. "Or we shall be here all night."

"As you wish."

The blessing was mercifully brief. I looked to Mrs. Medcroft to discover what was to come next. Her eyes closed and she swayed in her chair. All around could be heard the sound of irregular breathing, and my heart thumped against my chest.

"Is there anybody here?" Mrs. Medcroft intoned.

Silence.

"Is there anybody here?" she demanded again in a louder voice.

There was a soft rap on the table.

"Good Lord," said Eglantine, her teeth clicking across her words and her eyes bulging. "Who did that?"

"Please be quiet," Mrs. Medcroft exclaimed, struggling to maintain her trance. "I simply cannot work with interference."

"There's no need to get snippy about it."

A groan from Fanny shushed her.

"Is that you, White Feather?" Mrs. Medcroft continued.

This brought a second, louder rap.

"Who's White Feather?" Ursula asked in a loud whisper. Her angular face seemed to hover in the darkness, and her faintly slanted eyes glistened in the candlelight.

"Mrs. Medcroft's control," her sister replied. "Now, do be quiet."

"Don't you tell me to be quiet."

"Good Lord," Winnie muttered, giving his curls an impatient shake. "If you two are going to carry on we might as well all go to bed."

"It's a pity you didn't suggest that earlier," Ursula said. "I, for one, would have preferred a decent night's sleep to putting up with this tripe."

"Do you want me to continue or not?" Mrs. Medcroft demanded, opening her eyes and glaring across the table at the company seated there. "This was not, after all, my idea."

"Now, now, dear lady. There's no point in getting upset. Everyone's just a little nervous."

Fanny nodded. "Do go on. We won't make another sound. Isn't that right?" She levelled a sharp look on his sister, who scowled at her but said nothing.

Mrs. Medcroft relaxed against the back of her chair. "I shall try again. But if one more person interrupts then I simply will not continue."

She let a few seconds pass while she struggled to return to her trance. Around the table the tension grew. It billowed upward like a dark cloud and hovered above our heads. Just when I thought the pressure would be too much to bear, Mrs. Medcroft groaned loudly.

"Are you still there, White Feather?"

A loud rap.

"How are you, dear? Feeling better, I hope?"

Several raps in quick succession.

"Good. White Feather's granddaughter recently passed over and he's been helping her make the transition. It's been something of a drain on his energies, poor man."

"Well, give her our best wishes," Winnie offered.

Another series of rapping met his comment, and he laughed nervously.

"Is there anyone on the other side who wishes to communicate with us tonight, White Feather?" Mrs. Medcroft's voice rang out through the room, and I surmised she had regained some of her failing confidence.

There was a short silence, followed by a soft rap.

"I see . . . I see . . . Oh, dear, everything is so murky, it's hard to tell. Is it a child, White Feather? A young—"

"Robin!" Eglantine exclaimed. "Is it my brother, Robin?"

"Did he die at a young age?" Mrs. Medcroft asked. "This child is no more than ten."

"He was eleven, but he was always small for his age. He died of scarlet fever."

"What on earth is he doing here?" Fanny demanded.

"He's my brother. Why shouldn't he come?"

"Well, I'm sorry, but this is supposed to be my séance."

"You really are a self-centered little pig, Fanny," Ursula said.

"Not too self-centered to appreciate what's beneath my nose," she retorted obtusely.

"Will you two stop bickering. I want to hear what Robin has to say."

"He says . . . he says he loves you and that you mustn't worry so much. He's looking out for you."

"Ask him if he knows where I lost my pearl earrings. I've been searching for them everywhere."

"I'm sorry. It's too late. He's gone."

"Bother. Why couldn't he have stayed a few more seconds?"

"At least he came. No one's said anything to *me* yet, and this is *my* séance."

"It's difficult for them to remain more than a few minutes in the physical world," Mrs. Medcroft explained, apparently able to maintain her trance and contribute to the conversation. "It's painful for them to see those they've left behind. And it really does no good asking them about material possessions, because they realize the unimportance of such things."

"Ask White Feather if there's anyone else who wants to speak with us," Fanny prompted.

Mrs. Medcroft nodded. "Is anyone else present, White Feather? Oh, yes. Of course. I see her now."

"Who is it?"

"A . . . a woman. She's young and very beautiful. Her hands are reaching towards us, and she's calling . . . yes, yes, she's calling 'Fanny.' Could it be your mother, dear?"

Fanny eyes shone in the candlelight. "Yes, it would have to be her. She died when I was only ten."

"Oh, the sadness. It's unbearable. The utter, utter sadness. You cannot imagine what I am suffering. The poor, dear woman. How she hated to leave you."

"Oh, I know it's true," Fanny said, her face shining. "I've always known she wanted to stay with me. I've felt her presence around me all my life."

"She's calling to you again. I can hear her. She's crying, 'Fanny. Fanny. My dearest Fanny.' Call out to her, my dear, and let her know you love her."

Fanny licked her lips. "Mama? Mama, is that really you? Can you hear me? Please answer me, Mama."

There was a loud, excited rapping, not on the table, but on the parlor door. Our heads turned and the door burst open, as though pushed from the other side with great force. It struck the wall with a bang hard enough to shake the table, and a cold gust of air surged through the room and swept across us with icy fingers. In an instant, it extinguished all the candles, and we found ourselves in absolute darkness.

Before any of us could recover from the shock, a woman screamed.

4

In the corner of the room, a match was struck and a light flared in the darkness. It illuminated nothing more than Mr. Llewelyn's grim face, a sight that was not in the least reassuring. His mouth was set in a tight line, his hooded eyes only magnified his annoyance. The flame died almost immediately, and I found the darkness infinitely preferable to that forbidding visage.

"For God's sake, Edmund. Bring a lamp," Dr. Rhodes demanded. "Are you all right, Fanny?"

"Really, Kenneth." Ursula's disembodied voice floated through the gloom. "You might extend your concern to the rest of us."

"Can you answer me, Fanny?" he asked again, ignoring her remark. There was no reply, and he muttered to himself beneath his breath.

"Do get a move on, Edmund," Winnie said, his earlier exuberance noticeably absent.

With deliberate movements, our host obliged. A

second match burst into flame, and he lifted the glass chimney from an oil lamp that sat on the mantelpiece. That done, he turned up the wick. The mellow glow spilled across the room and across Fanny Llewelyn's limp body.

Dr. Rhodes gasped. "Good Lord, she's fainted."

He bent over her. She had collapsed against the back of her chair and her face was stark white. His color was not much better, but, whatever his emotions, he maintained a professional self-control.

He glanced over his shoulder. "Winnie, help me get her to the sofa."

"I don't think I'll be much use to you, old man. Feeling a bit weak myself."

"Good God. Edmund, come and give me a hand. Ursula, bring the smelling salts."

"I have some in my purse," Mrs. Medcroft told him. "I like to keep them on hand, you understand. In case the spirits—"

"Yes, yes. Give them to me."

"Well, really. That is hardly the way to talk to someone who only wishes to do a good deed."

"Shall I look for them, Mrs. Medcroft?" I offered.

She willingly passed her purse to me. While Dr. Rhodes and Mr. Llewelyn carried Fanny to the sofa, I rummaged through the wad of lacy handkerchiefs until my fingers touched the familiar vial. I immediately handed the smelling salts to Dr. Rhodes. He shot me a grateful look and turned back to his patient.

"Trust Fanny to make a fuss," Ursula muttered. "This was all her idea in the first place."

Eglantine Winthrop managed a faint groan. "I, for one, cannot blame the child. Never have I had such a scare. What on earth caused that rush of air?"

"Wind sweeping down the chimney." Mr. Llewelyn's flat statement issued from directly behind me, startling me almost as much as Fanny had done with her scream. I hadn't realized he had been standing at my back.

"Come now," Winnie protested. "Hardly a draft. I shut the damper myself."

On the sofa, Fanny moaned and her eyes flickered open. Crushed ringlets clung to the crown of her head. Her heart-shaped face was as white as the lace at her throat. She gazed up into Dr. Rhodes's face with a look of confusion. But even pale and shaken, she was delightfully appealing.

Dr. Rhodes gazed adoringly into her frightened, lavender-blue eyes. "Nothing to worry about. You'll be fine in a minute."

"And perhaps this will teach you a lesson," her brother added, again making me jump.

Hardly a charitable remark under the circumstances. I dared to glance upward at his face and was immediately raked by an accusatory scowl. He seemed to think a good share of the fault for his sister's distress—and his own bad temper—was mine.

I refused to accept the rebuke without delivering one of my own. "You might show a little consideration. Your sister has suffered a shock."

He stared at me, affronted by my nerve. "You are hardly the one to criticize."

"Certainly, someone needs to say something. It is bad enough that we must endure your attacks, but surely you must have compassion for your own sister."

"Compassion is wasted on fools," he retorted, not lifting his gaze from my face.

I forced myself to face his disapproval without betraying my sense of unease. That was difficult to do. He was passionate in his disgust of me. It emanated from him like black smoke from smoldering coals. Though why he chose to save the brunt of his assault for me alone, I couldn't fathom. Unless it was because I dared to challenge him.

Determined I should not be the first to avert my eyes, I kept my gaze leveled upon him and, using my sweetest voice, said, "Do you know, Mr. Llewelyn, all through my childhood I wished for a brother? But I cannot say I envy Fanny hers."

My rudeness stirred a flurry of gasps. Only the target of my insult remained unfazed. "Her fainting was none of my doing," he said in a silken voice that made me regret my hasty tongue. "That was due solely to the efforts of you and your friends."

Mrs. Medcroft pushed back her chair and stood. Exacting every inch from her considerable height, she said, "How dare you, sir? I did nothing that was not asked of me."

He rounded on her. "It was a ridiculous performance from start to finish, one designed to delude and frighten the gullible. Now look at your handiwork."

"Are you aware that I am welcome in the best houses in London?"

"Well, you are *not* welcome here!"

Dr. Rhodes glared over his shoulder at the three of us. "If you must continue this argument, will you please take it somewhere else. You are upsetting Fanny."

"I'm feeling quite a bit better," she murmured, sounding anything but well.

"She deserves to be a good deal more than upset," her brother retorted. "If it were up to me, she would be given a good spanking." Nevertheless, he stalked from the room and slammed the door behind him.

"Such a disagreeable man," Mrs. Medcroft said, and looked to Mr. Quarmby for agreement.

He nodded thoughtfully. "Sometimes I marvel at your patience, dear lady. To do so much for so many, and yet receive so little gratitude in return."

Ursula snorted. "Perhaps when and if Fanny fully recovers, she'll see you receive some of that gratitude." She regarded her distraught guests and weary sister with a hard eye. "Well, unless anyone would like a hot toddy, I think we ought to retire. Kenneth, I'll help you get Fanny to bed. Winnie, you and Eglantine can make your way to your rooms without me, can't you? I've put you in your usual suite."

Her words stirred Winnie. He placed both hands on the table and forced himself to his feet. There was a yellow cast to his skin and his balance looked precarious. Earlier, I had thought his protestations of weakness merely an excuse to avoid putting himself to the trouble of helping Dr. Rhodes. Now I realized I had been wrong.

Winnie gave his arm to his wife, who wobbled to her feet and leaned heavily on his arm for a support he seemed ill able to give. Her lips were gray, and the tip of her tongue flickered across them. She had also, I realized, been oddly quiet since the candles had blown out.

"What a night this has been," Mrs. Medcroft exclaimed, voicing my own thoughts, although not in the tone I would have used. Hers was decidedly pleased.

She took a deep breath and filled her lungs with air. Slowly, it whistled out between her pursed lips. "Ah!" she sighed. "I feel rejuvenated. What a pity we had to stop, just when we were getting somewhere. If your brother is home, we will try again tomorrow evening, of course."

Nobody, not even Fanny, looked pleased by that announcement.

Dr. Rhodes's brow wrinkled. "I think one séance is quite enough. Edmund is right."

After taking that strong stand he looked at Fanny and his conviction vanished. "Really, Fanny, I don't mean to take his side against you, and you know it isn't like me to protest, but this can't go on. It's not good for your health."

"Oh, tosh." Mrs. Medcroft brushed aside his words. "Fanny will be fine. She's just a bit shaken. That often happens the first time, and you can't count the evening with Mrs. Pritchard, because White Feather wasn't feeling well and nothing much happened."

Fanny glanced from her complacent face to Dr. Rhodes's grim countenance. "Well, I—"

"Don't you let your young man sway you, dear." Mrs. Medcroft waggled her finger at her. "I know the effect a young man can have on his young lady. But you have to insist upon taking the reins of your own life. Mrs. Pritchard told me how badly you want to reach your mother. What would she say if she learned I'd failed you?"

"I do want to talk to Mama," she agreed.

Dr. Rhodes came to his feet. "Perhaps this decision had best wait until tomorrow. Ursula?"

"Of course. Winnie. Eglantine. You both look dead on your feet." She gave us a dismissive glance. "I assume the three of you can manage on you own?"

"Of course," Mr. Quarmby agreed. "Do not trouble yourself on our account."

With Ursula and Dr. Rhodes supporting Fanny, they all departed. Mrs. Medcroft watched them go with a frown. "Annoying man," she muttered. "Another second and Fanny would have agreed."

"Nothing will have changed by tomorrow," Mr. Quarmby assured her.

I was less convinced. The banging door, the cold draft, and the dousing of the candles had badly shaken her. By tomorrow, she might have decided to abandon this foolishness. I fervently hoped she would. Then there would be no need for us to stay.

And the sooner we were out from beneath Mr. Llewelyn's roof, the happier I would be.

I prepared for bed immediately upon returning to my room, but didn't retire. The séance had somehow energized me, and my mind and body rebelled at the thought of sleep. Instead, I took out my stationery and wrote a letter to my father's solicitors to let them know I had arrived safely and was in Mrs. Medcroft's care.

I did not elaborate on the nature of her activities, for I could imagine their distress. They were fair minded, but fearful and suspicious of anything that was odd or out of the ordinary. Still, I did admit that I had not altered my intentions of looking for a position.

After carefully signing my name, I tucked the single sheet into an envelope and picked up my pen to write out the address. A woman's muffled laughter arose from somewhere beyond my bedroom door and made me pause. It was a provocative, flirtatious laughter, filled with intimacy and meaning, and I could not imagine the sounds coming from either Ursula or Eglantine. Fanny? I wondered. But Dr. Rhodes had intended to give her a sleeping draught.

I set down my pen and listened.

The laughter came again, soft, but distinct in the silence. The hair on my forearms prickled, and the light from the lamp on my desk dimmed, although the flame remained high and steady. My heartbeat quickened.

Were the sounds due to some ghostly presence, or had I succumbed to fancies because of the séance?

Determined to relieve myself of any nonsensical notions before they took hold of me, I rose and walked quietly across the room. There, I hesitated. What a fool I should look if I interrupted a tryst between lovers.

The doorknob glittered in the lamplight, tempting me. Was it better to have the answers to my questions or to act with discretion? Reluctantly, I reached out my hand. My fingers brushed across the crystal surface, and I drew them back with a gasp. I might have been touching solid ice.

Outside, the woman laughed again. Loudly, but without amusement. She had grown bored. Impatient.

Was she mocking me? Or someone else?

I grasped the knob again, ignoring the chill that shot up my arm, and opened the door. The coldness in the corridor hit me like a wave of seawater. I shuddered from head to toe and pulled the flaps of my nightjacket together. Everything was in darkness, and the sounds had stopped as abruptly as they had begun. And yet . . .

Something made me turn toward the landing.

It was quiet. But not empty. Someone was standing there. I squinted into the gloom and made out a slender, feminine shape next to the bannister. Before I could move or speak, the figure turned. My heartbeat pounded in my ears and I bit back a scream.

Then I realized there was something familiar about the graceful motion.

"Chaitra?" I demanded.

"Miss Hilary?" She moved out of the darkness, her long hair unbraided and swaying around her. "What are you doing out of bed?"

"I might well ask you the same thing. Was that you laughing?"

"So you heard her, too, did you?"

"I could hardly avoid hearing her. Everyone in this wing must have heard her."

"Do you think so?"

"What do you mean by that?"

She glanced down the corridor meaningfully. "No one else has left their room tonight."

"Nor do I blame them. After this evening's episode they were probably too frightened."

"Perhaps." Her tone was singularly unconvinced.

Not liking what she was implying, I asked, "Did you see who it was?"

"There was nothing to see."

"I thought it might have been Fanny. Or one of the maids."

"There was no one there," she said flatly.

I stared at her. She had left her room and reached the landing before I had opened my door. Before the laughter had stopped. If someone had been there she could not have failed to see them.

"Then who?"

She shrugged. "Whoever Mrs. Medcroft summoned to the house this evening."

"Nonsense," I declared. "That's quite impossible."

"If you say so, miss."

Her answer upset me more than outright disagreement. I wanted to argue with her, but she had given me no cause. Instead, she bid me goodnight and slipped past me to return to her own room.

"Chaitra," I called after her in a loud whisper. "Where is Mrs. Medcroft?"

She chuckled. "In bed, miss. Sleeping."

I did not sleep well that night. Chaitra's words had upset me more than I wanted to admit. It did not help matters that I had found something haunting and unnatural in the laughter. From the moment I had stepped inside the foyer, the house had seemed oppressive, as though a bad smell lingered in the air. Last night, the feeling had been stronger.

Had we, through the séance, given added strength to an unworldly being?

And who was that being? Fanny's beloved mother?

Or someone much more sinister?

I reached the breakfast room somewhat later than eight, but found only Mrs. Medcroft and Mr. Quarmby sitting at the table. Pale sunlight filtered through the chintz curtains on the French doors, and low-lying clouds settled on the gardens beyond.

In the corner of my eye, I caught a flash of motion, something dark fluttering at the edge of the curtains. I turned my head, but whatever had been there was gone. A blackbird, perhaps. Or a raven.

From the full platters of bacon and ham and shirred eggs on the sideboard, I realized I was not the only one who had slept late that morning. After bidding the others a good morning, I silently filled my plate and took the chair opposite Mrs. Medcroft.

She regarded me with concerned eyes. "Hilary? Are you all right? You look troubled."

"It's nothing, really."

"Come, now. You must not be afraid to confide in me."

I set down my fork. Perhaps it would be more sensible to speak. "It is this business with the séances. Do you think it wise to continue them? I can't help fearing that, through our efforts, we have disturbed and strengthened something that was better left alone."

Mrs. Medcroft exchanged amused glances with Mr. Quarmby. "You're a dear child. Just like your mother. She worried about everything and everyone. But you mustn't fear. I am completely familiar with the spirit world. No one knows better than I what should or should not be done."

"Indeed," Mr. Quarmby agreed.

"And last night went especially well, I thought. Didn't you, Mr. Quarmby?"

"Absolutely. Without question."

"One of my better séances."

"You were magnificent."

They exchanged smiles, and I suppressed a shiver. "Forgive me, but there is something about this house that frightens me. I felt it when we arrived, and again when the draft blew out the candles. Then, last night, after we had gone to bed . . ." I hesitated, realizing how foolish I sounded.

Mr. Quarmby leaned forward, suddenly interested in what I had to say. "What happened?" he asked.

I told them about the laughter, feeling more foolish than ever. "But I'm convinced we are disturbing something that should not be disturbed," I finished stubbornly.

Mrs. Medcroft tittered and shook her head. "Really, Hilary. You are very young and the very young are most susceptible. We cannot have your imagination getting the better of you."

"But Chaitra—"

"Nonsense. You mustn't listen to Chaitra or she will fill your head with all sorts of silly ideas. I'll have a talk with her and see that she doesn't upset you again." She yawned politely behind her hand. "Mr. Quarmby, I cannot eat another bite. If you would be so good as to escort me upstairs . . . ?"

He nodded politely, but his eyes flickered in my direction.

"And Hilary, dear," she continued. "When you're finished, would you come upstairs and help me with my correspondence? I have rheumatism in my fingers and, with all the wet weather we've been having in London, they've been bothering me."

"Certainly."

She kissed me on the cheek and gave Mr. Quarmby her arm. Together, they walked off, he was struggling to match his short strides to her long, flowing steps. I fought back a smile. In their own way they were as mismatched a pair as Winnie and Eglantine, although Mr. Quarmby was decidedly more devoted than his counterpart.

A soft click by the windows distracted me, and I glanced across the room. A man was standing just inside the French doors, his dark figure outlined by the splash of sunlight at his back. It was several seconds before I was able to see his features clearly, but I had no doubts as to his identity. His imposing height, the arrogant lift to his chin, and his aloof air made Mr. Llewelyn wholly unmistakable.

As my eyes adjusted to the brightness around him, I saw there was a slight curve to his full lips, a complacent smile that made me feel he had caught me at a disadvantage. How? I wondered. Then I realized there was something odd about his choosing those doors to enter the room, and remembered the dark flutter I had glimpsed upon seating myself at the table.

"How long have you been standing outside?" I demanded.

He delivered me a cool look that said I had no right to question him, while telling me everything I wanted to know.

I gasped. "You were eavesdropping on our conversation."

"You are hardly one to throw stones."

For a brief moment his gaze caught and held mine, and I found myself sinking into those mysterious gray depths. It was a strange sensation, rather like being adrift on shrouded waters. I felt chilled by his cold appraisal and yet the room seemed too close for me to catch my breath.

He arched a brow, impatient for a response I was not certain I could make.

Luckily, I was saved from my plight by a sense of indignation that rose through my confusion and swept the fog from my mind. "Had I been able to leave the balcony without drawing attention to myself, I would have left immediately. But you—"

"*I* thought it might be well worth my while to listen. And, after a fashion, it was."

He had not even attempted to excuse his behavior. The nerve of the man. "Did you expect to hear us making plans to bilk you of your fortune? You must have been sadly disappointed. I should think our *private* discussion proved us to be innocent of any wrongful intent."

"I would hardly make such a sweeping statement."

He sauntered across to the sideboard and peered disdainfully at the chafing dishes. His complete disavowal of wrongdoing was etched in his every motion. I had never seen anyone who seemed as comfortable in his body as Mr. Llewelyn. Even my rebuke failed to make him look the least bit disconcerted, and I fumed silently.

At last, he lifted his head and, with the air of one making a magnanimous admission, said, "But I have learned you have better sense than I had originally thought."

"I could hardly have less."

"I suppose that is no less than I deserve."

"I should say it was a good deal less."

"I did not come in here to argue with you. Only to admit that I owe you an apology. I must beg you to forgive my previous bad manners."

I barely refrained from gaping. Those words could not have come easily to a proud man like Mr. Llewelyn. From the hard line of his mouth to the stiff stance of those long legs, there was not an inch of him that was either pliant or reasonable.

I was left with no choice but to forgive him. That, or to behave in a manner that would be unacceptably rude.

"I shall accept your apology . . . to me," I said. "But I cannot forgive you for your opinion of Mrs. Medcroft and Mr. Quarmby until you also repent of your behavior toward them."

"Ha! More likely you will come to a realization of their dishonesty first."

I pushed aside my plate and rose from my chair. "I hardly think that possible. Nor will I continue to talk with you whilst you take that view."

Before I had gone three steps, he crossed the gap

that separated us and caught me by the shoulder. His rough seizure, unexpected as it was, sent a shock trembling down my spine. Before my cry of dismay could reach my lips, he twisted me about to face him. His hard fingers pinched into my flesh beneath the thin layer of taffeta, but he seemed to care nothing for the pain he was causing me. I winced and drew up my hands to defend myself.

His chin jerked up in surprise. "And what good do you think that would do you if it was my intention to harm you?"

Decidedly little. He towered over me by almost a foot and, despite the breadth of his chest, not one inch of him was excess fat. He needed only the one hand to hold me in place and seemed to exert little effort in accomplishing that feat. And greater than his physical strength was the aura of power that exuded from him. My struggles were nothing but ridiculous posturing in the face of that power.

I dropped my fists and glared at him. "If necessary, I will scream."

"Good Lord. Hasn't there been enough screaming in this house? I only wish you to remain and hear me out."

"Then there was no cause for you to assault me. You only had to ask."

Obligingly, he dropped his hand from my shoulder. "Is that better?"

"Immensely." I took a backward step.

"And you will give me a few minutes of your time?"

I hesitated, then slowly nodded lest a different answer cause him to resume his hold on me.

Satisfied, he folded his arms across his chest, pursed his lips, and fixed me with a fierce stare. The knowledge that he had developed a small measure of respect for my character failed to protect me from the force of his assessment. I fought with the urge to retreat yet another step and tried to forget we were alone in the room.

"This business with the séances *must* stop," he said abruptly, giving his words a curious emphasis. "They will do no one any good, I am convinced of it."

"I thought you did not believe in spirits, Mr. Llewelyn."

"I do not."

"And you say there are no spirits at Abbey House?"

He shot me a furious look. "There are not."

"Then what reason have you to be concerned?"

He deliberately stepped toward me, intimidating me with the nearness of his person as he had failed to do with his words. "You have met Fanny, Miss Carewe. She is high-spirited and headstrong. I do not think her equipped to look upon a simple matter like a cold draft with objectivity. None of this is good for her."

Something in his tone rang false, and I had the strongest feeling there was a great deal more at stake than his sister's state of mind. "You have only to order us to leave," I pointed out, quite reasonably I thought.

He tossed aside my suggestion with an impatient wave of his hand. "If I spoil what Fanny calls 'her fun,' she will go to great lengths to punish me. And since I am impervious to her barbs, she will undoubtedly take satisfaction in tormenting Ursula. Is it unreasonable of me to wish to maintain some level of peace in my household?"

"Of course not. But what do you want of me?"

"A favor. Since you and I both agree the séances should end, I hoped you would prevail upon Mrs. Medcroft to return to London of her own accord. Fanny could not possibly take exception at that."

"I have already told Mrs. Medcroft of my doubts with no result. As you yourself are aware," I added pointedly. "What makes you think I can do better if I speak to her again?"

His tone became markedly friendlier. "I am only asking that you try. And I will have Kenneth speak to Fanny and see if he can make her listen to sense."

Silently, I considered his request. While I believed he wanted us to leave, as much now as before, I did not for a moment believe the reasons he had given me. Instead, I suspected he, too, was afraid of unsettling something that was better left undisturbed. Something that already had a foothold in his home.

For that, I couldn't blame him.

I lifted my gaze to Mr. Llewelyn's expectant face. "I cannot promise to succeed," I said. "But I will do what I can."

"That is all I ask."

He gave me a nod of approval and my stomach fluttered. It startled me to discover how much I enjoyed that approval. But there was no question Mr. Llewelyn could be charming when it suited him, and his good looks gave him an outrageous advantage over most gentlemen.

I steeled myself not to surrender to that charm.

Fortunately, another thought distracted me. I put my hand in my pocket and pulled out the letter I had written the previous night. "Perhaps you can do me a favor in return," I suggested. "Is there someone who might post this for me?"

He took the envelope from me, unintentionally

brushing my fingers with his own. I hastily withdrew my hand. Luckily, his gaze rested upon the address and not upon my warm face. After a quick glance, he raised his head and nodded. "I will see to the matter this morning."

"That's very kind of you. And, now, if you will excuse me, I will go and see if Mrs. Medcroft needs my help."

He looked down at my barely touched breakfast plate and raised a questioning eyebrow.

"It seems I am not as hungry as I thought," I mumbled.

With his gaze heavy upon me, I made my retreat.

I filled the morning hours doing odd tasks for Mrs. Medcroft who seemed determined to keep me occupied. "I know what young people are like," she insisted, handing me some stockings to darn. "Too much energy for their own good. If their minds aren't kept busy, they fill up their heads with all sorts of silly ideas."

I supposed she meant well. After our conversation at the breakfast table, she must have thought the best medicine would be everyday tasks that demanded my attention without stirring my imagination.

Twice I tried to broach the topic of leaving Abbey House, and twice she changed the subject. At last, seeing I was not to be thwarted, she set down her reading and came and sat on the sofa beside me.

"Really, child. Just think what you are saying. We are here to help Fanny Llewelyn, and I will not leave until I have done just that."

"But both her brother and Dr. Rhodes say this cannot be good for her health."

"Neither of them are sensitives. This is a spiritual, not a medical matter. They are less qualified than I to give advice." She patted me on the hand. "Only be patient. You will see that I am right."

I sighed and let the subject drop. It was, after all, not my decision to make.

Nevertheless, there would be no séances that evening. Fanny felt too unwell to come downstairs that day, and her decision about holding other séances was delayed until tomorrow. To my surprise, she sent a message to Mrs. Medcroft asking if I might be allowed to come and read to her that afternoon.

"Of course you must go," she said, accepting for me.

The prospect of spending the afternoon with Fanny did not upset me in the least. Whatever her brother and sister thought of her, she had proved herself the most charming member of her family. The only charming member, if I overlooked her brother's brief friendly attempt at winning a favor and the nod of approval he had bestowed on me.

After luncheon, I washed my face and hands and asked the upstairs maid to show me to her room. The family suites were strung along the west wing, and I took the corridor that let out on the opposite side of the landing from the guest rooms. The maid bustled ahead of me. I fixed my gaze on her lace-trimmed cap, horribly conscious of the drafty landing at my back and the demonic faces peering at me from the enormous Gothic fireplace.

Those faces seemed to have lives of their own. There was a look of conscious evil in their stone eyes, and their lips curled back over toothy grins and pointed, darting tongues. The chill on the landing seemed to emanate from them and spread in all directions throughout the house.

Fanny's suite was a distinct relief. It was like stepping into a flower garden. Pink brocade hangings fell from a gilt and tasseled head canopy and swathed the baroque headboard. Scalloped and ornately carved rosewood framed chairs and two-seat sofas, upholstered in satin prints, were crammed into every nook, and tabletops were littered with ceramic urns and Parian figures.

She herself was sitting up in bed, surrounded by a mound of pillows. The fringe at her forehead was curled, the rest of her hair was pulled back into a low chignon, and her shoulders were swathed in a lacy wrapper. Ill? She looked more like someone prepared to hold court.

She smiled cheerfully and waved a hand to draw my attention to her circumstances. "It's all nonsense, really. But Kenneth does worry."

"And so he should," I agreed. "You had quite a start last night."

"Oh, bother. That was nothing. I've done myself worse harm falling off a horse."

"Not really?" I gazed at her with increasing admiration.

She nodded and, with a slender hand, shoved aside the pile of French fashion magazines surrounding her. "Do come and sit down. Or pull up a chair if you can't stand the clutter."

Something in her excited manner made me feel fifteen again. I slipped off my shoes and sat cross-legged on the end of the bed. She tossed me a pillow that I propped against the footboard at my back.

"What would you like me to read to you?" I asked.

"Goodness, let's not do anything so dreary. That

was only for Kenneth's benefit. I thought we might have a nice chat."

I couldn't see how that could do her any harm. "Did you ride much?" I asked, curious about the nature of her accident. "My father never would let me rent anything but the dullest old mares."

Her smile flashed. "Edmund's just as bad. He's been my guardian since Papa's death when I was fifteen. But I don't let him stop me. Look."

She pulled up the sleeve of her wrapper and displayed a faint scar that stretched from her wrist to her elbow. "I have another on my leg that's much worse. You cannot believe the fuss everyone made."

"What happened?" I asked, finding it difficult to match Fanny's delicate beauty with her obviously headstrong nature.

"I'm ashamed to tell you. I can only imagine what you'll think of me. I was a horrible child." Nevertheless, she shrugged and pulled down her sleeve. "Kenneth brought up this delightful mare for one of Edmund's hunts. He meant to ride her himself, of course. But I slipped down to the stables before breakfast and had one of the grooms saddle her for me."

"I suppose, given your relationship, he wouldn't really have minded."

"Oh, that was several years ago. I was only fifteen. Kenneth hadn't given me a second look." She giggled. "As I recall, he was a little afraid of me. He's always been awkward with ladies. Except for Ursula, and you can't really count her."

I felt a brief twinge of pity for her stern, unfeminine elder sister, but my curiosity made me dismiss her. "How did you dare take Dr. Rhodes's horse if you weren't close?"

"I was awfully wild. But Papa had just died, and I was feeling horribly sorry for myself. It had to do with being an orphan and desperately needing attention."

She glanced at a framed photograph on the table nearest her bed, one from which a bearded and bewhiskered gentleman glared in unsmiling disapproval. The light eyes were hard, the few remaining tufts of hair completely white. But Fanny's beautiful lavender-blue eyes misted, and no one could have doubted the affection she had felt for him.

I glanced about the room for a picture of her mother, but found none. Odd. I wondered if her mother had disliked having her photograph taken, or if Fanny couldn't bear to be reminded of her.

"At least you have a brother and sister," I remarked, wishing I had that much family.

"Half brother and sister," she corrected.

My eyebrows rose.

"Didn't you know? Mama was Papa's second wife. Edmund and Ursula had a different mother."

"I had no idea," I admitted. "But that does explain the differences between you."

"Goodness, yes. Aren't they a pair? Edmund is the most unreasonable creature on this earth, and my half sister's no better. Neither of them have a sense of humor, although I feel a little sorry for Ursula. She raised me and took care of our father after Mama died. Now, I suppose she'll stay here and look after Edmund until he gets married. After that, she won't be wanted."

"Surely that depends upon the woman your brother marries?"

Fanny shook her head. "You don't know Ursula. There's no getting along with her. She won't even share the task of managing the household with *me*. Not that I mind. Housekeeping's nothing but a lot of drudgery. Kenneth and I will be married soon and then I'll have my own home. He has a sweet little place in Smedmore and the dearest little housekeeper. We'll manage famously, I should imagine."

It was difficult to imagine Fanny not managing famously with anyone she should meet—unless that person was actively jealous of her good looks and social polish. "But what happened with the horse?" I prompted. "Couldn't you manage her?"

Fanny grimaced. "The silly thing simply refused to budge until I tapped her with the crop. Then she took off down the lane and through the fields as though all the hounds of hell were baying at her tail. The next thing you know, she came up against a stone wall, came to a dead halt, and threw me over her head and into the field beyond."

"Good heavens. You might have broken your neck."

"Or cracked open my skull, although Edmund swore it would have taken a sledgehammer to do that. Luckily, there was blood everywhere or they would have skinned me alive."

"Were you badly hurt?" From the pale scar, I had assumed she had gotten off lightly.

She laughed ruefully. "As it turned out, only a little of the blood was mine. The mare had thundered into the protruding rocks and cut open her legs."

I gave a cry of dismay.

She grimaced again. "Yes, well. She had to be destroyed, poor thing. She'd slashed the tendons in her forelegs. Edmund reimbursed Kenneth, naturally, but everyone was furious with me for weeks. Ursula wanted to strangle me. Instead, she insisted Edmund

pack me off to school in Switzerland. And over all my
protests, he did. Got me out of their hair for three
long years. It was my own fault, of course." She
dropped her voice and her eyes saddened. "It was a
horrible thing to do. I've never really forgiven myself.
Six months earlier or six months later, it wouldn't
have happened. But I was angry with the whole world
after Papa died."

Her slender fingers rubbed along the silver
frame she was still holding, and she stared at her
father's image behind the glass. Her lips drooped
at the corners, almost imperceptibly. Someone less
observant might have thought her merely thoughtful. The unhappiness that emanated from her was
as intangible as a vapor.

"It's terrible losing one's parents," I said quietly.
"It must be far worse to be an orphan at fifteen."

She nodded. "That's how it goes sometimes." With
a determined laugh, she dismissed her melancholy.
"But I've rambled on long enough. I want to hear
about you."

"You'll be bored stiff. My life has been horribly
dull."

"Nonsense. How did you meet Mrs. Medcroft?"
she demanded. "You can't say that living with a spiritualist is not out of the ordinary."

"No," I admitted. "But I've only known her for several days."

It was her turn to gasp. "Not really. But I supposed
she had been friends with your family forever."

I shook my head and explained what little I knew
of her connection with my mother. Fanny hung on
every word and filled my ears with her questions.
Each time I paused to catch my breath, she urged me
to finish, and she took from me a vow to let her see

the scrapbooks Mrs. Medcroft had loaned me.

Ursula, I decided, had badly misjudged her sister. She might have been headstrong and careless, even irresponsible as a child, but no one who was truly self-centered would have been as attentive to another's story as she was to mine. In the end, it was the maid who interrupted me by bringing up Fanny's tea.

"Your own is downstairs, miss," she told me.

Fanny pouted, but her irrepressible smile refused to be denied. "I suppose you had better go downstairs," she admitted. "It's that or Kenneth will be up to ask why I'm not resting. We can talk again tomorrow."

5

China and silverware clinking behind me, I left Fanny to her tea and the care of the maid. Mrs. Medcroft and the other guests would be awaiting me in the drawing room. Between that dubious sanctuary and me lay the first-floor landing, an area I could not help but associate with Mrs. Llewelyn.

It loomed ahead of me, poorly lit and oddly colorless. I forced myself to suppress a shudder. My fears were unreasonable and completely unacceptable. And ghosts, if they did exist, had no power to harm the living.

I lifted my chin and walked determinedly toward the stairs. A loud crash at my back brought me to an abrupt halt, and I spun about with a soft cry. Intent as I was on whatever lay ahead, the noise behind me caught me completely off-guard. I stared down the long corridor.

It was empty.

Good heavens. What a little ninny you are, I told

myself. Fanny's maid must have dropped one of the plates.

A second crash echoed down the tunnel-like passage, coming not from Fanny's room as I had thought, but from the farthest reaches of the wing. Nor did it have the sound of something falling. Rather, I would have said, something had shattered against a wall with great force. As though it had been thrown.

But what?

And by whom?

Certainly not Fanny. Although I could well imagine her throwing a cup of tea across her room in a fit of pique. But I could hear her talking in the nearest room, chatting happily to the maid.

Who then? This was the family wing. The idea of Mr. Llewelyn throwing crockery was utterly ridiculous. There was something entirely feminine in the act. Ursula, then. I would have thought her too restrained and proper to behave in that manner, but people did not always conduct themselves in private as they did in public.

A third crash persuaded me to act. I hurried down the corridor, stepping softly until I came to the room at the end. Hesitantly, I tapped on the door.

No one answered.

"Miss Llewelyn? Are you all right?"

Still no answer.

Even as I told myself there was no reason for me to intrude, I reached for the doorknob. My hand seemed to have a life of its own. I might have regained control of myself in another moment, but the door swung open at my touch.

I peered inside. It was dark and shadowy. The curtains were drawn across the windows, shutting out all but the palest light. As my eyes adjusted to the gloom,

I made out the squat and huddled shapes of tables and chairs. None of them appeared to be occupied, but I had the uncomfortable sense of being watched.

"Is anybody here?" I asked again.

There was no response. I took a deep breath and entered. Carefully picking my way between patches of light and darkness, I went to the windows and drew back the curtains. The muted afternoon light burst through the panes of glass and illuminated my surroundings.

I was standing in a sitting room. No one else was there. Nor, it seemed, had anyone been there for some while. Sheets draped the furnishings, and a layer of dust drifted across the floor. The imprints of my footsteps were markedly clear.

I pulled back one of the cloths to reveal a Louis XIV writing table. My reflection wavered across the polished surface. I ran my fingers over the gleaming wood and wondered why anyone would let such a beautiful piece of furniture sit in an unused room.

A noise in the doorway made me lift my head.

Edmund Llewelyn was framed in the doorway, his head brushing the lintel, his face as dark and severe as the close-fitting sloping-away coat he wore. "You?" he exclaimed, sounding both surprised and greatly annoyed. "What are you doing in here? I had supposed that trespassing was beyond you."

I watched the play of emotions on his face, like some fast-moving and ominous cloud that would, at any instant, break into a violent storm. His arms were held rigidly at his side, but his fingers twitched, and a wave of menace flowed from his person and surged over me.

"I was not trespassing," I protested. "At least, that was not my intention. I heard noises and thought someone might need my help."

"Do you expect me to believe that nonsense? No one uses these rooms."

"So it would seem. I must have mistaken the direction of the sounds."

Face wary, he considered my statement. All the while, he kept his gaze fixed upon me, pinioning me to the spot. I hardly dared breathe, although his broad chest rose and fell with the regularity of a well-disciplined soldier on parade. Yet despite his apparent self-possession, I sensed an emotional battle waging within him. Was he to treat me like a confused young lady or like a thief who had stolen in his home? And, for some unknown reason, it seemed the decision he reached was of utmost importance. As if he dared not be in error lest his mistake be turned to his own detriment.

"What kind of noises did you hear?" he demanded, seemingly in need of more answers before he could condemn me.

No longer convinced of the trustworthiness of my senses, I hesitated before admitting, "Something very like glass shattering."

"That is a complete lie. My room is across the corridor and I heard nothing."

"Your door was shut. I was standing in the corridor."

"Enough. Do you expect me to believe that it was only by chance you came to my stepmother's suite?"

I felt the color drain from my cheeks. "Were these her rooms?"

"Don't play the innocent with me."

He stepped into the room, making it small and close solely by his presence there. Downstairs, the high ceilings and exaggerated spaces had reduced him to reasonable proportions. Here, his full six foot four inches and excessively broad shoulders overwhelmed me, and my view of the corridor—my one escape— was obliterated.

I held my ground and refused to be intimidated. I was a guest in his home and, whatever he thought, I had done nothing wrong. Nevertheless, his glowering expression and determined stride made me wish I had been more persuasive in my own defense.

He stopped three feet from me, too short a distance for my liking. "It seems, Miss Carewe, I have mistakenly credited you with good intentions. I will not do so again."

"On the contrary. You have misjudged me yet again. I almost regret that I am not a charlatan. For if I were, Mr. Llewelyn, you would be the most easy of victims."

His eyes glittered. "Would I, indeed?"

"Of a certainty," I cried, ignoring the danger I read in his face. "Anyone who fails so persistently and determinedly to see the truth could not help but fall prey to those who hope to mislead him."

"If you think to win my confidence by these tactics, you have sorely underestimated me."

"I am doing nothing of the sort. How was I supposed to know what rooms were or were not hers?"

He paused, then swiftly answered, "Fanny must have told you."

"She did not. But if you don't believe me, you have only to ask her."

"All right," he said in a controlled manner that might have persuaded someone less wary to suppose he had undergone a change of heart. "Let us say I do believe you. Was anything broken?"

"No," I admitted, realizing how my answer would sound to his ears. "But I may have come to the wrong room."

"And how did you get in?"

"Why, through the door, of course. How else?"

"These rooms are kept locked, Miss Carewe. And I have the only key. You could not have entered without first picking the lock."

"Why, that's absurd. As I recall, I did not even turn the handle but merely touched the doorknob. Someone else must have been here and left the door ajar."

His gaze went to the floor and followed the tracks of my footsteps to the window and back again. Those, and the trail made by his own feet, were the only marks in the entire room. I stared at them with dismay, knowing that the evidence supported his worst suspicions.

"I am telling you the truth," I cried, my voice trembling.

"You do not sound either convinced or convincing, Miss Carewe."

He took one long step, covering the remaining distance between us, and grasped me roughly by the shoulders. "I thought you might have seen me through the French doors this morning. It seems your little display was all for my benefit. Is Mrs. Medcroft aware you have schemes of your own that have nothing to do with hers?"

"Just what are you suggesting?"

"I am thirty-two years old, Miss Carewe. Unmarried. Excessively rich. And considered more than passably handsome."

I gaped at him. The utter arrogance of the man. Did he really think I had deliberately led him to believe I was in accordance with him in order to win his approval? Another look at his derisive expression told me that was exactly what he believed.

"That is utter nonsense," I declared. "*Neither* of us

are scheming against anyone. And as for me, far from having designs on you, I would sooner live out my life a spinster than be forced to suffer your company one moment longer than is necessary."

"Do you think me foolish enough to fall for your lies?"

"I think your vanity blinds you to the truth."

"I am wholly familiar with the games women of your sort like to play."

"Of my sort?"

He nodded. "And the time when I was likely to fall prey to those games is long past. Be warned. If you use your wiles on me you will find yourself the loser." With one hard pull, he brought me up against him. My breasts flattened against his chest, and I struggled helplessly to free myself.

Ignoring my panic, he cupped my chin with his free hand and lifted my face to his. I gasped. He could not possibly mean to—

Before I could bring myself to admit to his intentions, his mouth descended on mine and he kissed me. It was a rough, hard kiss, not a lover's caress but a warning of what fate held for me if I dared cross him. It forced the breath from me, and his hard embrace made drawing new air into my lungs an impossibility.

I grew dizzy and my legs trembled. If he held me another moment in that iron grip I would surely faint. Desperately, I beat my fists against his shoulders.

With a snort of contempt, he released me.

I gasped for air and, with one hand grabbed for the back of the nearest chair to support myself. When my feet were steady, I raised the other and brought it across his face with all the force I could muster. There was a resounding slap and the marks of my fingers stood out white and distinct upon his dark cheek.

His eyes narrowed. "You would be well advised never to strike me again."

"Nor will I, if you succeed in keeping *your* hands to yourself."

"I did nothing you did not want and expect of me. Although perhaps you fancied something of a more romantic nature."

The suggestion infuriated me and only good sense kept me from slapping him again. Finding no physical satisfaction available to me, I cried, "You are the most contemptible man I have ever encountered. If my father lived you would not escape so lightly."

"If your father was an honest gentleman, he would likely beg me to give you a sound thrashing."

"Should you dare attempt such a thing, I vow it will not be accomplished without some damage to your own person."

"No doubt you are right. But do not think for an instant you would get the better of me. In *any* battle," he added. "And as you seem intent on helping this spiritualist with her charade, you may, in the future, expect my utmost cooperation."

"Your cooperation?" His words astounded me.

He nodded, his features a study in complacency. "Since I seem unable to rid my home of you, then I shall make it my business to *expose* you." The word lingered on his lips, as though he savored its taste.

So that was his game. "Well may you try," I replied, my confidence in Mrs. Medcroft complete.

He regarded me coolly. "You think your tricks too adept for even my eyes?"

"Don't twist my words. I mean only that Mrs. Medcroft has already produced a ghost without chicanery. No doubt she can do so again."

"Miss Carewe, I see that you, at least, have no reason to fear me."

"And why is that?" I asked warily.

He smiled. "Because with your pretty face and talent for deception you will no doubt find a new career on the stage. And likely find yourself in better company." He stepped to one side. "I believe our luncheon is waiting for us downstairs."

The man was mad. The thought of sitting at the same table with him, making polite conversation, made my head swim. "I would sooner break bread with a common thief. May you choke on your luncheon," I retorted and rushed past him and out the door.

Nor did I stop until I had reached the safety of my own room.

Mrs. Medcroft tapped on my door an hour later. I rose from my bed to admit her, hurriedly shaking out my dress and fluffing my curls to make myself presentable.

"Why did you not come down to eat?" she demanded, before she had taken a step into the room. Her gaze ran from my tousled hair to my crumpled gown. "Are you not feeling well?"

"A slight headache. Nothing more."

The faint crease faded from her brow and she squeezed past me into my room. Her gaze swept the room, taking in the rumpled bed and open window. Apparently assured that there was nothing more amiss than what I had claimed, she turned to me with a motherly smile. "I'll have Chaitra fix a posset for you. She's very good with herbal teas. We would not want you to be feeling poorly tomorrow."

"Are we leaving?" I asked, a faint lift to my voice.

Mrs. Medcroft destroyed my hopes with a quick shake of her head. "My work here has only just begun. Tomorrow Miss Llewelyn will have recovered and I shall attempt another séance."

I stifled a cry.

Oblivious to my distress, Mrs. Medcroft sauntered to the looking glass. She twisted back and forth before the oval glass, examining herself from every angle. Her figure was inclined to thinness, but her bearing and dramatic coloring drew the eye. Then, too, there was a heightened color to her cheeks, and her dress, a pale lavender silk, flattered her complexion.

She turned to me, a girlish brightness to her eyes. "You cannot know how pleased I am that we came. A success here could restore me to my former greatness, not to mention"—her voice dropped to a confidential whisper—"that Mr. Quarmby seems to be on the verge of making me a proposal."

"Of marriage?" I asked.

Her hands fluttered in the air, warning me to speak softly, and she glanced meaningfully at the door. "We have known each other for seven years, and his friendship means everything to me. But I never supposed his feelings could be as deep as my own."

"He greatly admires you," I pointed out. "I have never known a gentleman as complimentary to a lady as he is to you."

She nodded happily. "I knew when I received your letter that my luck was changing. There was a moment—a brief moment—when I doubted my own senses. First because of Mr. Llewelyn's threats, and then the unfortunate affair with Mrs. Broderick. But now I see that she was only the means the fates used to force me along the path I was meant to take."

Her mention of our host brought me back to unpleasant reality. "I fear that Mr. Llewelyn is determined to block that path in any way he can."

"But that is as it must be," she cried, her words lifting victoriously. "Convincing him will be my *tour de force*. It will prove to everyone that I am who and what I claim to be."

"I doubt that he is likely to recommend you to his peers. Regardless of your success."

"That will not be necessary. Mrs. Pritchard arrives tonight and the woman simply cannot be quieted. She is certain to relay every word that is uttered, every nuance of speech, every nod of the head to her friends of London. My triumph is assured."

She threw back her shoulders, and her face glowed. She needed only a lighted torch to complete the picture. But her enthusiasm was not contagious. How would Mr. Llewelyn react should his private life be displayed for the general public?

The thought made me shudder.

Hunger that a light tea had not quenched drove me to descend for dinner at seven-thirty. I would have made a poor martyr. One missed meal and filling my stomach had become more important to me than playing the wounded and misjudged heroine. It was ridiculous. The reproach made by my short absence would not have daunted a saint; Mr. Llewelyn was too great a villain even to have remarked upon my empty chair.

I took what comfort could be found in my companions. Mr. Quarmby insisted upon giving me his left arm, Mrs. Medcroft being draped about his right, and he escorted us down the wide stairs with the grace and flourish of a dancer. I wondered if Mrs. Medcroft could have guessed his intentions correctly. Always affable, tonight he was garrulous in his compliments.

Even I received a full share, although I found it difficult to listen. Whenever he turned to me, I could not help but notice the precise line his moustache drew above his upper lip. To have achieved such perfection, he must have trimmed the bristles individually.

As before, we gathered in the drawing room. Mr. Llewelyn glowered in the corner, embraced by the shadows that had collected there. Cloaked though he was in darkness, my gaze was drawn to him. Immediately I glimpsed his forbidding visage, I averted my eyes. It was impossible to look at him without remembering the way he had crushed me in his arms. Nor could I halt the rising warmth in my cheeks. Determined to do no more than pay him the merest civility—and that only when good manners required—I deliberately turned my attention to the others present.

In the wing chair nearest him, Ursula stared at me from behind exotically slanted eyes. Her wary look added shadows to her already dark face. This evening, she had changed into a watered silk dress of dark plum, a shade that would probably have flattered her olive skin had she been inclined to smile.

Apparently, she was not.

Given her brother's natural bent for authority, I suspected she was younger than he, despite her appearance of greater age. I wondered why she refrained from curling her hair or using any of those devices available to women who wished to enhance their femininity. Had she chosen, she could have been a handsome woman.

Fanny smiled from the sofa and beckoned to me. Her slight figure was enveloped in yellow chiffon. Double frills bounced at the shoulders and again at the hip. I felt decidedly dowdy and out of place in my plain black taffeta.

"Do come and join us, Hilary," she said, graciously welcoming me. "Have you met Mrs. Sally Pritchard?"

The woman seated next to her giggled. She was a good five years older than Fanny and faintly, but attractively, plump. She had fair hair, the shade of dark honey, and clear blue eyes that caught her viewers' gazes without involving their minds.

She gave me a quick glance, noted my quiet mourning dress and simple chignon, and smiled. The dimples in her cheeks immediately deepened and several linked bracelets of gold and brilliants jingled happily at her wrist.

"It is a pleasure to meet any friend of Mrs. Medcroft," she assured me. "I have depended on her ever since my husband's death two years ago. Fanny tells me you are recently come from Bath."

"From Bristol," Fanny corrected.

"Yes, of course. How silly of me." She laughed and a fringe of honeyed curls bounced on her brow. "My dear Mrs. Medcroft. I hear you are giving a séance tonight."

"Absolutely not," Dr. Rhodes said, giving his wire-rimmed spectacles a nervous push.

"But since Mr. Llewelyn has postponed his plans to go to London, I thought—"

"I will not hear of it. Fanny needs another twenty-four hours to recover."

I glanced with interest at Dr. Rhodes. When speaking as a doctor, he managed an authority and confidence he lacked in social affairs. Concern for Fanny had strengthened his gentle features, and I suspected he was a very competent physician.

Apparently sensing the same absolute command in the mild young gentleman, Mrs. Pritchard appealed to Fanny with stricken blue eyes. "But didn't you say—"

"No, Sally," she answered with a sigh. "I told you it would be tomorrow at the earliest."

"Oh dear, what a disappointment. But naturally you must do as your fiancé advises."

"If she was willing to do what I advised, she would forget this nonsense altogether."

"And that," her brother agreed, "is the best piece of advice you could be given."

Fanny chewed hesitantly on her lower lip, and she glanced around the room to see how the other guests felt. Winnie and Eglantine shifted uncomfortably in their chairs, and Ursula scowled at her with obvious reprobation. Even I mentally willed her to forget this foolish pursuit. It seemed our only hope of leaving this place.

But Sally was the first to speak. "Of course you must continue. You have been talking about contacting your dear mother for years. Now you have the opportunity. What possible reason could you have for stopping?"

"None, of course," Fanny agreed, immediately swayed by her friend's conviction. "I will be fine, Kenneth."

Mrs. Medcroft shot a triumphant smile at Mr. Llewelyn. He was scowling at Mrs. Pritchard and failed to notice. A fortuitous circumstance, I thought. Mr. Llewelyn was not one to let a challenge go unanswered, and I did not think my benefactress his equal. Certainly, the now-flustered Mrs. Pritchard would have agreed that it was foolish to cross him.

"Well, that's settled," Winnie said, his cheerful voice drawing all gazes to him. He was as comfortable with our attention as Fanny, and he tossed back his tawny curls with the flair of an actor. "Perhaps we can forget the matter for one evening and enjoy a hearty meal."

"I would like nothing better than to forget the matter entirely," Eglantine replied, speaking for the first time. Her severely braided knot and heavy velvet dress were in stark contrast to Mrs. Pritchard's low chignon and satin evening gown, and she seemed well aware of the difference between them. "Really, Edmund. One could only imagine what your father would say about this whole affair."

Sally giggled. "Don't be silly. The late Mr. Llewelyn indulged Fanny terribly. She was the most spoiled child I'd ever met. Never mind, darling." She shot her friend an apologetic look. "You have turned out quite the lady, despite all predictions."

"And more than a few of them yours," Fanny retorted with a pleasant smile.

Sally flushed and giggled behind her painted Japanese fan.

Mr. Llewelyn shifted his weight from one long leg to the other, and his dark look fell on Mrs. Medcroft. "I begin to wonder how many foolish young women you have drawn to your employ."

"Really, Edmund," Winnie protested, the gold flecks in his green eyes glittering. "That is most unfair, given the obvious intelligence of Miss Carewe. I think you owe her an apology." He bestowed a warm smile upon me.

Eglantine stiffened in her chair, and her prominent teeth clamped together in a fixed smile. Only the forbidding look in her host's eyes kept her from commenting.

Mr. Llewelyn strode into the middle of the room, pulling all gazes with him. There he paused, and he regarded me from down the length of his straight nose. "You are quite right. Miss Carewe neither needs nor should receive our pity. She is well aware of her role in this affair. Aren't you, Miss Carewe?"

Good Lord. He meant to do more than try to expose us as charlatans. He meant to humiliate me in front of his friends and mine. It was outrageous.

I would not give him the satisfaction of blushing. "If you are in any way suggesting that my behavior would be less than honorable, you are mistaken."

"Edmund, come now," Winnie protested. "You're being most unfair and horribly rude. I would not have thought it of you."

"Ah! But I forgot. You were not aware that I caught Miss Carewe sneaking through my stepmother's rooms this afternoon."

Ursula gasped and even Mrs. Medcroft blanched.

Refusing to sit quietly through his accusations, I rose and faced him. "I have explained my reasons for being there. I heard the sound of breaking crockery and thought someone needed assistance."

"Good Lord!" Winnie stared up at me, and beads of perspiration dotted his brow. "Lily . . . that is, Mrs. Llewelyn had a habit of breaking dishes when she was upset. Do you think—"

"Nonsense," Edmund countered. "She was searching the drawers for information that could be of use to her employer."

"And how was I to know that those were her rooms?"

"Fanny told you, did she not?"

"No, I didn't, Edmund," Fanny whispered in a tiny voice.

"Damnation. You must have."

"But we didn't once mention Mama. I swear to you."

Mr. Quarmby cleared his throat. "I think that is quite enough," he ventured cautiously. "You have attacked this young lady's character unfairly and I insist upon an apology." His moustache quivered and no one in the room had any doubt that he was not able to insist upon anything where our host was concerned. I marveled that he found the courage to try.

Not at all contrite, Mr. Llewelyn measured me between narrowed eyes, like a merchant visually weighing a sack of oats that he knew to be several ounces light. "I am not convinced I was mistaken. But since I am unable to prove my claim, I will retract my statements until such time that I can gather evidence against you."

And that was as much apology as I was likely to get. Not that I cared in the slightest. My back stiff, I returned to my place on the sofa.

"Really, Mr. Quarmby. You were quite marvelous," Mrs. Medcroft whispered and he bowed his head to me.

At eight, we entered the dining room. The table had been set with silver candlesticks and long-stemmed crystal wine glasses. The cut-glass water goblets were of the same pattern, and the light from the candles flashed across the array of cutlery.

One had only to look at the display to appreciate Mr. Llewelyn's immense wealth. And glance at Mrs. Pritchard's wistful face to realize how many women thought he would make a desirable husband. No wonder he had supposed my apparent compliance had been born of a desire to win his approval. I doubted he met many single or widowed young ladies who did not want him to admire them.

Not that that excused his complete arrogance.

Despite the hour, the chafing dishes hadn't been set upon the buffet. Ursula pinched her lips together, but nodded for us to take our chairs. I found myself at the lower half of the table—across from Mrs.

Medcroft and next to Dr. Rhodes. I wondered what disgrace had sentenced him to my company when he should have been seated next to Fanny.

"I'm afraid we had an awkward number of ladies," Ursula said serenely before her sister could question the arrangements. "And Edmund would insist on sitting in his usual chair. I did the best I could under the circumstances."

This was a blatant lie. Dr. Rhodes could easily have exchanged places with Mrs. Pritchard, leaving her to sit with me. Clearly, Ursula's decision to separate them had been deliberate. Her brother scowled at her from the head of the table, but said nothing. If Fanny intended to protest, her words were cut off by his silencing frown, and the two sisters glared at each other from across their place settings.

Oblivious to everything but her own thoughts, Sally touched her friend's puffed sleeve. "Do you suppose Miss Carewe *could* have heard your mother's ghost?" She shivered dramatically.

"Of course she didn't," Mrs. Medcroft answered. "The child is not mediumistic. I suspect one of the maids was careless in performing her duties."

"The maids at Abbey House are not careless," Ursula said in a tight voice. "More likely, Miss Carewe suffers from a surfeit of imagination."

Winnie's thick eyebrows drew together. "Still, given Lily's quick temper and penchant for hurling ornaments at people's heads, it does arouse certain questions."

"Hasn't there been enough said about the matter?" Edmund demanded. "There were no noises. I was in the next room and heard nothing."

"But you aren't a sensitive," Sally insisted. "Only certain people can hear spirits. Isn't that right, Mrs. Medcroft?"

"Well, yes. Naturally. But I'm certain the child was mistaken."

I let the argument rage around me. I had too many questions of my own and not a single answer. Why had the door been ajar if it was kept locked? Had someone gone in ahead of me? If so, where had they gone? And what about those sounds? From which room had they emanated? It was surprising I didn't give myself a headache.

Eglantine's strident voice drew me back to the conversation. "It is unfortunate that Lily's more common habits have survived in our memories. But given her background—"

"I think you have said quite enough," her husband warned, with a glance toward their host.

Eglantine's eyes were bright in the dim light. She looked around the table at her audience and continued blithely. "Perhaps some of you are unaware that Lily sang in a music hall before she married Mr. Llewelyn."

"Good heavens," Ursula said. "Must you dredge up the past?"

"It would be better if you said nothing about her," Mrs. Medcroft agreed. "I would not want my responses to be affected by anything that is said here tonight."

Mr. Llewelyn's chin lifted and he nodded to Eglantine. "Then by all means, continue. You can say nothing that can't have been learned with a minimum of research, and it will prevent our guests from claiming to have received the information from unseen sources."

"I assure you those practices are beneath me," Mrs. Medcroft protested.

"Then you will not have known that my father married a woman who was one-third his age. A

woman who made her living as a singer of questionable ballads."

"Edmund, that is enough." Ursula looked meaningfully at Fanny. Her gaze fell upon the clock at her
back. "Good Lord. It's quarter past eight. What on
earth is the matter?" She reached for the bell at her
side.

Before her fingers touched the silver handle, the
door swung open. A white-gloved butler stepped into
the room, his features as stiff as his back. He crossed
to Ursula's chair and, in a muted voice, asked
politely, "Did you wish to continue to wait dinner,
mum? Cook says the roast will be ruined if you delay
any longer."

"What?" Ursula was too startled to keep her voice
low. "Whatever gave her the impression that I wanted
her to wait dinner?"

"Elsie said one of the guests hadn't come downstairs. A young woman, I believe."

There was a prolonged silence. It took me several
seconds to recall that Mrs. Pritchard was the only late
arrival; there were to be no other guests.

The faces grouped around the table had paled.
Mrs. Pritchard pulled nervously at her bracelets, and
Winnie reached for his water glass, realized it was
empty, and promptly set it down. His wife snapped
her fan open and shut, and looked anxiously at
Ursula.

Mr. Llewelyn cleared his throat. "Whoever Elsie
is, she is mistaken. We are all here and growing quite
impatient. Kindly bring in the platters immediately."

The butler nodded. "Certainly, sir." He disappeared with as much haste as he could manage and
still maintain his dignity.

Ignoring the curious faces around him, Mr.

Llewelyn turned to his sister and demanded, "Who on earth is Elsie?"

"The new maid." Ursula frowned. "She seemed quite reliable and came with excellent references."

He snorted in disgust. "Likely written by someone who wished to be rid of her. If this happens again, she will find herself looking for a new position."

And that was all anyone dared say of the matter.

Our dinner showed only the faintest signs of not having been served at the right moment. The creamed soup was a touch too thick, the salad a shade less crisp than might have been desired, and the roast vaguely dry. Undoubtedly, our palates were predisposed to find fault, our minds attuned to failures that would otherwise have gone unnoticed. But no one, least of all Edmund, who presided over us with a bleak face, had a word of criticism for the meal.

Our conversation was desultory and dull. Even Sally Pritchard lost her voice. Light chatter was impossible when our minds were distracted with disquieting thoughts we dared not speak aloud. Through each course, Elsie's name hovered on our lips, and she was as much a part of our gathering as if she had sat at the foot of the table and demanded her own plate.

And if we refrained from speaking of Elsie, we dared not even think of the woman she had passed on the landing.

6

"May I come in?"

Fanny poised in my doorway, her cheeks pink, her lustrous eyes showing nothing of the strain she had suffered two days earlier. Even yesterday's silent dinner and this morning's subdued breakfast appeared not to have wilted her. Grateful for any distraction, I smiled and stepped aside.

She swept into the room, leaving a trail of rose scent and the rustle of petticoats in her wake. "You promised to show me your scrapbooks. I thought we could have a look at them before lunch. Unless you would rather join Sally and Edmund. But that might not be wise."

Her advice was quite unnecessary. I had enough reasons of my own for avoiding her brother. Nevertheless, I wondered about her reasoning and asked, "Why not?"

She yawned, politely covering her mouth with a slender hand. "Edmund can be a terrible host when he is forced to entertain a lot of silly women." Realizing how her words must have sounded, she shrugged apologetically. "Those are his words, not mine, and I don't mean to imply that you are silly. Only that *he* can be remarkably unpleasant company when he chooses."

"Mrs. Pritchard has my deepest sympathies," I murmured.

Fanny laughed. "You need not worry about her. Half of his insults will escape her notice entirely. The other half she will have misconstrued as compliments before the day is out."

She flung open the French doors and poised in the sunshine like a flower soaking up the warmth and light. She was quite theatrical in her movements and actions, something she had no doubt inherited from her mother. If she also resembled her in appearance, the woman must have been a beauty. Beautiful enough to lure a man like Edmund's father to the altar, despite the obvious loss to his respectability.

I wondered if his son and daughter had vocally disapproved the marriage and strongly suspected they had.

The scrapbooks lay in the middle drawer of my dressing table, beneath a woolen shawl that had belonged to my mother. I took them out and carried them to the gateleg table next to the balcony. Fanny promptly deserted her pose, took one of the two chairs, and avidly reached for the topmost book.

We pored over the articles together. If there had been unflattering accounts written about Mrs. Medcroft and her activities, she had not saved them. The pages were filled with her many successes. After several pages, they began to be repetitive.

"I never would have guessed," Fanny mused aloud.

"Her popularity has sunk to such a low ebb in the last twenty years. I had not heard of her before Sally brought her to my attention."

My mother's name appeared often as "the spiritualist's assistant and constant companion." And there were many photographs of them together, although none as intimate and flattering as the photograph that had been given me.

Perhaps because of her own mother's background, perhaps because of our friendship, Fanny was particularly absorbed in those accounts that mentioned her. "Your mother seems to have attended Mrs. Medcroft through the height of her popularity," she pointed out. "I imagine she was also quite the celebrity."

"I cannot think that anyone attached much importance to her."

"Under the circumstances, they could hardly have overlooked her. Her face must have been known throughout London. Still, you may be right." Her brow puckered. "Do you ever dream of being famous?"

I laughed at the notion. "My father had strong opinions on the subject. Any profession or behavior likely to draw attention to one's person was not an acceptable pursuit for young ladies from good families."

She grimaced. "He sounds like Edmund. How awful for you."

"I know he meant well. But given what I have learned of mother's background, I think his words must have hurt her."

Fanny rose and walked back into the stream of sunshine cascading through the open French doors like bright lights falling on a stage. She threw back her shoulders and lifted her face to receive the gentle glow. Unlike Mrs. Medcroft, she seemed to have no need of looking glasses to be aware of the picture she presented. I half expected her to burst forth into song.

Instead, she looked down at me and smiled. "My mother used to tell me about her life on the stage when I was small. It sounded quite wonderful. Everyone adored her and she was the center of attention wherever she went. Even the scandal caused by her marriage to father delighted her. She used to mimic the shocked faces of London's well-bred ladies for me. She'd pinch her nose and parody their conversations until I rolled on the floor with laughter."

It seemed an improper way to bring up a child, teaching her disrespect for her elders, but I suppose it was better to laugh at those who repudiated you than let them hurt you. Certainly, Fanny seemed to have a healthy self-esteem and a cheerful nature.

She grinned wickedly, as though guessing my thoughts. "Mama desperately missed the stage and the applause. I think she found life with father a terrible bore. She used to sing for me and demand that I applaud when she was done. As loud and as long as possible, until my hands hurt and my arms ached. But it was never enough."

"Do you think she was unhappy here?"

"Not in the least. Mama had a talent for finding audiences. Whenever someone was expected, she would pose on the landing and wait for Ursula to open the door. Even when she was my age, my sister insisted upon acting like a housekeeper," she added with a hint of derision. "As soon as Mama's guests stepped into the foyer she would sweep down the stairs to welcome them, commanding everyone's attention. It was one of her favorite performances."

I stifled a shudder. Was that why her presence lingered there? Why the new maid Elsie had passed a strange woman in that very place, and why I had felt that cold wind rushing down the stairs the day of our arrival? But there had been nothing light or welcoming about that incident.

There was a knock at the door, and my questions faded. Chaitra waited in the corridor. Her gaze wandered curiously to Fanny, then back to me. In a soft voice, she explained that Mrs. Medcroft was waiting for me in her sitting room. There were a few notes she wanted to record in her journal. Doubtless about the apparition on the stairs.

"But we were having such fun," Fanny protested before I could reply, her blonde ringlets bobbing adamantly against the back of her neck. "Surely that can wait for another time."

Chaitra's brown eyes noted the open scrapbooks and Fanny's petulant face. "Another time will serve as well," she agreed, a slight frown wrinkling her smooth skin. "My mistress would not want to spoil your pleasure."

"Oh, but—"

Chaitra shook her head, ending my objection. "It was a small matter and one that is easily put aside," she assured me. She slipped out of the room as quickly as she had come.

"Is that what you want for yourself?" Fanny demanded the second the door had closed behind her. "A life as Mrs. Medcroft's assistant?"

"Heavens, no." The strength of my reaction startled me. I had not thought myself particularly disturbed by these last few days. Apparently, I was unaware of how greatly the odd events had unsettled me. "She has been very kind," I continued in a milder tone. "But I am determined to find myself a post as a governess where I can be of real service."

Her brows arched above their natural line. "Then you think her a fraud?"

"In face of the evidence, I cannot. But there is simply too much of my father in me. I would rather help children prepare for life than serve those whose lives have ended."

"If you wish, I might be able to help you."

"In what way?"

The ideas churned behind her eyes and she chewed on her lower lip with small, perfectly straight teeth. There was no lack of intelligence in that face. I suspected her veneer of frivolity was due only to her youthful high spirits and her family's determination to view her as immature. Had she been treated as level-headed and responsible, she might have responded in a different manner. Perhaps marriage to Dr. Rhodes would make the difference. For her sake, I fervently hoped it would.

"I have a friend with a young daughter who has outgrown her nanny," she said slowly. "Unless they have hired someone since we last spoke, they will be needing a governess. Do you have references?"

"I can get them from my minister and my father's solicitors."

"Then you must let me see what I can do."

"Indeed, I would be grateful for your help," I admitted. "I had intended to look through the advertisements in the London papers. But coming here made that impossible."

"Think nothing of the matter. It will be my pleasure to do whatever I can."

She smiled happily, and a pleased glow lit her face with a brightness that the sunshine could not have given her. There, I thought. Only give her the opportunity to do someone a kindness, and she comes alive. What a pity her brother and sister regard her as a burden thrust upon them by their father and his socially unacceptable second wife. I felt rather sorry for her. No wonder she wanted to reach beyond the grave to her mother. The only surprise was that she did not also wish to contact her indulgent father.

Something of my feelings must have been reflected in my face. "Do you think me foolish for chasing after a memory?" Fanny asked.

I shook my head, but it was more out of politeness than anything else. "It seems unnecessary," I confessed. "Your memories of your mother will always be in your possession."

"It was all so long ago." She sighed heavily and returned to sit beside me. The glow had gone from her face and, without a visible transition, she had become a portrait in despondency. Every curl on her head drooped, and her eyes glistened with unshed tears.

"Perhaps you would understand if you had lost your mother when you were only ten. And under tragic circumstances." She glanced up at me. "I suppose you know how she died."

I shook my head.

"She fell from the gallery in the church and cracked her head open on the stones."

I gasped.

Fanny nodded. "There was blood everywhere—or so I am told. What a horrible way for someone as beautiful as she to die, don't you agree?"

"For anyone," I murmured.

She nodded. "Since then, the church has been kept closed. Services hadn't been held there for years, anyway. Mama liked to go there in the afternoons to pray. She said that given the unpleasant dispositions of her husband and stepchildren, it was the one place where she could be assured of peace and privacy."

Her words surprised me. Considering what she had told me of her mother's nature, I would not have thought her the kind of woman to find pleasure in a quiet church. I had also supposed that Fanny's father had been as indulgent a husband as he had been a father. Obviously, there was another side to them both that I had yet to discover.

Fanny rose and shook out the creases from her dress. "I ought to go. There are those letters I promised you I would write, and I have had enough of the past for one morning."

"Are you all right?" I asked, worried that she might have upset herself unduly.

She nodded, but there was a faintly harried air about her. I wondered if I should say something to Dr. Rhodes. Certainly, she would not thank me if I did. Fanny plainly disliked the restraints that were placed on her and only viewed them as trials that had to be borne.

Oblivious to my concerns, she crossed the room. She squared her shoulders firmly, as though she knew she could not avoid life but must confront each assault. No one watching her could have failed to admire her courage.

At the door, she paused. "If I were you, I would not tell anyone else of your mother's history."

"Why ever not?" I asked, astounded.

"Listen to someone whose mother sang in a music hall. Your background will always raise eyebrows, no matter what you do or where you go. Edmund has already taken a dislike to you and, presently, he and Ursula assume your mother was one of Mrs. Medcroft's well-to-do but foolish clients. If he knew the truth, he would not let me spend these hours alone with you."

"Do they think I would corrupt you? What awful snobbery." I spoke without thinking and immediately regretted my words. They were, after all, her half brother and sister.

Fanny only shrugged. "It is because of Mama. She married my father for his money, and they despised her. It was no secret," she added, looking at my face and realizing how her words had shocked me. "Papa was forty years her senior, devoted to making money, and rather unpleasant. Except to me," she added with an impish grin. "Unfortunately, Edmund assumes all attractive women whose behavior or circumstances are questionable have the same intentions. Did you not wonder why his slights are more for you than Mrs. Medcroft?"

I admitted I had.

"Then do be careful what you say. I would not like to give up our friendship." Her smile said more than her words.

I sighed, knowing how easily she could be disappointed. "I promise to say nothing, but I cannot guarantee that no one else will speak."

She laughed. "Who else knows but those of us who are your friends?"

After she had gone, still musing on her words, I returned to the table where we had been sitting. The second scrapbook lay open to the last page, and I started to flip the back cover into place. Then I stopped. Something didn't look quite right.

I lifted the book to eye level and took a closer look. There, in the crack where the pages fitted together, was a ragged edge of paper.

The last two pages had been torn out.

With Fanny gone, I went directly to Mrs. Medcroft's room and made the requested notation in her journal. As I had expected, it was a detailed account of all that had happened during the séance and the odd events afterwards. Omitted was my strange experience with Chaitra, neither of us having convinced her that our encounter was anything but nightmares brought on by her own successes. As for what I had heard in the west wing, that had already been dismissed, and I was happy not to broach the subject again.

She did, however, ask if anything about Abbey House bothered me and agreed that she also had a particular distaste for the first-floor landing. "I do hope I have not instilled my concerns in you."

Although I assured her this was untrue, she wasn't convinced and insisted on blaming herself. "You are a lot like your mother," she added. "I would have called her . . . empathic. I had only to tell her I had turned my ankle, and immediately she would walk with a limp."

I laughed, but thought her account unlikely. Mother had certainly been sympathetic, but her sympathy had always found a constructive outlet. Nor were the other stories any the more likely. They ended with the appearance of one of the kitchen maids. Ursula had decided to have everyone served luncheon in their own rooms, affording us all the chance to collect ourselves. I wondered if the decision had been a wise decision on her part or merely reflected a desire to be rid of us for a few hours.

In the midafternoon, Mrs. Medcroft decided to take a nap, and my time was my own again. I wondered downstairs, thinking there must be a library at Abbey House and wondering if anyone would object to my borrowing a novel. A noise led me to the drawing room. A young maid was dusting the mantel and a collection of porcelain elves and gnomes.

As I entered, she glanced up and peered at me from beneath the frill of her cap. Her face was full and round and her complexion ruddy. But despite her look of good health, her eyes were rimmed with pink, and the corners of her full lips drooped.

She gave a little sniff. "Can I help you, miss?"

I hesitated. I would have liked to have asked her if she was all right, but that would have been prying. Her personal affairs were none of my business. Reluctantly, I said, "I was looking for the library."

"Down the hall, third door to your right."

I thanked her and started to leave.

"Miss," she called after me, "are you with that spirit woman?"

I turned back to her. "If you mean the spiritualist, Mrs. Medcroft, yes, I am."

"I thought you was and I wondered if . . . if you don't mind my asking . . ." A tear slid down her cheek.

"Why don't you sit down and tell me what's wrong?" I suggested.

Her eyes widened in horror. "Oh, I couldn't sit down in here, miss. That wouldn't be proper. Miss Llewelyn would skin me alive. But—"she glanced over her shoulder "—I was hoping you might speak to *Mr.* Llewelyn for me."

"I don't understand."

"My name's Elsie, miss."

Some of my confusion disappeared.

She caught my expression and nodded. "Yes. *That* Elsie. Mr. Llewelyn thinks I made up the story about a lady on the landing. And I didn't, miss. She was there. All dressed up, real fancy like. I supposed she was one of the houseguests, but now that I think on it, she was a bit . . . fancy for this household."

"And what did you want me to talk to Mr. Llewelyn about?"

Her voice dropped to a horrified whisper. "He thinks I took money from *that woman* to tell lies, and he didn't believe me when I said I didn't. I'm afraid he'll turn me out without references. I can't find another position if I don't have references, miss. If you could tell him none of you gave me any money, I wouldn't be half grateful. He'd believe *you.*"

I frowned. If I was her only hope, she was in dire straits. "I will tell him he is mistaken," I promised. "But I have grave doubts that he will believe me."

"It can't hurt, miss."

I was not even convinced of that. But Elsie's anxious face made refusing impossible. I sighed. "Where would I find Mr. Llewelyn at this hour?"

"He's with Miss Fanny's friend, miss. I believe they're in the conservatory."

With her directions to guide me, I made my way to the conservatory. It was a sunlit room, set with marble floor tiles and filled with orchids, bougainvillea, ferns, potted hydrangeas, and a few palms. Even before I entered, I could hear Sally chattering happily and the occasional terse reply. Mr. Llewelyn sounded cornered and decidedly irritated. I wondered if he would look upon my interruption as a blessing or an added trial.

"—and what do you think of—"

I circled a bushy fern and stepped into view. Sally Pritchard was leaning intimately toward our host, her dimples cutting deeply into her full cheeks, her vacuous blue eyes widened to saucerlike fullness. Upon hearing my approach, she turned, and her honeyed-brown ringlets bobbed a protest against the back of her neck. "Oh, Miss Carewe. How nice of you to join us."

Mr. Llewelyn's face was angled away from me. Keeping his body fixed in that position, he deigned to glance over his shoulder. His expression was as rigid as his body, and there was a wintry cast to his eyes. Hardly an auspicious beginning.

I forced a pleasant smile. "Forgive me for interrupting. I was hoping to have a word with Mr. Llewelyn. But if another time would be more convenient . . . ?"

"Not at all," he countered hastily, unbending enough to adjust his posture to include me in their conversation. "Mrs. Pritchard and I were not discussing anything important.

"Well . . . no. Not really. You must come and join us," she offered reluctantly. "And please, call me Sally. Everyone does." She peered hopefully at Mr. Llewelyn from beneath her fair eyelashes.

I hesitated. "I'm afraid it is a private matter, but one that will take no more than a minute." Or such was my hope.

Mr. Llewelyn nodded grimly but, when he turned back to the woman at his side, his scowl lifted. "I'm certain Mrs. Pritchard will excuse us. We have already lingered rather a long while in the conservatory and no doubt she would like the chance to go and refresh herself."

"Oh, well, that . . ." She glanced at his face and her polite protest died on her lips. Pouting, she amended, "I suppose I must."

Her heels tapping out her annoyance on the marble tiles, she swept out of the room. It was an exit that Fanny could have done to perfection, but Sally only succeeded in looking like an outraged hen.

Mr. Llewelyn spared one contemptuous glance for her retreating figure before rounding on me. "And now, Miss Carewe. I hope we can keep this brief."

I thought his rudeness unwarranted, since my appearance had freed him from one unpleasant duty. A duty that he had apparently fulfilled with only a modicum of civility. But with me, he seemed to see no need for manners.

Still, for once, we were in agreement. I, too, wanted to keep our conversation brief. "I require only a minute, Mr. Llewelyn, and even that need I regret. But it has come to my attention that you believe either I or one of my friends bribed your maid to disrupt dinner last night. I merely wanted to assure you that we did nothing of the sort."

"And why, pray tell, should I believe you?"

"Because I am telling the truth." For all the difference that was likely to make. But on my walk to the conservatory, I had given the matter some consideration. "And," I added, "because a girl like Elsie would burst into tears and confess to any wrongdoing the moment she was questioned. If you were any judge of character, you would have realized that for yourself."

His fingers twitched at his side and I became very conscious that I came no higher than his shoulders and was only half his weight. And more than his size made him physically overwhelming. He appeared to be the kind of man who was familiar with all the muscles in his body and exercised them regularly. I already knew, to my misfortune, that more than his glare was stony. His grip was equally hard. There could not have been a worse moment to recall that memory.

His gaze was fixed upon me, and I had the uncanny certainty that his thoughts had followed the same path. But I need not have worried. In a detached and dispassionate manner, he assured me, "As it happens, I am an *excellent* judge of character. Otherwise she would no longer be in my employ."

His statement deflated me, as he had no doubt intended. Nevertheless, I lifted my chin and stared back at him defiantly. "Then I am sorry to have wasted your time. But you can take comfort in knowing these few seconds spent enduring my company served to rid you of Mrs. Pritchard."

He started and, caught off guard, laughed out loud. I was amazed at the transformation in his face. For that moment, he looked almost human, but he quickly recovered himself. Pretending he had not been caught in any lapse, he said severely, "I hope you do not expect me to thank you."

"I have learned not to expect any kind of civility from you, Mr. Llewelyn, deserved or otherwise. And now, since my being here is needless, I shall bid you good afternoon." Brushing past a spiky palm, I started for the door.

"Wait a moment."

I turned, to find him regarding me with a puzzled look.

"Perhaps you would be good enough to tell me

why you concerned yourself with the troubles of one of my maids?"

"You did her an injustice. Our presence here could, after a fashion, be considered the cause."

"It damn well was the cause," he retorted, anger flashing back into his eyes.

"Nonsense. Your determination to think the worst of us was the real cause."

"I would have to be a fool to think anything else."

"That sir, is your opinion. In my mind, your inability to view us in any but a predetermined light proves you the fool. Now, if you will excuse me, we have had this argument before, and it does not bear repeating."

"Indeed, it does not. You would be wiser to save your energies for others more gullible than I."

There was, I thought with a sense of amazement, something of my father in this man. That should have made him easier to understand and tolerate, but it did not. Perhaps it was because my father's gentleness and unfailing kindness were absent. In its place, there were only a forceful personality and the authority and confidence that often accompany wealth and good looks. A poor substitute for good character.

"Is something wrong, Miss Carewe?"

"There is not."

"Then you might answer one more question for me before you go."

"And that is?"

"Did Mrs. Medcroft send you in the maid's behalf? Or was the decision solely your own?"

"Mrs. Medcroft knew nothing of the matter, or undoubtedly she would have come herself."

"Undoubtedly," he agreed in a manner that made me want to slap him.

Deciding it would be wiser for us to part company

before I lost my self-control, I started for the door a second time. I did not attempt a haughty exit lest, like the poor Mrs. Pritchard, I only gave him cause for amusement. I was within inches of making my escape when he called after me to wait. I turned reluctantly.

"It occurs to me that, as long as you are a guest here, you might be interested in learning something about the estate."

"Are you offering to show me around Abbey House?" I asked incredulously.

"If it pleases you. Or does my company make you uncomfortable?"

It was a blatant challenge, one I would have liked to refuse. But the taunting look in his eyes made that impossible, as well he knew. "It would take more than your incivility to upset me," I said coolly. "But are you not concerned that anything I learn will immediately be put forth in tonight's séance?"

"I intend to acquaint you with the house's history, not my own." He smiled complacently. "I think a tour is is order, don't you?"

He offered me his arm and, reluctantly, I accepted. With a cold smile, he led me into the hallway that had so recently promised me my freedom. The muscles beneath my hand were as hard and tense as I had guessed they would be, and I knew he had not relaxed his guard but was merely positioning himself for a different sort of attack—one for which I would be given no warning.

But if someone had chanced to come upon us, they would have seen nothing amiss in his manner. He steered me through the house with a smooth authority and graciousness. And, although his smile never reached his eyes, neither did it leave his lips.

"No doubt you have guessed from the name that

originally the building was used as an abbey," he said smoothly. "It fell into disuse at the end of the fifteenth century and one of my ancestors purchased the land."

He paused and, seeing that he expected me to hold up my end of our odd conversation, I asked, "How old is the main building?"

"Seven hundred years."

"That much? I would not have guessed."

He nodded at me with approval. I had agreed to abide by the rules of his game. We were host and guest, strolling through his manor, with nothing more on our minds than filling an hour as pleasantly as possible. It would make his attack, when it came, all the more startling.

"It has been remodeled many times," he continued, the words falling easily from his lips. "My father was the last to make changes, but like his father and grandfather, he limited himself to the living quarters. There are several parts of the abbey that remain untouched since the medieval ages. As a child, I found them fascinating."

I dared to glance up at him, receiving a noncommittal smile for my efforts, and wondered what he had been like as a child. Surely he could not have been so unyielding and unfriendly. Or had he developed those traits during solitary explorations of those drafty stone halls and gloomy chambers?

Unaware of my speculation, he continued his narrative. "There are catacombs under the house, long since bricked up, naturally. And, although I have never come across any entrances on the estate, the hillside was supposedly honeycombed with tunnels and the house with secret passages."

"Whatever for?"

"In case the monks needed to slip away without being noticed. England was forever changing religious persuasions and it would have been unwise of the monks to assume themselves safe from persecution."

"A difficult life."

There was a quick flash of even, white teeth. "I imagine there were compensations."

"Such as?"

"A life without women strikes me as a peaceful existence."

Curse the man and his rudeness. And my own foolishness for allowing him to lead me into that trap. It was exactly the kind of response I should have expected from him. But he would not desert the fray unscathed.

Pretending only the mildest interest, I said, "From what I recall of my history lessons, chastity was a virtue practiced by few monks during the medieval period."

"Then those individuals deserved whatever befell them. I, on the other hand, would not have invited such a fate."

"Are you saying *you* dream of a life of quiet contemplation, Mr. Llewelyn?" I lifted my eyebrows.

He glanced down with a haughty air. "That surprises you?"

"Indeed, it does."

"And why, pray tell?"

"Scholarly pursuits require an open mind. What could you do but fill your hours with pointless memorization?"

His smile tightened, the only sign that he had felt my barb. Nevertheless, he nodded politely. "Very good, Miss Carewe. You have avenged your sex for my earlier remark. I shall be more cautious in the future. Still, I must disagree. It is not my opinion that my mind is closed on any subject."

"Except for that of the female of the species."

"Hardly a subject worthy of scholarly examination."

"I begin to wonder, Mr. Llewelyn, whether you were born or hatched."

He was saved the necessity of making a retort by a loud banging. Our stroll had led us far from the remodeled portions of Abbey House and taken us into the past. All around me rose the ancient walls of the abbey. Low doors opened onto small stone chambers, and there was the smell of mold and mildew in the air.

The noise echoed down the corridor, becoming a pounding beat that shook my eardrums. Unconsciously, my grip tightened on Mr. Llewelyn's arm.

He glanced down at me, faintly surprised. "There is no need for alarm. Merely some workmen finishing a few tasks I set for them."

Cheeks warm, I loosened my fingers. Of all the stupid things to have done. It was bad enough he regarded me as a devious version of Mrs. Pritchard. I did not have to add to his suspicions.

Luckily, at that moment, we rounded a corner and we were both distracted. At the end of a long tunnel, I saw the men he had hired. They were pulling wooden boards off a set of double doors that had been set into a Gothic archway. Each plank they removed, they hurled to the flagging.

"You look curious, Miss Carewe."

I nodded.

"But I told you, did I not, that I meant to support your efforts."

"Your meaning escapes me."

"Are you not at all curious what lies beyond those doors?"

I regarded him warily, knowing we had come to the reason for his tour.

"Come now, Miss Carewe. You haven't guessed. They are opening up the old church. I thought it an appropriate place for Mrs. Medcroft's next séance."

7

The company sitting around the dinner table might have been a gathering of long-dead wraiths. No one drew a breath. Not so much as an eyelash fluttered in their pale faces. And no one stirred to set down their glass or fork. Of those of us listening, only I had been given any warning of Mr. Llewelyn's intentions, and the intervening hours hadn't made the prospect any less unsettling.

The fervent hope that he had been deliberately baiting me had kept me from voicing his intentions to Mrs. Medcroft. It would have been unkind to have upset her unnecessarily. Now I regretted leaving her in ignorance.

Ursula shuddered, breaking the stillness. "Open the church? You cannot be serious?"

"A poor jest, Edmund," Dr. Rhodes added in a dry voice, and hastily reached for his water glass.

Winnie's fork clattered against his plate. "Absolutely. In very bad taste, old man. Upsetting to the ladies."

Mr. Llewelyn buttered his roll with two easy passes of his knife, a complacent smile on his face. "I assure you my remark was wholly serious."

"This is nonsense." Ursula straightened in her chair, and some of her lost composure returned to her. "The church has been shut for a decade. Do you expect us to sit amongst the dust and the cobwebs?"

"Not to mention the mildew and the foul air," Eglantine contributed. "Think of the harm we would be doing our lungs."

"I have already anticipated your concerns and set four men from the village to work in your behalf." He turned to Mrs. Medcroft. "I imagine you have no complaints."

"Well, I . . ." She glanced doubtfully at Mr. Quarmby.

He managed a weak shrug.

Finding no help from that quarter, she looked hopefully at the other guests. "I suppose it would be all right, if everyone else agrees."

"Then the matter is settled." Mr. Llewelyn was the genial host in both voice and manner. "Nevertheless, those of you who wish to forget this evening's festivities are certainly excused. The rest of us will meet in the church at midnight. A more precise hour than eleven, don't you agree?"

Sally Pritchard gave a faint moan, but her normally vacuous eyes glowed.

Dr. Rhodes regarded her as he might have regarded a member of the audience at a cockfight. "I think the final decision should rest with Fanny."

She, who had said nothing since her brother's announcement, found herself the focus of everyone's attention. "Of course I have no objection," she declared, the color high in her cheeks. "Why should I?"

If it was not the response Mr. Llewelyn had desired or expected, there were no signs of disappointment in his expression. He bestowed his smile on each one of us sitting at the table, glancing quickly over me as though I was not there, and then gave his attention to the last bite of roast beef remaining on his plate. He chewed with a deliberateness that was maddening, and his sigh of satisfaction upon setting down his fork might or might not have been directed at the meal.

I suspected it was for something else entirely.

"He is up to something, mark my words."

Mrs. Medcroft's hands danced in the air, and she fluttered about her sitting room like a very large and startled lavender butterfly. Mr. Quarmby darted to her side and slipped his arm around her waist. Inconsolable, she dragged him along at her side, and he let himself be carried the length of the room without a murmur of protest.

"It might have escaped *your* notice," she continued, hardly catching her breath. "But my senses are too acute for his tricks."

"But he has outsmarted himself, dear lady. I have considered the matter, and I believe he has done us a service."

"A service?" She rounded on him. "Are you mad or merely deluded?"

"Not at all. Not at all," he said soothingly. "But what better spot could there be for your séance than the very place where the poor lady died?"

"Good heavens, you *are* mad. The very notion appalls me." Her chiffon gown shivered from neck to hem. "Can you imagine the pain Lily Llewelyn suffered in her fall from the gallery? I will be completely overcome."

"Who told you she had fallen to her death?" I asked. Certainly, nothing had been said by me. I stepped away from the windows where I had retreated to avoid being trampled.

Mrs. Medcroft came to an abrupt halt in the center of the room. "What? Oh, Sally Pritchard. It was the reason she gave for bringing Fanny to our regular séance unexpectedly. What did you suppose?" she demanded, her face aggrieved.

"Nothing, really. But Fanny told me the story herself this afternoon, and I didn't know it was one with which you were familiar."

"And what else did she say to you?"

Both of them stared at me with sudden interest, and I felt much the way Fanny must have felt downstairs—forced to produce an answer I was not prepared to give. It had, after all, been a private conversation, and she wouldn't have wanted her feelings openly discussed.

"Most of the morning we looked through your scrapbooks," I claimed with complete honesty. "I doubt the subject of her mother's death would have been mentioned had we not been talking about my own mother."

Mrs. Medcroft frowned. "You must be careful, dear. Mr. Llewelyn already thinks you are seeking information on my account."

"But that is nonsense."

"Indeed, but ladies in my position are often forced to endure slanderous attacks." She forgot me and turned back to Mr. Quarmby. "Do you think that awful man could have arranged some kind of trickery to amuse himself and make me look the fool?"

"Surely he would not stoop to such depths. But if he has, we will expose him."

There was a tap on the door and Chaitra stepped

softly into the sitting room, carrying a heavily laden tea tray. Her sari billowed around her like a peaceful blue cloud, and there was an amused look in her dark eyes. Her air of serenity contrasted sharply with the turmoil around her.

"I thought you would be needing something to settle your nerves," she announced, putting the tray down on the nearest table.

"Obviously, you have heard," Mrs. Medcroft said in a petulant voice.

"The downstairs staff cannot stop themselves from talking, although they lower their voices in my presence." Slyly, she glanced at her mistress and arched an eyebrow. "I suspected you wouldn't be pleased."

"You know how I hate unexpected changes. I swear you delight in seeing me distressed." Her legs wobbled, and she sank onto the sofa. "Dear me, I am undone. This night will be a disaster. Nothing less than a disaster."

"It is nothing but stage fright," Mr. Quarmby assured us. "I knew an actress who suffered this way before every performance." He caught Mrs. Medcroft's sharp look and, without either blinking or faltering, continued, "An elderly woman who had spent sixty of her seventy years in the theater. That was years ago, of course. I would not have remembered her, were it not for the similarity of your current circumstances."

"I am not an actress," she snapped. "I am a sensitive. The two professions are completely dissimilar."

"Of course, dear lady. Yours is a noble calling."

Her gaze lifted to his and, with glistening eyes, she mutely apologized for her brief loss of temper. "What are we to do, Mr. Quarmby? White Feather will be expecting to find us in the parlor."

Before he could respond, Chaitra roughly shoved a cushion behind Mrs. Medcroft's back and forced a cup of tea into her hands. "If he can return from beyond, he won't be troubled by a short walk from one part of Abbey House to another. Have a sip of that and you'll feel better."

"Spiteful creature. What do you know about these things? White Feather was an Apache warrior and a pagan. Likely he will not set foot on holy ground."

"If that were true, he wouldn't have set foot in any part of the abbey."

"Oh, why do I waste my energy trying to reason with you? Don't you realize, I have mentally and spiritually prepared myself to work in the parlor this evening?"

The state of her nerves surprised me, although I had already discovered she was highly emotional. Still, her fears seemed wildly exaggerated. I sat next to her on the sofa, took her hand in mine, and gently rubbed her fingers. It was what my mother had done for me whenever I had been frightened as a child.

"Dear Hilary," she murmured. "You cannot know how much I have already come to depend on you. You must be my strength this evening."

"You succeeded well enough our first night, with no kind of preparations," I pointed out.

"But this evening they will be expecting more from me."

Mr. Quarmby clicked his heels. "And you, dear lady, will not let them down." He glanced at me, a faint uncertainty in his eyes, and added, "I am convinced. Utterly convinced."

Despite the various protests, all of the houseguests appeared in the drawing room. Oil lamp in hand, his long strides setting a fast pace, Mr. Llewelyn led us to the church. His shadow flattened against the stone walls of the corridor, tall and straight and no less austere than its master. The rest of us clumped together in a silent mass, unwilling to be left behind in the dark, but none too eager to close upon his heels.

The church stood at the end of the long tunnel I had already viewed, and was separated from the rest of Abbey House by those heavy oak doors. They had been propped open to admit air and a meager warmth as well as to allow us to enter. As I squeezed through the opening, my dress snagged on a splinter, and I glanced down. There were deep scratches and holes in the thick wood where the iron nails had recently been pried loose.

We clattered across the flagstone floor, and our steps echoed through the empty chamber and bounced off the ceiling. I peered upward through the shadows. Oak tie beams and braces arched overhead, looking as sturdy and durable as they must have done on the day they had been erected.

As Mr. Llewelyn had promised, the dust and cobwebs had been swept away, and the stone walls smelled faintly of lime. But in spite of the men's efforts, the smell of must lingered in the air, and there was a dampness that made the fringe of my hair droop limply across my forehead.

Mr. Llewelyn lifted his lamp, spreading a pool of light through the church. Most of the pews had been removed, but it fell across a circular table that had been set with eleven chairs. Two brass candlesticks glowed dully from its surface, waiting to be lit.

"You seem to have thought of everything," Winnie said. His jovial words reverberated from one end of the church to the other, sounding falser with each repetition.

Ursula frowned. "All right, Edmund. You have played your little game. You cannot really mean us to go through with this."

"As I recall, I was the one who said from the start that this whole affair was a mistake. If Fanny is content to end this matter here and now, we can all go upstairs to bed."

Dr. Rhodes took his fiancée by the arm and whispered something in her ear. Whatever his suggestion, it had no effect. Fanny pulled out of his grip and stared over his shoulder, seemingly hypnotized by something far beyond our small circle.

I turned and followed her gaze. Against the wall, a row of wooden steps rose upward to a broad gallery. It was the only gallery to be seen and must have been where her mother had stood before she fell to her death. It was no more than twelve feet above our heads, and a carved railing ran its full length to protect the occupants. Apparently, it had not been protection enough for Fanny's mother.

I shivered and risked a glance at Mr. Llewelyn.

His gaze was not upon the gallery as I had expected but on me, and there was a strange expression on his face. The instant our gazes met, the look vanished and he scowled and turned to his sister.

"Well, Fanny? I shall ask you again. What is it to be?"

"I will be fine," she assured him. "If Hilary will sit by me."

Mrs. Medcroft immediately caught my arm. "Oh, but that is impossible."

"On the contrary," Mr. Llewelyn countered. "I think it is an excellent idea. Furthermore, I should like Mr. Quarmby and Chaitra to be separated from you also. I shall sit on your left, and Ursula on your right."

"But that is not how I work," she protested. "I need the support of my friends if I am to guarantee any success."

"Nevertheless, you will do as I say or pack your belongings and leave my house tomorrow."

To my surprise, even Fanny didn't protest this edict. I had only to look at her brother's grim face to understand her silence. It would have taken a stronger character than she possessed to quarrel with him at that moment.

Mrs. Medcroft turned mournfully to Mr. Quarmby. He patted her hand nervously and assured her that if there were no results, no one could fault her. Nevertheless, he urged her to try.

"Yes, do," Sally begged, her bracelets jingling in the gloom. "You know how important this is to Fanny."

Mrs. Medcroft sighed heavily. "I will do my best. But under the circumstances . . ." She shrugged helplessly.

One by one we took our seats at the table, slipping into our chairs like condemned men waiting for their turn to stand before the noose. Our positions were all dictated by Mr. Llewelyn. I found myself between Fanny and Winnie, and Sally discovered she was to be seated next to our host.

It was not a place I envied her.

Mrs. Medcroft looked decidedly miserable. She cringed when Ursula settled into the chair on her left, and delayed giving her hand to Mr. Llewelyn until she had no other choice. Her face a pale triangle caught in the glow of the candles, she asked Mr. Quarmby to give the blessing.

His prayer wobbled through the church, fainter than the memory of the chanting monks. If that prayer was our sole protection from the spirits, I was not much impressed with our chances. It dwindled into a hasty and apologetic silence. Mrs. Medcroft's eyes closed briefly, flickered open, then closed again.

The seconds dragged into minutes, and she seemed to take much longer to slip into a trance than she had in the parlor. I was beginning to think her nerves would not allow her to continue when she began to sway in her chair. At first her movements were jerky and awkward, but slowly they grew more fluid and her breathing deepened.

"Is anybody here?" she asked in a quavering voice, and the tense lines faded from Mr. Quarmby's forehead.

"Is anybody here?"

There was a hard rap on the table and the candlesticks wobbled.

"Is that you, White Feather?" she asked, drawing courage from this slight success.

Another rap shook the table.

"Thank heavens, you found us. I was deeply afraid you would not."

The reproach in her voice was obvious, but I sincerely doubted the guilty party appreciated he was being rebuked. Mr. Llewelyn was glaring around the table, no doubt assuming that one of us had managed to circumvent the obstacles he had set. His gaze ran from Mr. Quarmby to Chaitra, at last, reaching me. His scowl deepened but, after a faint hesitation, he fixed his stare on Mr. Quarmby. Forced to endure the accusation in those grim eyes, Mr. Quarmby shifted uncomfortably in his chair. Even in the pale light, his cheeks looked flushed.

"Is there anyone who would like to speak to us tonight, White Feather?" Mrs. Medcroft continued, her closed eyes keeping her blithely unaware of her friend's discomfort.

There was no answer, but the candles flickered and lengthened, and wax flowed down their slender sides and dripped off the candlesticks to the table. I shivered. The temperature in the church was dropping, and my fingers were numb. Fanny's, too, were icy, and even Winnie's beefy hand felt cool.

"Anyone at all?" Mrs. Medcroft asked.

There was a plaintive note to her question, and her lashes fluttered. From her growing anxiety, I suspected she was unaware of the subtle changes around her. A glance at the nervous faces to either side of me proved that most of the others were not. Only Chaitra appeared serene. And Mr. Llewelyn, while not seeming fearful, looked anything but pleased.

In the stillness, something scratched against the stones. It was faint at first, like a field mouse scurrying into its hole. But the noise persisted, growing steadily louder until it could not be ignored. Neither could it have been mistaken as a mouse; nor even a rat, unless they grew as large as badgers in Dorset.

"White Feather, is that you?" Mrs. Medcroft opened her eyes; they were wide and startled.

The scratching had an evil undertone. It emanated from beneath the flagging, as though skeletal fingers were attempting to loosen the stones. The sounds of their struggles poured between the cracks, and echoed through the church until nothing else could be heard.

And then they stopped.

The silence was as dramatic and frightening as anything that had gone before. Inherent in its depths was the promise—or warning—that everything thus far was merely a preliminary to what was to come. Mrs. Medcroft moaned and sank against the back of her chair.

"Good heavens, she's fainted," Ursula cried.

"No, no. The dear lady has merely gone into a deep trance. We must not disturb her or break the circle."

"That is exactly what we must do," Dr. Rhodes cried, with a worried look for Fanny. "This cannot continue."

Someone sighed from the gallery. A woman's light footsteps pattered across the boards, and they creaked beneath a ghostly weight. At first, I could see nothing, but within seconds a line of mist drifted through the stone wall and became a luminous streak in the darkness. It drifted along the length of the gallery, and there was a sensuous quality to the movement, like a woman seductively swaying her hips for an audience.

In the middle of the gallery, the footsteps stopped, and the mist hovered inches above the boards. It poised there, motionless, for a period that seemed endless.

And then evaporated into nothingness.

"Dear God, is it over?" Ursula demanded.

Mr. Llewelyn thrust back his chair in order to rise. "It most certainly is."

He did not reach his feet. There was an unearthly howl and a horrid thud. The floor of the church trembled beneath my feet. It seemed to me that my heart had stopped beating, and a cold and ghastly stillness swept over our gathering.

And in that stillness, a voice cried, "Murder!"

All faces turned to me, and I realized with horror it was I who had made that dreadful accusation.

After enduring the sinister encounter in the church, the Gothic drawing room seemed cheerful and warm. But our faces reflected none of that cheer.

All of us were, in our own fashion, reliving the séance.

Mr. Quarmby bent over Mrs. Medcroft and solicitously urged her to take a sip of brandy. Arousing her from her trance had been difficult. His attempts had only been successful after I had dug through her bag for the vial of smelling salts. Mrs. Medcroft had returned to consciousness, bewildered and frightened, with no memory of anything that had happened.

She gulped down the brandy and returned the empty glass to the hovering Mr. Quarmby. "It is quite common for me to have no knowledge of what has occurred," she admitted, with an apologetic glance for those around her. "But rarely do I need assistance to return to consciousness. I cannot think what was wrong with White Feather."

"It was my contention you had fainted." Ursula peered sharply at her, suspicion etched across her sharp features.

"Good heavens, no. Although, to the *layman,* the two states appear similar."

"I assured Miss Llewelyn she was mistaken, dear lady. Thanks to our long-standing friendship, no one is more familiar with this process than I."

Sally squirmed anxiously on the cushions of her chair, and her bracelets jangled an off-key melody. "*I* certainly felt like fainting. It was simply awful. When Hilary cried 'Murder!' I thought my heart would stop beating." She placed a plump and dimpled hand atop her breast. "The beat is still irregular. Mr. Llewelyn, do be so kind as to tell me if you think I am in any danger."

"Dr. Rhodes would be of more use to you than I." He glanced distastefully at her pounding bosom, and she wilted beneath his censure. Apparently satisfied that he had dispensed with one foe, Mr. Llewelyn levelled his dark scowl on the rest of the gathering. "If no one else has need of me, I would like to have a few words privately with Miss Carewe."

I started in my chair. "Me? Whatever for?"

"You cannot blame Hilary for crying out as she did," Mrs. Medcroft protested. "She is not at all to blame."

He rounded on her, a black fury emanating from his eyes. "Is she not? Then am I to presume you put that unforgivable word in her mouth?"

"D-dear me, no. At least, *not intentionally,* I assure you. Forgive me, Hilary. You were no more than an innocent vessel through which I projected the energies that possessed me. They would only have flowed to someone I trusted, someone with whom I was in great empathy. As you know, the bond we share is deep and powerful."

"In that, we are in complete agreement," Mr. Llewelyn retorted. "And it is the nature of that bond that bears discussing. If the rest of you will wait for us here, I believe you will have your explanations shortly." He turned to me and arched one dark brow. "Shall we adjoin to my study, Miss Carewe?"

My stomach shriveled into a tight knot. "Surely this can wait until tomorrow."

"As it happens, it cannot."

He stared down at me, forcing me to obedience with the strength of his will alone. I found myself rising to my feet in spite of my desire to remain rooted to the sofa. Immediately, he grasped me by the arm and, fingers pinching into my flesh, he steered me into the adjoining room.

I was carried along, unprotesting, with no more ability to resist than the shadow that had followed him down the corridor and into the church. Whatever

I thought of Edmund Llewelyn, it was impossible to ignore the power and force of his personality. My dread of the confrontation to come was mingled with a kind of perverse physical pleasure for having been singled out for his attentions. Never before had my body warred with my mind, and the struggle left me as bewildered as it did flustered.

The study was a cramped little room with poor lighting and sparse furnishings. Not a room for guests nor comfortable conversations. Mr. Llewelyn banged the door shut behind us and twirled me about to face him. His rage seeped from every pore.

"Exactly what kind of game are you playing?" he demanded.

"I assure you I am not playing games."

"Do you really expect me to believe you had no hand in tonight's events?"

"I cannot think what possessed me to cry out as I did, if that is what troubles you. Certainly, it was not my intention."

His scowl deepened and his fingers twitched at his sides. He seemed unaware of their motion, but I was not. There was a threat in that unconscious movement, and I suspected he wanted to place his hands about my neck and squeeze. Nor did I place much faith in his self-control.

He glared at me through narrowed eyes. "I think crying out as you did was exactly your intention. Having failed to win my admiration—"

"Good heavens. As for wanting your admiration, I can only promise you I look upon you with complete and utter loathing. I would sooner have the affections of an adder." I stepped back lest he attempt to assault me as he had done in his stepmother's suite to prove to us both that I was not invulnerable to his physical magnetism. "For that matter," I taunted from a safe distance, "I think you completely incapable of affection."

"Indeed." He delivered me a haughty stare. "And how do you come by that opinion?"

"Your dislike of women is obvious. You sneer at Fanny and Miss Pritchard. You repeatedly insult Mrs. Medcroft and myself. Eglantine is, at best, tolerated. If Ursula were not your full sister and your mirror image in both thought and personality, you would no doubt have less tolerance for her."

The reproach poured from me in an unbroken flow. Mr. Llewelyn regarded me in much the same fashion as he might have regarded his boots had he accidentally stepped on soiled ground. His nose wrinkled, and he delayed taking a breath until it became a matter of filling his lungs or expiring. Even then, he appeared most dissatisfied with the choice he had to make.

He met my unchastened glare with a hard smile. "May I assume you are finished?"

"You may. For the moment," I added, in a deliberate attempt to infuriate him.

He remained coolly controlled. "Good. Because now you are going to go back into that drawing room and make your confession."

"What confession? I have done nothing wrong."

"Don't lie to me. It had to be you."

"What had to have been me?"

"Do not attempt to pretend you were not behind that little performance in the church. It is the only logical conclusion."

"I fail to see that logic."

"Then let me help you." He stepped toward me, forcing me into a retreat. "It was you, was it not, who cried murder?"

"I never said otherwise, but the word burst from me unbidden."

Another long stride brought him near enough to me that I could see the closely shaven jaw and the strong tendons in his neck. I gathered up my dress to avoid stumbling on the hem and took another backward step.

"And then there is the matter of the scratching on the stones."

"You cannot think me responsible for—"

"It was not your Mrs. Medcroft. Positioned between my sister and me, she could not have whimpered without one of us being aware. She had, therefore, an assistant."

He bore down upon me, intent on taking revenge for the insults that had been paid him. For each step he advanced, I retreated two, but the distance between us dwindled with frightening rapidity. I could see each dark lash distinctly, and count the number of dark flecks in his gray irises. My heart thundered in my ears, and panic made my movements clumsy. In my haste, I bumped against the chair and barely saved myself from falling to the carpet in an undignified heap.

"I suspected Mr. Quarmby," he continued mercilessly. "Since you entered her home but recently. And it was upon him I fixed my gaze after the rapping began. Had he twitched a muscle it would have been instantly apparent."

"Of course Mr. Quarmby would not have taken part in any deceit," I agreed. "But that is no reason for you to accuse me of wrongdoing."

My words had no effect whatsoever. He neither slowed his pace nor wavered from his attack. He was like some hunting dog who, having scented his prey, could not be shaken from its trail. It seemed he would soon be upon me, and I must either defend myself or give way to embarrassing screams to summon help. My hand rose convulsively to my throat.

Mr. Llewelyn followed the gesture with his eyes and smiled. "The maid Chaitra, you remember," he said in a deceptively pleasant tone, "was between Winnie and Eglantine. No doubt Winnie's attention was on you, although not in the manner I would have wished. But Eglantine can be shrewd when the occasion demands, and I warned her where her attentions must be focused."

"Perhaps you will recall that my hands were also clasped."

"On the one side by Fanny. I need hardly give you my opinion of her reliability. Your own remarks prove you are already cognizant of my feelings. That left only Winnie to police your actions, and you had only to flutter your eyelashes at him to do exactly as you pleased."

I stopped abruptly, forcing him to do the same. "I do not flutter my eyelashes at any man."

"I recall a certain coyness in the breakfast parlor the other morning. Have you developed scruples in less than forty-eight hours?"

"How dare you. If you were not blinded by your ego—"

"If I were blinded by my ego, I would make the mistake of assuming your interest in me genuine."

"You assume an interest that does not, and never did, exist."

"What I assume is that you are willing to use your charms in any manner that promotes your purposes."

"And how, pray tell, did I manifest your stepmother's ghost? Or do you think her merely a hallucination?"

He frowned and I prayed I had found the one flaw in his "logical" solution. But far from appeasing him, my statement only deepened his fury. His lips twisted into a cynical line. "It was dark. I could duplicate the scratching noises myself. I doubt you were expecting the added dimension the church's odd acoustics would give those scratches—although you made full use of them. After that, we were all susceptible to suggestion. That, or you somehow rigged the church."

"That is a slanderous accusation."

"You were the only one who knew my plans."

"Good heavens. I am not a magician. Furthermore, what reason would I have for doing these things?"

He reached out and caught me by the shoulders, and I realized my mistake in having paused in my retreat. Holding me tightly to prevent me from slipping out of his grasp, he covered the last step between us. I stared at the sharp line of his lips and told myself I would scream if he attempted to kiss me a second time, no matter what the loss to my dignity.

But it was only his gaze that fastened upon my face, and that was impassioned by rage, not desire. "You had two very good reasons," he said between clenched teeth and his words hissed into my ears. "To ingratiate yourself with Mrs. Medcroft—and to ruin me."

"Ruin you? That is insane."

"You would not be the first woman who attempted to destroy me after she discovered I had no interest in her."

"Is that why you dislike my sex? What a fool that woman must have been. Had she any real appreciation of your character, she would have blessed her good luck in failing to appeal to your tastes."

His eyes glittered. "I recommend you do not treat

the matter lightly. She nearly cost me dearly, and I will not have my life destroyed by another like her."

"And how am I supposed to be destroying your life?" I demanded, careless of the danger to my person.

"Do not play the innocent with me, Miss Carewe."

"Are you so caught up in your precious image of yourself that you could not bear seeing your family become the subject of gossip?" I demanded. "Do you fear that a murder in your home might make others slight you as you are wont to slight them? It would do you good to suffer a little humiliation. It might teach you to be more thoughtful of others in the future."

"Enough! I will give you but one chance. Confess what you have done and leave my house tonight, or force me to discover your secrets and expose you. If you choose the latter, I will have the lot of you arrested."

"I will not be bullied into confessing to a crime I did not commit."

He thrust me from him roughly. "Then I shall do what must be done. You may return to the drawing room, Miss Carewe. But do not expect the remainder of your stay at Abbey House to be a pleasant one."

"Then I need expect no change in your behavior."

With that last sally, I stalked from the room.

8

I stepped back into the drawing room, my heart pounding in my ears, and the hushed conversation ended abruptly. All heads turned in my direction, and Winnie pushed himself from his chair and lumbered toward me.

"Are you all right, my dear? We have been most concerned."

"There is nothing the matter with *me*," I assured him. "But nor are any mysteries likely to be explained tonight, since Mr. Llewelyn mistakenly thought me to be in possession of answers I do not have."

"Ridiculous assumption, of course," he agreed, patting me on the back.

The effort was too familiar to be soothing, but his support restored me to better humor. A glimpse of Eglantine's pinched face and clenched hands told me that any gratitude I might have shown must be minimized. I sighed inwardly. Staying under the Llewelyns's roof was like walking across a path strewn with thorns. There seemed to be no safe place to set one's foot.

I thanked Winnie in a stiffly polite manner that, judging by his disappointed face, could have offended no one. "Mr. Llewelyn's accusations *are* ridiculous," I agreed. "And if he were not desperately seeking some way to prove the séance a hoax, he would see that for himself."

"Well, his reasons aren't to be wondered at. Not really. But I don't suppose he bothered to explain them to you."

"I think that is quite enough, Winnie," Ursula warned.

He lifted his large head and looked at her reproachfully. "It's nobody's fault but his own. If he is going to bully this young lady, I think she deserves to know why."

"That is hardly your decision to make. This is a family matter."

"Well, I am a member of this family," Fanny said. Her clear voice traveled from one end of the room to the other. "If Edmund wishes to abuse my guests, then he deserves to suffer the consequences."

"Not another word, Fanny." Her sister fixed her with a dark glare that was akin to those I had received in the study.

Fanny gave her head a toss that set her ringlets bouncing and rose from her chair. She glided smoothly into the middle of the room, drawing all gazes along with her. "Father and Edmund had a falling out," she announced, tossing a defiant glance at her sister.

Ursula stiffened in her chair.

"And Papa had threatened to disown him."

"Sheer gossip. You were only ten and can hardly be regarded as a reliable source."

"Of course, Papa held strict views about the place of women, and he would not have countenanced leaving his fortune in *our* hands."

"For which we can be eternally thankful. If you had any control of the estate, we should have been paupers in less than a year."

Fanny lifted her chin, threw back her shoulders, and smiled victoriously. "But this was when Mama was alive and she was *expecting.*"

Her revelation had the desired effect. There was a gasp from half the members of her audience, although clearly the Winthrops and Ursula had known where the quarrel was leading. Fanny paused to enjoy the stir she had caused, and her face shone.

In a satisfied voice, she finished, "If the child had been a boy, then, without doubt, Edmund would have been disinherited."

"What difference does that make?" Ursula demanded. "None of us knew she was expecting until after the autopsy."

"It had not been openly announced. But she might have told Edmund. We have only his word she did not."

"Ridiculous. She barely tolerated him. She would have been more likely to tell you or Papa. Really, Fanny. You're worse than your mother. This is nothing more than an opportunity for you to indulge yourself in meaningless theatrics."

"Nevertheless, you must agree it was most fortunate for Edmund that Mama died before the child could be born."

There was the sound of slow, deliberate clapping at my back.

I turned. Mr. Llewelyn stood in the doorway that connected the two rooms, an ominous figure outlined by a pale light. From the expression on his face, I suspected he had heard a good deal more of the conversation than anyone would have liked. He surveyed his sister's houseguests, a bored smile on his lips.

"Excellent, Fanny. Truly a worthy performance. And now, if you are quite finished, I think you should let your audience retire. They look decidedly tired."

"Good Lord." Mrs. Medcroft briskly fanned herself with her hand. "Can you believe the man's audacity? The look in his eye chilled me to the very marrow of my being."

"An evil character," Mr. Quarmby agreed, but his gaze rested thoughtfully upon me.

I was too caught up in my own thoughts to pay either of them much attention. What had we done by coming here? Stirred up restless spirits and possibly uncovered an eight-year-old murder. We had no evidence that Lily Llewelyn had been murdered, but since that moment in the church when the word had slipped past my lips, I had been convinced of its truth.

"Are you all right, Hilary?" Mrs. Medcroft asked. "You look a little peaked."

"A slight headache. Nothing really, but . . ."

"Yes, dear?"

"Oh, Mrs. Medcroft. Surely you realize we *must* leave here now. If Mrs. Llewelyn was murdered, we can only place our own lives in jeopardy by remaining here."

"Now, now, dear. You have nothing to fear. Only my life is at risk, and I will not let fear drive me from this house. It is my duty to see the murderer unmasked."

"Laudable, dear lady. Laudable."

Laudable, perhaps. But hardly wise. This was a matter for the authorities, not spiritualists. Nor was I convinced, as both of them seemed to be, that Mr. Llewelyn was the murderer. He was almost rigidly bound by convention. Would such a man kill his stepmother?

But, if he had murdered solely for gain, would he refrain from murdering again to save himself from the hangman?

Mrs. Medcroft didn't share my fears. She sighed rapturously, told Chaitra to fetch her a footstool, and beckoned for Mr. Quarmby to sit beside her. "Tell me what happened again," she begged. "It really is unfair that I should remember almost nothing of this evening's triumph. Was I a complete marvel?"

"There was not one person at that table who was not spellbound."

Despite his words, his response seemed rushed, and he didn't accept her invitation to join her on the sofa. His finger brushed impatiently across his moustache and, again and again, his gaze drifted in my direction.

Mrs. Medcroft regarded him with faint surprise, then turned to me. "It's late, and you look tired, dear. Why don't you run along to bed?"

"You had better let me take you to your room," Mr. Quarmby offered. "I will not feel at all happy until I know your door is locked and you are secure on the other side."

"But that's silly. Hilary is in no danger."

"And my room is only a few steps up the corridor."

"Nevertheless, I insist. And with your permission, dear lady, when that is done I will also retire for the night. It is nearly three, and you have given us much to contemplate."

"Well, if you must," she agreed. "We can talk tomorrow."

Mr. Quarmby followed at my elbow, taking short, hurried steps, his fingers still nervously brushing his moustache. I had yet to overcome my distaste for his person, although his good manners and concern for my well-being made me ashamed of my feelings.

"Quite an evening, don't you agree?" he asked politely, unaware of my thoughts.

I nodded. "One that I am glad is over. Indeed, I wish it had never begun."

"Ah, you are very young, Hilary. You do not mind that I call you Hilary, do you?"

"I see no reason that you should not," I agreed slowly. "You are, after all, Mrs. Medcroft's long-standing friend." We reached my door and I turned to him and gave him my hand. "And now I must bid you good-night."

"Of course, my dear. But there is one thing I would like to say before we part company. You must promise to come to me if ever you need help. No matter what that help might be, you will find me at your service."

"That is very kind of you."

Thinking my words had sounded less appreciative than good manners demanded, I forced a smile. Still, Mr. Quarmby seemed satisfied. He bobbed his head and his heels clicked together. Before he could say more, I bid him a hasty good-night and slipped into my room.

I slept late but did not arise well rested. Too many thoughts troubled me. Eglantine made no secret of her distrust for her husband, no more than he made a secret of his attraction to me. Indeed, his interest was blatantly obvious, almost as though he wanted to upset her. That, or make her jealous. For despite all his smarmy glances, I never felt any underlying passion. Nevertheless, I wondered how much longer Eglantine would restrain herself to hostile looks and cold civility.

As for our hostess's family, Ursula and her brother had been cut from the same cloth, and neither wanted us here. But he was infinitely more threatening. Although there was no evidence to prove he had harmed anyone, it would have been foolish to dismiss the possibility.

Then there was Mrs. Medcroft herself, a curious woman who appeared vastly insensitive on some occasions and yet proved herself to be an efficient medium when the moment demanded. Her recent successes were backed by years of recorded triumphs. She had been kind to me, but I thought her actions ill-advised and incautious. And almost certain to create greater troubles if she refused to discontinue the séances.

I rose and went to my dresser drawer. I had several guineas in my purse, enough to see me back to Bristol if I desired. I held them in the palm of my hand, taking comfort from their weight. I did not want to burden the reverend or his family with my company and, just the day before, I had written and asked them for references. What would they think receiving this second request immediately after the first?

But I knew they would not have wanted me to remain somewhere where conditions were untenable. I sighed. Either way good manners would not permit me to descend on them unannounced. Nothing could be done until I had written and advised them of my intentions. Unfortunately, it meant remaining at Abbey House for several more days, long enough for the Smythes to have received my letter and to be allowed the necessary time to prepare for my arrival.

A great deal could happen in a few days.

But soonest started, quickest finished. That was my father's favorite homily. I took out my pen and a sheet of writing paper, and hastily composed a few lines. I had only to sign the note when Chaitra appeared at my door.

Her sleek plait fell across her shoulder, and her hands were clasped tidily at her waist. "Mrs. Medcroft will not be going down to breakfast and says you are not to wait for her."

Her gaze dropped to the sheet of paper in my hand, and when she lifted her head, there was approval in her eyes. "You have decided to leave. I think that is wise. This is not a good place for you."

I didn't ask how she had guessed my intentions, but only nodded. Chaitra had already proved herself to be remarkably astute. "But please say nothing about this to anyone. I have yet to tell Mrs. Medcroft."

"Nor should you. Not for a day or two, I think."

I frowned. Now that I had reached a decision, my announcement could not be postponed. It was unfair to a woman who had been my mother's friend and had tried to be mine. But at least I would wait until after my letter had been posted.

I hoped to find Fanny in the breakfast parlor, pre-ferring to relay my missive through her rather than her brother, but the room was empty. Chafing dishes heaped with scrambled eggs and links of sausages sat on the sideboard, waiting for those of us who had risen. None of the food had been touched. Finding no recourse but to wait until some-one appeared, I helped myself to a muffin and some blackberry preserves.

I had cleared my plate and was sipping at my tea when I heard footsteps. I looked up into the magni-fied and startled eyes of Dr. Rhodes. He hovered in the doorway, as much out of the room as in, and his finger pulled nervously at his starched collar. His suit—one I had not seen before—was neat and qui-etly respectable. Probably the suit he wore for making his rounds. One look at him would have told his patients that Dr. Rhodes was not the kind of physi-cian to put on airs and scorn them, either openly or privately, for their complaints. I smiled warmly and bid him good morning.

"Oh, M-miss Carewe." He brushed back a length of drab brown hair that had fallen across his fore-head. "I didn't expect anyone else to be up this early."

"Force of habit. Will you join me, Dr. Rhodes?"

"I wouldn't like to disturb your solitude."

"Nonsense. I would enjoy your company."

"Oh. Well, then. Perhaps I will have something."

His step hesitant, he crossed to the sideboard and reached for a plate. His sleeve brushed over the cutlery, and two forks clattered to the floor. He apologized hastily and stooped to pick them up. On his ascent, his head collided with the corner of the sideboard with a hard thud.

"Good heavens," I cried. "Are you hurt?"

"It's nothing, really," he assured me.

He pulled out his handkerchief and mopped his forehead. When he pulled it away, there was a red stain on the linen.

"You have hurt yourself." I pushed back my chair and rose to help him.

He shook his head. "Just a slight cut. Really not worth mentioning."

Under protest, he let me lead him to a chair. After I was certain he had done himself no real harm, I filled a plate and set it down in front of him, along with the necessary cutlery. I glanced doubtfully at the silverware, not entirely certain he should be trusted with a knife.

"Nice of you to go to the trouble," he mumbled. "Sometimes I can be a bit clumsy."

"We all have accidents. And I doubt that any of us will be too well rested after last night's disturbances."

"What? Oh, yes."

Neither of us were in any doubt that his awkwardness had nothing to do with lack of sleep. Dr. Rhodes was simply one of those men who found themselves ill at ease in the company of young women. I wondered how he had succeeded in winning Fanny's devotion. I would have thought a man like Winnie, or even her brother, more to her tastes. That this unassuming doctor had captured her affections was remarkable.

But I did not want to add to his embarrassment by revealing my real opinions. "Did you know Mrs. Llewelyn?" I asked, in an attempt to lead his thoughts away from his current situation.

"What? Oh, y-yes. Not very well, you understand. I was only twenty the first time I came to the house. And twenty-three when she died," he added, his eyes clouding. "An unfortunate affair. Most unfortunate."

"Were you at the house on the day of her accident?" I asked eagerly, convinced that he was. Something in his tone and posture suggested he was well acquainted with the tragic events.

Dr. Rhodes fumbled with his spectacles and

nearly dropped them in his scrambled eggs. "Yes, as a matter of fact, I was. Well, we all were. Except for Mrs. Pritchard and your group. But Lily—Mrs. Llewelyn —enjoyed house parties. I suppose that's where Fanny acquired the taste for them."

Fanny had been ten at the time of her mother's death, hardly an age when she would have entertained gentlemen friends. So the doctor had known the family for many years. I supposed it was through Mr. Llewelyn he was acquainted with them, guessing they had been school chums. Fanny may well have had a youthful crush on the young man. It would certainly explain her interest in him as a young woman.

"Speaking of Fanny"—Dr. Rhodes's voice dropped to a confidential whisper—"there's something I've been meaning to ask you. It's a bit of an imposition, really. I hope you don't mind."

"I'd be glad to help you in any way I can."

"Would you mind keeping an eye on her until this business with the séances is finished?"

I thought of the letter in my pocket. "I'm not sure I will be able—"

"It would mean a lot to me. I'd even be willing to pay you to act as a sort of companion to her for the duration of your visit here."

"But I couldn't possibly take your money."

"F-Fanny is a lot more important to me than a few pounds, Miss Carewe. I wouldn't ask, but she seems to have formed an attachment to you."

"But surely the members of her own family are both better able and better suited to take care of her."

"Good Lord, no!"

His outburst startled both of us and I studied him carefully. His nervousness had been replaced by a desperate intensity. His mouth quivered, and the color was high in his pale cheeks. It seemed that, whenever Dr. Rhodes focused on matters important to him, he lost his awkwardness. As a doctor, he was a complete professional. As a concerned fiancé, he was passionately devoted to his beloved. What a charming man Fanny had decided to marry. Once again, I had to acknowledge her good sense.

Caught beneath my stare, he dropped his gaze. "I suppose I had better explain. Neither Edmund nor Ursula are terribly fond of their half sister. And the séances are upsetting her. She doesn't let on, but I am a doctor and I notice these things. She needs a friend, Miss Carewe, and you seem a good deal more reliable than Mrs. Pritchard."

I sighed inwardly. Refusing him was impossible. Fanny had already offered to help me. She had a right to expect something in return. Nor could I help but be reminded of Mrs. Medcroft's kindnesses and remember that if any of us was in real danger, it was her. It was utter selfishness to run away and leave them to manage without me.

Sadly, I reached in my pocket and crumpled the letter I had hidden there. "Keep your money, Dr. Rhodes. I will do whatever I can."

Soon afterward, I left him and went upstairs. Chaitra met me in the corridor, a breakfast tray in her hands. She took one look at my face, and her usually smooth brow furrowed.

"We will only be here for another week and a half," I said before she could speak. "And it was unfair of me to think of leaving. There are others who are in greater danger than I am."

Her fingers tightened on the tray and she stiffened. A mist passed over her dark eyes, and she stared at me without seeing. Instead, she seemed to be looking through me and beyond to some dark world visible only to her.

It was unnerving to be caught in the path of those unseeing eyes. Worse, I seemed to be trapped in her vision, for I could feel a cloud of icy air sweeping toward me. Nor was it the clean, fresh air of wintertime, but the dank blast released from a long-closed burial vault.

"Two and one," she muttered. "Danger on two sides, and one caught in the middle. One who will bring them together . . . to join what never should be joined." She reached out and gripped my arm. "Leave this place. Forget what you think you must do, and do only what must be done."

I shuddered and fought to maintain my composure. To my relief, Chaitra stirred and blinked and the awful sensation faded. Only a trace remained, visible in the goose pimples on my forearms.

"Good heavens," I said. "What did you mean by all that? You were speaking in riddles."

She shook her head, as confused as I, and the plates rattled on the tray she held. "I only know I do not like this place. It drains the energies from me. But I must stay. You are free to go." Her eyes fixed on me. "Leave here, Hilary. If you do not go quickly, I fear you might end your days at Abbey House."

Chaitra didn't linger, but hurried off to the kitchens. Her feet had no sooner pattered down the stairs than I had shrugged off the warning. She did not say I *would* end my days at Abbey House. Only that she feared I would. And I had the same fears for her mistress. She was the one caught in the middle, the one attempting to join the two who should not be joined. But who were the two? Lily Llewelyn and . . .

Her murderer?

I shuddered and hurried into my room, convinced more than ever that I must stay at Mrs. Medcroft's side until this whole affair had come to an end.

Mrs. Medcroft and Mr. Quarmby felt inclined to spend the day together in quiet pursuits. They, or rather Mr. Quarmby, graciously invited me to join them, but I refused. I wanted to fill my hours with activity until I had rid myself of the sense of foreboding that had engulfed me after hearing Chaitra's prophecy. Nor did I think, judging by Mrs. Medcroft's coy smile and hopeful eyes, that my company would be much missed.

If Mr. Quarmby would propose to her, perhaps we could return to London. Surely Mrs. Medcroft would be too excited and busy to think of séances with wedding plans to consume her attention. I said a silent prayer that he would accomplish the deed before the day ended.

With my promise to Dr. Rhodes in mind, I set off in search of Fanny. One of the upstairs maids kindly told me she was in her sitting room. "And would be glad of a bit of company," she added. "She's full of high spirits, that one, with not enough to keep her busy."

With that blessing for encouragement, I hurried past the first-floor landing and stepped into the family wing. It was quiet, and a muted sunlight filtered through the window panes at the far end. I paused and glanced down the long corridor to assure myself that I was not likely to meet Mr. Llewelyn. Seeing no one about, I walked briskly to Fanny's rooms.

At my knock, her door swung open wide. Fanny's blonde curls tumbled wildly about her face, and she

smiled with feverish brightness. "Hilary, thank goodness you've come. I am bored to distraction."

Beyond her, ensconced on the two-seat sofa, Sally
Pritchard stiffened. "Really, Fanny. Since I have been
keeping you company for this last hour, I cannot find
that remark anything but rude."

Her friend burst into laughter. "Oh, don't be silly.
You know I adore listening to all the gossip, but I
simply cannot sit still a moment longer."

She caught me by the arm and dragged me into her
sitting room. She took two small steps for each one of
mine, dancing at my side like an excited child. Sally
followed us with her eyes, her mouth pursed, and I
wondered if she was remembering the last occasion
when I had been an unwelcome intrusion.

"Why don't we go riding?" Fanny suggested.
"Hilary has seen almost nothing of the estate and it is
a lovely afternoon."

"You know I cannot abide horses. They make me
sneeze and my eyes get runny."

"Then Hilary and I shall go. You don't mind being
left alone for an hour or two, do you, Sally?"

"Why would you think—"

"Go and find Ursula. It would do her good to talk
to someone. And I imagine Edmund is somewhere
about," she added with a sly smile.

A light flickered in the young widow's eyes, and
her frown faded. "Perhaps I will." She rose and gave
Fanny a kiss, nodded to me, and slipped out of the
room.

Fanny waited until the door had closed and then
rolled her eyes. "Edmund will be absolutely furious
with me."

"Do you really think you ought to—"

"Sally's company will do him good." She tossed

her ringlets back from her face. "Do you ride? You said you did."

"A little," I admitted. "But I haven't a riding habit."

"You can borrow one of mine. It's certain to fit."

Fifteen minutes later, we were making our way to the stables. They were a rambling affair of gray stone and sloping slate roofs. Stable hands and grooms traipsed in and out of the open doors, their boots clapping against the flagging, and the smell of hay and fresh droppings mingled in the warm air.

Fanny had dressed me in a dark jade habit, an outfit that allowed me to maintain the semblance of mourning. It was not, she admitted, one of her favorites, the fabric having been chosen for her by Ursula. Her tastes ran to brighter hues; she swept down the path, swathed in rose velvet, a pert hat perched above her recently tidied curls.

A middle-aged man with a protruding stomach and a cap pulled low on his forehead met us outside the stable. He glanced from Fanny's face to my own, and he shifted from one foot to the other.

"Good morning, Sam," Fanny said, a childishly sweet smile on her lips. "Saddle up Ginger and Stockings for us, there's a dear."

"Can't do that, miss." He pulled at a button on his coat, refusing to meet her eye. "You know Mr. Llewelyn's orders."

"Bother. He said I was not to ride alone. And I am not alone, am I?"

I smiled politely, but I couldn't help feeling that Fanny was doing something that I should not support. I remembered her account of her youthful misadventure, but that had been several years ago when she was little more than a child. That could hardly be the reason for her current problem.

The groom shook his head doubtfully. "I don't know, miss. I'm not familiar with this young lady."

"You cannot expect to know all my friends, Sam. Now run along and do as I ask."

He hesitated, reluctant to move.

"I should not have to tell you twice," she said, impatience sharpening her tone.

Her words brought his head up, and he opened his mouth to make some kind of protest. The words never came. Instead, he looked over her shoulder and relief washed down his face. Fanny whirled about, her riding skirts flying around her.

I turned unwillingly, guessing, as she must have done, that Mr. Llewelyn stood at our backs. It was an uncomfortable situation. Without knowing why, I felt as though I had been caught filching the silverware. Certainly, something was amiss.

On this occasion, Mr. Llewelyn's dark scowl was for his sister. "What are you doing?" he demanded, with barely a passing glance for me.

"Oh, it's you, Edmund." Fanny politely covered a yawn. "Hilary and I are going to take a ride around the estate."

"You have been forbidden to ride unless someone accompanies you."

"I'm with Hilary, am I not?"

His gaze raked me with contempt. "I do not consider Miss Carewe a suitable chaperone."

"Bother. What a lot of trouble over nothing. Then send Sam, if you must, but I refuse to sit twiddling my thumbs all day."

"It takes more than Sam to control your antics, as well you know."

"Really, Edmund. You're impossible." She gave a quick toss of her curls. "Join us if you must. But I will not be deprived of a ride."

There was a second's pause, then he nodded. "But, in the future, I would prefer an hour's notice."

It was not the inconvenience he would have liked us to believe. He was already dressed for riding, in a tailored suit that showed off his square shoulders and lean frame to good advantage. Apparently, he was also looking for some kind of distraction, and it was only our company that was a nuisance.

His formidable presence dampened even his sister's lively spirits, and our conversation was desultory. Nor did he feel any need to be civil, but left us to talk quietly between ourselves. Every few minutes, Fanny glanced across at him, but he ignored her with an equanimity that escaped her.

The estate undulated in all directions, rolling green waves of pastureland and wooded copses. We could not have ridden more than a mile before we spotted a solitary rider cantering in our direction. As he drew nearer, I recognized the slight figure of Dr. Rhodes.

"Kenneth," Fanny cried with pleasure and spurred her horse forward, riding with a skill and grace that proved her brother's caution unnecessary.

He frowned, but let her go without comment. I watched enviously, wishing I could have followed. But Fanny would want a few moments alone with her fiancé. I did not like to intrude, even though that meant remaining in the company of Mr. Llewelyn.

With whom I was now obliged to make conversation. "You must be pleased that your sister has found a worthy man to marry," I said, choosing a subject that I thought would not offend him.

A muscle in his cheek jumped. "As it happens, I am not. Kenneth ought to have more sense."

"Good heavens, what is the matter with you?" I asked, forgetting myself in my surprise. "I would think, as her brother, you would at least try to be happy for them."

"Do not attempt to tell me what I should or should not feel, Miss Carewe. And, as long as we are alone, there is another matter I would like to discuss with you."

"When is there not?"

He glanced at me sharply, and his fingers tightened on his reins. "In the future, I will thank you *not* to abet Fanny in her attempts to thwart my discipline."

"What are you talking about? That affair at the stable?"

"Exactly."

"Until your groom protested, I was not aware there was a problem," I said, matching his cold civility with my own. "Even now, I do not understand your reluctance to trust her. She is obviously an excellent rider."

"When she chooses to use her head—which is rarely."

The wind caught at the collar of his coat, slapping it against his clean-shaven jaw, and he impatiently brushed the offending flap back into place with his free hand. His action reminded me of the wisps of hair that had escaped my chignon and were blowing across my eyes. He turned to me, and I half expected him to make some derisive remark about my unruly appearance.

Instead, he said stiffly, "I suppose I must make you an apology. In *this* instance," he immediately added. "It was unreasonable of me to assume that Fanny would have informed you. It is well within her character to use deceit if it suits her purposes. A habit she acquired from her mother."

Good heavens. He might have been referring to a stranger and not his own flesh and blood. His attitude was reprehensible. "Admittedly, I have only known your sister a short while, but I have seen nothing in her that warrants such absolute condemnation."

"Are you measuring her by your character? For by those standards, she cannot help but shine."

"And if your assessment of me is any measure of your ability to judge, I must, perforce, ignore all you have said."

I was spared having to hear his response. The drumming of hoofbeats cut across his words, and Dr. Rhodes and Fanny cantered down the path. She tossed her brother a victorious smile. "Kenneth will take me about the estate. You and Hilary may ride on without us." She appealed to me with an apologetic smile. "You don't mind, do you, darling?"

Utterly and completely.

"No," I mumbled. "That will be fine."

"Then we'll see you at dinner."

Without waiting for Dr. Rhodes, she urged her mare along the path. He nodded to us, deliberately avoiding his friend's gaze, and hastened after her. Within seconds, they had disappeared behind a copse of trees and we were alone. Indeed, I could not recall a time when I felt more alone than I did at that moment.

"There is no need for us to continue on together," I said quickly. "I only came at Fanny's insistence. As long as she has no need of my company I will return to the stable."

I attempted to turn my horse. His hand reached

out and he caught my mount by the bridle, pulling her to an immediate halt. Controlling both horses with unconscionable ease, he shifted in his saddle to face me. With nothing to distract my attention from the nearness of his person, I found it difficult to breathe, and my heart faltered from its usual beat.

Luckily, he was too absorbed in his own thoughts to be cognizant of mine. "There is something you should know before you leave, Miss Carewe," he explained, speaking to me as he might to a willful child. "Fanny's careless riding habits resulted in the death of a fine animal. One that did not even belong to our stable. I will not let that happen again."

"But she was only a child."

"Then she did tell you."

"About the accident, yes."

"Hardly an accident. It was deliberate negligence."

I frowned. Fanny had admitted as much herself. But she had also told me something of the circumstances surrounding the incident. It was easy to understand the emotions that had driven her, and pity her for the tragedy that had resulted. Clearly, Dr. Rhodes had forgotten the matter, and it was he who had suffered the loss of a beloved animal.

"Surely, after all these years, you could bring yourself to forgive her?"

His expression hardened. "Fanny neither wants nor needs my forgiveness. Nor do I intend to see another animal harmed because of her carelessness."

"But she was a child whose only remaining parent had just died."

"I see she has persuaded you to make excuses for her." The contemptuous look on his face told me I had sunk even lower in his estimation, something both of us had believed impossible. He smiled grimly.

"Well you may save your breath, Miss Carewe. This had nothing to do with my father's death. Fanny was, and is, irresponsible and willful."

"Have there been other accidents?"

"There have not. But solely because of the precautions I have taken."

He deserved to be slapped hard. The intensity of my outrage surprised me. I had never before succumbed to feelings of such complete hostility. But when, I asked myself, had I met anyone who was as convinced of his own superior judgment as Mr. Llewelyn?

And with less reason.

I glared into his complacent face. "If your sister is irresponsible, you have only yourself to blame. She is a grown woman and you treat her like a child."

"She *is* a child. And I will thank you not to tell me how to run my household."

"I can only be glad for Fanny that she is about to be married and will soon be out of your household. Perhaps then she will have a chance to live a normal life."

"Despite what you may think, she manages to keep herself amused—usually at someone else's expense. It is my sister and I who are continually denied the pleasures of a normal life through her antics."

He spoke as though he only had one sister. I stiffened in shock. The mare sensed my tension and skittered sideways, forcing Mr. Llewelyn to pay more attention to the hold he had on her. He seemed glad of the distraction, and I noted a crack in his composure. Was it caused by shame? He couldn't have failed to appreciate the cruelty of those words.

Poor Fanny. No wonder she sought attention wherever it could be found.

"I think this conversation has been exhausted," I said, struggling to keep my tone civil. "Will you kindly release my reins?"

"As you wish. But I will accompany you."

We rode back silently. I wondered if his determination to remain at my side was because good manners demanded that he did, or because he feared for my mount. The answer came when we reached the stables.

Instead of dismissing me, he determinedly strode up the path at my elbow, escorting me until we entered the house. It was ironic. In actions, he was the perfect gentleman. Considering his bad temper and many rudenesses, I wondered why he bothered.

He paused in the foyer to bid me a terse good-afternoon, and his gaze fell on the narrow table that stood near the door. A letter lay atop its marble surface. Hastily, he reached down and stuffed the envelope in his inside pocket.

And what, I wondered, was the need for that?

9

I returned to Mrs. Medcroft's suite to find Mr. Quarmby gone and her spirits at a low ebb. A harried Chaitra shot me a grim look and promptly excused herself to fetch a pitcher of hot water.

She had no sooner closed the door behind her than Mrs. Medcroft wailed, "What is the matter with the man?" Her hands fluttered in the air, the long, thin fingers grasping at invisible strands for support.

"Has something happened?" I asked politely.

She shook her head. "More to the point is that something hasn't happened. I fully expected Mr. Quarmby to propose this afternoon. I know how much impressed he has been with me of late."

"Perhaps he feels this is not the proper place." I took her by the arm and led her to the sofa. "There has been so much happening, it seems a bad time to talk of marriage."

"Nonsense. There is never a bad time to talk of marriage. Something is wrong with him. I am convinced of it." Her gaze snapped to me. "You were not gone more than a few minutes before he excused himself with a headache."

"There is your answer. He was not feeling well."

"Then why wasn't he in his room when I went to check on him?" she demanded.

I smoothed back a wing of white hair that had fallen across her damp brow. "He may have decided to take a walk in the garden. Fresh air is excellent for removing headaches."

"Did you see him? Where have you been?"

"I have been riding with our host." I did not elaborate, thinking this a poor moment to tell my tale.

Surprisingly, Mrs. Medcroft immediately dismissed her own troubles and reached for my hand. "You must be careful around him, Hilary. He is not at all to be trusted around young women."

"Surely you are mistaken? Never have I met a man who seems less interested in female companionship."

"He took you riding, did he not?"

"Only because he would not let Fanny ride alone."

The tension smoothed from her brow and she settled back against the cushions. "The ride was her idea? The three of you rode together?" She lay her hand across her forehead and rubbed her temples.

I nodded. "At first. Then we met Dr. Rhodes and she decided to ride with him. But—"

"Without you?" She sat upright and ignored my attempts to press her back onto the cushions. "Dear me. What have I done by bringing you here? Tell me he did not make any improper advances."

I burst into laughter. "Whatever I expect from him, it is not that."

"Really? You would not deceive me?"

"I hope you think better of me than that."

She apologized immediately and reached for her handkerchief. Dabbing at her moist eyes, she begged, "Please do not be cross. It is just that you are such an innocent, and it frightens me to see you subjected to the attentions of that awful man."

"The attention he pays me is not of a sort to be desired."

She studied my face, searching for a greater reassurance, one she did not seem to find. The faint lines around her eyes deepened, and her tongue flickered over her dry lips. "I suppose I should have said something before now," she said slowly. "But it is a distasteful subject."

"Of what do you speak?"

Before she could answer, Chaitra appeared with the hot water for her mistress's washstand. Her gaze went immediately to the tearful Mrs. Medcroft, then to me, hovering at her side.

"Can't you see we are having a private conversation?" Mrs. Medcroft demanded. "Go on about your business and leave us alone."

Chaitra frowned, but silently disappeared into the other room. Mrs. Medcroft shook herself. "I really wonder why I tolerate that woman."

"What was it you wanted to tell me?"

She shifted uncomfortably. "It is about Mr. Llewelyn. It is best you know he has a reputation as a womanizer."

"Mr. Llewelyn?" From what I knew of him, it was completely out of character. He did not like the company of women, and the standards he set himself as a gentleman would have made the practice unacceptable to him. "I think that most unlikely. If that is what troubles you, then—"

"I am quite serious, my dear. He keeps a townhouse in London and often takes women there. Of all kinds. But he seems to take particular pleasure in ruining the reputation of young women from good families."

I gasped. "But that kind of behavior would not be tolerated."

"Oh, my poor child. He is a very wealthy man, Hilary. And he chooses his victims carefully. Young ladies with no father or brother to defend them." She looked at me meaningfully.

I knew what she was suggesting, but she was wrong. Even if Mr. Llewelyn was the depraved character she described, he had made no attempt to seduce me. And her charges were probably based on nothing stronger than gossip.

"Perhaps you should tell me how you came to hear of this," I suggested gently.

Her hand clutched spasmodically at her handkerchief. "In my line of business, you meet many kinds of people. Including desperate ladies who have been spurned by their lovers and wish to know if they will return."

I stared at her. Could she possibly be right? Or had someone misled her with an outrageous tale? Either way, I did not feel myself to be in danger. In Mr. Llewelyn's estimation, I did not fall into the category of "a young woman from a good family." He had made that very clear.

But for Fanny's sake, I hoped she was mistaken. How awful to have such a man for a brother. I could even bring myself to feel sorry for Ursula. And more than ever, I was convinced we needed to leave Abbey House.

Mrs. Medcroft reached out and patted me on the knee. "You will be careful, won't you, dear."

"You have my promise."

I left her in better spirits, and Mr. Quarmby's failure to propose seemed forgotten. There had been more than enough excitement and disappointments for one day. I prayed the evening to come would be a quiet one.

Either my prayers were answered, or good fortune had decided to descend upon Abbey House. No one suggested holding a third séance that evening, not even Mrs. Medcroft. She had not, as I had thought, completely recovered from her disappointment. Gathering from the repeated glances she gave Mr. Quarmby when they were together, communicating with otherworldly beings was not uppermost in her mind.

I think we all retired early that night, glad of a quiet evening in which to do nothing but sleep. The moment my head touched the pillow, I was lost to consciousness and Abbey House. Nor did I awaken until well after the sun had risen.

Sally Pritchard traipsed into the front parlor in a pink silk morning gown, nodded briefly to Ursula, and hurried to where Fanny and I were reviewing sketches of wedding gowns. She gave them a brief glance and dismissed them with a jangling wave.

"How you can think of weddings is beyond me. Naturally, you can have no real happiness until your mother's murderer has been brought to justice."

"Naturally." A secret smile played upon Fanny's lips. "But I should not wonder if Edmund refuses to let us continue. He has, after all, a great deal to lose."

Sally gasped. "Surely you did not mean the things you said in the drawing room. I thought that was nothing more than theatrics."

"It was." Ursula set her needlework aside to give us her full attention.

"That or merely wishful thinking."

Winnie's words resonated through the parlor, and we looked up to see him standing in the doorway. He was dashingly dressed in a tailored suit of mustard-colored serge, the jacket fastened only by the top button. His curls had been carelessly thrown back from his face in such a manner as to make his hair look fuller and his head larger and more imposing. He needed only a gold-knobbed cane to complete the picture. That, he had either wisely or reluctantly foresworn, since a cane had no place in the parlor.

He nodded to our small group and strolled into the room. "It would mean a tidy inheritance for you if Edmund was convicted of murder, wouldn't it, Fanny? I imagine your father's will left everything to you and Ursula in the event that something happened to your brother."

"To be administered by the barristers," Fanny responded with a pout. "And they are just as bad as Edmund."

"Never mind. You will get around the lot of them by marrying Kenneth." He settled himself in the chair next to me, and clasped his hands behind his head. "Good morning, Miss Carewe. We have seen too little of you during the day. Where do you hide yourself?"

"Usually I am with Fanny or Mrs. Medcroft."

Sally sniffed. "When she is not bothering Mr. Llewelyn with trifles."

"Goodness, I hope you haven't become enamored of our Edmund. That would be most unwise."

I wondered if he was merely jesting or if he had heard the same tales as Mrs. Medcroft. But I realized he had made no effort to advise Sally, unless he had said something to her privately. If so, his warning had failed to take effect. She flirted with Mr. Llewelyn whenever they were together and had been crushed by the possibility that he might be to blame for Lily's death.

Seeing that the others were involved in their own pursuits, Winnie took the opportunity to engage me in conversation. He stretched out his legs, crossed one boot comfortably over the other, and invited my opinions on the séances.

"It was I who introduced Lily to Mr. Llewelyn," he said, reflecting back over the years. "I had heard her sing in London and recommended her for a week-end's entertainment. Edmund's father thought it good manners to invite his business associates and their wives to Abbey House every year, but he never did know what to do with them when they got there. My suggestion could not have been more welcome."

Ursula sniffed audibly.

He chuckled, not at all discomfited. "No one could have been more surprised than I when they became engaged. Good Lord. I never would have thought it of the old man."

"You have known the Llewelyn family long?" I asked politely.

He pulled idly at the narrow lace frill on his sleeve. "Twenty years, is it, Ursula? Yes, of course. We met shortly after my marriage to Eglantine. Her father's estate lies to the east of Smedmore—a lovely old manor house. A shame you can't visit us there, but we are using these few weeks of absence to have the kitchens renovated." He covered his mouth with his hand to smother a yawn. "It was Eglantine who introduced us. She had been friendly with the first Mrs. Llewelyn. It seems I acquired all of my wife's connections when I married her. Can't say that she approved much of mine."

The admission appeared to amuse rather than annoy him, and I suspected the notion of having a wife who approved of his friends would have severely damaged his image of himself. Once again, I was made to reflect on what an odd couple they made.

Discovering his audience was distracted, Winnie promptly recalled my wandering attention by asking how I had been spending my hours at Abbey House.

"I did go riding about the estate yesterday afternoon," I admitted, without much enthusiasm.

Fanny pushed the wedding sketches aside. "Poor Hilary. It was unkind of me to desert you yesterday. Tomorrow I'll ask Kenneth to drive us to Durdle Door," she promised. "That will make up for everything."

"You might remember that he has been making his rounds every day this week," Ursula said. "And that he sat up all last night delivering Mrs. Wattle's baby."

"Oh, hush. A day at the beach would do him good. Anyway, Kenneth doesn't mind."

"If he had any sense, he would. And if you had any real feelings for him, you would not ask him to exhaust himself on your account."

Winnie lifted his head from his hands and cleared his throat. "Surely it is a little early in the day for this argument, ladies. Who else can we discuss but the good doctor? I, for one, would be interested in learning more about Miss Carewe." He turned his smile on me.

Fanny saved me from the necessity of demurring. "Kenneth is my fiancé, not hers. I should not have to endure her orders where he is concerned."

"I wish it was unnecessary. I would far rather you

found it within yourself to show him a little consideration."

"You are hardly one to talk. At least with *me* he does not suffer from neglect."

"How dare you criticize me."

"You are perfectly willing to criticize me. Everybody knows your behavior was far worse than mine."

"Not everybody," Winnie reminded her pointedly. "But they will if you continue this argument." He rose from his chair and smoothed the wrinkles from his waistcoat. "Miss Carewe, can I persuade you to join me for a walk in the garden?"

I hesitated. His question put me in an awkward position. Any excuse to leave the room was welcome, but walking alone with Winnie would cause different problems. "You will want to join us, won't you, Sally?" I suggested.

"Goodness, no. The damp air would wilt my dress. Do go on, Fanny."

Ursula surveyed the silk and chiffon concoction Sally was wearing and her nose wrinkled. "It might teach you to wear more appropriate attire. But I imagine you will take great pleasure in adding her lies to your collection of inaccurate tales."

"Well, really."

"And they are hardly lies," Fanny countered. "You let Kenneth dangle for ten years."

"How dare you discuss my personal—"

"Why shouldn't I? You never hesitate to point out my failings. Perhaps you have forgotten that you let him propose five times and never once gave him a straightforward yes or no."

All thoughts of a walk in the garden were forgotten. I gaped at the two women, finally understanding the reason for the bitterness between them. And for Edmund's disapproval of Fanny's engagement. Naturally, he would favor Ursula over his younger sister.

The color had blanched from Ursula's face. "If you saw Kenneth was in love with me, you should have had the decency to stay away from him."

"I saw how unhappy he was," Fanny retorted. "If I hadn't returned from Switzerland and caught his eye, you would still be making his life miserable."

"Caught his eye? You threw yourself at him, as well you know. It was disgraceful."

Fanny threw back her head, displaying the graceful line of her neck, and peals of laughter burbled from her throat. "What nonsense. I had only to smile at him and speak a few words of praise and he came running to me like a lapdog."

"You had no right to encourage him."

Hatred for her younger sister smoldered in Ursula's eyes. Her fingers spread wide on the arm of the chair like drawn claws. Winnie's eyes widened in his handsome face, and Sally gripped the folds of her dress with an unconscious lack of concern for the damage she did the fabric. My heartbeat pounded in my ears like a reverberating drum. Only Fanny seemed unaware of the danger.

Her eyebrows arched. "Should I have waited until you refused him a sixth time? Or a seventh and eighth? If you wanted to marry him, you should have said yes when you had the chance."

"There is a lot you don't understand."

Her lips curved at the corners. "You might be surprised what I know."

"You couldn't . . ." She broke off, horrified, and her pupils became black dots in her gray irises.

Fanny glanced mischievously at her audience. "Would you like to hear why my sister refused to marry Kenneth, in spite of her feelings for him? It's because he—"

Ursula lunged at her. Winnie threw himself in her path and spread his arms to catch her before she could reach her target. The two collided hard and, despite his solid frame, Winnie quivered beneath the force of the impact. Ursula crumpled to the floor, gasping for breath. Fanny fell back against her chair and burst into hysterical giggles.

The door to the parlor banged open, and Mr. Llewelyn regarded the chaos with a cold eye. "Do you realize you can be heard from one end of the house to the other?"

Neither woman answered.

"Perhaps you enjoy humiliating our family in front of guests?" he continued.

"I shouldn't worry about us, old man," Winnie replied, helping Ursula to her feet. "We're practically family."

"I'm sorry, Edmund," Ursula said between gasps of breath. "It won't happen again. Will it, Fanny?"

She pouted and said nothing.

His gaze moved from her to Sally Pritchard, and he managed a warm smile. Even that was enough to give a charming tilt to his eyes, and my heart fluttered. Goodness. I despised the man and still he could have this effect on me. I could only wonder what that smile did to poor Sally.

In a silken voice, he said, "You will not, I hope, describe any part of this deplorable scene to your many friends, Mrs. Pritchard. Your discretion would mean a great deal to me."

"Oh dear me, I won't say a word," she promised, and her face glowed with adoration.

He turned to me. The smile didn't fade, but there

was none of the ingratiating warmth, only a stiff politeness. "And you, Miss Carewe. I assume I may also count on your silence."

Only my mother's good training kept me from gaping at him. *Assume?* Yesterday, he would have been convinced that nothing but money would have bought my silence. Now he appealed to me as he might have appealed to any well-bred gentlewoman.

Which, of course, I was.

"You did not need to ask," I murmured.

He nodded, and something flickered in his eyes. Sally stirred anxiously in her chair, drawing his attention back to her. Whatever emotion had played there disappeared, replaced by the syrupy warmth I had seen earlier. Coyly, she lowered her gaze, and the dimples in her cheeks deepened.

With a final, severe look for his sisters, he left the room. Sally immediately turned to me and shot me a victorious smile. Had she displayed any likable traits in the short while I had known her, I would have been inclined to pity her.

Edmund Llewelyn did not lack for intelligence. He had known he must not appear to favor me over Sally Pritchard lest he risk losing her cooperation. And had he tried to manipulate me with his charm, I would have been insulted. Instead, he had appealed to my good manners, thereby immediately gaining my support.

But how had he known I would reflect my breeding when he was convinced I had none?

There was little time for me to reflect on his behavior. The door to the gardens opened, and Eglantine Winthrop stepped through the French doors into the parlor. Judging from her heavy tweed walking suit and leather walking boots, she appeared to have been strolling in the garden. But instead of the satisfaction I might have expected to see on her face, her horsey features were tightened into a grimace and her eyes had an added bulge from the stress of overexertion.

The ruddy color in her cheeks was also too deep to be attributed to mere exercise, and she scanned the room with the eye of a general preparing to ambush or be ambushed. From the angle of her entrance, she was not able to see all the occupants of the parlor. Only Winnie, who had returned to his chair where he sat with his legs on the footstool.

And, directly across from him, me.

"I thought as much," she said, bearing down on us. Her headlong thrust carried her another yard and she caught sight of Fanny and a smirking Sally. She faltered and came to an awkward halt.

"You always were able to guess in which room we would collect," Ursula said, neatly saving her from complete humiliation. "Do come and sit down and help me with my needlework. There's a stitch that escapes me."

Eglantine smiled gratefully at her friend and joined her on the sofa. Slightly more collected, she looked at her husband reproachfully. "You told me you might take a walk in the garden. I have been searching for you up and down the paths for the last hour."

"Forgive me, my darling. I'm afraid at the first sight of a comfortable chair all my good intentions were undone."

Silently, I thanked heaven that Winnie and I had not escaped the parlor, even with Mrs. Pritchard in tow.

That afternoon, since Chaitra was busy with tasks of her own and Fanny was nowhere to be seen, I decided I would take a walk in the gardens—although in nobody's company but my own. The day was warm and dry, and a gentle wind was blowing up from the south—a perfect afternoon for a stroll.

Stone paths meandered through the flower beds and across the lawns. I wandered through a maze of rosebushes, pushed along by gusts of air and a desire to reach the dense woods that sprawled across the southeastern portion of the estate.

My brisk strides carried me to the edge of the lawns and into the tangled mass of oaks and beech trees. Springy moss cushioned my steps, and thick clumps of ferns pulled at the hem of my dress. Narrow paths twisted and turned in all directions, and branches intertwined above my head, blotting out the sun and sky.

My feet moved of their own accord, taking me down first one fork and then another. I passed through quiet green tunnels and open glades spattered with foxgloves and splashed with sunshine. My pace became hurried, and my thoughts were all for what lay ahead and who waited there.

Twice, I thought I heard twigs snapping underfoot somewhere behind me, but instead of growing wary, I became suffused with a need to reach some unknown destination. All my senses sharpened. Leaves brushed against my face, and I could see each vein in their smooth surfaces. Birds chirped and twittered a warning at my approach, and each note hung in the air, crystalline in its perfection. The fragrance of the rich earth emanated from the ground at my feet, a sultry, provocative scent that stirred my blood and made my head swim with the unaccustomed richness. I could taste my excitement, sweet and thick like a honeyed wine.

Abbey House was nothing more than a bad memory, a prison I had escaped and would escape. Again and again and again. Whenever I chose, for who was there to stop me? Certainly not Edmund. Poor deluded Edmund who knew everything about money and nothing at all about women.

I threw back my head and laughed—wanton, shameless laughter—and my hand moved to my head to pull the pins from my hair. Long russet curls fell down about my face and shoulders, and I burst from the shade of the trees and into a large glade.

A white gazebo stood in the center, the latticework overrun with briar roses. Tendrils dangled from the archways, and the perfumed air lured me toward the peeling white steps. Already drunk with the richness of the day and unable to bear confines of any sort, I unbuttoned the neck of my dress and threw off my high-buttoned shoes and dark stockings.

I was free, free, free. Enjoying the coolness against my warm toes, I twirled and danced in the sunlight. My energy was boundless, as overwhelming as the wild exultation that drove me. My eyes closed, but rather than diminishing my awareness, my loss of sight allowed my other faculties to expand.

I sensed rather than saw I was not alone.

I opened my eyes. Edmund Llewelyn stood on the edge of the clearing, a black figure in my sunlit world. I laughed and sashayed toward him, heedless of the warning in his grim face. Nor did I stop until my bare toes brushed the hard leather of his boots and the top of my head bumped against his chin.

"Did you follow me, Edmund?" I asked coyly, in a voice that did not sound like mine. "I knew you would." I lifted my hand and trailed my fingers across his cheek.

He flinched and jerked his head backward.

"Dear, dear Edmund," I cooed. "Are you afraid I will bite?"

"What is the matter with you?" he demanded. "And how did you learn of this place?"

"Is it a secret?" I laughed gaily and tossed back my hair from my face. "Then let it be our secret. Yours and mine, Edmund," I said in a throaty whisper.

It took only one small step to bring my body against his. One swift motion to lift my arms and lock them about his neck. Shamelessly, I pulled his lips down onto mine and my mouth parted in anticipation.

He did not resist. His arms tightened around me and a small groan escaped him. His tongue pressed against mine and I savored the taste of him. It was like partaking in an exotic spiced wine, rare and stimulating. A wine that, once sampled, would always be craved. I trembled with the pure physical pleasure that washed over me.

But he did nothing to me that I did not also do to him. A shudder coursed through him and I reveled in my power. I was the master here, not he. I was the one who took without asking. I pulled my lips from his and laughed at his startled face.

He groaned again and his fingers bit into my arms. "Damnation, Hilary. What has possessed you?"

At the sound of my name, the enchantment shattered. The power and the excitement rushed from me, leaving me weak and shaking. I stared up at Mr. Llewelyn, realizing what I had done and in whose arms I stood. Horrified, I gasped. What had happened to me?

"Forgive me," I mumbled, pulling out of his embrace and hurriedly closing the open neck of my dress.

He stared at me, saying nothing, his brows drawn together in a dark line. Conscious of his gaze leveled upon me, I fumbled with my buttons and searched for my stockings and shoes. They were strewn about the glade, where I had apparently tossed them. Cheeks burning, I gathered them up in my arms and carried them to a fallen log where I could sit with my back to Mr. Llewelyn and dress myself in relative privacy. My heart pounded against my ribs, the sounds echoing in my ears. Nothing about my behavior made sense to me, but I imagined it made perfect sense to him. I had, through my actions, convinced him that everything he thought of me was true.

My hair still tumbled about my face and I searched my pockets for the pins. But they were no longer in my possession. I looked around miserably, guessing they were scattered through the grass and knowing that finding them would be impossible. I was in complete and utter disgrace, and it was all my own doing.

"Are you ready?" he asked.

Unable to speak or meet his gaze, I nodded.

His hand descended on my arm and firmly he escorted me to one of the many paths that cut through the trees. I had not noticed how many there were until then. All of them looked the same, and any one of them could have been the route I had taken to get there. I realized then that, if he had not followed me, I would have been lost before I had gone a hundred feet.

For several minutes we walked in silence with only the pad of our footsteps on the soft ground and our own rough breathing to fill our ears. Undistracted, my thoughts were all for what I had done, the brazen manner in which I had kissed him and forced him to kiss me.

What had been wrong with me? Certainly, I had not been myself. Never had I behaved in such a fashion. Could the fresh air have unbalanced me? But that was ridiculous. I had consumed plenty of fresh air in my lifetime and never before displayed any odd susceptibility.

Had Mr. Llewelyn cast some spell on me or affected my emotions in a way I had not realized? I glanced at his dark visage and shuddered. Nothing about the man appealed to me.

Nothing and everything.

But why had my thoughts and emotions seemed to belong to someone other than myself? Why had my behavior seemed more suited to a fallen woman than a properly raised gentlewoman? The answer was unthinkable. Beyond unthinkable.

It was as though I had been possessed by some wild energy that was not my own. Even the thoughts had not belonged to me. Inwardly, I shuddered. If not mine, then whose? There was only one possible answer.

Lily Llewelyn.

Could it have been her husband she had been mocking? The Edmund she despised? And had she gone to the glade knowing her stepson would follow? Wanting him as I had wanted him for those few brief minutes. It was too incredible. I could barely believe in the possibility myself. Certainly, Mr. Llewelyn would not listen to my tale.

I dared not glance at his face. But the tension between us was tangible, impossible to ignore. I began to feel, if one of us did not speak soon, I would scream. But my tongue did not respond to my commands

Abruptly, Mr. Llewelyn demanded, "Who told you of that place?"

"No one. I found the gazebo by accident."

"That is hardly a spot one happens upon unawares."

"Nevertheless, I did."

I expected him to accuse me of lying, but he did not. Instead, grim face looking neither to the right nor left, he propelled me forward. Brusquely, he guided me around the thick roots that jutted across the paths. Despite the obstacles, he neither paused nor hesitated, but maintained a steady pace. He seemed determined to put the glade and the gazebo far behind us.

"Is there some reason I should not have gone there?" I asked, determined to keep him talking until this torturous walk had ended.

"Those who know the estate far better than you have gotten lost in these woods."

His mouth was a tight line, and I knew he had deliberately misinterpreted my question. "And the gazebo?" I prodded, knowing there was little I could say or do to damage myself further in his eyes.

He scowled. "It was one of my stepmother's favorite haunts. Rarely a sunny day passed that she did not go there." I stumbled and he glared down at me. "If I were you, I would spend less time asking questions and more time watching where I was putting my feet."

Mutely, I complied. At least he did not accuse me of searching for information to give Mrs. Medcroft. I wondered why he had not. He had never been loath to think the worst of me before. But he had not found me searching the glade for clues to her personality. Instead, I had been wantonly awaiting his arrival. My shocking performance must have convinced him my sole interest was in seducing him.

I realized with a start that those had been my

intentions. If he had not brought me back to my senses by calling my name, to what lengths might I have gone? I grew sick and dizzy at the thought.

Mr. Llewelyn broke off his stride and I looked up to find we had reached the edge of the woods. Still, he did not seem anxious to leave the sheltering branches. I forced myself to remain motionless and resist the temptation to pull out of his grasp and flee across the broad stretch of lawns.

He regarded me solemnly, seeming to compare my quiet person with the creature who had flaunted herself in the glade. Only my unpinned hair remained to remind him of that stranger.

He brushed one of the long strands back from my face with his free hand and asked gently, "Do you think your parents would approve of your association with Mrs. Medcroft?"

"My father would not," I admitted, startled by the tenderness in that one act. "As for my mother . . ." I shrugged, not knowing the answer. "But if it were not for Mrs. Medcroft's kindness, I would have had nowhere to go."

"Is that it?" His chin lifted and I found myself staring at the even line of his jaw. "Then let me advise you—no, rather let me make a suggestion which I can only pray you will take to heart."

"And that is?"

"That you find yourself a post of some kind, and get as far away from Mrs. Medcroft and others like her as is humanly possible."

"That is unfair," I protested. "She is one of my few friends, and I pray she and I will always maintain contact. But I do not think myself suited to be her assistant," I confessed, willing to be honest since he had dropped his arrogant stance. "As for a post, Fanny has already offered to recommend me to friends of hers who need a governess."

"Has she, indeed? Then she has better sense than I would have believed." His eyebrows arched sharply. "I assume you have accepted."

"I have."

"Good. A wiser decision you will never make." He managed a short nod of what I supposed was dismissal rather than farewell. "And now I shall bid you good afternoon. You can find your own way from here with no trouble. I think it would be wiser if we did not return together."

With my hair flying loose about my face, his statement needed no remark. I nodded and he released my arm. But something niggled at my mind and urged me to speak, something I had tried to deny but failed. "Would you object if I asked you something of a personal nature?" I asked, my throat dry.

I could feel his withdrawal. "That would depend entirely on the question."

"It is not at all offensive. I only wanted to know the name of your father."

"My father?" His face was wholly perplexed. "It was Edmund Llewelyn, the same as my own. Why do you ask?"

"Simple curiosity," I lied, but a chill spread from the tips of my fingers into the depths of my heart.

10

Mr. Llewelyn watched me at dinner that evening, always when I turned my head away from him to address Mrs. Medcroft or Mr. Quarmby or when the level of excited chatter had risen and briefly captured everyone's attention. But I felt the warmth of his gaze upon me, and the hairs at my nape prickled. My embarrassment had made me acutely aware of him, and I couldn't dim the memory of my arms about his neck and my fingers tangled in his hair.

Nor was I the only one who caught his surreptitious glances. Twice, Ursula noted the direction of his gaze and her lips pursed. Sally Pritchard, squirming in the chair next to mine, babbled desperately at those moments he scrutinized me. Even Mrs. Medcroft wore a faint frown, but her glances fell most often on Mr. Quarmby.

Whatever his thoughts, Mr. Llewelyn did not reveal them. And immediately after supper, he and the other gentlemen politely withdrew and closeted themselves in the gaming room. Dr. Rhodes had a helpless shrug of apology for his fiancée, and Mr. Quarmby's moustache drooped at the corners. Winnie trailed after them, a sad look for the company he was deserting. But whatever they might have wished, none of them dared argue with their host.

The door swung shut behind them and Ursula surveyed our motley group with a dismayed air. "What about a game of bridge?" she suggested.

Eglantine promptly agreed, but Fanny and Sally demurred with equal haste. Ursula looked doubtfully at Mrs. Medcroft and me. Having to either accept or disappoint them, we let good manners prevail. Led by Ursula, we traipsed into one of the sitting rooms.

It was a cozy room, decorated in walnut furnishings upholstered in assorted blue paisley fabrics, a room that held no unpleasant or awkward memories. Sally wandered over to the harpsichord and idly sorted through the sheet music. Finding something that appealed to her, she carefully sat down and spread the full skirt of her dress around her. Before starting to play, she removed the array of jangling bracelets that adorned her plump wrists. I wondered at her forethought, but the instant her fingers touched the keys, I realized she was an excellent musician and had the sense not to distract from her obvious skill.

Without coaxing, Fanny drifted across the room and started to sing. Our cards were promptly forgotten, and it was ten minutes and several songs later before we remembered to pick them up. Fanny, it seemed, had inherited her mother's voice—an exquisite soprano that was impossible to ignore. Each word hung in the air like a frozen ice crystal, perfectly formed, then slowly melted into nothingness.

Listening to them, I realized what bond had forged

their friendship. Both showed the other off to greater advantage than could ever have been accomplished separately. Immediately the thought entered my mind, I chided myself for my lack of charity. It could just as easily have been their love for music and not vanity that had brought them together.

But the impression, once received, never completely deserted me.

The enchantment slowly faded, and we took up our cards. Ursula and Eglantine usually partnered each other, but, since both were excellent players and Mrs. Medcroft and I merely novices, it was necessary for them to separate.

"I will take Hilary," Ursula offered before anyone else could speak.

Mrs. Medcroft bristled silently, clearly supposing her decision to be yet another slight. I knew better. Thanks to Winnie's unwelcome attentions, Eglantine would never have countenanced playing with me, and her friend's quick thinking saved us all from an awkward moment.

Throughout the game, Ursula politely but determinedly questioned me about my background. Remembering Fanny's warning, I was careful in phrasing my answers. Fortunately, Mrs. Medcroft was too busy struggling with the bidding to ask why I failed to mention my mother's early association with her. Several hours later, Ursula's taking me as a partner proved a fortuitous decision. We won most of the sets, mainly due to Mrs. Medcroft's peculiar inability to judge the content of Eglantine's hands.

"I never did have a head for cards," she admitted, after a particularly blatant error. "I think the spirits have a distaste for gambling and deliberately lead me astray."

The evening came to an early close, for none of us were at our best. Ursula appeared to be suffering from some secret dissatisfaction that had nothing to do with her sister; neither Eglantine nor Mrs. Medcroft were pleased with the outcome of the game; and the events of that afternoon still haunted me. Only Fanny appeared cheerful, pleased at having been given a chance to entertain us, and her happiness did not seem to be shared by her friend.

"I was much impressed with your talents," I said, and thanked them both before I retired.

Sally merely shrugged. "I love to play, but what a pity there was no one here to listen."

Fanny stifled a giggle, and I managed a polite smile.

Whether or not Sally had the pleasure of meeting Mr. Llewelyn again that evening, I didn't know. Nor did I much care. My thoughts were all for my quiet room and the comfortable bed that awaited me.

It was quiet in the foyer and on the stairs, but it was not a peaceful quiet, more the kind of gloomy hush that descends around deathbeds and empty graves. All the stone faces around the fireplace leered at me with expectant gloating, and the air shivered with a dreadful anticipation.

I was glad to reach the safety of the corridor. The atmosphere on the landing was growing steadily worse and had begun to spread. What had once merely been a vague sense of evil had become a living, palpitating force. More than a mere force. That was simply undirected energy, and what I sensed had both direction and . . . I struggled for the word to fit the sensations that overwhelmed me.

Personality.

That was it. There was a distinct personality to the

energies spreading throughout Abbey House. God protect us all, I murmured.

With those thoughts to see me to bed, I did not sleep well. My head whirled, and my dreams were filled with feverish dancing. I was caught in a man's embrace, but his face was shrouded in shadows. I struggled to make out his features, but just when I thought I recognized him, he changed into someone new. Sometimes it was Winnie, sometimes Dr. Rhodes, sometimes men I didn't recognize.

And then the music grew louder, the pace faster, and my partner stronger. I did not have to study the dark, stiffly polite face to know I danced in Edmund's arms, that I rested my cheek against his strong chest. It was exhilarating, intoxicating, and I was happier than I had ever known myself to be.

Laughter streamed from my lips and mingled with the strains of the waltz. At first melodic, the gay sounds changed, becoming harsher and coarser. The notes of the unseen musicians faded, until only that harsh laughter remained.

My laughter. It echoed about my ears, driving me faster and faster. Edmund's expression had grown distant, hostile, and he tried to free himself from my grasp. I dug my fingernails into his neck, raking his flesh and refusing to release him.

Beneath my feet, the dance floor had darkened into a black sea. It clung to my feet like tar, and I found myself sinking into those gruesome depths. My grip tightened on Edmund, not out of fear but out of determination. I would never release him. Never. Not even if it meant dragging him with me. I wanted to drag him down, to punish him, to sentence him to the same fate to which he had sentenced me.

It was his fault. All his fault.

Anger mingled with desire, and I burned with the heat of my passions. How dare he have done this to me. With a ferocious cry, I tore at his face with my fingernails.

And started into consciousness.

The sounds of a clock chiming midnight echoed somewhere deep within the house. My pulse was racing, and my brow was damp with perspiration. The blankets entwined about my arms and legs, capturing me in their heavy folds. I pushed back a damp lock and waited until my heartbeat slowed.

It was warm in the room. Too warm. The sultry heat invited nightmares. Determined not to endure a repeat of what I had just suffered, I rose and threw open the doors that let out onto the balcony. My efforts brought no relief. The night was still; if there was any breeze, it did not reach the house.

I stumbled back through the darkness to the far side of the room and pulled my door ajar. A cold draft wafted from the hall and stirred the air. The room would soon be cooler than I wanted. Leaving only a four-inch crack, I returned to my bed.

I had plenty of questions to occupy my thoughts. What had caused the dream? Did I have some intuitive awareness of Lily Llewelyn, or was I troubled by my own questions and imagination? Probably the latter. There had been too much talk and too many odd occurrences. It was no wonder I slept badly.

And to believe there was any reality to my dream would be to believe that Edmund Llewelyn had caused his stepmother's death.

I fell asleep quickly but awakened again, this time to the sound of voices coming from the direction of the stairwell. Through the darkness, I heard the tread of feet, and a voice that could only have belonged to

Mr. Llewelyn said, "What were you thinking about, Ursula? There is no excuse for that kind of behavior."

"I'm sorry, Edmund," his sister replied.

Neither of them could have realized that my door was ajar and I could hear them. Nor would they have been pleased if they had known. I tried not to listen, but their voices became more distinct, strengthened by emotions that they usually kept under control.

"You know how Fanny infuriates me," Ursula said, appealing to him for sympathy. "She does it deliberately."

"Good Lord. You are ten years her senior and should be capable of ignoring her silly remarks."

"They were hardly silly. She said she knew about my quarrel with Kenneth."

"Nonsense. She was only a child and could not possibly have known."

My first feeling was one of pity for Ursula. Her brother had no patience with feminine foibles and was not likely to appreciate her pain. Then I realized that by coldly dousing her notions, he probably gave her more comfort than he could have done by holding her hand and commiserating with her. But Ursula was hard to convince.

"You didn't see her face," she protested.

"Nor is that necessary. Use your head, Ursula. If Fanny had known, the truth would have spilled from her years ago. She loves upsetting you."

"I suppose that's true."

"Of course it's true."

There was a short silence, broken only by their muffled steps on the carpet. Outside, in the corridor, the darkness lifted several shades and the yellow glow of a lamp spilled through the open crack in my doorway and fell across the floor. I found myself holding my breath, not wanting to be accused of eavesdropping on a second occasion.

But Ursula had no thoughts for her guests. "Fanny positively gloats about having stolen Kenneth from me," she said, incapable of dismissing her sister from her thoughts.

There was a rude snort from her brother. "It's your own fault. You should have forgotten your silly pride and married him years ago."

"I've tried. God knows I've tried. Perhaps in time . . . but how was I to know what she would do?"

"If it hadn't been Fanny, it would have been somebody else. You couldn't keep him dangling forever."

There was the sound of snuffling, and Ursula blew her nose.

I heard a typically male groan. Mr. Llewelyn sounded much like any man who found himself with a weeping female on his hands. In a kinder tone, he suggested, "You ought to go and have a talk with Kenneth and straighten all this out. He'd be far better off with you than Fanny."

Good heavens. Did he want Dr. Rhodes to break off his engagement with Fanny in favor of her elder sister? What was the matter with him? That was far worse than anything they accused her of doing. She had merely encouraged a man her sister had been determined to refuse.

If Ursula thought her brother's suggestion outrageous, she didn't bother to tell him. It was the futility of the idea that discouraged her. "He wouldn't look twice at me," she protested. "Not any more. She's got him wound round her little finger. She's her mother's child, from head to toe."

"More's the pity. Oh Lord, Ursula. Give him a few months. He'll come to his senses."

"They'll be married long before then. And he'll never divorce her. He's too good to walk away from any responsibility, even a bad marriage. Damn Fanny. I swear there are times I wish she had never been born. Or that she'd broken her neck when she fell off Kenneth's horse."

There was a muffled laugh and a fervent, "Just be grateful there aren't two of her."

"Oh, Edmund."

Neither of them said anything else for a few beats, then Ursula muttered, "If you *had* killed her, Edmund, I wouldn't blame you."

"No more than I would have blamed you," he retorted. "And that's quite enough about that."

"You don't think anything could come of this séance business? Not really?"

"Yesterday, I would have said it could not. Today, I'm not certain."

Their voices had been fading steadily as they moved into the west wing. If anything else passed between them, it escaped me. I lay back against my pillow, reflecting on what I had heard. It would have been an easy matter to pity Ursula, had she not made those final remarks. And apparently both of them thought the other capable of murdering their step-mother. Worse than capable.

Justified.

Instead of pity for the thwarted Ursula, all I could feel was fear for Fanny.

I left the breakfast room and strolled toward the foyer and the curving stairway that would take me back upstairs. The corridor was empty. I seemed to be the only one who liked to rise at an early hour and was becoming used to my quiet mornings. But sausages and disquiet thoughts, I discovered, did not sit well on my stomach.

Vacant doorways that led off to empty rooms lay in both directions, and the patter of my steps bounced back to me from distant walls. Without warning, Mr. Llewelyn stepped from one of the parlors, appearing directly in front of me. His tall frame blocked my path and startled me into dropping the book I was carrying.

He neither hesitated nor blinked, but impatiently scooped up the small book of Dorset sights I had borrowed from Fanny. Instead of returning it to me, his fingers tightened on the spine and he peered beyond me, as if to see if I was accompanied. Immediately, his gaze returned to me.

"Miss Carewe, would you mind giving me a few minutes of your time?"

I frowned, bothered not by the request, but by the civil fashion in which it had been phrased. It was the third time he had displayed unexpected good manners—although once, admittedly, had been when he sought a favor.

"Is something the matter?" I asked warily, uncertain as to what would be forthcoming.

His expression gave me no indication. "Could we not step into my study?"

I hesitated.

"I assure you, there is no need for alarm."

In that, he was mistaken. I found a polite and respectful host very much cause for alarm. Every part of me suspected a trap. Especially after my deplorable antics in the glade.

Reluctantly, I let him usher me into his Spartan study. Daylight did nothing to improve its atmosphere.

Stepping into the room was like stepping back into the medieval ages, into the office of the abbot. All that was missing was the wooden cross that should have hung on the plastered wall.

"If this has anything to do with what happened yesterday—"

"It does not." He pulled out the heavy Jacobean chair from behind the scarred desk and invited me to make myself comfortable.

Bewildered, I did as he asked.

Hands clasped behind his back, he stared at me. Why, I did not know. But he scanned my face as if searching for something he had not seen before, for something he had missed. His earnest scrutiny did nothing to help my composure. Must I always feel awkward with this man? I wondered. Must I always feel the need to check my buttons or pat my chignon to see if the heavy strands had unwound and fallen down my back?

"There was something you wished to say?" I prodded, determined to end his discomfiting study of my person. "Something else I have done that has upset you?"

He took a deep breath, held the air in his lungs for an excessive length of time, and then let it issue from between his lips like a sigh. "In fact, it is *my* behavior we must discuss."

"Yours?"

"This is most awkward. I hardly know where to begin." He ran his fingers through his dark hair, and his eyebrows drew together in a straight line. "Do you recall the letter I posted for you?"

"Yes. To my father's solicitors."

"I took the liberty of first copying down their address."

"For what reason?" I demanded.

He had the grace to avert his eyes before admitting, "In order to contact them myself and enquire into your character."

The gall of the man. I gave him a stare that should have made the tips of his ears redden.

"I considered myself well within my rights," he argued. "I am, after all, Fanny's guardian. To your solicitors, I said only that you were her guest and that, since your acquaintance has been of short duration and your parents were dead, I wished to learn something of your background."

No amount of rationalizing made his behavior acceptable, at least not in my eyes. Nevertheless, my lips twitched with amusement. I had the great satisfaction of knowing that Papa's no-nonsense solicitors would have added a few cutting remarks about his effrontery to what would have been a long accounting of my fine upbringing, my parents' admirable characters, and my own basic honesty.

"I imagine you were disappointed by their response," I murmured.

He grimaced. "I suppose that remark is deserved. But, despite the upbraiding I received, I was pleasantly surprised by their response. It appears I owe you an apology."

"Several, at least."

"Will you take one that is all-encompassing? If it is sincerely offered?"

His gray eyes brightened, flickering with something very like amusement. A rueful amusement. Brought on by a knowledge of his own faults instead of mine. It was a look that almost made him likable. Good Lord. I had thought him many things. Unpleasant. Rigidly honorable. Autocratic. Certainly physically compelling, even charming.

But *likable?*

Mrs. Medcroft would have been horrified.

I was horrified.

Good manners forbade me to refuse his apology. And with the memory of the affair in the glade still fresh in both of our minds, I thought it wise not to make too great a fuss about *his* failings. As for the conversation I had heard, in the morning light, it seemed like nothing more had passed between brother and sister than the admission that both thought the other capable of having murdered their stepmother. Neither was necessarily capable.

And neither had confessed to the deed.

However, I could not restrain myself from adding, "I hope this means I will not have to endure any more insults."

"I am deeply ashamed of myself. And can offer no excuse save for having been misled by the companions you have chosen for yourself."

The brief flash of liking I had felt for him disappeared and I rose, my back stiff. "If you mean to make me listen to a litany of Mrs. Medcroft's supposed faults, we can bring an immediate end to this conversation."

"There is more that must be said before I can give you leave to go." He waved me back onto the chair. "I may have misjudged you, Miss Carewe. But if I can no longer believe you dishonest, then I must assume you to be horribly naive. And since you are a young lady under my roof, I must take upon myself the responsibility for your well-being."

It was the sort of speech that would have won my father's approval. I could easily imagine the same words coming from his lips, but with a good deal less arrogance. But nor would my father have looked like a dark Galahad, with silvery lights glinting in his eyes and dark curls brushing the edge of his collar.

Nevertheless, I responded only to the arrogance. I did not wish to appear as silly as Mrs. Pritchard, nor could I completely dismiss the conversation I had overheard from my bedroom. It was *his* character that was questionable.

"You overstep yourself, Mr. Llewelyn. I am quite capable of looking after myself. And if I need assistance, I shall go to Mrs. Medcroft. She was, after all, my mother's friend."

"Which is something I may never understand."

Apparently, my solicitors were either ignorant of this piece of Mother's history or they had decided to say nothing of the matter. Certainly, he would not get his explanations from me. I smiled politely and said nothing.

He lifted his chin, presenting me with a view of his smooth-shaven jawline, and stared over my head at the wall. "Privately, you may do as you wish. But until you leave Abbey House, I take full responsibility for anything that befalls you. With that in mind, you will obey the same rules I have set Fanny. On your own, you may go where you wish in those parts of the house that have been restored. The older sections are off-limits unless you are accompanied by me or Ursula. You are free to enjoy the gardens, but please avoid the woods"—he glossed over that statement hastily—"and if you wish to go riding, I ask only that you consult me first and allow me to make the arrangements."

Assuming he was finished, I stood again. "I will respect your house rules, Mr. Llewelyn," I promised in an even voice. "But I will not be treated like a child. Or," I added pointedly, "as your ward."

He stood in front of me, his legs slightly apart, his weight braced on his heels. A faint line creased his brow. "I do not think you a child, Miss Carewe." He ignored the second half of my comment. "But nor am I convinced you do not need my rules. And I assure you, it is only your safety I desire."

"I am, and shall continue to be, most circumspect. But should I feel the need of guardianship, I will apply to my father's solicitors. And now, if you will excuse me . . ."

He hesitated, his mouth a tight line. Then, unwillingly, he stepped aside to let me pass. "But I wonder if you would mind satisfying my curiosity before you go?"

"If I can," I agreed, once again wary.

"Why did you choose to go to Mrs. Medcroft, rather than to your father's family?"

His question was entirely unexpected. But it was neither upsetting nor offensive. "They are all dead. And my mother is also an orphan."

A shadow passed over his face. It was as if a storm cloud had blown across Abbey House, shutting out the daylight. "Prevarication, Miss Carewe? After the glowing report I have had of you, it seems ill-timed."

"I am telling you the truth."

"Nonsense. You forget, your father's solicitors have advised me of your background. Coincidentally, I have done business with your father's brothers only this year, and I have not heard that they or their families have suffered either accident or illness."

"You are mistaken. Neither of my parents had family."

He glowered, leveling his annoyance on me with an intensity that made me grab the back of the chair for support. But it was a momentary weakness.

Furious that he would question my veracity after having been assured of my good character, I returned stare for stare. His anger swelled, darkening his face. It hovered there while he searched my face, clouded with confusion, and slowly withdrew. Only his doubt remained visible.

He pulled at his collar with his finger as though it had suddenly grown tight. "There is no question of my being mistaken. Henry Carewe had two brothers and, although I am less certain of this fact, a sister. And, if memory serves me, one of your uncles mentioned that his parents were remarkably healthy for their years."

"But that is quite impossible," I protested, but my own doubts stirred.

"Do you mean to say you were unaware of this?"

My legs wobbled and I sank back into the chair.

"Forgive me. I had no idea or I would not have asked."

I looked up into a pair of concerned eyes. "You must be mistaken."

He frowned and shook his head.

"But it makes no sense. We had no contact with them. None whatsoever."

"If you like, I could make inquiries for you."

I wavered, near acceptance. Slowly, almost of its own accord, my head shook in refusal I raised my gaze. "Thank you for your kind offer, but if my father had no wish to speak to any member of his family, then I am certain it was with good reason. Nor would I want them to think I was looking for charity now that my parents are gone."

He nodded, and I glimpsed the faintest look of approval. It was the second time he'd approved of some act of mine, and I felt ridiculously like Sally

Pritchard. Good heavens, I thought. What was wrong with me? Perhaps I was truly as naive as he accused me of being. Certainly I should have known better than to allow good looks and a strong male physicality to undo me.

"Is it still your hope to find a post with Fanny's friends?" he asked, unaware of my thoughts.

"It is."

"Then I will hope we receive word before it is necessary for you to return to London. Or, if it is your wish, you may remain here until word comes."

"I couldn't possibly—"

"I see no reason why you should not. You will be entertainment for Fanny, and my sister is a suitable chaperon."

The offer was unbelievably generous, especially considering our past disagreements. I wondered if it had been made because his outmoded code of honor demanded that he protect any maiden who needed assistance. Or was it because he regretted having upset me with the news of my father's severed family connections? His expression was impossible to read. I found him studying me with equal interest.

Another thought occurred to me, and I gasped.

He cocked his head.

"It's nothing," I assured him. "But you have told me things here today that will take some while to absorb."

He nodded, and the color of his eyes made me think of a soft mist; they were the same mysterious hue, mesmerizing and alluringly tranquil. I smiled and relaxed, and sent a silent thanks to the heavens that he had no notion of what had passed through my mind.

But it had occurred to me that, in the space of one

day, I had ceased to be of questionable character and had become "a young lady from a good family."

Could that have been what had aroused his interest?

That afternoon it was my intention to join Fanny, but a short hunt proved she was nowhere to be found. Nor had any of the maids seen her for several hours. Sally, who had accompanied me in my search, pulled impatiently at the lacy ruffles on her sleeve.

"Trust Fanny to escape the house and leave us to suffer her sister's company alone. Selfish little pig. Well I, for one, intend to take a nap."

She trotted off down the corridor, her head twisting from side to side as she walked. Her gaze searched each room she passed, no doubt for our host. But he, like his sister, had managed to find a sanctuary and succeeded in eluding her guests.

I considered spending my day closeted in my room if Mrs. Medcroft didn't need any help with her correspondence. It seemed easier than fending off Winnie for an entire afternoon with no one to support me but possibly Ursula. Nor did I wish to come upon Mr. Llewelyn accidentally, lest something else embarrassing occur.

Then, too, it would give me a chance to consider what he had told me. I had yet to absorb the fact that I had relatives that were unknown to me. Why had I never been told? And what had caused the break? Mrs. Medcroft had accused my father of severing all ties after his marriage because of his jealousy. But that did not explain why he had separated himself from his own family. Perhaps a letter to my father's solicitors would help me find some kind of explanation.

I was saved the trip upstairs by Mr. Quarmby. He was hurrying down to the foyer, taking short, brisk steps, a plaid overcoat folded neatly over his arm. "There you are, dear girl. Mrs. Medcroft sent me to find you. We were going to take a stroll in the garden and she hoped you would join us."

Since the offer had originated with her, I assumed she hadn't intended the walk to be a romantic encounter, and I accepted. I had not given Mrs. Medcroft much of my time since coming to Abbey House and thought she deserved better treatment from me. We talked quietly in the foyer, waiting for Mrs. Medcroft to join us, but five minutes passed, and still she had not appeared. Mr. Quarmby begged me to wait while he made certain that she was all right.

A few minutes later, he appeared at the top of the stairs, a faintly disappointed look on his face. "Chaitra advised me she was taken ill. A migraine, I suspect. She gets them occasionally."

"Never mind. We can take our walk together another afternoon."

"But me must not cancel our plans. She would insist we did not."

I hesitated, then decided that although I was not fond of Mr. Quarmby, I would be perfectly safe in his company. "If you are absolutely certain there is nothing else you would rather do," I said politely.

"Not a thing." He gave me his arm. "Besides, I would very much like to become better acquainted with you. Mrs. Medcroft and I are such close companions, we will be seeing a lot of each other. Perhaps more than you realize."

He seemed to be alluding to their possible marriage. I felt a surge of relief. Until that moment, a part of me feared Mrs. Medcroft had overestimated the depth of his affections. Once again, she was right. I smiled at Mr. Quarmby, rather more warmly than I might otherwise have done, and the bristles of his moustache quivered.

A light morning rain had spattered the gardens, and sunlight glanced off tiny droplets that hung at the tips of leaves and nestled in the hearts of the roses. Damp patches shrank on the paths, and a light mist hovered above the tops of the trees. I drew the freshness into my lungs, while letting the breeze sweep away the gloom of the house that seemed to cling to my garments.

"It is unfortunate we have had so little opportunity to speak," Mr. Quarmby said as we walked.

"It has been a harrowing week."

"But highly successful, don't you agree?"

"I am hardly one to say. But I still fear elements have been roused in the house that would have been better left alone."

"This is another . . . feeling you have?" he asked, focusing his black stare on me.

I nodded. "I suppose you think me foolish."

"Not at all." He regarded me with the restrained eagerness of a well-trained dog waiting for a scrap of meat to fall from the table. "Perhaps you, too, have the elements of a sensitive within you. Have you had other . . . odd experiences?"

"A few. But my father soon squelched them. He had no patience with mystics."

"And your mother?"

"Was more sympathetic, but she also discouraged me."

Mr. Quarmby glanced upward at the row of windows that ran down the top story of the house, frowned thoughtfully, and guided me down a hedge-lined walkway. The gardens were an elaborate maze of flower beds, lawns, wooded copses, and stone paths. More than once we wandered out of sight of the house, only to emerge from around a stand of beeches and see the rooftops reappear above the trees.

"I wouldn't wonder if some of Mrs. Medcroft's abilities hadn't rubbed off on your mother," he said after some thought. "They did, after all, work together for several years, didn't they?

I nodded.

"From 1855 until 1857, I believe?"

"Oh, they met several years earlier," I corrected, trying to recall the dates that had been printed on the articles. "I believe they were together in 1851. Possibly before. The first press clipping in Mrs. Medcroft's scrapbooks was printed in December of that year, and my mother was mentioned as being her assistant."

His lips curved into a pleased smile. "Ah. I stand corrected. Then they were together for . . . ?"

"A good five years."

"A long period, indeed. I wouldn't wonder if she hadn't developed a few talents of her own in all that time."

"I suppose it is possible."

We came upon a marble bench, sheltered by a semicircular holly hedge, and Mr. Quarmby suggested we take a respite. He waited until I had made myself comfortable, then sat down at a slight distance, taking great care not to crumple my dress.

"You aren't aware of any, I suppose?" he asked.

"Any . . . ? Oh, odd talents." I shrugged. "She did have an uncanny knack for knowing when a certain neighbor intended to visit and would draw the curtains and tell the maid to say we were not at home."

We both laughed, and he plucked a sprig of holly and twisted it idly between his fingers. "A useful trick, admittedly. But hardly enough to make a living as a clairvoyant."

"And I believe she used to read tea leaves for the minister's wife," I added. "But I cannot be certain."

"And why is that?"

"Because neither the minister nor my father would have approved. They simply closed the door of the parlor on occasion and refused to admit anyone, even me, for a good hour. I have no proof that was what they were doing, but . . ."

"But?" he prodded.

"I cannot say, really. It was just a feeling I always had."

He leaned forward. "Did you ever try to develop those feelings? You . . . you might be more use to Mrs. Medcroft if you did not censor them."

I could hardly tell him my intentions to find a post as a governess when I had yet to inform Mrs. Medcroft. Nevertheless, I shook my head. "I fear my current habits are entrenched in me. And I do not see that Mrs. Medcroft is in need of my help."

"True, true," he agreed hastily. "Nevertheless, I think you might be underestimating your own capabilities. Are you not even the least bit curious about your . . . your powers, shall we call them?"

I couldn't refrain from laughing. "Hardly powers. At best, I am susceptible."

"But what else is a sensitive but an individual who is susceptible to those influences that escape the rest of us? Really, my dear. These abilities are God-given and should not be ignored. Promise me you will consider what I have said."

His tidy face struck me with its intensity, and I could not refuse. "But I make no guarantees," I warned, and privately I told myself I would wait a few days and then tell him my efforts had come to nothing.

He bobbed his head, pleased with his success. "And do you remember the other promise you gave me?"

"To come to you if I needed help?"

"You will not forget."

"I will not. But I suspect I will have no more difficulties while we remain at Abbey House."

Something in my tone caught his attention, and he fixed me with his starry gaze yet again. "Has something changed?"

"In a way, yes. Mr. Llewelyn saw fit to check on my background and has decided my character is not as shady as he originally thought. Instead of threatening to alert all of London to my dishonest dealings, he now insists on taking responsibility for my welfare. But I fear his good opinion does not extend to you and Mrs. Medcroft. He can be a most unreasonable man."

Mr. Quarmby grimaced, and his hand went to his stomach as though to ease a pain. "Naturally, I am glad he will not be harassing you further. But you must be cautious. You are an attractive young lady, and gentlemen like Mr. Llewelyn cannot always be counted on to behave themselves around beautiful young women."

I laughed off his warning, although not with absolute conviction. But if I were to listen to him and Mrs. Medcroft, I would soon think myself the target of all men who wandered across my path. But, in truth, it was only Winnie who seemed at all interested in me, and his interest extended to women in general. Certainly, his attentions were not enough to inflame one's ego.

By odd chance, we looked up to see Eglantine striding up the path. Her tweed skirts flapped at her legs, and her sturdy walking boots clapped impatiently against the flagstones. At her side hurried an anxious Mrs. Medcoft. Some of the pins must have fallen from her hair, for a wide silver wing flapped across her eyes, and a black tendril clung to her neck.

It was Eglantine who reached us first, a few steps in advance of Mrs. Medcroft. She stared past Mr. Quarmby to me, and demanded, "How long have you been walking in the gardens together?"

I gaped at her, too startled by her rudeness to think of a reply. Before I could speak, Mrs. Medcroft reached us, and Mr. Quarmby replied, "Hardly more than a few minutes. Had we known you were interested in joining us, we would certainly have invited you."

It was a blatant lie. We had been in each other's company for a good half hour or more. I glanced at Mrs. Medcroft puffing heavily, and understood his reasoning. With her gaze, she was anxiously measuring the quite respectable distance that separated us. Astutely, he had recognized her doubts without once looking in her direction and hastily dispensed with them. Rather than upset Mrs. Medcroft, I didn't contradict him.

Eglantine glared at me. "And where were you before that?"

"I hardly see what business that is of yours," I replied shortly, determined to end her interrogation even if it meant employing that same rudeness with which she addressed me.

She straightened, and her mouth tightened. Between clenched teeth, she said, "We shall see whether or not it is my business."

With that she stormed off, leaving us all flabbergasted by her common behavior.

Mrs. Medcroft turned reproachfully to Mr. Quarmby. "You did not advise me you were taking a walk."

"But that is untrue, dear lady," he protested, rising instantly and offering her his place on the bench. "I asked Chaitra to tell you. And when I enquired after you, she said you had a headache."

"She did not say a word to me."

"Then you must have a talk with her. Likely she forgot the message and made up a lie to cover her mistake."

I frowned. That did not sound at all like Chaitra. And hadn't Mr. Quarmby said that Mrs. Medcroft had suggested I join them? Otherwise, I would not have agreed to come.

Nevertheless, I said nothing. It would not do to create contention between them when I suspected both of them had their hearts set on marriage. Instead, I excused myself and left them in each other's company.

11

It was a short walk to the house. Mr. Quarmby and I had taken a circuitous stroll that had almost brought us back to our starting point. I took firm strides, cutting across the lawn to make it impossible for anyone to approach me without my noticing. I did not fancy another encounter with Eglantine.

Undoubtedly, she had been searching for Winnie and assumed he had been spending his hours with me. By saving himself, Mr. Quarmby had unwittingly led her to believe that he and I had only been in each other's company a short while, leaving her to think I might have but recently separated from her husband. I hoped she would soon discover her error.

And why had Mr. Quarmby arranged our solitary stroll? To learn more about my mother? Or myself? Apparently, both. His interest had been in our mediumistic abilities, and he had encouraged me to develop mine. Unlike Mrs. Medcroft—and my father—he did not dismiss my feelings as mere fancies.

But for what reason?

He had suggested I might be of real help to Mrs. Medcroft in her profession. The assumption that she would want my help seemed faulty. She had managed well enough without help for many years and, like Fanny, jealousy guarded what she considered her territory. Surely he knew her that well.

Near the house, I heard the sound of voices and raised my head. Mr. Llewelyn stood in the driveway, his tall frame and broad shoulders impossible to mistake. He was bidding farewell to a man I didn't recognize as either one of his guests or one of the servants, a burly man with gingery hair and bushy sideburns. Nor was I able to see his face, for he was clad in a plaid overcoat with the collar turned up about his ears and a cap shading his eyes.

My gaze went to his mount. The roan gelding was a sturdy animal, but it lacked the sleek lines and glossy coat of the horses I had seen in the Llewelyn stables. It could not have come from there. Nor did the man appear to be a gentleman, someone whom Fanny would have invited to her houseparty.

I wondered if he could be one of Mr. Llewelyn's business associates, then immediately dismissed the notion. The man's attire was respectable, but his coat fit poorly about the shoulders and the fabric was inexpensive. Nor was the cap appropriate to someone in business.

A tradesman, perhaps, I mused.

Mr. Llewelyn noted my approach and promptly ordered the fellow to be off. He used the same civil but authoritative tone he used with his servants, convincing me I was right about the man's purpose there. With a satisfied expression, he turned to me and waited for me to reach him.

"Good afternoon, Miss Carewe." His cool gaze brushed me, illogically leaving a tingling warmth in its wake.

I nodded, pretending not to see the slight curve of his lips or the way the sun highlighted the prominent cheekbones. I had enough on my mind without adding to my troubles.

He gave me his arm to escort me into the house, making it necessary for me to draw near enough to him to catch the faint whiff of shaving soap and feel the hard line of his muscles beneath his sleeve. My own muscles tightened across my chest, making it difficult for me to breathe. The tension was understandable, or so I told myself. Part of me was not convinced of the change in our relationship.

But his manners were faultless. He held open the door, asked if there was anything I needed before he left me, and suggested I might like to join his sister in the parlor. And yet there was something odd about his manner, something too careful about his tone, and his words were too well-chosen.

Because he still held doubts about me?

Or because he meant to impress upon me how different a man he could be?

I glanced toward the parlor he had indicated. By his sister, I assumed he meant Ursula and suspected she would be chatting with Eglantine—or possibly the missing Winnie. I thanked him but decided to return to my room in order to collect myself.

"But have you seen Fanny?" I added.

Faint lines of irritation creased his brow. "Has she disappeared again?"

"Again?"

"It is a talent she has had ever since she was a child. She manages to drop out of sight and cannot be found again until she chooses. You must forgive her bad manners, Miss Carewe. For the most part, she reserves her tricks for Ursula and me. Her guests usually fare better, since she likes to entertain."

"I have managed well enough," I assured him. "I only worried that she might be in need of company."

"You need not fear on her behalf. When she needs you, she will certainly find you."

I started to leave, but paused on the stairs and glanced back over my shoulder. He was still standing there, watching my ascent with the eye of a man who was struggling with himself and had not yet won or lost the battle.

I had struggles of my own, simply to recall what I had been about to say. The words came back to me in a rush. "Mr. Llewelyn, perhaps if you expected more from Fanny, she would surprise you."

"I will keep that in mind, Miss Carewe," he replied, his voice devoid of emotion.

And that attempt had met with great success.

But I did leave his company convinced that he had meant everything he had said that morning.

Since Mrs. Medcroft was gone from her suite, I decided to pay Chaitra a visit and put some questions to her. She cracked open the door and peered through the gap. Upon seeing it was me, she hurried me inside her room.

Bewildered, I studied her. Her face looked strained, as though she were suffering from a severe headache, and her eyes were puffy and tired. Even her sari appeared rumpled, and I suspected she had been taking advantage of her mistress's absence to take a nap.

"You don't look well," I told her. "Is there anything I can do for you?"

"All my tasks are done," she assured me.

She even sounded weary, not at all like her usual self. "Would you like to tell me what's bothering you?" I asked.

"I . . . I slept poorly last night."

She averted her eyes. That slight movement and her hesitance to speak told me that if she was not lying, then certainly she had not admitted to the entire truth. "I thought we were friends," I chided her. "If there is some problem, then surely you can bring yourself to tell me."

She sank down on the edge of her narrow bed and pressed her palms together. "I did not like to frighten you. But I fear this house has been opened to a great evil."

"You feel it too?"

"The evil presence?"

I nodded. It was what I felt when we first arrived, and it has grown stronger with each passing day. "At first I thought myself foolish because Mrs. Medcroft said there was only sadness in the house."

"She knows nothing. She feels only what she expects to feel, sees only what she wants to see. There are forces here that are beyond her ability to recognize or control."

"Good heavens." I sat down on the edge of the bed beside her and caught her hand in mine. "Please, tell me why you didn't open the door when I knocked."

"I was . . . afraid." She shivered, and her warm brown skin had a sickly yellow cast. "Last night, I said I could not sleep."

I nodded. "It was warm. I was restless myself."

"It was not the heat. In this country, I have never suffered from the heat. Only the cold and damp."

"What disturbed you, then?"

"Music. The sounds of dancing and laughter."

The goose bumps rose on my arms, but I said nothing.

Unaware of my distress, she continued. "It was not long before midnight. I had been sleeping, but the noise awakened me. It was loud, too loud to be coming from downstairs, and I went to my door to look outside. When I touched the doorknob—"

"—it was cold," I finished.

She looked at me and nodded. "And an icy draft blew beneath the door."

"Did you go outside?"

Her head shook emphatically. "I hung my charm bag on the knob and hurried back to my bed. But sleep had left me and did not return."

I frowned and quickly gave her an accounting of my own experience. This was the second time we had heard the same sounds, although last night the music and laughter had become entwined in my dreams. "What do you think it was?"

"It was her. She seeks to return to this place where she was murdered. It cannot bode well for those who live here."

Or those of us who are guests at Abbey House, I thought.

Chaitra's thoughts must have taken the same turn. "The charm I made," she asked. "Did you bring it with you?"

"But I promised not to take it from the wardrobe."

She muttered a few sharp words in Hindustani. "I cannot obtain the proper herbs to make you another while we are here." She rose and hurried to the door and removed the scarlet pouch that dangled from the knob. "You must take this one," she insisted, returning and pressing the herbal concoction into my hands.

"I couldn't possibly," I protested, giving it back to her. "Besides, you are more attuned to these things than I, and therefore more likely to be disturbed."

She frowned, but no amount of argument would convince me to accept the charm. Chaitra put more faith in them than I ever could or would. Its lack was certain to affect her adversely.

"But things are certain to get worse," she said slowly. "Mrs. Medcroft told me there would be another séance tonight."

"God forbid," I said, and my throat tightened.

"Another séance?" Upon hearing Mrs. Medcroft's announcement, Eglantine turned to Fanny with undisguised horror. "You can't be serious. Wasn't Thursday's performance awful enough to satisfy you?"

Sally stepped back from the looking glass that stood over the mantelpiece in the drawing room and reached for one of the chocolate creams on the silver platter. "But her mother's spirit cannot possibly rest until the truth is revealed. Isn't that right, Mrs. Medcroft?"

"Indeed it is."

"I suppose we need not go back to the chapel," Fanny offered.

Ursula glared at her. "I should think not."

"I've had the door boarded up again," Mr. Llewelyn said. His gaze wandered to me, almost as though he were seeking my approval and, for an instant, there was no one else but us in the room.

I dropped my gaze, warm with embarrassment and something horribly like pleasure.

Winnie clapped him on the back. "Bloody good thing, too."

"I really think you must listen to Mrs. Medcroft in this matter," Mr. Quarmby advised. "She is, after all, a professional."

"The decision is mine," his host retorted. "Fanny, if you must play this foolish game, you will restrict yourself to the parlor."

"Are you afraid, Edmund?" she asked sweetly. "Some of us might suppose you were harboring some secret guilt."

"Only if they were as simple as you," Ursula returned, before he had a chance to defend himself. "Besides, I had planned on a musical evening tonight. Providing you and Sally are willing to entertain us again?"

Sally hastily pulled her chocolate-smeared finger from her mouth. "Surely there is time for both?"

"I think not." Ursula bestowed a complacent smile on her sister. "Make up your mind, Fanny."

She hesitated, but what was intended to look like uncertainty struck me as something entirely different. She's enjoying this, I decided. All of us had strong feelings about whether or not the séance should be held, and Fanny had the power to please or disappoint us as she chose.

She ran the tip of her pink tongue across her upper lip and sighed. I dreaded the moment when she would speak. Among her audience, there were only two people who desperately wanted to summon her mother's ghost, and she had no reason to feel any animosity toward them. On the other hand, she delighted in upsetting her family members, and I was certain of what her answer would be.

"There is always tomorrow," Sally pointed out.

"That's no good. Kenneth promised to take us to Durdle Door, and we might be tired afterward."

"These matters shouldn't be delayed too long," Mrs. Medcroft protested. "I have built a bridge into the spirit world, but they are fragile structures. Another day and I might have to begin all over again."

"But a musical evening would be such fun," Sally pleaded, appealing to her with glistening blue eyes and a childishly innocent smile. It was a look her friend could have done to perfection. On Sally it merely looked vacuous.

Fanny tossed her a contemptuous glance. "Oh, all right. If that's what you all want."

No one could have been more startled by her response than I. I chided myself for paying too much attention to her brother and sister. Now I, too, was underrating Fanny.

Ursula rose, and her plum silk dress rustled softly about her. "Shall we all go into the music room? We have a grand piano in there."

"That's where Mama used to sing," Fanny volunteered. "Although usually only for my father and me."

"As much as you miss her, it is good of you to make this great *sacrifice* for your friends," Mrs. Medcroft offered. "I doubt I could be as charitable." She watched her hostess's face hopefully, but if Fanny was tempted to reconsider her decision, she successfully hid her doubts.

My thoughts were interrupted by the sudden appearance of Mr. Llewelyn at my elbow. "May I be your escort, Miss Carewe?" He didn't wait for me to accept, but wrapped my arm around his.

Surprised, I looked up and was met with the flash of a devastating smile, its force all the greater for the lack of warning that preceded its appearance. I suppressed a gasp and told myself that the glow from his face was merely a trick of the light and not a special warmth intended solely for me.

While I fought to recover my composure, he promptly offered Ursula his other arm. The act convinced me that his intention was to avoid Sally rather than seek out my company. Still, that did not lessen the effect of his nearness, and I could feel my cheeks flush, a flush that did not stop with my face but rushed down the full length of my body.

We walked through the parlor and across the hall to reach the music room, a walk that was both endless and delightful, although not a word was spoken and our every movement was made in full view of the entire gathering. And yet, I might have been dancing, not walking. Swept along in strong arms to music that had been written especially for us. I said a silent prayer that the events of the glade were not repeating themselves, but there was a difference to the sensations that made me feel they were mine and mine alone.

When we reached our destination, I suppressed a gasp. The room was was long and narrow with a raised dais at the far end. A black lacquered grand piano stood on the dais, and there was a backdrop of red velvet curtains hemmed with gold fringe. Overhead, a two-tiered crystal-drop chandelier hung from the vaulted ceiling.

Despite the warm colors, the room was cold. Unnaturally cold. I tried unsuccessfully to suppress a shiver. Mr. Llewelyn felt the tremor and turned to me with questioning eyes. From his curious expression, I guessed he found nothing out of order.

Fanny rescued me from having to make an awkward explanation by announcing, "My father had the room redecorated to please my mother. She liked to sing for their guests."

"And nothing short of her own theater would please her," Ursula muttered. "I should have redone the room years ago."

"You might at least wait until after Kenneth and I are married," Fanny returned cheerfully.

Mr. Llewelyn's arm stiffened beneath my hand, and I wondered if his tension was merely an attempt to warn Ursula to control her temper or if it was his own anger he was attempting to control. I endured a moment's irritation with Fanny for upsetting her brother, a feeling that would not have arisen in me a mere twenty-four hours earlier.

"There is room for rows of seats," Fanny continued, oblivious to our distress. "But we store them in the attic until they're needed. This arrangement is enough for smaller parties." She indicated the horse-shoe arrangement of chairs and settees that ran around the room.

Leaving us to sit where we chose, she dragged Dr. Rhodes to the chair nearest the dais. "I shall sing especially for you," she murmured in his ear. Her words managed to carry down the length of the room, although whether that was because of the acoustics or her desire to aggravate Ursula, I didn't know.

And having misjudged her once, I thought, I will be careful not to do so again.

"Is there somewhere particular you would like to sit, Miss Carewe?" Mr. Llewelyn murmured in a voice that suggested he was offering me much, much more.

I looked up at him to discover that same smile on his face, a smile that had nothing to do with the glow of the fire or mere civility. "Anywhere," I said, too disconcerted to make a quick decision.

There were two fireplaces along one wall, and fires had been lit in both of them. Mindful of my earlier shiver, Mr. Llewelyn led me to the settee nearest one of those fireplaces. His thoughtfulness came as another surprise. But the warmth from the fires seemed to radiate no farther than the hearths. The air in the room remained, at least to me, clammy and dank.

Several minutes passed before it occurred to me to wonder why the fires had been burning in a room that was rarely used. The decision to enjoy a musical evening had been made only a few minutes ago.

Or had it?

If that had been entirely true, the room would have been cold and unusable. Somebody had hoped, if not intended, that there would be no séance held this evening. But who? Ursula or Edmund? He feared what the séances might reveal, and she was devoted to him.

Could one of them possibly have committed the murder?

I shivered again, but this time it was not from the cold.

"Would you like me to send one of the maids to fetch your wrap?" Mr. Llewelyn asked.

I thanked him but refused. It would take more than a shawl to remove the chill that had settled upon me.

"I hope you are not catching a chill."

"It is kind of you to be—"

Sally had been watching our conversation from the dais. Before I could finish speaking, her fingers touched the keys and she began to play. Her start was precipitous and unexpected. Fanny glared at her, and she was forced to stop and wait until her friend was ready. But her actions brought an abrupt end to the scattered conversations.

Her second attempt was more successful than the first. With Fanny poised in the center of the dais, Sally bent lovingly over the keys and her plump arms moved with the grace of a dancer. I wouldn't have believed her capable of improving upon yesterday's performance, and yet both ladies excelled when supplied with a "real" audience.

A quarter of an hour passed, but I could not lose myself in the music. Our presence should have helped warm the room, but the chill had grown worse. My feet were numb, my arms covered in goose pimples. Out of the corner of my eye, I saw Ursula briskly rub her hands together, and Eglantine wore a puzzled frown.

On the dais, the song ended and Fanny turned to Sally and said, "Play 'Greensleeves.'"

"Not that one," Ursula countered.

"Why not? It was one of Mama's favorite's. She used to sing it constantly."

"You have answered your own question," Winnie told her. "I believe we intended to spend an evening without your mother."

"It's only a song. And it happens to be one of my favorites, too."

She nodded to Sally. Her friend hesitated and looked toward Mr. Llewelyn for advice. But he had noticed my attempts to warm myself and had turned to ask me again if I would like him to have the maid fetch a lap robe. Annoyed, she lifted her hands and the first bars flowed through the room.

Halfway through the first line, another voice picked up the words—a deeper, throatier voice. Startled, I looked to Ursula, not understanding why she would join her sister in a song she had not wanted to hear. But she was rigid in her chair, her eyes coated with a glassy sheen.

I did not need to look around me to know that the new voice did not belong to either Eglantine or Mrs. Medcroft. On the dais, Fanny broke off and the keys clanked beneath Sally's fingers. The flat notes reverberated down the length of the room, but the ghostly singer didn't miss a note. The song echoed around us, catching at us, taunting us.

And none of us dared or was able to move.

The last note dwindled away, and there was a brittle silence. Then a woman's laughter rushed into the emptiness, like the tide pouring through a narrow crevasse in the rocks. But this was not the careless laughter Chaitra and I had heard on the stairs. It was a vicious attack.

To my amazement, its target seemed to be Dr. Rhodes.

The laughter echoed around him, drenching him in waves of sound. It was, to all of us, a frightening manifestation, but Dr. Rhodes shuddered and twitched as though a festering wound had been laid bare. As we stared, his face blanched and he twisted in his chair, seeking for some sign of his tormentor.

There was none.

But that did not lessen the intensity of the assault. A scarlet hue crept from beneath his collar and spread upward, consuming his neck and crawling across his face until he was the same color as the curtains at his back.

It may have been his embarrassment, it may have been the effects of some strange power from beyond, but the years seemed to be falling away from him. There was only a trace of his fair moustache. The faint wrinkles at the corner of his eyes melted into smooth skin. He looked like a young man barely out of his teens, a deeply and intensely embarrassed young man.

Lily's laughter grew louder and harder. It was steeped with sensuality and scorn. The object of that scorn—the young man who had been courting her stepdaughter at the time of her death—dropped his gaze and could not bring himself to look at any of us.

Her tones darkened, revealing an angry disappointment. It reminded me of a day I had gone for a walk in the park and watched a bespectacled, unassuming man attempting to fly a kite for his son.

The boy had been contemptuous and spoiled, but his father had only tried harder to placate him. Moments after the breeze caught the kite, its direction changed and the toy blew down into the trees and crumpled into a mangled lump of torn cloth and broken sticks. Denied the treat he had been expecting—not because someone had had the sense to refuse him, but because his father had failed him— the child had mocked his father in those same tones.

It was the laughter of a bully for his hapless victim.

I stared at Dr. Rhodes. What had he done to Lily Llewelyn to throw her into such a fury? What reason had she to be upset with her stepdaughter's mild-mannered and nervous suitor who was at a loss in the company of ladies? I could imagine him attempting to pay her a polite compliment and somehow offending her with an ineptly turned phrase. I could see him spilling his drink on her and ruining her dress. Trivial accidents, but Lily seemed to be emotional and temperamental.

Still, Dr. Rhodes was not. A lapse in social manners could not possibly have caused him the deep and abiding shame he presently suffered. The contention between them had to have been more substantial.

I glanced around the room and noted Ursula's pinched lips and the high color in her cheeks. In that instant, my mind made a connection between their combined discomfort and led me to a possibility that was unthinkable. One that could not possibly be admitted by any well-mannered lady or gentleman.

And yet the conviction that I was right was somehow steadily impressed upon me by a force or personality that was not my own. Lily, it seemed, had not yet finished her game.

Without my closing my eyes, an image sprang into my mind. That of a woman's bedroom and two naked figures sprawled clumsily on a bed. Dear Lord. It had to be. Lily Llewelyn had seduced her stepdaughter's gentleman caller. And he, inexperienced and horribly shy with women, had failed her.

Ursula must have learned the truth. It would not have been beyond Lily to tell her. And that poor, betrayed young woman had been unable to forgive Kenneth for his disloyalty. Until it was too late and he had turned to Fanny.

Was that the secret Fanny had threatened to tell in the drawing room? And how could she have known? Unless Lily was so completely without shame that she regaled her small daughter with accounts of her infidelities.

I looked around at the shocked faces of the others sitting to either side of me and saw that those who had not already known the story had come to the same conclusion I had reached. Only Winnie looked remotely amused. The others struggled with a mixture of embarrassment and shock.

Abruptly, the laughter ceased and the music room

felt stiflingly warm. Dr. Rhodes rose from his chair, mumbled an excuse, and fled. Ursula started to rise, but her brother stopped her with a frown.

"Let him go. He will want to be alone."

The rest of us stared at each other, and none of us seemed to know what to say. What we were thinking was too awful to mention, but all other thoughts had deserted us.

Mrs. Medcroft slapped her hand on the arm of her chair. "There! I warned you, did I not? We simply cannot ignore the crime that has taken place here if we expect her spirit to find peace."

Actually, that had not been the fear she had expressed in the drawing room, but nobody cared to argue. We were all too grateful to have our attention removed from poor Dr. Rhodes.

"But mightn't that be dangerous?" Sally Pritchard asked, her voice a frightened squeak.

"Only to me," Mrs. Medcroft assured her. "And this will not be the first time I have risked my life to help others. On both sides of the veil."

"None of this would have happened if it weren't for your coming here," Ursula retorted. She snapped her fan shut and rose to her feet. "I suggest we all forget what has happened tonight."

"A little difficult, don't you think?" Winnie unbuttoned his jacket and wiped his handkerchief over his damp brow. "And this does rather suggest that Dr. Rhodes and Lily were more intimately acquainted than most of us knew."

"Nonsense. It's ridiculous to make that assumption based wholly on what has happened here."

"Not wholly, my dear. There is also your mysterious reason for refusing to marry him when everybody knew how much you loved him."

Fanny stepped down off the dais, her face tragic. Her ringlets had slipped from their sapphire ribbons and tumbled about her face. Unconsciously, her slender fingers plucked at the silk rose pinned to her bosom. "None of you can think Kenneth *murdered* my mother. He is too kind and good and . . . and . . . too gentle a man."

Unwittingly, she settled on a description that brought to mind an image of Dr. Rhodes that would have been best to avoid. The expression on our faces told her what she had done and she stamped her foot. "I simply will not believe it of him. Oh, Kenneth," she wailed. Tears flooding from her eyes, she dashed out of the room.

Mrs. Medcroft dabbed at her own eyes. "The poor child. But it is better to know the truth. And I am not convinced that her fiancé is at fault." She looked meaningfully toward Mr. Llewelyn.

He ignored her and turned to me. "Miss Carewe, would you mind if we spoke privately?" His request was softly made, but his eyes demanded that I accede.

"If that is your wish," I agreed, more calmly than I would have thought possible.

Mrs. Medcroft reached for Mr. Quarmby and clutched at his sleeve. "As the child's guardian, I must protest. I am not happy with her being the constant recipient of your attentions. You are not at all a suitable character."

That statement invited a withering retort, but he said only, "Miss Carewe is an adult and, according to her father's barristers, has no legal guardian."

"And how would you know that?"

"I have made it my business to know." Dismissing her, he turned and nodded to me. "Are you ready, Miss Carewe?"

"I will be perfectly all right," I assured her, and let him lead me from the room.

I expected him to take me into his study, but he suggested we step outside. "The evening is quite mild," he added, seeming eager to escape the house.

It couldn't have been colder than the air in the music room. And the thought of fresh air and a brief respite from the house's oppressive atmosphere held an appeal that was not to be resisted. I nodded willingly and, with a grim light in his eye, he steered me through the foyer and out the door.

It was cool on the steps. Cast-iron lanterns flickered from either side of the double doors, sending patterns of light dancing across the stones. Mr. Llewelyn paused beneath the tower arch and immersed himself in the shadows, apparently content to go no farther.

I remained at his side, not wanting to release his arm, nor even convinced he would allow me to escape him. His fingers stroked my hand, sending tiny shivers up my spine, but he seemed unaware of either his actions or the effect he was having on me.

After a difficult silence, he cleared his throat. "I am not a believer in spirits and suchlike, Miss Carewe. But I would have to be a fool to pretend that something is not terribly wrong."

"I am glad you are not going to suggest this was some flummery concocted by Mrs. Medcroft," I replied stiffly, desperately trying not to betray the emotions he had aroused in me.

But his distraction was complete. "It would have taken greater talents than hers to have pulled off this evening's stunt. I am forced to conclude that, through these ridiculous séances, an unwelcome force has been summoned to Abbey House."

"But surely there were problems before we came?"

"Nothing," he said emphatically. Too emphatically. And his fingers halted at my wrist, as though frozen there. I said nothing but waited. Seconds passed, and then he grudgingly admitted, "A few cold drafts and inexplicable noises—things common to all old houses. But we weren't troubled by spirits until after you came."

"And yet something—or someone—greeted us when we arrived."

"Are we to have yet another account of Mrs. Medcroft's divinations?" He shot me an askance look.

I blushed and confessed it had been my own impression.

His irritation faded. "Forgive me. But it is difficult for me to admit to being wrong twice in one day. Still, I am glad the impression was yours. Although it may be prejudice, I am more inclined to believe you."

"Why on earth would you place any confidence in my reactions?" I placed little enough in them myself.

"I think I am correct in assuming you were the first to be aware of her presence tonight."

"Whatever gave you that idea?"

He looked down at me from his great height, a faint trace of amusement in his eyes for what he seemed to think my innocence. I could feel the wave of protectiveness that issued from him, a protectiveness that made my stomach flutter. It was, I admitted to myself, a feeling I liked.

"None of the others were cold," he explained, and it took me a second to realize he was answering my question. "Not at first. Your senses seem to be more finely attuned than ours."

"But Mrs. Medcroft—"

"Whatever her capabilities, I cannot bring myself to trust her. Nor would I seek out her help."

"And yet she has enjoyed a history of successes." My temper rose, but I regretted losing the precious bond that had briefly linked us.

He sighed wearily. "I suppose you have had that by her own word."

"That, and the many news accounts she has saved over the years."

"Really. That is a matter that bears investigation."

My heart missed a beat. If he asked to look at the scrapbooks, then he would certainly learn the truth about my mother's involvement with Mrs. Medcroft. I would once again be regarded as "someone from a questionable background" and . . . and Fanny would be denied my friendship. I held my breath, waiting for the inevitable.

To my relief, instead of pursuing the matter, he squeezed my hand and asked, "Miss Carewe, do you really believe my stepmother was murdered?"

"I do."

"And have you any notion who that murderer might be?" His gaze searched my face for clues to what I might be thinking.

Relieved that he did not possess the talents to know my thoughts, I shook my head.

"No suspicions of any kind?" he prodded, sensing that there was something I was hiding. "You need not be polite. I am aware that I had as good a reason as any to wish her dead."

"As apparently did Dr. Rhodes. And Ursula."

Who knew to what lengths she could have been driven by her wounded pride? The image of her lunging at Fanny was still vivid in my mind. I glanced up to find Mr. Llewelyn's eyebrows had lifted sharply, and I blushed. Their particular reasons for murder should have escaped the understanding of any well-

brought-up and unmarried young woman. Nor did
they bear mentioning in mixed company. He bent his
head and coughed quietly into his hand, politely pretending to be too distracted to have caught my soft
murmur.

"There were others in the house, were there not?"
I asked gratefully.

He nodded. "Winnie and Eglantine. And Fanny,
although she was but a child of ten."

"And your father, I suppose."

"He was bedridden at the time."

"And had no reason to wish his wife harm."

"On the contrary. Everyone who came into contact
with my stepmother had reason to wish her harm."

All the muscles in his body seemed to contract and
tighten, and I could feel the tension electrifying the
air around him. My usual calm having fled the second
he had taken my arm to escort me from the music
room, I was quickly overwhelmed. I shivered convulsively and swayed toward him.

Either he thought I was cold or supposed our
recent experience had upset me. He shrugged off his
jacket and laid it across my shoulders. I found myself
engulfed in a warm layer of fine woolen cloth that
smelled indescribably delicious. Nor could I help but
wonder if any man's jacket, had its user washed with
that particular soap, would have had the same intoxicating effect on me.

Seeing that I was still unsteady on my feet, Mr.
Llewelyn wrapped an arm around my waist to support me. There was nothing suggestive or untoward
in the action, and yet I found it increasingly difficult
to speak.

"Do you think your father was aware of her . . .
indiscretions?" I managed.

"I find it hard to believe he was as blind to them as he pretended. Nor could I blame anyone for lashing out at her. Justice seems a more appropriate term for her death than murder. I would be willing to let the name of her executioner go to the grave with her."

"Surely she could not have been—"

"Absolutely and wholly evil."

His words horrified me. Not only was he confirming the impressions Chaitra and I had received, but he was condoning his stepmother's murder. And, from his manner, I was convinced he wanted me to do the same. But what did my opinion matter?

"Even if I agreed with you, winning my compliance would serve you no purpose," I protested. "Mrs. Medcroft is convinced Lily's spirit will not rest until she has named her murderer."

His grip around my waist tightened and he drew me closer. "Then you must convince her otherwise," he insisted in a husky whisper. "This matter must be allowed to die. For all our sakes. Once you said you would help me. Can I not count on you again?"

"You can," I breathed, and flames of desire roared through me, drowning out my words and deafening me to the promise I was making.

The corners of his lips curled and his breath wafted gently across my cheek. "At times, you can be a most irritating young lady, Miss Carewe. It is nice to know you can also be a comfort."

12

My promise to help Mr. Llewelyn might just as well not have been made. Mrs. Medcroft was determined to see Lily's murderer exposed, if not actually brought to justice, and my attempts to plead with her to reconsider were regarded by her as the foolishness of an inexperienced young woman—a young woman who saw and felt compassion for those around her without appreciating the needs of those in the spirit realm.

She was utterly determined to finish what she had begun.

And, now that I was no longer influenced by Mr. Llewelyn's charismatic presence, his request bewildered me. Why had he asked *me* to persuade Mrs. Medcroft to stop her activities when he had only to order us out of his home? Because of a commitment he had made to Fanny? Or because he feared to cast suspicion upon himself by such a direct act?

It was not a reassuring thought.

Our trip to Durdle Door was cancelled. The reason given us was that Dr. Rhodes had been summoned to attend the blacksmith's sickbed, but I suspected his practice would keep him out of our company for longer than a day. He had been humiliated before both friends and near strangers, and he was too sensitive a man to dismiss the memory easily.

Fanny appeared at the breakfast table for the first morning that week, rubbing her eyes and claiming to be famished. Nor was she the only one who had been unable to sleep. Both Sally and Ursula had made unusually early appearances. Fanny heaped her plate with poached eggs and sausages, and plopped down on the chair next to me. But after nibbling on a buttered muffin, she pushed her plate aside.

"You make me feel like a pig for eating more than two bites," Sally complained, jealously eyeing Fanny's slim figure.

"Kenneth thinks I am too thin," she said amiably.

"Then it's a pity you don't eat your food instead of letting it go to waste," Ursula retorted.

Fanny shrugged and demanded to know if she had received any letters. Her finger tapped impatiently on the edge of the table, and she shot me a conspiratorial smile. From that, I gathered she was expecting to hear from her friends.

I wondered what their response would be. Certainly, securing a post would simplify my life. But Ursula disappointed us both by saying nothing had come for her, and I had to resign myself to showing a greater patience.

Fanny downed her tea and deserted us, and Sally followed soon afterward, mumbling an excuse about needing to consult Edmund about a financial matter. Ursula and I were left alone at the table, facing each other over a bowl of fruit. She smiled pleasantly at me, patted her mouth with her napkin, and offered me another cup of tea.

"I think two is enough, thank you." I set down my fork and removed my own napkin from my lap.

"If you're finished . . ." She hesitated. "I wonder . . . would you mind if we had a talk, Mi—Hilary?"

The request surprised me. Ursula had pointedly avoided me on other occasions and had shown no interest in becoming better acquainted. I regarded her more closely. Outwardly, she looked unchanged. She had again donned a black taffeta dress. Her hair was knotted high on the crown of her head, drawing up the outer corners of her eyes.

But now her well-cut facial bones looked gaunt, as though strain had been etched into them with a sharp chisel. And there was a cloud of misery in the depths of her eyes. She looked tormented, like an animal who was being hunted and was unable to find a safe hiding place.

Still, I had no reason to refuse her. "Of course I don't mind," I said, but a faint edge of suspicion crept into my voice.

"Not here," she said hastily. "We are certain to be interrupted. Why don't we go upstairs to my suite?"

"As you wish," I agreed, more startled than ever.

We walked upstairs together, talking about the weather and the countryside, dull topics that did nothing to distract me from the cold drafts sweeping through the house or the conversation yet to come. In the corridor, muted conversation drifted from beneath Fanny's door and I assumed Sally had failed in her quest to find Mr. Llewelyn. Ursula's gaze met mine, and I caught the trace of a smile on her lips.

Her suite was in the middle of the west wing, and she hurried me inside. It was a vastly different sitting room from the one used by her sister. Elegant and understated. The furnishings had been upholstered in cream brocade, the pattern discreetly picked out with gold thread, and the same fabric had been used for the draperies.

I hesitated near the Louis XV sofa—a modest creation with little carvings and gently curved finger molding—then decided to take the straightback chair by the fire. I was not yet ready to drop my guard in her company, and the hard seat would guard against too great a relaxation.

Ursula sat at the end of the sofa, directly across from me. "Do you mind if I call you Hilary?" she asked with a disarming smile.

"Not at all," I murmured.

"And I would be pleased if you would call me Ursula." Her straight brows drew together over her gray eyes, and she reminded me very much of her brother. No one could have mistaken the relationship.

"I gather Edmund has reversed his opinion of you," she said, as if she had guessed my thoughts.

I managed to nod, and added, "With good cause."

"Yes. He showed me the letter." Her composure faltered and her hands twisted in her lap. "I feel I should also make you an apology. We have allowed our distaste for Fanny's parlor games to affect our judgment. Consequently, you have been treated most unfairly."

It was a startling admission. But, always, there was an oversight. "As has Mrs. Medcroft," I reminded her. "But no one has made any reference to her."

Ursula sighed, and I expected her to protest. Instead, she struggled inwardly with her emotions, mastered them, and regarded me with a civil expression. "Admittedly, she seems to be in possession of talents that are beyond my ability to fathom. But that does not mean her motives are exemplary."

"You might at least reserve judgment until you can produce proof to the contrary."

"Since you think highly of her, I will reconsider my opinions."

I hadn't expected to win even that slight victory. Struggling to conceal my amazement, I thanked her. What had come over the woman?

"And now, perhaps, we can be friends," she added. "Tell me, Hilary—if you do not mind my asking— what are your plans for the future?"

I was beginning to think that everyone was concerned with what I would do and where I would go. I told her my intentions, even admitting to Fanny's helpful offer. But rather than showing surprise over her sister's generosity, Ursula skipped over the matter completely.

"Then you have no young gentleman interested in marrying you?" she asked instead.

"I do not."

"That surprises me. You are easily as attractive as Fanny—"

"Not by any means," I protested.

"On the contrary. Her looks are more flamboyant, but you have the appearance of good breeding and a pleasant disposition. Fanny has neither."

There was a bitter edge to her words that was impossible to miss. "You do your sister an injustice," I countered.

Her fingers tapped impatiently against the sofa's dark molding. "You think it is out of jealousy. Well . . . you may be right," she admitted grudgingly, but even that was more than I had expected. "Still, if I thought Fanny would make Kenneth a good wife, it would be easier for me to accept their engagement."

"Perhaps you underestimate her."

"I make every effort not to underestimate Fanny," she retorted, and there was an inference to her statement that I did not fully understand. Nor did she give me time to unravel the mystery. Hastily, she amended, "But maybe you see something in her that we have missed. I shall hold a pale hope for the success of their marriage, regardless of my doubts. But enough about Fanny. Tell me, is it by choice or necessity you seek a post?"

"Mostly necessity," I admitted. "I could remain with Mrs. Medcroft, but I would prefer to go elsewhere."

"Yes, yes," she agreed. "You are not the type for her kind of life. Too"—she searched carefully for the word she wanted—"sensible, I think."

"It would delight my father to hear that said of me."

"Was he a sensible man?"

"Eminently."

"And I am right in thinking you favor him?"

"Perhaps a little."

"I hope more than a little." She plucked at the fringe of an embroidered silk cushion, unconsciously twisting the strands between her fingers. "There is something I must say to you that will be meaningless unless you possess good sense."

"I am intrigued."

"It is about Edmund."

Her flat statement startled me. I would not have thought her willing to discuss her brother with me. "Go on," I prompted, keeping my features impassive.

She dropped the fringe and regarded me with a direct look. "I love my brother, Hilary. There is no one to whom I feel closer."

"That is quite obvious."

"Then you will appreciate how difficult this is for me to say."

"I will make every effort to understand."

She took a deep breath. "Edmund is not fond of women."

Her announcement did not come as any great surprise. I myself had already come to that conclusion. Indeed, his recent behavior was confusing for that very reason. I waited. Surely she had more to say.

After a short pause, she continued. "It is not without reason, you understand. There was an . . . unfortunate incident when he was a young man."

"But surely this is no business of mine."

"I fear it is. I would not speak of this matter, if it were not absolutely necessary."

Her skin had a gray cast and, although she tried to hold them still, her hands trembled. It was easy to see she was under a great strain. Her usually straight back was hunched over, and her arms held tightly and defensively across her chest.

"All right," I agreed. "Please continue."

She relaxed slightly. "My father made a foolish mistake in marrying my stepmother. The kind of mistake often made by middle-aged men who have a great deal of money but are inexperienced in social affairs. They make fools of themselves over any charming and attractive young woman who knows how to put them at ease and flatter them shamelessly."

"But what has this to do with your brother?"

"My stepmother enjoyed being the wife of a

wealthy man, but she was used to other pleasures that he could not provide."

Her words shocked me. This was not a conversation we should be having, no matter what the circumstances. I started to protest, but she put out her hand and caught me by the arm. "It is a distasteful subject, but please hear me out, I beg you. It is for *your* sake this must be said."

"Then I wish you would come to the point quickly."

"I will. My stepmother's interest in Kenneth was passing. He was nothing more than an afternoon's distraction. It was Edmund she wanted. My brother."

My thoughts flashed to my odd dream and the afternoon in the glade. Ursula's announcement reflected the sensations and feelings that had consumed me on both occasions. I had tried, not entirely successfully, to dismiss them from my mind. Was I now to believe they were reflections of the truth? My stomach rolled and I could feel the warmth drain from my face and hands.

Ursula's gray gaze flickered over me, noting the change in my demeanor. The ring of dark lashes around her eyes quivered, but otherwise she remained completely still. "My father caught them"—she glanced back at me, hesitated, and delicately finished—"together. He was furious, of course. He told Edmund to leave the house and threatened to disinherit him. If Lily hadn't died, I doubt they would have reconciled."

"Are you suggesting—"

"That Edmund killed my stepmother? I neither know nor care."

I gaped at her. But her honesty could not be questioned. It was exactly what she had said on the stairs to her brother. But if that was how she felt—"What possible reason could you have for telling me this?" I demanded.

Ursula rose from the settee. Wringing her hands together, she wandered to the windows and stared out at the gardens. But her eyes were glazed over and she seemed to be looking back to a different time or place. I shifted in my chair to study her, and had the unaccountable sense that she was more than upset.

She was also frightened.

Of what? I wondered.

Or whom?

Her own brother?

Ursula sighed heavily. "Lily almost robbed Edmund of his home and his future. I am convinced that she instigated any romance they might have had but, after they were discovered, she claimed Edmund had seduced her. Had used force against her."

"But he would not—" I broke off, startled by my immediate attempt to defend him.

Ursula regarded me with sadly knowing eyes. "My father believed her because he wanted to believe her. It was only after her death that he came to his senses. Since then, Edmund has never trusted women. Nor has he treated them with much kindness."

"And what has any of this to do with me?"

"I should think that was obvious. If you were the person we had supposed you to be, I would not have troubled myself to protect you. But now I am forced to warn you. For your own protection, Hilary, please do not allow yourself to become involved with Edmund."

"But we are not involved."

"No," she agreed. "Not yet. But I know my brother

very well. And you . . . you seem very quick to defend him."

I could think of no answer to her accusation, but she did not seem to expect one. Her warning had been given, and there was nothing more for us to say. I left her suite shortly thereafter, and wandered down the corridor, still contemplating her remarks.

Her words had been more subtle, but had certainly echoed Mrs. Medcroft's tale. And while the latter could have been mistaken, I thought it unlikely that Ursula would slander her brother's character without cause.

And more and more it became harder to tell myself that I had not been influenced by Lily in the glade. Was that why Mr. Llewelyn had not rebuked me? Because he recognized her hand in my behavior and could not hold me accountable?

I reached Mrs. Medcroft's suite before I had come to any conclusion. Chaitra admitted me. Her mistress was lying on the sofa with her curtains drawn, and the sitting room was lit only by candles. Incense wafted from a brazier on the occasional table.

"Hilary?" Mrs. Medcroft lifted her head to peer at me through the gloom. "Run along and find Fanny. I will not be needing your help today."

"Are you ill?" I asked, my gaze running over her supine form.

"Not at all. I wanted to prepare myself for tonight's séance."

I groaned silently and returned to my room, not yet prepared to face anyone else. Not with Ursula's last remarks still uppermost on my mind. Was she right? I had been quick to defend her brother. Could I possibly be falling in love with him?

I flung myself on the bed. It was all too improbable

to be true. The sooner I was gone from this place, the happier I would be.

Or was I lying to myself?

There was a knock on my door, and I hastily rose, glanced at myself in the looking glass, and hurried to the door. "Did you need me—" I began, the words slipping from my tongue before the door had fully opened. I broke off immediately. It was neither Chaitra nor Mrs. Medcroft, but Mr. Llewelyn who stood in the corridor.

He wore a short jacket of biscuit-colored cloth and low-laced shoes, and the brim of a straw boater twisted between his fingers. The light, casual attire gave him a jaunty, boyish appearance, and there was an unfamiliar brightness to his eyes and expression.

"Need you?" he asked, his lips curling upwards. "As a matter of fact, I do. It is most obliging of you to ask."

"Oh! I did not think it was you."

His smile broadened. "Fortunately, you are mistaken. I have agreed to take Sally and Fanny to Durdle Door to make up for their missed outing with Kenneth. Fanny insisted you must accompany us."

He could not have chosen a worse moment to make his invitation. I knew that, at all costs, he was to be avoided—at least until I had come to grips with my own emotions and the feelings he aroused in me. Even standing in his presence made something within me stir, like a dormant bulb coming to life in spring. Something was awakening within me, something young and new and wonderful.

A feeling that must not be allowed to put down deeper roots.

I forced a smile. "That is very good of her, but no.

Mrs. Medcroft will almost certainly need me this morning. She has several letters—"

"Nonsense. Surely she will not miss you for a few hours." His eyes willed me to accept and I found myself teetering dangerously near surrender.

"Perhaps I had better ask," I tried, convinced she would object, thereby settling the matter.

Mr. Llewelyn smiled victoriously. "An excellent idea. But there is no need for you to bother. I shall have a word with her myself."

Ignoring my objections, he strode off down the corridor, his broad strides covering the short distance in a heartbeat.

And that, I thought, was the end of that. Mrs. Medcroft would crumple before him and my excuses would be handily swept aside. My resolution to avoid him had been broken only seconds after it had been made.

He returned within minutes, a slight swagger to his walk, and advised me to bring my hat and coat. "A breeze often sweeps up in the afternoons."

Sally and Fanny were waiting in the foyer, an enormous wicker basket at their feet. To look at them, they might have been sisters. Fanny was, of course, taller and prettier than her rounder, less golden friend. And her movements and mood were lighter and gayer, childlike rather than vaguely immature, as Sally's often seemed. But both of them looked cool and fresh in flared linen skirts with sailor blouses. Curls of fair hair peeped beneath the straw bonnets they had worn to protect their milky complexions.

By comparison, my own black taffeta dress was completely inadequate. Sally looked disdainfully at me. "That is hardly suitable in this heat. You will be horribly uncomfortable."

"Oh, for goodness' sakes," Fanny protested. "She will be fine. Besides, she's in mourning and has little choice."

"And what about Mrs. Medcroft?" Sally persisted. "Surely she will be needing you."

"On the contrary. She is spending the day meditating in preparation for tonight's séance."

I glanced at Mr. Llewelyn, wondering how greatly my news upset him. His expression remained unchanged, but a muscle jumped in his cheek, and it was as if a dark pall had been cast across our merry gathering.

Fanny caught me by the arm and pulled me toward the door. "Don't listen to Sally," she whispered. "She wants Edmund all to herself."

It was too late to escape. I followed them to the carriage waiting outside the double doors, a light calash with facing seats and a raised leather hood. Somehow, after Mr. Llewelyn had helped us into the carriage, I found myself seated next to him and across from Sally. It was unfortunate positioning, more for her than for me. During the entire hour's drive, she struggled between directing smiles toward our host and scowling at me. I began to fear she might do herself an injury.

Mr. Llewelyn seemed oblivious to her distress. Back straight, his arm resting comfortably on the edge of the carriage, he nodded to the driver. The reins snapped and, with an almost imperceptible jolt, we started off.

The Dorset countryside was attractive and peaceful. Flocks of sheep clustered on the heath-covered moors that rose and fell about us with the gentle motion of a calm sea. Plaster and thatch cottages appeared at every bend and dip in the lane, and I began to feel as though I were thumbing through the pages of a book of fairy tales. I shrugged off my reservations and gave myself over to the pleasure of absorbing the scenery.

"Did Winnie and Eglantine not wish to come?" Sally asked with a hint of petulance. "Surely, if anyone else was to be included . . ."

"They had some private matters to discuss," Mr. Llewelyn replied, and his mouth set in a hard line.

Fanny giggled, a knowing look in her bright eyes. Because of some secret she knew about the Winthrops? Or because she was amused by her friend's jealousy? It was difficult to judge. Nor was there time. Her brother shushed her with a cool look and turned to me.

"Are you familiar with the local countryside, Miss Carewe?" There was a warmth in his voice that was more intense than the sun's rays, and I felt my cheeks flush to the color of the leather seats.

I managed a shake of my head and admitted, "Except for a few holidays in Wales, we rarely left Bristol."

What a pity," Sally said politely. "I went to school on the continent, and my late husband and I made repeated trips to Italy and France. One cannot truly be educated unless one travels."

"And some of us not even then," Mr. Llewelyn added in a silky and inoffensive voice that almost made it possible to overlook his meaning.

Sally lifted her head to respond, then stopped, suddenly realizing what he had implied. The soft color faded from her round cheeks, and she stammered something unintelligible.

Fanny smothered what was supposed to be a yawn behind her hand and wriggled impatiently. "I hope we are not going to have to put up with yet another of your unpleasant moods, Edmund. Otherwise, I am sure we would *all* have stayed at home."

"I was not aware that I had said anything to give offense," he replied, looking mildly surprised.

I had no doubt his innocence was an act, but Sally recovered her smile immediately. She lightly swatted Fanny on the arm and chided her for harassing her brother. "The two of you ought to be ashamed. Always assuming the worst of each other. Today you must call a truce and try to enjoy yourselves."

Good advice, I thought, but it was unlikely to be heeded.

It was a half-hour drive to the beach, a drive interspersed with brief snatches of conversation and notable only for the scenery beyond our carriage and the restraint displayed within. When she was not openly commanding his attention, Sally studied our host surreptitiously. He ignored her, giving most of his attention to Fanny. She pretended complete uninterest in anything but the breeze and the smell of salt air, which she inhaled prodigiously. As for me, by rights, I should have felt completely neglected. Instead, I suffered from the odd sensation that I was uppermost in all their thoughts. It was, to say the least, discomfiting.

The driver brought the carriage to a halt on the top of high, downward-sloping bluffs. Chalk cliffs lined the coast. Beyond them lay a narrow stretch of sand and jutting out of the blue-green waters to the west was Durdle Door. The arch had been cut into the primeval rocks by the sea, and was linked to the mainland by a narrow isthmus. Gulls swooped and screeched over our heads, and the tang of salt and seaweed filled my nostrils.

"I'm famished," Fanny exclaimed. "Has it really only been two hours since breakfast?"

"That should teach you to eat properly at mealtimes," Sally retorted, but she peered hopefully at the wicker basket.

In the end, we decided to eat the picnic luncheon before making our way down to the sandy beach at the bottom of the cliffs. Forty-five minutes later, with Edmund's strong arm to support us, we clambered down a sloping cleft in the bluff. The tide was out, leaving shallow pools and scattered rocks jutting upwards, naked to the sun.

As soon as we set foot on the warm sand, Fanny kicked off her shoes and stockings, caught up the folds of her dress, and dashed happily toward the distant water. Her bonnet flew back from her head, and her ringlets streamed behind her in a golden flow. I paused to watch her mad flight, struck by her beauty and grace. One could not help but be captivated by her.

Sally plopped to the sand and hastily dispensed with her own footwear. Seconds later she was struggling to catch up with Fanny and fighting with the ties of her own bonnet. It was an obvious attempt at imitation, done for Mr. Llewelyn's benefit. But Fanny's magic eluded her, as it would have eluded most mortals. And, I thought sadly, had she considered Fanny's strained relationship with her brother, and the scowl that darkened his face when he watched her, she would not have wanted to instill a similar image in his mind.

Finding myself alone in his company, something I had promised myself to avoid, I threaded my way between two rocks and started after them.

Mr. Llewelyn hurried in my wake and caught me

before I could escape. His fingers molded around my arm, gently squeezing. It was too light a touch to cut off the circulation, but still the blood pounded in my temples. Feeling like a cornered rabbit, I swallowed and turned to face him.

"Would you like to take a stroll along the water's edge?"

"Why, I am sure we all—"

The sunlight glanced across his eyes, making them flash like a steel blade drawn from its sheath. "I was not inviting anyone but you."

"But that would be rude."

"Not rude. Merely discriminating."

It was difficult to thank someone for a compliment when that compliment insulted others. I tried to meet his remark with a disapproving frown, but he shot me a disarming grin that made his previous remarks seem like nothing more than light jests made for my benefit. I found myself smiling back at him, although I knew he had twisted the situation to suit himself.

"Didn't you promise Fanny you would be pleasant?" I demanded.

"I can hardly be offensive if I am not in their company," he pointed out. "If the four of us remain together, however, I can make no such guarantees. By walking with me, Miss Carewe, you will be doing us all a favor."

"Thank you, but—"

"Surely you would not refuse me?"

Not waiting for my reply, he took me by the arm and guided me up the beach. There was a strength in that arm that forbade resistance, and an energy that propelled me along at his side. He matched his pace to mine, but I could feel the constraints he had placed upon himself. It was like being shackled to a stallion who presented only the appearance of docility. Had he decided to disregard his training, he would have been completely unmanageable.

We strolled along beneath the shadow of the cliffs, protected from the direct sunlight by the overhang. It was several minutes before I realized that by choosing that route, he had made certain I need not suffer unduly from the heat.

Nor had he brought his thoughtfulness to my attention to win my appreciation.

Sometimes, Mr. Llewelyn made it very difficult to dislike him. Or even to remember that he was an undesirable character. But after everything that had been said to me, how could I dare to think otherwise? I sighed heavily.

He glanced down at me curiously. "You surprise me, Miss Carewe. There are very few young ladies who would be unhappy to find themselves in my company."

"So I have been told."

"Really?" He gazed upon me with greater interest. "By whom?"

I realized my blunder. Just thinking of the conversation I'd had with Mrs. Medcroft made me flush. Nor could I refer to his sister's remarks, for they had been no more charitable. I struggled for an acceptable answer, and stumbled on the only other response I could make.

"By yourself, if you remember. In your stepmother's suite."

And that brought back other memories. My gaze traced the line of his full lips and my cheeks grew warmer. Even my arms prickled where he had gripped me.

His sculptured face showed no trace of emotion,

but he could hardly have failed to be aware of my thoughts. Purposely, he looked off into the distance, and I felt the muscles in his arm tighten beneath my hand.

"You are being uncharitable, Miss Carewe."

"How is that?"

"I thought you had forgiven me my misdeeds. Apparently, you have not."

"That is untrue."

He twisted his head to glance down at me, and a curl fell across his brow. "What other reason could you have for refusing to walk with me?"

None that I cared to confess. "I merely thought the others would wish to join us," I lied.

He caught and held my gaze. It was a long, steady look, one that both appraised me and made me aware of the foolishness of attempting to lie to him. I became very conscious of the way he kept my arm tucked beneath his. Of the long, even stride that he fitted perfectly—and effortlessly—to mine. And of the strong emotions held in check beneath the perfect manners, the tailored suit, and the immaculate grooming. At one and the same time, I felt safer and more vulnerable than I had ever before felt. I trembled, overcome by a kind of fearful ecstasy.

If he noticed the slight tremor, he pretended he had not. "Has Fanny had word from her friends?" he asked in a voice that only a stranger would have mistaken as casual.

"Not yet," I admitted, my throat dry. "I believe she expects to hear shortly."

"And if they wish to meet with you immediately, what will you do?"

"Of course, I would go," I said, barely conscious of whether or not I was making a sensible response, and tiny waves of electricity prickled down my spine. "Mrs. Medcroft would be disappointed, but certainly she would understand."

"I wonder if that is true?"

"Now it is you who are being uncharitable," I retorted, breaking free of the spell he had cast on me.

He was instantly aware of what he had done, and regret clouded his eyes. "Forgive me. I suppose you look forward to leaving Abbey House." It was a statement, but there was the hint of a question in his voice. And something more, something very much like disappointment.

It was a disappointment I shared, although I knew my emotions were leading me astray. "You seem uncertain," I challenged, preferring to war with him than with myself. "Was it not you who thought I should remove myself from Mrs. Medcroft's influence?"

"I did. And do. But I must admit that . . . I wish we had more time to become acquainted." He finished in a hoarse voice that might or might not have been due to the breeze blowing off the water.

I turned from him to stare with interest at the pre-historic rocks, pretending a fascination I could not make myself feel. My gaze fixed upon them, I murmured, "You surprise me, Mr. Llewelyn. You and I have rarely agreed on any topic. I would not have thought of us as friends."

"I have yet to make an effort." His even smile glinted in the shadows, pearly white against the streak of darkness outlining the cliffs. He bent over me, deliberately dropped his voice and, in an intimate murmur that said a great deal more than his words, claimed, "I am told I can be quite charming."

By whom? I wondered. Other "young ladies of good character" who had fallen prey to his charms? Or had Mrs. Medcroft and his sister overstated his faults? I scanned his face and tried to garner some impression of him beyond that which was naturally available to me. Instead, by opening my senses, I left myself vulnerable to the stunning smile and the erotic warmth that emanated from his eyes.

I hastily lowered my gaze. "I think your interest in me . . . sudden."

"Not at all. I have always thought you attractive and intelligent. But until recently, I also supposed you unsuitable. Highly unsuitable," he admitted with a rueful grin. "I was pleased to learn otherwise."

"You must meet many young women who are both attractive and intelligent. There is no reason to take a special interest in me."

He shrugged. "They are too willing to hurl themselves at me. I find their lack of modesty offensive."

Because of his stepmother's adulterous habits? I caught his eye on me and flushed again. Only the knowledge that he couldn't possibly be aware of the things Ursula had told me saved me from complete humiliation.

He cleared his throat. "That day in the glade . . ."

I relaxed slightly. He had presumed that my own wanton dance had been the cause of my discomfort. "I have no notion of what came over me. You may be certain it will not happen again."

"You must not be embarrassed. It was not characteristic of your behavior. I see no need to mention it again."

Once again, I found myself the grateful recipient of his kindness. My embarrassment faded, and I realized it was his offhand chivalry that completely undid me. His good looks and charm had far less effect.

Still, although it remained unsaid between us, both of us were aware there was something unnatural about the incident in the glade. I wondered why he didn't mention the possibility of his stepmother's influencing me. Was it because he wanted to say nothing of their affair? Or did he refuse to admit that anything out of the ordinary had occurred?

"Why don't you tell me something about yourself," he suggested in an obvious attempt to change the subject.

For my sake or his?

I shrugged. I had already been through this with Mr. Quarmby. "There is little to tell. I lived a quiet life with my parents. Almost reclusive."

"Was one of them unwell?"

"On the contrary. They enjoyed excellent health, until . . ."

"Forgive me." He squeezed my hand. "It was an insensitive and thoughtless remark."

I frowned. It was only a slip, one that anyone could have made. Mr. Llewelyn was anything but insensitive, as I was quickly discovering.

Unaware of my thoughts, he noticed only my frown. "I seem to be forever making apologies when you and I are together," he said, chagrined. "I hope you will allow me to make amends in that short while you remain at Abbey House."

"There is no need."

"On the contrary. Besides, I enjoy your company." He smiled down at me. "You are a most interesting young woman, Miss Carewe."

"And that is nothing but shameless flattery. I am

not the least bit interesting, as Mrs. Pritchard has but recently reminded me."

He snorted. "She hasn't the intelligence to appreciate subtleties. You are a furled rose, Miss Carewe. I think I would enjoy watching your petals open."

"I think, Mr. Llewelyn," I said, determined to let the conversation go no further, "that my petals must wait for another day. Fanny and Sally will be concerned for our safety."

13

The tide had turned, and the stretch of sand was rapidly narrowing. The wind, too, swept with greater force off the water, rustling through the grass on the top of the cliffs and catching at my skirts with a determined hand. I was forced to cling to Mr. Llewelyn to keep my balance. He, far from objecting, seemed to take pleasure in my difficulties.

It was ten minutes before we reached the narrow cleft in the cliffs, and we scanned the beach for Fanny and Sally. Neither of them were in sight.

"I doubt they would attempt to climb the bluffs without assistance," Mr. Llewelyn said with a slight frown. Nevertheless, he lifted his head and called out their names.

Neither of us heard any response.

The furrows across his brow deepened. "They may have returned to the carriage and failed to hear me."

He glanced further up the beach, knowing we would have met them if they had walked in an easterly direction. A short distance from us, the bluffs jutted outward, and it was impossible to see beyond them.

"There's a small cove around the bend. That may be where they have gone." He twisted his head to gauge the approach of the incoming tide. "Perhaps you had better wait here. I will be faster on my own, and they may need my help in returning."

"You need not fear for me," I assured him, sitting down on a flat-topped rock. "I will wait here until you return."

Distracted, he nodded and set off at a fast pace. Within minutes he had traveled beyond the sound of my voice. Only then, with my mind and gaze wandering, did I chance to notice Sally's straw hat.

It lay atop a piece of driftwood. I rose and picked my way through a mass of dried seaweed to collect the gaily ribboned hat. Why had she left it here? It was unlike Sally to forget about the damage the sun could do her fair skin. Thoughtfully, I turned around and cast my gaze about for any other sign of them.

There was a dark opening in the cliffs. I would have seen it earlier, but a protruding rock hid the cave from the sight of those looking in a westerly direction. Mr. Llewelyn, his gaze intent on the end of the spit, would have hurried past the entrance without ever being aware of the cave's existence.

Had Fanny and Sally gone inside? That would certainly explain their failure to notice the incoming tide. And the forgotten bonnet. I stepped cautiously into the dark hole.

"Fanny? Sally?"

A muffled cry came back to me, but it was impossible to tell if someone had answered, if it was merely the echoes of my own voice, or a combination of the two.

If they had entered the cave, they could not possibly have gone far. Not without a lantern. I glanced over my shoulder for Mr. Llewelyn, but he had disappeared around the headland.

And by the time he returned it might be too late.

Picking up the hem of my dress, I bent my head and descended into the cave. The ground declined sharply for several yards. Gradually, it leveled out and I was able to walk without stooping. Fifteen feet back, the opening narrowed, but the sandy bottom made walking easy. I waited for my eyes to become accustomed to the gloom and plunged onward.

A thin light trickled down from high above my head, and I looked upward to see pinpricks of light in the blackness. There were small openings in the rock ceiling, letting sunlight into the cave. Slowly, the ground began to rise, and I wondered if there was an exit on the top of the bluffs. If so, Fanny and Sally might have found their own way back to the carriage. It was possible they had been making their way through the cave when Mr. Llewelyn had called for them.

I hesitated. Would Fanny really have attempted anything this adventuresome? She would, I thought, answering my own question. And she'd drag poor Sally along with her, regardless of her friend's protests.

I shook my head, amused rather than exasperated, and told myself I would have to do the same. If only to be assured they had safely reached the other end. Around me, the walls of the cave narrowed, and my pace slowed. Every few minutes, I called out for Fanny, but had no answer save for the muffled and plaintive cry that was neither intelligible nor recognizable.

I walked for what seemed a great distance, slowly moving upward as I moved deeper into the cliff face. Surely it could not be much farther? An instant later, I came to an abrupt stop. The cave dead-ended in a sheer rock face.

I groaned and cursed myself for my stupidity. Now, I would have to turn around and go back. It was the second time I had underestimated Fanny. Clearly, she had never been in the cave. Which proved she was capable of showing a good deal more sense than I.

I twisted about and slowly began the descent. Part way down I heard muffled noises and cried, "Mr. Llewelyn? Is that you?"

The echoes of my own voice returned to me, and this time I had no doubt the plaintive cries were mine. As for the odd sounds I'd heard, I took comfort in knowing they were too low-pitched to have been bats.

That comfort quickly died.

The rumbling noises grew louder and I recognized them for what they were: waves rushing into the cave.

My heart raced. I couldn't waste any more precious seconds trying to protect my dress from the jagged rocks. It was imperative I get out of the cave. I rushed forward blindly, holding my arms in front of me to protect my head. Twice, I hit my wrists on the walls, and I felt a warm trickle of blood stream down my upraised arms.

The sand sucked at my shoes with wet, smacking noises, and the rumbling had become an angry roar. Another few steps and the water was rushing about my ankles and soaking through the hem of my dress. With every step I took, the water rose about me. In less than a minute it had reached my knees. A few more seconds and I was floundering, waist-deep.

My feet were numb with the cold, and my petticoats tangled about my legs and threatened to trip me with each step. Then, too, seawater poured down from the cave entrance and slapped against me, knocking me backward each time I tried to reach the opening. I grabbed at the rough walls, but they were slick with spray and my hands slipped from the rocks.

I rushed forward again, determined to reach the rapidly diminishing arch of sunlight. The sands rolled beneath my feet, and a wave hit me full force across the midriff. I tumbled backward, screaming as I fell.

The water rushed over my head and threw me into the depths of the cave. Sand clogged my nostrils, and my head slammed against a rock. A shower of lights exploded in my head and twirled around in circles like a hive of swarming bees, and I could no longer distinguish up from down. For one what seemed to me endless moment, an overwhelming panic gripped me and I believed my death inevitable.

The voluminous fabric of my dress snagged on something—a rock, a piece of driftwood—and remained caught. I was startled out of my unreasoning terror, but it was not a pleasant return to consciousness. As my dress became more and more entangled, I was being pulled deeper and deeper. I flailed and kicked out madly, but the last of my strength had gone and my struggles failed to secure my freedom. Inexorably, I was being dragged to my death.

I resigned myself to my fate and relaxed.

Immediately, my head emerged from the waves and blessed air rushed into my lungs. I spluttered and coughed and my vision cleared. Mr. Llewelyn stood above me, framed by the light at his back, hauling on the folds of sodden taffeta until his strong hands reached my waist.

Fingers biting into me, he pulled me upright and sheltered me from the current's onslaught with his body. The waves slapped against his legs and back, but were unable to reach me. I was safe in a peaceful lagoon, and he was my coral reef.

The need for fear gone, I gave way to hysterical laughter. My confused senses had told me I was being towed beneath the water. Instead, Mr. Llewelyn had been battling to bring me to the surface.

And I had been fighting him. Had I not relaxed . . .

I shuddered and fell against him.

His arms wrapped around me. "Good Lord, Hilary. Are you all right?"

"Edmund. Dear, dear Edmund."

I clung to him, wrapping my arms around his neck and pressing myself against him. My breath came and went in harsh sobs, and my fingers wound into his wet curls. The waters that swirled about us were the chill waters of the English Channel, cold even in the midst of summer, but between us a fire flared.

Edmund tightened his embrace. Again and again, he murmured my name, his mouth pressing against my ear. It was like listening to music, a sweet, rich melody that was more beautiful than anything mortal instruments could have created. Each time I heard my name upon his lips I knew I was alive. And safe within his arms.

He held me to him with bone-crushing force, impressing me not with his strength and power but with the safety he offered. Although I could not see his eyes, I could feel the intensity of his gaze upon me, searching my face for confirmation that I was not a dream, but truly there. Alive and in his arms.

"Edmund. Oh, Edmund. Thank God you came for me."

I buried my face into the hollow of his neck, muffling the other words that poured from my mouth. With the roar of the waves around us, he could not possibly have heard me cry, "Edmund, I love you. I will never stop loving you." Fortunately, my words did not even reach his ears, and I was saved from complete humiliation. But nothing could have convinced me to release him, not Mrs. Medcroft's warnings, not my inner voices softly reminding me that my behavior was—if understandable—still not entirely correct.

"Damn propriety and damn Mrs. Medcroft," I mumbled with more emotion than clarity.

"What did you say?" he asked, sounding faintly startled.

"I . . . I . . ."

"I think we had better get out of here," he said firmly.

Gratefully, I nodded.

With Edmund to support me, I had little difficulty in escaping the cave. We clambered up the incline step by step, pausing to brace ourselves against each oncoming wave, and splashing forward again as they retreated.

Within minutes, we were standing on a narrow stretch of sand and rocks that had not yet been devoured by the tide. My sodden dress clung to my legs and arms, and I shivered uncontrollably, suddenly aware of the icy water and the bite of the wind.

Edmund gathered me up and strode toward the path that led to the top of the bluffs. Despite my protests, he made the awkward ascent with me in his arms.

Fanny and Sally stood near the carriage, anxious looks on their faces. Upon seeing us, Sally gave a little shriek and vigorously fanned herself with her hand.

Fanny rushed toward us. "Good heavens, what happened to you?"

"She wandered into a cave when I went searching for you," Edmund said with ill-concealed temper. "And was nearly drowned."

"Goodness, Hilary. What a silly thing to do." Her gaze swept over me and she wrinkled her nose in dismay. "What shall we do with you?"

"*We* are going to get her home as quickly as possible. Before she catches pneumonia."

Edmund covered the last few strides to the carriage and his driver hastily opened the door. He dropped me on the seat, paying no notice to the stream of saltwater that ran in rivulets across the leather upholstery. With a snort of impatience, he pulled a lap robe around my shoulders and threw another across my legs.

"Get in, both of you," he said impatiently to his sister and Sally, nodding to the driver to give them a hand.

Doubtfully, they took their seats across from us. Sally glanced distastefully at me, and drew her skirts to the side. But puddles of water collected on the floorboards and pooled about her shoes.

Fanny looked more amused than discomfited. "Thank goodness you are all right, Hilary. But you really must be more careful."

"I imagine Miss Carewe knew exactly what she was doing," Sally said, her mouth tight. "I am just beginning to appreciate her cleverness."

"Oh, do hush," Fanny told her in a bored voice. "Edmund, you might at least tell us what happened."

His reply was terse, and focused on my near death rather than his heroism. Nor, I realized, had he guessed my reasons for entering the cave. Nevertheless, he didn't reproach me for what he must have thought was sheer foolishness.

Shivering, I stammered, "I f-found Sally's bonnet on a piece of driftwood nearby. I thought they had gone inside and didn't know the tide had changed."

Across from us, the two of them exchanged glances, and Sally's cheeks turned a bright pink. She opened her mouth to speak and emitted a high-pitched and meaningless squeak.

Fanny shook her head impatiently. "We were looking over the cliffs for you, and a gust of wind swept it right off her head. If we'd known what was going to happen, we would have sent Jim after it."

"I was hoping one of you would notice and bring it up with you. I suppose—" Sally glanced from me to Edmund's outraged face, and hastily finished, "Never mind. I have others."

Edmund scowled at them. "You both deserved to be strangled with the ties of that bonnet."

"It's as much your fault as ours," Fanny protested. "You slipped off without a word to either of us. And you should have known we wouldn't have stayed on the beach once the tide started to turn. You never give me credit for any sense."

"And the trouble we had getting up by ourselves. Fanny practically had to push me all the way to the top of the cliffs," Sally added, quick to come to her friend's support. "*I* wanted to wait for you," she added self-righteously, spoiling her attempt at loyalty.

With a look of disgust for both women, Edmund threw his arm about my shoulders and pulled me against him in an effort to keep me warm. His behavior might not have been proper, but I nestled against him and closed my eyes, too exhausted to care.

But now that we were back in the carriage, moving steadily away from the cold waters at the base of the cliffs, I was grateful he had not heard everything that I had said to him in the cave.

He could not possibly have heard me cry, "Oh, Edmund, I love you."

Mrs. Medcroft fluttered around my bedside, her hands battering at her bosom. "Are you certain you're all right, Hilary?"

"Perfectly," I assured her.

And I was. Upon returning to Abbey House, I had been given a hot bath and a glass of brandy and sent to bed. Blankets had been heaped upon me, pillows had been stuffed beneath my head, and I had been treated to a constant parade of concerned visitors and well-wishers, all of whom were subjected to Mrs. Medcroft's anguished description of my acute suffering.

"I knew something was wrong," she claimed, the first moment we found ourselves alone. "I felt it in my heart. Only ask Mr. Quarmby."

As if on cue, he tapped on my open door and, having heard her remark, promptly agreed. "She has been most distressed. Ever since you departed."

"I knew I should have refused Mr. Llewelyn," she wailed. "But he has such a forceful character."

"It was he who saved me," I reminded her, still

feeling the residue of warmth and gratitude that had engulfed me. "Were it not for him—"

"None of this would have happened! Forgive me, Hilary, but if you leave this house again, it *must* be in my company. I could never forgive myself if something had happened to you."

I said nothing. She was too distraught for me to remind her that it was not her place to set rules for me. Nevertheless, I realized it was time that I faced the unpleasant duty of telling her of my intentions to leave her.

Tomorrow morning at the latest, I promised myself.

I remained in bed for the rest of that day, and Mrs. Medcroft refused to leave my side. Even Chaitra's efforts to minister to me were usurped. Our dinner was served to us on a tray and, had I allowed her, Mrs. Medcroft would have fed me herself. All thoughts of her holding another séance that evening were forgotten.

"I simply could not concentrate," she insisted, and nobody had the inclination to protest.

She retired at nine o'clock, after firmly turning down my lamp and shutting my door to make certain nobody would disturb me. I lay back against the mountain of pillows, grateful for the first quiet moments allowed to me, and my mind wandered back to those terrifying minutes in the cave.

And yet I could not help smiling.

I awakened with that same smile upon my face. My left temple was sore where I had been thrown against the rocks, and I suffered a slight headache. Neither troubled me. I was more cheerful than I had been for days.

Remembering my intention to speak to Mrs.

Medcroft, I dressed quickly. As I brushed my hair, I debated whether to catch her before breakfast or to wait until after she had something in her stomach to brace her for my announcement.

But she could have plans to walk in the garden with Mr. Quarmby after breakfast, and there might be no chance to catch her alone for the rest of that day. Steeling myself for an unpleasant task, I left my room and went directly to her suite.

Chaitra admitted me with a warm smile, her brown eyes soft with compassion for my frightening escapade. Her mistress was staring out the window, rubbing her bare ring finger thoughtfully, and muttering to herself. Her dark hair had not yet been combed back into her chignon, and it fell about her face.

The morning sunlight glanced across the crown of her head, shimmering off each strand. There was, I realized, more silver in her hair than I had realized.

"Hilary, my dear," she cried, looking up and pushing a lock back from her face. "Would you not have been wiser to stay in bed?"

"I have never felt better," I vowed. "Besides, if you have a minute, I was hoping to speak with you."

"I always have time for you." She motioned for Chaitra to fetch her brush and hairpins. "She can fix my chignon while we talk."

"I think you should sit down."

"Good heavens." Her wandering attention promptly returned to me. "Do you mean to tell me . . . ?" Her hands twisted together. "Oh, please say it is not so."

"Say what is not so?" I asked, wondering if she had guessed the truth.

"That awful man. He has defiled you."

I gasped, too shocked by the suggestion to make an

immediate response. Could she really think that I . . . that Edmund . . . that Mr. Llewelyn . . . that either of us would even harbor the notion? I struggled to find my tongue and declared, "He has not. Indeed, he has not."

She sagged in the middle and sighed audibly. "Thank the Lord. I had feared . . . but, never mind. I am glad to know you have not been misled by his *apparent* heroism."

"Apparent? But he saved my life."

"He should never have left you alone. Never. It was disgraceful." She glanced at my face and hastily added, "But that is enough about him. What is this terrible news you have for me?"

I stifled my outrage, determined not to be swayed from my intent, and tried to speak in a pleasant manner. "It is not terrible news, although I admit you might be disappointed. Miss Llewelyn has offered to find me a post as a governess with one of her friends, and—"

"You refused her, naturally."

"No. I have accepted."

"But why?" she wailed, and her hands clutched at her throat as though she were trying to ward off strangling hands. "Haven't I been like a mother to you?"

"You have been . . . wonderfully kind, but—"

"Then why would you choose to leave? Are you afraid of being a burden?"

My irritation with her earlier remarks faded and I smiled. Whatever she thought of Mr. Llewelyn, she had been kind to me. Indeed, were it not for her, I would not have met Fanny and been able to avail myself of the opportunity she had offered me.

"Nothing you have said has made me feel I would be a burden."

I hurried to her side and took her hand in mine. It felt dry and papery, and I could feel the quick throb of her pulse beneath my fingers. I looked up to see her eyes glittering with tears, and rebuked myself for having broached the subject in an abrupt and heartless fashion.

"Then why would you want to leave me?" she asked, in a tremulous voice that made my heart ache for her.

My explanations did nothing to lessen her disappointment. To my remarks that I thought I could be more useful as a governess, she protested that I had not given myself the time needed to judge the value of her contribution to society. When I pointed out that my father would have objected to my living in this fashion, she countered that my mother had been happy with her and would have wanted the same for me. In the end, we came to no resolution, and I was forced to agree to give the matter greater consideration, although it was only my intention to give her a few days to accustom herself to my leaving.

I did not immediately go downstairs for breakfast, my appetite having deserted me. Fifteen minutes later, someone knocked at my door. Expecting to see Mrs. Medcroft, armed with new arguments in her behalf, I opened the door.

Mr. Quarmby stood in the corridor, his moustache neatly trimmed, his eyebrows looking as though he had fastidiously brushed them into smooth alignment. He pressed his pudgy hands together, and a faint crease between his brows wrinkled his otherwise smooth face.

"Forgive me for disturbing you—I do hope you have recovered from your recent misadventure."

"I have, thank you."

He nodded. "I thought as much. You are a sensible young lady, and sensible young ladies rarely dwell on their misfortunes." He coughed delicately. "I know this is none of my business, but I have just spoken with Mrs. Medcroft and thought I ought to have a word with you."

"Is it absolutely necessary?" I asked reluctantly, assuming he hoped to change my mind.

"I will not tire you," he promised. "I only wished to learn whether or not you were certain you had come to the best decision."

"I believe I have."

He shook his head. "Never have I seen the dear lady this distraught. She cherishes your company."

"I do not mean to be cruel."

"Of course you don't. And, naturally, you must choose for yourself the life you wish to lead. I only hope you do not act in haste. There may yet be *other* choices for you to consider."

I looked at him blankly. What was he suggesting? I thought of the interest Mr. Llewelyn had shown in me. Could Mr. Quarmby have noted his interest and believed him sincere? Or was he referring to his statements in the garden about my possibly having mediumistic abilities?

Seeing my confusion, Mr. Quarmby reached out and gave my hand a squeeze. "Think carefully, my dear. You can always find a post as a governess. Take a while to explore other . . . avenues. I am certain you will not be disappointed."

No wiser than I had been a few moments before, I managed a smile and thanked him for his concern.

Seemingly satisfied, he wished me a restful morning and returned to Mrs. Medcroft's suite. I watched him go, his short legs taking brisk little strides, his footsteps quiet and discreet.

It was ten o'clock before I decided to leave my room, only after I had finished writing a letter to my Bristol neighbors. Twice, I had crumpled the sheet and begun again, having written several paragraphs in praise of Mr. Llewelyn that would have persuaded them I had fallen in love with him. And surely it had been gratitude, not love, that had stirred my emotions. In the end, I gave up and dashed off a short note that said nothing.

Downstairs, Fanny and Sally were nowhere to be seen, and both may still have been abed. I heard voices in the parlor and thought them to belong to Ursula and Eglantine, but did not care to join them. Ursula may have wished to show me friendship, but her mother's dear friend did not.

Knowing the breakfast platters would have been cleared from the buffet, I wandered out into the garden. I was not in search of company, but a peaceful nook in which to sit and consider my current situation. Remembering the curved marble bench behind the holly bushes, I strolled down the path Mr. Quarmby and I had taken.

I reached my destination only to find the bench already occupied. Winnie lifted his leonine head, shook his gold and silver curls, and smiled broadly.

"Ah! And how is our erstwhile mermaid?"

"A very poor mermaid," I retorted. "A few more seconds and I would have drowned."

"And that would have been a terrible waste." Blue eyes shining flirtatiously, he came to his feet and waited for me to sit down.

I hesitated, but it would have been rude to ignore him and walk off. Especially after his polite inquiry into my welfare. I decided to linger a minute or two, then pretend to remember that Mrs. Medcroft was expecting my help before luncheon.

Cautiously, I took my place at the opposite end of the bench. Winnie promptly sat down at my side, stretched out his legs, and peered at my face with great interest.

"Is that a bruise I see?" He deliberately brushed my brow with his forefinger.

I tilted my head to avoid his touch. "Only a small one. But it is still sore."

He dropped his hand. "Edmund should have warned you about our tides. It was unforgivable carelessness. Unless, of course—"

"Unless?"

He threw back his head and chuckled. "I would not put it past him. I might have done the same myself."

"I hope you will share the jest," I prompted, my doubts about sitting with Winnie replaced by a deep and genuine interest in what he had to say.

He seemed to be enjoying himself immensely. The laugh lines around his mouth deepened, and he wiped a tear from the corner of his eye. "Our Edmund is a clever fellow. I do believe he would have endangered your life purely for the pleasure of saving you."

I gasped. "But that's nonsense."

"Not really. Nothing like playing the knight in shining armor to impress a fair maiden. Only think how grateful young ladies can be to those who save their lives. I wager you've forgiven him all his many rudenesses."

In fact, I had. That made Winnie's statement all

the more offensive. The protests surged from me. "He couldn't possibly have known I would go into the cave."

Winnie shrugged. "I think it was a safe assumption. He happens to notice Sally's hat, knows you are unacquainted with the tides, and vocally announces his concerns for his sister. He only has to make himself absent and . . ." He opened his hands and then clapped them shut.

"I think you have read one too many fantastic tale, Mr. Winthrop," I said severely.

He grinned. "Perhaps. But you must not let Edmund take advantage of your gratitude."

"There is no fear of that."

The laughter faded from his eyes and his handsome face became grave. "You must know I am fond of you, Miss Carewe. Let me give you a word of warning. Edmund can be very cruel to women when he chooses. Be careful around him."

"If I am not, it will not be for lack of advice," I said crossly. "If you will excuse me, Mr. Winthrop, I think it is time I was getting back to the house."

I stalked off, all my good intentions forgotten. It served him right if I was rude, I thought. Insulting a man who had just saved my life.

I rounded the holly bushes and almost stumbled across Eglantine. She was crouching on the ground, oblivious to the damage she did her dress on the dew-soaked grass. Her taut hairknot always gave her a look of permanent surprise, but I thought she looked more startled than usual.

"Good morning, Mrs. Winthrop," I said politely, convinced she had heard me leave the house and followed me to discover if I was meeting her husband.

"Good morning," she said brusquely, and her cheeks turned a bright scarlet. "I was looking for—"

"Your husband is a short distance up the path," I said politely. "Sitting on the bench. I am surprised you did not hear us talking."

"I was looking for an *earring*. It dropped off and rolled beneath the bushes."

"May I help you?"

"I . . . I . . . ." She bent over and reached beneath a thicket of pointed leaves. "There. I have it now. Thank you, but you see there is no need."

"Then I shall leave you." I nodded to her politely and continued on my way.

As soon as the distance between us guaranteed me some privacy, I released the sigh I had been holding. It was not yet midday, and already I had fallen afoul of three of the five people I had encountered. It was as though we were all feeling and reflecting the tension around us without quite knowing what had ruffled our nerves.

I glanced up at Abbey House. The gray stone structure blotted out a large portion of the sky and cast a broad, diagonal shadow across the lawns toward my feet. It was as if some dark and ominous hand were pointing at me, singling me out for some evil fate. It was not the kind of thought to reassure someone who had nearly drowned the previous afternoon. I shivered and hurried into the house.

I nearly collided with Fanny.

She was running down the stairs, her yellow silk dress billowing around her, her cheeks pink with excitement. "Hilary!" she cried. "There you are. I was coming to find you." She waved a letter in the air in front of my nose, narrowly missing my eye. "I have had word from Mellie Spensser. What do you think she says?"

"It must be good news," I said, letting her high spirits chase away my somber mood.

She giggled, caught my arm in hers, and waltzed me into the parlor. Ursula, if she had ever been there, had left, and there was no one to disturb us. Fanny collapsed onto the sofa, dragging me with her.

She leaned back against the cushions and scanned the page. "Listen to this: 'Jane is getting too old for her nanny, and if this young woman comes with your recommendation we would be glad to interview her. Stuart will be driving back from London on the fourth'—that is today," she interjected—"'and will stop at Abbey House on the fifth to meet Miss Carewe. If she is suitable, he will expect her to leave with him. It will save us the trouble of sending the carriage back for her.' There!" She set the page on her lap and turned to me. "You could not have hoped for anything better. They are lovely people, and their daughter is a sweet little girl who could not possibly give you any trouble."

"Everything seems to be set," I managed to say, my emotions churning within me.

Fanny peered at me suspiciously. "What's the matter? You don't seem terribly pleased."

"I am," I insisted. "It's . . . it's just rather sudden."

"But it has been over a week. And you said this was what you wanted."

"Forgive me. I don't mean to appear ungrateful. I'm just a little overwhelmed."

Her brow puckered and then she smiled, and the doubt vanished from her face like clouds routed from the sky by a brilliant sun. "Of course you're overwhelmed. You haven't really recovered from your fright on the beach." Impulsively, she gave me a hug. "But there's nothing to worry about. You'll absolutely love them. You have my word."

"I'm certain I will," I agreed, finding any other response impossible in face of her conviction.

But, to myself, I said only that no decision needed to be made until tomorrow afternoon. I might not like Stuart Spensser. And, as Mr. Quarmby had pointed out to me, it would always be possible to obtain a governess's post.

Who knew what other avenues might be open to me?

14

Mrs. Medcroft set down her wine glass, wiped her mouth with her serviette, and looked at us from across the recently emptied desert plates. Her height gave her a commanding air. Simply by straightening her back and adopting a still pose, she drew all gazes to herself.

Fanny was the last to stop her chatter and twist in her chair to discover why she had lost her audience. She caught sight of Mrs. Medcroft's grave demeanor and choked off her rambling sentence. A smile flickered hesitantly on her face.

"Is something the matter?" she asked sweetly, relinquishing the stage without a murmur of protest.

Mrs. Medcroft took a deep breath and slowly released the air from her lungs. Appearing to have reached a state of perfect calm, she said, "Now that Hilary is feeling better, I am ready to continue my work. Tonight is the perfect night for a séance."

A mixture of gasps and groans met her announcement. Edmund jabbed his fork into the remains of his trifle and pushed his plate aside, nearly knocking over his glass of brandy.

Fanny paid him no notice. Excitement brightened her eyes. "Really? And why is that?"

"This is *Midsummer Night's Eve.* We could not ask for a more auspicious occasion."

Dr. Rhodes sank back against his chair and, although they had not slipped forward, he gave his spectacles a nervous push. It was the first evening he had joined us since the unfortunate incident in the music room, and everybody had studiously avoided mentioning the subject.

Until now.

Sally dropped a hand onto her friend's sleeve, and her pearl eardrops shivered against her neck. "Isn't that fortuitous, Fanny? Perhaps tonight you will learn the truth."

"And justice will be done," Mr. Quarmby finished with the fervor of a minister closing a prayer.

Ursula glared at the two of them. "Good Lord, haven't you caused enough trouble with these stupid games? It is time you put a stop to this, Edmund."

Instead of agreeing, he leaned back in his chair. His gaze darted to me, then returned to his sister's disgusted face. "This is Fanny's party, and I will not interfere."

Out of the corner of my eye, I saw Dr. Rhodes's cheeks flush.

"It has to be done," Mrs. Medcroft insisted, directing her arguments to Fanny. "Your mother's spirit will never find peace until her murderer has been caught."

"That's true," Sally agreed. "Really, Mr. Llewelyn. As an intelligent and reasonable man, don't you think

Fanny must do whatever she can to help her dear Mama?"

Mrs. Medcroft beamed at her. "My dear, your wisdom is refreshing. When I think of the ignorance I must battle . . ." She rubbed her temples and gave a little moan.

Fanny shook her arm free of Sally's hand, and glanced at me, her eyes solicitous. "How are you feeling, Hilary? Have you fully recovered?"

"Certainly she has," Mrs. Medcroft replied, giving me no chance to respond for myself. "Do you think I would risk her health?"

I sighed inwardly and wondered if her determination to hold this séance was due to my anticipated departure. I had, only an hour ago, warned her of the impending arrival of my prospective employer. Mrs. Medcroft had shrieked, collapsed on the sofa, and cried for her smelling salts. Between loosening her topmost buttons and gently slapping her cheeks, I had been forced to soothe her by telling her that nothing was definite. The decision to hire me hadn't been made; nor had I decided to accept.

I suspected she wished to use what might be our last evening together to show me the value of her profession.

"Hilary?" Fanny prompted, insistent on my answering her question.

I glanced at Mrs. Medcroft's anxious face. My feelings about the séances hadn't changed, and I knew the answer Edmund would want me to make. And yet a part of me knew I owed her something. I could not be the one to deny her.

"There is nothing wrong with me," I assured Fanny. "You need not consider me in your decision."

"Then, naturally, we must continue." She lifted her chin bravely. "It is what Mama would wish of me."

It was decided that we would meet in the parlor at midnight, Mrs. Medcroft having chosen the hour. Eglantine shuddered, but there was no changing Fanny's decision now that it had been made. Until then, we retired to our own rooms to wash and prepare ourselves.

Eglantine and Winnie were the first to retire, followed by Dr. Rhodes, who expressed a need for "a little fresh air." Edmund offered to accompany him, although not without a backward glance for me. There was a faint wistfulness to his expression, and I thought that, given the opportunity, he would rather have remained in my company. We had had no chance to speak alone since those frightening moments in the cave.

Sally, finding no reason to remain downstairs once Edmund had gone, decided her curls needed repair. Mr. Quarmby took Mrs. Medcroft's arm, and I followed upon their heels.

I was barely out the door, when Ursula said, "For goodness' sake, Fanny. I would think you would have more consideration for Kenneth. How do you think he feels about this?"

"Don't be silly. Kenneth didn't kill Mama. The truth could only be good for him."

"Does it ever occur to you that you are capable of making a mistake?"

"Really, Ursula. We both know I have made my fair share of mistakes. But having faith in Kenneth's innocence is not one of them. That," she added pointedly, "was your error."

If Ursula made any response to this, it escaped my ears.

*   *   *

In the parlor, nothing but the polished surface of the cherry wood table, the silver candlesticks, and our anxious faces were illuminated. Somewhere, a clock ticked and one of the chairs scraped against the floor. Mrs. Medcroft's incense tickled my nostrils, making it impossible to breathe without sucking in the sweet-smelling perfume, and I struggled to thwart a sneeze.

Serenely confident, she surveyed her gathering. "You cannot believe the emanations in this room tonight. They are overpowering. Already, I sense White Feather hovering at my shoulder."

She tilted her face, catching the candles' glow. With her raven hair melting into the darkness at her back, only the silver wings at her temples were visible. They arched away from her white face like thin streams of ectoplasm.

If she had tried to impress or startle her audience, she could not have done better. Eglantine muttered something under her breath, and I caught the word "witch." I had a feeling it was a good thing that the rest of the remark escaped me.

Edmund had taken the chair next to mine and captured my hand in his. His touch gave me a sense of safety I enjoyed only with him. Otherwise, he'd ignored the seating arrangements, saying nothing even when Sally slipped into the place on his left. Was that, I wondered, because of his unsuccessful efforts in the chapel?

Or was he distracted for another reason?

As I was distracted whenever he and I found ourselves in the same room?

He gave my hand a squeeze, immediately reminding me that it was those strong hands that had pulled me from the water. I glanced up at him to find his gaze resting on me, and his eyes shone with a glow brighter than any that could have been caused by the candles' flames.

In the darkness of the room, it was a simple matter to remember standing in the cave, caught in his embrace, and a pleasant shiver traveled up and down my body. From the slight smile curving at his lips, I suspected he was remembering those same moments. And with the same warm feelings.

As if to prove me right, he said, "Forgive me for not enquiring after you this morning. I . . . had some business matters that demanded my attention."

Instinctively, I knew he was lying. And all my suppositions were immediately brought into question. I frowned, once again confused and uncertain whether or not to trust him.

Sally smothered a titter. "Hilary said she was fine. Anyway, I imagine she doesn't want to be reminded of her own foolishness."

Stiffly, he turned to her. "I believe she was trying to make certain neither you nor Fanny were in danger."

"Or so she says."

Mrs. Medcroft frowned impatiently. Her loud sigh distracted Sally from the glare Edmund delivered her. As for me, I did not care what Sally either thought or chose to think. It was enough that Edmund did not suspect me of playing tricks to win his attentions. If only I could have been equally convinced of his own innocence.

"If we must do this, can we please get on with it?" Ursula said, her voice strained.

"It is not *my* fault we have not begun. I told you that I already felt White Feather's presence."

"I'm surprised the whole blessed tribe hasn't had time to file into the parlor," Eglantine muttered.

"Is it necessary to have an argument each time we do this?" Winnie asked cheerfully. "No wonder Lily is in a vile mood when she appears. She always was the most impatient creature."

Mrs. Medcroft nodded seriously. "You are quite right, Mr. Winthrop. Spirits are dependent upon the energies we exude. If we welcome her with love in our hearts—"

"She would think she had stumbled onto the wrong séance and depart," Eglantine finished. "That or that we had gone mad. Lily knew what we all thought of her."

"Now, now," Winnie protested. "Not all of us. I always admired the lady. You cannot say she was not a talented singer."

"It was what those of us with any sense thought," Ursula snapped. "You think the best of anything in skirts."

"Unless the lady in question is his own wife," Eglantine added.

"This is hardly the place or the time, my darling. And you do me an injustice. You know the depth of my feelings for you."

"Indeed I do."

Mr. Quarmby cleared his throat, thereby winning a grateful look from Mrs. Medcroft on his left. "And now, dear lady, shall I give the blessing?"

She nodded and, his moustache quivering, he rattled off the prayer. It was enough to bring an end to the verbal sparring, and the silence hastened around us like a guest who was impatiently waiting to be included. I could feel its weight upon my shoulders, heavy and forbidding. The darkness, too, seemed to come alive and fill with watchful faces. They swelled and retreated, and I was horribly reminded of the ebb and flow of the tide near Durdle Door.

"White Feather?"

Mrs. Medcroft's question met with a firm rap. Not the table-shattering rap of the chapel, but a good solid knock on the table's thick, cherry wood surface.

"There. I told you tonight would be a good night, did I not?" With eyes shut and body swaying, Mrs. Medcroft still managed a complacent smile. "White Feather, can you put us in touch with Mrs. Llewelyn?"

Her approach also showed greater confidence. Always before she had taken a circuitous route toward reaching Fanny's mother. Now she thrust headlong down a straight path, almost as though she knew her destination were within her grasp. I guessed her recent successes had had their affect on her.

"Perhaps you should say Mrs. Lily Llewelyn," Fanny suggested. "There were, after all, two of them, and I would hate for him to become confused."

Mr. Quarmby politely shushed her. "You mustn't distract her after she has gone into a trance. It breaks the link she has forged."

"But—"

"Shut up, Fanny, or we shall be here all night." Ursula cast a worried glance toward Dr. Rhodes.

He said nothing. Nor had he spoken since we'd entered the parlor. Was he hoping not to draw Lily's attention to himself again? What must he be suffering? And was proving his innocence worth subjecting him to this torture of anticipation? I was inclined to side with Ursula and say it was not.

Mrs. Medcroft's swaying grew more exaggerated. "I feel . . . I feel someone. Yes, yes. I'm certain it is she. But she is . . . she is hesitant."

"Then it can't be Lily." Eglantine chuckled at her own jest.

No one else joined her.

"She is afraid. She fears . . . she fears someone at this very table. That is why she is slow to appear." Mrs. Medcroft sighed victoriously as though she had leaped a great hurdle.

Ursula shifted in her chair. "More likely she wants to make an entrance."

"Please," Mrs. Medcroft protested. "White Feather says you must be more considerate of her feelings. She is delicate and sensitive. And very like her daughter."

"I would agree to the last statement," Ursula muttered. "The rest is sheer nonsense."

"There is someone here she loves deeply. Very deeply."

"Mama," Fanny said hopefully. "I love you too, Mama."

"No . . . no. This is . . . a different kind of love . . . the kind of love a woman can only feel for a man. It is for"—Mrs. Medcroft opened her eyes and stared directly at Edmund—"Mr. Llewelyn."

Sally gasped.

"I suppose she felt something for Papa," Ursula said, her voice cutting deliberately across the table. "No matter what we might have thought."

"Yes, I'm sure she did," Dr. Rhodes agreed, speaking at last. No doubt because he wanted to save Edmund the humiliation he had suffered. But I imagined Edmund would handle the situation with a great deal more aplomb than his future brother-in-law had done.

"But Mrs. Medcroft said she loves someone here," Fanny protested. "Papa is not here. She could only mean—"

"That Papa is also here in spirit," Ursula said

sharply. "I'm not surprised. He deserves a turn at the table."

I had to admire her loyalty to her brother. But even if she had not told me the truth—or if Fanny had not spoken—I would not have been fooled by her statements. I wondered if anyone else had been misled. Probably only Sally, and that because she refused to believe anything about Edmund that did not fit her image of him.

And, yet again, Mrs. Medcroft had said nothing that was not the truth. There had to be at least two people in our circle who were impressed with her abilities, however little they wanted to believe her.

She closed her eyes again. "I feel . . . I feel such an enormous outflowing of love, but there is also . . . *betrayal.*"

Here, she hesitated.

Thank the Lord. Let this end here. Let the roof fall in on us. Let the ground give way beneath our feet. Let anything happen save that she speak another word. I held my breath and gave all my concentration over to willing her continued silence.

Mrs. Medcroft opened her mouth to speak.

And was forestalled by the sound of a woman's footsteps.

They came from outside the parlor. It should have been impossible to hear anything softer than a heavy tread through the thick door, and yet these footsteps succeeded in being both light *and* impossible to ignore. They started upstairs. On the landing, I guessed without a moment's hesitation.

But each step brought them closer.

Our small circle froze. No one spoke nor moved. Not an eyelash flickered on the pale faces I saw around me. Indeed, it seemed we hardly dared breathe. The tension flowed through our tightly clasped hands and, although Mr. Llewelyn didn't stir, I could feel his anxiety.

For himself?

Or for someone else in this room who he suspected of murder?

A log—I thought it was a log—crackled on the hearth, a dry, papery crackle, like an old taffeta dress being removed from tissue where it had been stored for a decade or more. It mingled with the sounds of the footsteps, one seeming to incite the other. And the fragrance of attar of roses seeped beneath the door and drenched the air like a heavy smoke.

"It's Lily. That's her scent. I always said you could smell her coming from fifty yards." Eglantine shuddered and leaned toward her husband.

Winnie shifted in his chair. "I hardly think this is the right moment for insults."

"For God's sake, Edmund," Ursula urged. "Get up and light one of the lamps."

"You must not break the circle," Mr. Quarmby protested. "It could be dangerous."

"To hell with your circle," she countered. "I simply cannot stand a repetition of the last two . . . appearances."

"And nor can Fanny," Dr. Rhodes added. Despite his agreement, he didn't—or couldn't—budge.

Edmund alone seemed to have retained his presence of mind. He dropped my hand and pushed back his chair, but did not immediately leave the table. Instead, he struggled with something on the other side of him.

"Will you please release me, Mrs. Pritchard?" he demanded abruptly, providing us with the answer to that mystery.

"I can't," she whimpered. "Dear God, I can't."

Any response he might have made was interrupted by a quick series of raps on the parlor door. It popped open, revealing a dark and empty corridor.

Eglantine shrieked. Edmund forgot his struggle with Sally and placed a protective arm about my shoulders. I raised my hands to guard the candle flame and waited for the gust of cold air I expected to come.

It didn't.

The temperature dropped and something like a fine mist swirled or rather danced into the parlor. Unlike the mist in the chapel, this had a definite shape. There were the head and gracefully sloping shoulders of a woman. A slender figure with nipped-in waist and a provocatively high bosom. Although the features of her face were indistinct, I felt rather than saw the arched brows, the upturned nose, and the full, sensuous lips.

You are imagining things, I told myself sharply.

If so, it was not an image I could shake.

Lily Llewelyn—if indeed it was she—drifted toward the table, and that cold amusement I had felt on the landing and again in the music room flooded my senses. A mixture of pity and apprehension welled within me, and I surreptitiously glanced at Dr. Rhodes. He looked pale and his hands were trembling splashes of white against the blackness that surrounded us. But whatever he was feeling, he devoted his attention to Fanny and not himself.

She was rooted to her chair, her fingers clenched tightly around her fiancé's wrist, her gaze following the apparition's approach. Her mouth opened and she whispered, "Mama? Mama—"

Instead of moving toward her, the white shape

oozed around the far side of the table and from some-where above our heads came a throaty, satisfied chuckle. Not at all the sound of a woman who was displeased with her lover.

I held my breath. Was it to Edmund she was walking?

To my relief and even greater surprise, the pres-ence hovered near Winnie's shoulder, and a lazy warmth spread over the room like a thick blanket. Good Lord, was there anyone this woman hadn't seduced? Although I doubted Winnie had objected to her attentions. He may well have invited them. But Mrs. Medcroft had talked about a deep love. This was nothing more than satisfaction.

A purely physical satisfaction.

In the still room, something ruffled through Winnie's tawny hair. Invisible fingers? Or had unseen lips pursed to blow warm air through his curls? The tips of his ears looked red, even in the candlelight, but only his unnaturally rigid posture proved him to be both aware of and discomfited by her ghostly caress.

There was a soft, derisive titter that might have come from anywhere in the parlor. But it wasn't directed at Winnie, as Lily's laughter had been directed at Dr. Rhodes. Instead, it was shared with him. It floated around his head, inviting and coaxing him to join her. And, although he neither moved nor spoke, I had the feeling that he had, in the past, taken part in that cruel amusement.

And, with a gasp, I realized it was at Eglantine they had laughed.

Eglantine Winthrop must have reached that same conclusion an instant later. She rose with a shriek and lunged at the mist. Her fingers tore at the intangible white drifts. They parted around her attack, only to congeal again the instant her nails had raked them.

Although she must have been nearly fifty, she was a strong woman, large-boned and used to regular exercise. But her strength was useless against a phantom. The titters grew louder. They hardened. They blotted out every other sound in the room, like black oil pouring over a painting.

"For God's sake, stop. You're making things worse." Winnie caught his wife's wrists and held them fast, ending her onslaught but not her angry tears.

"Damn you, Lily," she screamed through her hiccups. "Why can't you stay dead? You never loved him. You only wanted to torment me, the way you tormented any woman who had the good sense to despise you. The way you tormented your stepdaughter by taking her—"

"That's enough, Eglantine," Ursula protested, yelling to be heard over the laughter and her friend's sobs. "Do be quiet. This is a game she's playing. And you're doing exactly what she wants you to do."

"Why should I be quiet? It's a game she played with my husband for more than ten years. Since the day she came to Abbey House. Don't any of you try to pretend otherwise."

"You're upsetting yourself for no reason," Winnie argued, neither admitting nor denying the accusation.

His wife glared at him. "No reason. She stole you from me, and she didn't even want you, whatever she might have pretended when you were alone together. Not after she learned that you had no money outside of the allowance my father paid you."

Abruptly, the laughter stopped. The mist melted into nothingness. The fire spread a warm glow over the room. Only the faint scent of attar of roses lingered to prove that anything odd had occurred.

In the silence, Sally groaned and collapsed against Edmund.

Had she fallen in the opposite direction, her misfortune might have been taken more seriously. But we had all been stretched to the end of our patience. None of us was prepared to deal with another disaster, especially not one that had been created for no more reason than to gain Edmund's attention.

Irritated, he propped her back into her chair and asked, "Would you mind seeing to her, Kenneth?"

"Are you all right, Fanny?" he asked, reluctant to leave his fiancée's side for an attack we all knew was pretense.

She nodded, not much distressed, and her Cupid's-bow mouth pursed thoughtfully. Dr. Rhodes hesitated. Impatiently, she brushed him away with a wave. "You're being silly, Kenneth. There's nothing the matter with me."

He rose and glanced briefly at Sally's healthy pink cheeks. "By any chance do you still have those smelling salts, Mrs. Medcroft?"

Immediately, Sally moaned and her eyelids fluttered open. "Where am I?" she mumbled and hopefully cast her gaze about for Edmund.

He was setting a lamp on the table, his broad back to her, and he had the forbearance and good sense not to glance in her direction. His expression, captured in full detail by the lamplight, would have crushed her.

An awkward silence followed Sally's question. Ursula looked meaningfully at her sister. "Fanny, since you aren't upset by this latest encounter, perhaps you would be good enough to help Kenneth take

Sally to her room." Without giving her a chance to reply, she immediately addressed Edmund. "Do you think she's really gone?"

"There isn't any reason for her to stay."

"And what do you mean by that?" Winnie demanded.

Edmund surveyed the table's occupants, a badly concealed sneer on his face. "She's done what she came to do, hasn't she? I imagine we've heard the last of her. For tonight, at any rate."

"And just what is it you think she came to do?" Mr. Quarmby asked.

Mrs. Medcroft looked apprehensively at Eglantine and Winnie. "Surely she meant to name her murderer."

"On the contrary," Edmund countered. "Lily delighted in provoking people. She will not deliver the last line to this performance until she has exacted every ounce of enjoyment there is to be had."

"But she must." Mrs. Medcroft's hands fluttered to the amber lavaliere at her throat. In a softer voice, she mumbled, "She simply must. I cannot maintain the connection between us forever. Even now, it may be gone."

"We can always hope," Ursula retorted. "Would anyone like a cup of tea?"

That night, we again retired late. Edmund, or rather Mr. Llewelyn—I told myself I must not allow that one all-too-brief moment in the cave to affect my perceptions, but must force myself to remember we were little more than strangers—Mr. Llewelyn glanced at me wistfully, as though he hoped to speak with me alone, but Mrs. Medcroft hurried me upstairs. I could do nothing but glance helplessly over my shoulder at him.

Our gazes met, and there was a connection between us that was tangible. We might have been linked by an invisible cord. My heart tightened, causing an unfamiliar ache. I desperately wanted to call out to him, but there was nothing to say that could be said in a roomful of people.

And had we been alone, what could I have said save that I was grateful to him for having saved my life? That was something he already knew.

Mrs. Medcroft lingered at my door, her hands pulling at the knot in her strand of pearls. "You cannot know the fondness I have come to feel for you in this short while we have been together. Losing you would be like losing your dear mother all over again. I doubt my heart can bear the strain."

"I have not yet made *any* decision," I reminded her. "Nor is there any need for us to separate completely now that we have become acquainted."

I kissed her firmly on the cheek. Her skin was papery and smelt faintly of lavender. She herself looked much like the dried flower, rustling in mauve taffeta, a sense of determined and careful preservation clinging to her. I had the sudden conviction that she was markedly older than she either professed or appeared. Nearer her late fifties than forties.

Was that why she clung to me? Because she feared being old and alone? I gave her a second kiss, a more compassionate and willing kiss than the first.

Something of my greater understanding was clear to her. She managed a brave smile and dropped her beads. "I shall say a prayer to your mother, begging her to give you the necessary guidance. I know this life is what she would wish for you." She bid me good-night and retired to her own rooms.

I wished I shared her confidence.

Sleep came quickly, and with it an odd dream from which there seemed no escape. I knew myself to be in bed and yet I found myself walking down a dark corridor. My bare feet padded across a coarse carpet, and my nightgown flapped against my legs. Not the flannel nightgown I remembered, but a concoction of lace and silk that clung to me, defining and revealing those parts of my body that were not already revealed by the dangerously low neckline and thin, almost transparent, fabric.

All around me it was dark. The doors to either side were tightly shut. No light escaped the rooms that lay beyond those forbidding doors. But finding my way was easy. It was as though I had walked that corridor again and again, both in my mind and in actuality. I had no need of anything but my own memory to guide me.

I should have been frightened. The overwhelming darkness. The narrow corridor confining me. The sense of being completely alone. These were the ingredients of a nightmare.

Instead, I was utterly happy, serene with a confidence that was hitherto unknown to me. I felt an energy within myself that told me I could do anything, have anything. Have *anyone*. Had I been awake, I might have realized that there was something unnatural, even insane, about my attitude. No one could be possessed of that much power.

But I was not awake.

I was dreaming.

And in my dream all things were possible.

My heartbeat quickened and my excitement rose within me, burning like a fire that could not be quenched. Something flared in my mind, and I knew where I was going. To whom I was going.

Edmund.

Handsome, desirable Edmund.

The only man who had ever struggled to resist me. Who stubbornly refused what I had to offer. I had been foolish to think he would surrender to a mere kiss. To unbound curls and a glimpse of cleavage. It would take more than that to break down his resistance. A great deal more.

And he would have more. Tonight. This time he would not push me from him as he had done in the glade. This time he would welcome me into his arms.

Into his bed.

I shivered happily and envisioned his surprise to find me there, saw his smile flash, his arms reaching for me to pull me against him. I imagined the feel of his mouth, enjoyed the pleasure of those strong, full lips sweeping over mine. I nuzzled against him and mentally traced the line of his upper lip, lingered at the indentation beneath his nose to savor the brush of air from his nostrils against my face.

A light sigh escaped me.

What it would be like to take his hands and press them against my naked breasts, feel their softness flatten beneath his palms, my nipples harden between his fingers. He hadn't the strength to resist those warm, compliant mounds of flesh that had been made for his caresses.

It would be exquisite. I trembled with happy anticipation.

The silken nightgown shivered down the full length of my body, brushing across my thighs with the slight abrasion of a man's fingertips. Edmund's fingertips. Sweet, sweet Edmund. I was almost glad he had made me wait, made us both wait for the joy that would be ours.

And when I knew Edmund was mine, truly mine, I would leave him. It would be his punishment for making me wait. For making me beg for his touch.

I threw back my head, aware without benefit of a looking glass that my throat would be a delicate arch of white against the darkness. Unbidden, the laughter rose in my throat. Like a thick, golden syrup it streamed through the night, a honeyed stream that flowed through the corridor ahead of me, rushing to Edmund's door.

I hurried in its wake. Edmund. Already, I could taste him. A delicious male taste. Salty like sea spray, faintly dry like an expensive champagne. And equally intoxicating. In my mind, I ran the tip of my tongue across his chin and down his throat. I could feel his neck muscles constrict, sense the groan that escaped him and feel his arms tighten around me.

Tonight, they would not release me.

A carousel of erotic sensations and images spun in my mind. His hands sliding eagerly down my naked back to my waist. His fingers encircling me. His eyes amazed by the slender perfection they encompassed. The weight of his body atop mine, crushing me, flattening me beneath him with a lover's cruelty. His legs entangled with mine, wrestling them apart. The sweet, burning delight of being entered. Of being possessed and possessing. Of wrapping my legs around him and squeezing, imprisoning him, taking from him what he had unkindly withheld. Enslaving him as he had enslaved me.

My head spun. I was drunk with anticipation and desire. My hand lifted of its own accord; my fingers brushed a knob and turned. The door was unlocked and opened silently.

Easily.

Had it always been this simple to go to him?

Moonlight spilled through the open window, and the curtain billowed and swayed with a gentle summer breeze. Edmund was asleep in bed, his dark head outlined against his pillow. His chest rose and fell, and the only sound in the room was the soft exhalation of his breath.

I stared down at him, savoring what was to be mine. One by one, I undid the pearl buttons of my nightgown and impatiently shrugged it from my shoulders. It fell about my feet, forgotten. I sighed and leaned forward until my fingers brushed across his cheek.

He stirred and his eyes flickered open. His gaze fell on me and I waited happily for him to reach for me. For one drawn-out moment he gaped up at me, and his gaze swept me from head to toe, absorbing every inch of me, wanting me as I wanted him.

Slowly, his gaze returned to my face, and he drew a ragged breath. "Good God. Hilary. What in heaven's name are you doing?"

15

His question shocked me into full consciousness. I was awake. Standing above Edmund's bed. Naked.

Wholly and humiliatingly naked.

I gasped. The room spun treacherously around me. And I crumpled to the floor.

I awakened disoriented and confused. That I was in bed, I quickly realized. Also that it was still night, for the room was dark and a silvery moon trailed across my coverlets. But my French doors had become windows, and they had moved to the opposite wall. And the room smelled faintly of a man's shaving soap.

I struggled to make sense of where I was and what was happening. The remnants of an odd dream clung to me, like a soft echo that would not completely fade. Slowly, memory returned, and with that memory its devastating conclusion.

I gasped and tried to sit up.

Firm hands pushed me back onto the bed.

Edmund. Dear Lord, what had I done? And what could I expect from him? What could any woman expect who came to a man's bedroom in the middle of the night and disrobed? I moaned and twisted my head about and buried my face in the pillow.

"Hilary," he murmured in a hoarse voice that was barely recognizable as his. "Are you all right?"

Nothing would be right again. What would he think of me? He'd never believe my tale of dreaming and sleepwalking. I would be no better than Sally Pritchard in his eyes, just another woman who wished to seduce a rich and handsome man. And compared to my deplorable behavior, she was a model of virtue and discretion.

"Hilary? For God's sake, answer me," he insisted, fear seeping into his voice.

Mouth dry, I croaked, "Forgive me. I . . . I . . ."

"There's nothing to forgive." He reached for my hand and pressed my fingers to his lips. He held them there, unwilling to release them, and I did not resist.

"Do you think you can get dressed?" he managed finally.

Dressed? He wanted me to leave? It was not enough that I had ruined myself forever, he did not even want me. All he asked was that I pull myself together and put on my nightgown. I burst into hysterical giggles.

His hand covered my mouth, smothering my laughter. "Sorry, my darling," he muttered. "But you must be quiet. If anyone were to guess you were here . . ."

What would they do? Expect him to marry me? Was that what he feared? Of course it was. He was the last man to want to be burdened with a wife, let alone a wife who had shown herself to be everything he despised.

But why had he called me his darling? Or had I heard only what I wanted to hear?

"I can manage," I said. "Please, give me a minute alone."

I stifled another burst of hysteria. It was a little late for either modesty or decorum. But I simply could not have dressed before his gaze. And struggling to pull on my nightgown beneath the covers would have left me open to greater ridicule.

"If you are certain you will be all right," he said politely.

"Yes, thank you."

It was inconceivable. Here I was, lying in his bed, his blankets pulled up to my throat to hide my nakedness, and our remarks were unquestionably well-mannered and correct. We might have been at tea, passing a plate of finger sandwiches.

The cucumber is very fresh, don't you think?

I do. Did they come from your greenhouse, Mr. Llewelyn?

They did.

Truly delightful. I have always had a taste for cucumbers.

Unaware of the insane dialogue running through my head, he rose and left the room. His room. I immediately threw back the blankets and reached for my nightgown. It had been laid neatly across the bottom of the bed. As though it belonged there.

As though I belonged there.

I dressed, fastened the buttons, and pulled down the sleeves to cover my wrists. It was not enough. Had I been wearing my traveling suit with a heavy mantle thrown over my shoulders and a veiled hat atop my head, it would not have been enough. I would never again feel properly dressed in his company. Even the thought of sitting down to a meal in his presence made my cheeks burn.

Thankful that he had no lamp to shed light on my embarrassment, I walked into the corridor. His head lifted, a dark shadow against a background of shadows. And I, thank God, would be the same to him. I caught the movement of his arm, reaching toward me, and hastily stepped backward.

In a low voice that could not have been heard in any of the nearby rooms, he apologized for frightening me. "I thought you might need some support."

"I can manage, thank you."

"Nevertheless, I intend to see you to your room."

"I can find my own way. There is no need."

"Forgive me, but I would not rest easily if I left you here."

Did he think I would come creeping back? Or did he merely intend to bury this incident beneath a continued wealth of good manners? If so, I would certainly support his efforts.

There was a sense of unreality to everything that was happening to me. Perhaps I would awaken a second time, this time to discover that, from start to finish, it had been nothing more than a dream.

Or a nightmare.

We padded down the corridor together, neither of us speaking. I wondered if he was as aware of me as I was of him. Another horrible possibility, for I could think of nothing but the length of his stride. His nearness. The warmth of his body. And worst of all were the vivid memories of my waking dream. I had not known myself to be capable of such thoughts.

Another question struck me and my stomach lurched into my throat.

Did the memory of my nakedness linger in his mind?

It took forever to reach my door. Each second was like an hour. We might have trudged in silence for miles. For days. I gazed upon my room with unbelieving eyes, incapable of understanding that the torture had come to an end.

Edmund caught my arm, preventing me from making my escape and sending hot shivers coursing up my spine. "Hil . . . Miss Carewe, before you leave, there is something you must know. I have given the matter some thought and have come to a decision."

"Yes, Mr. Llewelyn?" I said, civil to the end.

"You cannot remain at Abbey House."

"Of course." I smiled inanely, a smile he could not see, but could have heard in my voice. "It would be better if nothing were said of this, you understand. I will think of some explanation—if one becomes necessary. There is every chance I will be leaving tomorrow with Fanny's friend."

"Who?" he demanded, in a manner that had suddenly ceased to be civil.

Oh, Lord. Would he ruin any hope I might have of departing his home with a modicum of dignity? Surely he would not refer to what happened rather than let me enter a respectable house. If he did, where would I go? And what would I say when I got there?

"Who is she expecting?" he demanded again.

I forced myself to answer. "A Mr. Spensser. She received word of him today. He is stopping here tomorrow to interview me."

"Good Lord, I had forgotten about the governess post."

"There was no reason for you to remember. Why should you concern yourself with my affairs? You have more than enough troubles of your own to—"

"Nonsense." He cut across my words. "I promised to take responsibility for you while you were here. It seems I have let you down badly," he added ruefully.

Let me down? Surely the reverse was true.

"Go to bed, Hilary," he ordered softly. "We can talk about all of this tomorrow."

I did not go downstairs that morning, being both tired and thoroughly embarrassed. Instead, Chaitra brought me up my breakfast on a tray. I deliberately ate late, thereby giving myself an excuse to avoid luncheon as well—or, more accurately, to avoid Mr. Llewelyn.

Mr. Spensser arrived shortly after midday, his carriage pulled by a sleek pair of matched chestnut geldings that were the equal of any in the Llewelyn's stables. They came to an abrupt halt directly across from the arched double doors, and he jumped down, a broad grin on his face.

I glimpsed him from my balcony, a gentleman in his late twenties with bushy side whiskers, sandy hair, and sculptured features. Looking down at him from above, he seemed short and slight of build, but he may have been taller than the angle suggested. Unaware he was being watched, he raised his head to the second-story windows and called loudly for Fanny.

Rather an unconventional young man, I thought, knowing by that single act he would have destroyed himself forever in my father's eyes.

But surely I was capable of being more open-minded.

Fifteen minutes later, Fanny pounded on my door. Too impatient to wait for a maid, she had rushed upstairs in search of me herself. Her ringlets quivered around her face and there was a delicate pink flush to her cheeks that might or might not have been caused by her dash up the stairs.

"Do hurry, Hilary. Stuart's waiting to talk to you."

She hastened me into the front parlor. I took a deep breath, half expecting to smell attar of roses, but there was nothing but the aroma of pipe tobacco and the sweet scent of fresh air sweeping through the open windows.

Mr. Spensser rose as we entered. "It is a pleasure to meet you, Miss Carewe. Fanny has been extolling your virtues." He flashed a smile at her, disclosing a crooked front tooth that did little to mar his good looks.

"That is very kind of her," I said politely. "She has been very good to me in the short while we have known each other."

"If you overlook my almost getting you drowned," she retorted with a cheerful grin. With Sally's help, of course.

Far from looking startled, Mr. Spensser laughed ruefully. From the sound, I suspected he had suffered a few accidents around Fanny himself. Although I didn't blame either her or Sally for my near disaster; the windblown bonnet's landing near the cave had caused an accident that could not truly be blamed on anyone.

"Shall we sit down?" Fanny suggested, comfortably settling herself in a tufted armchair to oversee the proceedings.

I took the straightback chair and left Mr. Spensser in full possession of the sofa. He leaned back against the cushions and crossed his legs at the ankle. His careless sprawl, while inappropriate, made him look taller than his five feet eight inches.

"Perhaps you would be willing to tell me something of your history," he suggested.

"I am completely without experience," I admitted, rather more eagerly than I should have done.

"But she has excellent references," Fanny said in my behalf.

I nodded and handed him the letters written by the minister and my father's solicitors. They had arrived the day before yesterday. Both were lengthy, being several pages apiece, and filled with accounts of my reliability, my honesty, and my excellent character. I had blushed in reading them and had to remind myself that neither of the two writers wished to be responsible for my upkeep.

Mr. Spensser gave them a cursory glance. "Well, everything certainly seems to be in order. I think you will be exactly what Jane needs."

"Naturally, you will wish to do a thorough search into my background."

He looked faintly surprised, as though the idea had not occurred to him. "I see no need. Anyway, you'll find my wife and I are simple people. Just keep Jane out of our hair and we'll be satisfied. She can be a pest at times."

I didn't wonder. Her father, at least, showed a horrible lack of concern for her welfare. Fanny hadn't known me long enough, and was too frivolous, to be regarded as a competent judge of either my character or my capabilities. And he had practically ignored the letters of reference. What kind of a man was he?

"Are your bags all packed?" he asked, startling me yet again.

"As a matter of fact, they are not."

"We only got your letter yesterday," Fanny said hastily. "Anyway, you'll want to stay for tea. Hilary will have plenty of time to get her things together."

"Fair enough." He dismissed me from his thoughts and turned to her with a smile. "Now, how about a glass of brandy for the weary traveler?"

I left them together, ostensibly excusing myself to go and pack my bags. But what I really needed was time to think. Was this what I wanted? To go with this handsome, careless stranger who thought more of creature comforts than he did of his own child?

What kind of life could I anticipate in his household?

Was that the life I wanted for myself?

And how could I possibly answer those questions in the few short hours remaining to me? I threw myself on the bed and buried my face in the soft pillows, determined to shut out all distractions—the sunlight cascading through the French doors, the cheerful flowered wallpaper, the glossy walnut furnishings—and concentrate only on the decision that had to be made.

The image of Edmund Llewelyn floated into my mind.

I rolled over on my back with a groan. This was not a simple matter of choice. He had insisted I leave his house. With good reason. And having been offered a post with the Spenssers, I could hardly protest I had nowhere to go. I should have been grateful he was willing to accept me into his home. After all, it was either that or make plans to return to Bristol immediately.

Or tell Mrs. Medcroft the truth and beg her to take me back to London.

None of the options appealed to me. I wandered out onto the balcony, stared across the rolling lawns, and tried to sort through my confused emotions.

I did not want to hurt Mrs. Medcroft, but nor did assisting her in her calling appeal to me. Our coming to Abbey House had caused nothing but trouble. And if we had discovered a murder, we hadn't unmasked the murderer. Nor were the authorities likely to accept the word of a ghost and a spiritualist. All we had done was disrupt the lives of a number of people, and only one of them could have been guilty of the crime.

But returning to Bristol would be like stepping back into the past. That, too, held no appeal. I would only be a burden to those who took me in—and they were too good to refuse me. As for me, I would not be happy confined to a way of life I had outgrown.

That left only the Spenssers and what promised to be a careless, disorganized household. Mr. Stuart Spensser reminded me too much of Winnie. Would I be forced to fend him off for the years I lived beneath his roof? What woman would tolerate me in her household under those circumstances?

I smiled ruefully. Mr. Quamby had been right. There were several avenues open to me. What he hadn't realized was that none of them would be acceptable.

Nor did it help that what I wanted was the most preposterous and unlikely possibility. Despite all the warnings I had been given, I had fallen in love with Edmund. Why else would I have traipsed to his room in the middle of the night? I was being led by emotions I had tried and failed to suppress.

There was a noise behind me, and I glanced over my shoulder. Fanny was letting herself into my bedroom. She gave the door a quick push, banging it shut behind her, and twirled around to look for me. Finding the room empty, my portmanteau laying open and empty on the bed, her happy smile faded and her eyebrows drew together in a concerned frown.

"I'm out here," I called.

She looked up, saw me, and recovered her smile. "I came up to give you a hand. Is something wrong? Now that I think about it, you did seem a bit flustered in the parlor."

I nodded slowly. "I was not overly impressed with Mr. Spensser's manner."

"Why ever not? I thought he was perfectly charming."

"Charming, yes. But . . . he would have given more care to purchasing a horse than he did to hiring me," I said, reluctant to admit to the real reason for my doubts.

She shrugged. "Oh, that. Edmund's always accused the Spenssers of being irresponsible. But compared to him, who isn't? Anyway, that's all the more reason for you to accept the position. Poor little Jane needs someone who'll look out for her."

It was a fair argument, one that might have been designed to appeal to me. I had, after all, expressed a desire to do something worthwhile. Now that the opportunity had arisen, it was churlish of me to object. Nor was there anything to keep me at Abbey House, whatever I might have wished. Nevertheless, I simply couldn't bring myself to remove my dresses from the wardrobe. It was as though something had drained the will and energy from me and all I wanted to do was lie down and go to sleep.

Fanny studied my face, and her lavender-blue eyes shimmered with expectation. Unable to meet her gaze, I stared down at my hands and fiddled with the buttons on my sleeve.

"Oh, good heavens, Hilary," she cried. "You can't back out now. Everything's all arranged. I thought you wanted to escape from Mrs. Medcroft."

"Hardly escape," I protested. "It is only that I didn't think myself suited to life as her assistant."

"Well, nothing has changed. Or has it?"

I shook my head.

"There. Stop being silly and let's get your belongings packed. Stuart will want to leave right after tea."

Ringlets bouncing at the crown of her head, she hurried to the wardrobe and began pulling my dresses from their hangers. One by one, she tossed them on the bed, until they lay in a heap next to my portmanteau.

I trailed after her and watched her work, but could not bring myself to help. Having emptied the wardrobe, she opened the drawers of the dressing table and gathered up the oddments she found there.

"Is Mr. Spensser in love with you?" I asked, surprising myself with my own question.

She looked up, faintly surprised, then smiled complacently. "He might have been. Once. Perhaps he still likes to think he loves me."

"He asked you to marry him, didn't he?" I continued, pursuing a course that was none of my business, nor made any sense to me.

She looked at me curiously. "Aren't you the astute one? Yes, he did. He was quite crushed when I refused."

"Why did you refuse him? I would have thought that . . ." I stopped, reason returning to me. My next remark would have gone far beyond the boundaries of good manners.

Fanny gave her ringlets a toss and laughed. "That he was more to my taste than Kenneth?"

I nodded.

"But Kenneth has something that Stuart did not." Her lips curved at the corners. "I shall let you discover the answer to that question. If you are able before you leave here," she added cheerfully.

There was little likelihood of that. As well she knew. But I had a strong suspicion that whatever her reasons, she wished to keep them to herself. Likely because they would not show her off to good advantage.

"You need not finish," I said quietly, nodding at the pile of garments on the bed. "Chaitra will come and help me if I ask."

She paused in the middle of folding a cotton petticoat. "As you wish. Only remember, you'll have to hurry if you wish to eat before you go."

"I won't forget," I promised.

She dropped the undergarment in my portmanteau and carefully smoothed out the wrinkles. Then she straightened, brushed my cheek with a kiss, and glided to the door. Her hand touched the knob and she paused. "Shall I invite you to the wedding? The Spenssers will be driving up from Weymouth."

My heart jumped. It would be my chance to see Edmund again. Perhaps, in the intervening months, he would have forgiven me for my behavior. He might remember our brief friendship and that fleeting moment in the cave.

I caught Fanny's amused look. "That would be most kind of you," I managed.

"Then we shall expect to see you." She disappeared into the corridor, leaving me to my thoughts.

And the hope she had stirred within my breast.

With a sigh, I began sorting through the muddle of garments she had left in her wake. It was a slow process, made slower by my own reluctance. I had only half-finished when I realized I had said nothing to Mrs. Medcroft. Good Lord. How could I have forgotten? I dropped the dress in my hands, shocked by my complete lack of consideration.

I hastened from my room, forgetting everything but the need to speak with her and tell her of my decision. If such it could be called. The carpet muffled my footsteps, but I hadn't gone more than a few feet when Mr. Quarmby emerged from his doorway.

"Hilary, my dear. I thought that might be you. Have you a minute to spare for me?"

I glanced doubtfully at Mrs. Medcroft's suite.

"It is a matter of some importance," he added.

I sighed inwardly, but nodded.

He motioned for me to join him and, completely ignoring propriety, hurried me into his bedroom. It was much like my own but had no balcony, and the furnishings were of dark oak instead of walnut. His personal possessions were nowhere to be seen, but were all tucked out of sight in either the large wardrobe or the dressing table. Even his straight razor and shaving brush had been removed from the washstand.

Mr. Quarmby started to close his door behind us, but a glance from me stopped him. "Of course, of course," he muttered. "I wasn't thinking." His forefinger nervously brushed his moustache.

"What was it you wanted, Mr. Quarmby?"

"I have something to show you."

He reached into his inner coat pocket and produced a small wad of tissue. The tip of his tongue flickered nervously over his lips and, tissue crackling in the silence, he folded back the corners. Trembling, he produced a narrow golden band that was set with a small diamond.

"What do you think?" he asked, his black eyes glittering more brightly than the stone.

The tension that had been building within me seeped away in a rush. So that was it. He did intend to ask Mrs. Medcroft to marry him. I almost staggered beneath the weight of my relief. If he meant to propose to her this same afternoon, he could not have chosen a more fortuitous moment. In the excitement of planning her wedding, Mrs. Medcroft would hardly notice my absence. Actually, my presence would be more of an unwelcome intrusion than a blessing.

I took the ring from Mr. Quarmby's shaking fingers. "It's lovely. Absolutely lovely."

His shoulders sagged, making me realize the depth of his anxiety.

I gave him an encouraging smile. "Mrs. Medcroft will be very pleased. She loves you dearly."

He blinked rapidly, looking horribly like a startled frog. "But it is for you. I am asking for your hand in marriage."

"Me?" I gaped at him.

He nodded. "You seem surprised. When we spoke yesterday, I assumed you understood."

"But I had no idea this was what you meant."

"Surely you are pleased."

"No. I mean, I'm sorry, but your offer is entirely unexpected." Oh, good heavens. Now what was I to do? Desperately fumbling for words, I pressed the ring back into his hands. "Forgive me, but I couldn't possibly accept. I've always supposed that you and Mrs. Medcroft were"—I could hardly say lovers—"friends. No, more than friends."

"But we are merely business partners. You are the lady who has captured my heart." He deliberately ignored or forgot the numerous occasions I had sat in their company, listening to him blatantly flatter her, and boldly proffered the ring I had returned to him. "Will you not consider me? I wish only to make you happy. It does not matter if you do not love me. Our love is destined to grow over the long years we will share with one another."

If he had been less earnest, and I less discomfited, I might have burst into laughter. His words sounded as though they had been culled from a badly written melodrama. Part of me was convinced they had been.

"Forgive me, Mr. Quarmby. But Mrs. Medcroft thinks more highly of you than you realize. Were I to accept your offer, she would deem it a betrayal of gargantuan proportions."

My answer might have been drawn from the same script as his proposal. I managed to stop myself before I added something about "a love that could never be." After all, I did not want him to decide we were star-crossed lovers, doomed to die by our own hands.

But I had underestimated my suitor.

"I tell you, she means nothing to me. Why, she is a good fifteen or twenty years my senior." The flowery speeches were gone, and his voice had a cold edge. "And you, my dear, are faced with the choice of becoming a poorly paid servant to some spoiled brat, or the companion of a whiny old woman. What kind of life would that be for a beautiful young lady?"

"Not all children are spoiled. Any more than all elderly women are whiny. Certainly, Mrs. Medcroft—"

"You cannot imagine the kind of life you could have with me," he bragged. "I could give you all of

London. We could travel the continent together. What young person would not want that kind of life?"

There was a passionate gleam in his eyes, but that passion did not seem to be for me. Something told me it was only for himself. That conviction made a firm response easier. "Forgive me, Mr. Quarmby," I said flatly. "But I am convinced I would not be happy with you. Indeed, I find your person quite distasteful. And now, if you will excuse me."

Startled by my vehemence, he withdrew a step and I found my path clear. I thanked God for my escape and rushed from his room.

I didn't pause to catch my breath until I stood outside Mrs. Medcroft's suite. After gathering the shreds of my composure, I knocked on her door.

There was no answer.

Neither she nor Chaitra were in the suite. I realized that it was past midday and that both of them were probably downstairs having luncheon. And possibly Mrs. Medcroft would be learning from Fanny or Mr. Spensser of my new position. I could not let that happen.

Picking up my skirt, I dashed for the stairs. It was an unladylike rush, but one I thought no one was likely to see. To my dismay, I reached the landing only to find Edmund—or rather Mr. Llewelyn, as I had told myself I must address him—coming up the stairs. I skidded to a halt and dropped my skirts, wondering if I could possibly sink any lower in his estimation than I had already done.

To my surprise, he paid my unruly haste no notice but looked greatly relieved to see me. Before I could speak, he said, "I hoped to catch you before you went downstairs. We must talk. About last night," he added unnecessarily.

Wearily, I shook my head. "There is no need. I will be leaving with Mr. Spensser this afternoon, directly after luncheon. I am this moment looking for Mrs. Medcroft to tell her."

He paused two steps from the landing, his large frame blocking my descent, his handsome face much on a level with my own. "You've accepted his offer?" I found myself staring directly into his gray eyes and struggling to remember my purpose for going downstairs. It had completely fled my mind.

His own emotions seemed to be churning behind those somber eyes, but he succeeded in maintaining his self-possession. His square jaw set resolutely. "Forgive me, but I cannot let you leave with him."

Dear God. Did he mean to deny me the only reasonable choice left open to me? I could hardly continue in Mrs. Medcroft's company after Mr. Quarmby had confessed his desire to marry me. Life with the two of them would be untenable.

I straightened and defiantly lifted my chin. "If you mean to give Mr. Spensser a full report about last night's . . . sleepwalking episode—"

"It was hardly that."

"—then you will almost certainly be disappointed by his indifference," I finished, deliberately ignoring his protest. "The knowledge is unlikely to prevent his employing me. More the reverse, I would think, from what I have seen of his character. Nevertheless, it will make living conditions in his home extremely difficult for me."

"What nonsense is this? What happened last night is nobody's business but our own. I am unlikely to say anything."

I stared at him, confused. "Then what is there to discuss? You ordered me to go and I am going."

"Ordered? I said only that you must leave this house. But that was for your own safety."

My legs wobbled dangerously and I braced myself against the railing. He was concerned on my behalf? Did that mean he was not disgusted by my behavior, but still felt something for me? Or was he merely making good on his promise to see that I came to no harm while I remained beneath his roof? Unfortunately, given his sense of honor, the latter was the more likely of the two. But that did not explain his refusing to let me leave with Mr. Spensser.

It was all too much for me. The sleepless night. The fears for my future. Mr. Quarmby's proposal. My jumbled emotions. My fingers loosened on the railing. "Edmund," I murmured. "I . . . I . . ."

He bounded up the two remaining stairs and his arm encircled my waist. "I think we had better go into my study. We can talk privately in there."

16

The aroma of roast lamb and freshly baked rolls wafted from the dining room, carried along with snippets of conversation and bursts of Fanny's laughter. Her happiness permeated the melodic sounds and lingered in the air like an alluring fragrance. It seemed her brother's absence, and Mr. Spensser's presence, had heightened her usual good spirits.

Edmund determinedly steered me away from the cheerful gathering and through the hall to his study. He closed the door firmly behind us, obliterating any and all noises. Still supporting me, he led me to the Jacobean armchair and pressed me down onto its thin cushion. With only a murmur of protest, I let him place my legs upon a footstool. From high above me, he surveyed his efforts. A satisfied smile played about his lips.

"I am hardly an invalid," I said, enjoying the solicitous attention but feeling like a complete charlatan.

My moment of weakness had passed as quickly as it had come.

He scratched his lower jaw thoughtfully, his gaze still fixed to my face and whatever he saw there. I tilted back my head and searched his face for some explanation for his recent statements. All I discovered was that the warmth in his eyes sent an unaccountable shiver down my spine and the curve of his lips made my stomach flip-flop like a floundering fish.

Hastily, I averted my eyes lest they betray my emotions. "You had something to say to me, did you not?" I asked, in an attempt to divert his attention.

He nodded, straightened, and wandered across to the windows. There he pretended to stare out into the gardens, deliberately keeping his face hidden from my scrutiny. Arms clasped behind his back, he rocked on his heels.

"It is not that I wish to see you go. But it is imperative that you do not spend another night in Abbey House."

"You said something about my not being safe."

A red flush crawled up the back of his neck. "I wish this need not be discussed. But twice you have come under . . . strange influences that have undeniably affected your behavior. Last night—"

"I was sleepwalking and had no notion of what I was doing," I protested.

His hands tightened at his back. "And how was it you came to duplicate exactly two incidents from my past?"

I gasped. "Then I was not mistaken. I thought . . ."

"What?" He turned on his heel. "What did you think?"

"That my mind had been playing tricks on me, or that—"

I stopped abruptly, and he stared at me curiously. The warmth rose in my cheeks, a flaming warmth that he could not possibly have overlooked. I tried to hide behind my hands, but he strode back to the chair and pulled them aside. With my wrists captured in his strong grip, he peered into my face and tried to decide for himself what it was I had thought.

"Hilary?" he demanded, but his tone was gentle.

I bit my lower lip, hoping to forget the wave of embarrassment that had flooded through me.

"Come, now," he chided. "I think it is time we trusted each other. Tell me, what you supposed?"

Choking on my words, I admitted, "That I had allowed my emotions to get the better of me and used Lily as an excuse to ignore propriety."

He chuckled softly. "A flattering notion, but not, unfortunately, a likelihood."

"You really think it was her?"

"I am convinced of it."

"But what purpose could she have?"

"Who knows what motive lies behind her tricks? I only know she hated me."

Once again, his statement startled me. If it had been Lily's emotions that had taken me to his room, then it was not hate she had felt for him. Admittedly, it might not have been my idea of love, but certainly there had been passion. Intense passion.

Unaware of my thoughts, Edmund crouched before my chair, his hand resting atop mine. I wondered if he realized how his touch drove reason from my mind. But he seemed to be lost to his own thoughts.

"Twice, she attempted to seduce me," he claimed. "I warned her if she did not stop, I would go to my father. That was a grave mistake. Fearing I might expose her, she went to him instead and accused me of having raped her. He worshiped her and chose to believe her lies."

I frowned. That she wanted to seduce him was consistent with my "dream." But Ursula had said her father had caught them together in bed. Which of them was lying? Which of them had the most reason to lie?

Edmund slowly rubbed my fingers, sending prickles of electricity up my arm. His gaze captured mine, and the crinkles at the corners of his eyes deepened. They were seductive, beguiling eyes, eyes that made you want to believe the things he said. Eyes that made it impossible to disbelieve.

He raised his free hand and brushed my cheek. With his forefinger he traced the line of my lips, coaxing them into a smile. Having ensured himself of a sympathetic audience, he murmured, "My father and I quarreled. He might well have disinherited me, had Lily not fallen to her death."

I noted he did not say "had Lily not been killed." Was that intentional, or did he simply refuse to admit to the possibility? I could not ignore the fact that had he set out to calm my suspicions, he could not have made a more concerted effort.

"Afterward, we reconciled," he finished, unaware of the turn my thoughts had taken.

"Why would her spirit return?" I asked. "If not to denounce her murderer?"

"Perhaps through these cursed séances we have given her the opportunity to make mischief. As for her attempts to seduce me"—he shrugged—"Lily never could take no for an answer."

"But why would she use me?"

He shrugged. "Perhaps because she felt the attraction between us."

Startled, I looked up. A wayward curl fell across his brow, giving him the look of a child, and there was a youth and tenderness to the line of his mouth. What had happened to change him? And then I realized what was missing. It was the faint bitterness that had clung to him, like a scent that never completely disappeared. Where had that gone?

"You look surprised," he murmured.

I nodded.

"Good Lord, Hilary. This is not the first time I have voiced my feelings."

"I thought you respected me. That is not love. And after last night—"

"Last night only made me realize how much I wanted you."

He leaned forward and, his breath brushing across my eyelids, kissed me on the brow. My eyes closed and I waited for him to withdraw. Instead, I felt his lips on the bridge of my nose. I tilted my face upward, mouth parted, and silently offered myself up to his caresses. He hesitated, then his mouth covered mine.

It was as if we had melted into each other. We were neither one nor the other but something of both. Heaven must be like this, I thought. Was it for this that Lily had yearned? For this that she had returned from the grave? But she had not loved Edmund. What I felt for him was much stronger than mere passion. Mere passion could never have made me feel like part of him, as though we belonged together, had been meant for each other's arms.

I sighed. At one and the same time, I felt invincible and wholly vulnerable. Had it been his wish, he could have crushed me simply with a disapproving look. Even his disappointment would have been too horrible to bear.

Slowly, he pulled away. I fought against opening my eyes, lest I should see something I did not want to see. But I could not sit there with my eyes closed forever. Against my will, they flickered open.

His face was very close to mine, the tip of his nose almost brushing my forehead. I did not need to look into his eyes to know that he no more wanted to part from me than I from him. Sighing, I leant forward and rested my brow against his square chin.

Do not ask me to leave you, I begged silently. Ask anything of me but that.

He cleared his throat and I stiffened. "I have an aunt in Swanage, only a few hours' drive from here. She needs a companion, and I want you to go and stay with her."

"But why?" I pulled away to stare at him, too confused to fully realize he still wanted me to go. "And what about the Spenssers?"

"Let them find another governess for that spoiled brat they call a child," he said, his temper flaring. "Oh, good Lord, Hilary. Please trust me to do what is best for you and do not ask questions."

"But your aunt?" I protested, rather more weakly than I should have done. "How will she feel about this?"

"She will adore you."

He grinned, completely confident that not only would his request be met, but also that she would not dare to think any differently of me than he commanded her to think.

I stared at him, not knowing how to reply. "And whatever will I say to Mrs. Medcroft?"

"You might say farewell. I am sending her back to London. It is the only way to get rid of Lily. I would have sent her packing a week ago, if . . ."

I looked at him questioningly. If what? If that would not have made him look guilty of murder? The more he talked, the more confused I was becoming. And the less certain I was that I should trust him.

He scanned my face and frowned. "Damn. I am making a poor job of this. I had intended on waiting but I begin to wonder . . . must I make a full confession?"

I started.

He caught the slight motion and nodded. "Perhaps it would be best. I could not send her away until I made certain I would not"—he tensed and I steeled myself for what I was convinced I did not want to hear—"also be losing you," he finished.

I gasped, completely taken aback.

Edmund rushed on. "I thought in sending you to my aunt's I would give us . . . give you more time to . . . to consider me."

"In what light?" I asked, my voice little more than a squeak. He could not possibly mean what I thought he meant.

"As a husband, naturally. I know I have not always behaved in a manner that—"

"You want to marry me?" I demanded, needing to hear him speak his intentions again before I could believe I had heard him correctly.

He nodded, his face grave. "And if you give yourself a chance to come to know me, you might find me a desire—a suitable choice," he amended hastily.

I stifled what threatened to be a burst of hysterical giggles and said, "Yes, I believe I would. Indeed, I am convinced of it."

It was his turn to gape at me. "Are you quite certain?"
I nodded happily.

"Then I see no reason for you to leave Abbey House. Ursula will make a perfectly respectable chaperon for us until we can arrange the wedding. Something small, I think. Under the circumstances." He indicated my mourning dress with a quick glance.

"Anything you say, Edmund."

He grinned. "I see you will make me a most obedient wife."

"Only until you grow bored with me."

"Then if you become quarrelsome, I will remember to blame myself." He gave me a quick kiss on the cheek. "If you can bear to have a late tea, why don't you go upstairs and unpack. I shall inform Mr. Spensser that you will not be needing the post after all."

I gasped. "Oh, my dear heavens. By now, either he or Fanny is certain to have said something to Mrs. Medcroft. She will be terribly upset. I've got to find her."

With a few hasty words, we separated and I dashed out of his study and through the empty drawing room. The sounds of muted voices and the polite tinkling of silverware still emanated from the dining room, but I knew I had waited too long to find her there. My dress swirling about me, I rushed upstairs to her suite.

Her sobs echoed down the length of the corridor, punctuated either by tiny shrieks or Mr. Quarmby's voice. It variously protested deep outrage or vowed never-ending devotion. Good Lord. All because of my thoughtlessness. That I had tried twice to speak with her and been intercepted on both occasions meant little in the face of her distress.

Her door stood open, and I hesitated. Mrs. Medcroft lay supine on the sofa, her feet raised above her head, a damp cloth on her forehead. Mr. Quarmby hovered at her head. In his hands, he gripped a water pitcher. His coat had been slung across a chair, his sleeves were rolled back from his wrists, and the front of his waistcoat was splattered with water. Chaitra was nowhere to be seen. Either she had been sent to fetch more cold water to replace that which had been wasted on Mr. Quarmby, or she had not yet returned from her own luncheon.

It was several seconds before Mr. Quarmby caught sight of me. His cheeks paled and his upper lip twitched. "Only look what you have done to the dear lady," he cried. "I doubt that she will ever recover."

Mrs. Medcroft pulled the cloth from her brow and raised her head. The instant our gazes met, she fell back with a moan and her sobs doubled in strength. Her friend set the pitcher down on the side table with a thump, and straightened to his full five foot five inches.

"Never mind, dear lady. *I* will never desert you."

"Perhaps just for a few minutes," I suggested, making no effort to conceal my irritation. "To let us speak privately."

"I think it a little late for speeches."

Nevertheless, he stalked out, chin high and back rigid. His attempt at regality was ruined by the damp stains spreading across his narrow chest. As soon as he had gone, I walked into the suite, sat down on the edge of the sofa and began smoothing strands of wet hair off Mrs. Medcroft's face.

She moaned and rubbed her temples. "How could you? After all that I've tried to do for you. To accept a governess's post."

"It is a little more complicated than you realize. I will be leaving you, but not to go with Mr. Spensser."

She sat up, and the wet cloth flopped into her lap with a wet smack. "What do you mean?" she demanded, heedless of the damage she was doing her favorite dress.

I hastily removed the cloth and laid it across the top of the pitcher. "I hope you will be happy for me. Edmund has asked me to marry him."

"What?" She gaped at me. "And you have accepted without even consulting me?"

"I . . . I am afraid I did." There was no tactful way to point out to her that I needed to consult with no one.

"Oh, good heavens. You poor child." She swung her feet off the cushions and pushed herself to her feet. "Do you not see what he is doing?"

"What is that?" I asked suspiciously, not wanting to listen to her if she intended to criticize Edmund.

Mrs. Medcroft threw her arms about me and hugged me in a crushing embrace. "My poor, poor Hilary. He does not love you. He merely hopes to ensure my silence by marrying you. He knows that you are as dear to me as any child of my own could be. And that I would do nothing to hurt you, even indirectly."

"Edmund proposed to me because he loves me," I protested. "Your suggestions is sheer . . . sheer nonsense."

And yet the first thing he had said after arranging my future was that he intended to send Mrs. Medcroft back to London.

She scrutinized my face and gave a satisfied nod. "It may not be what you want to hear, but you know I'm right. I have been convinced for days that he is the reason Lily Llewelyn cannot rest in peace. But what can I do? She must unveil her own murderer or it will mean nothing."

"You are wrong. Absolutely wrong. Of course, he wishes to rid his home of her disquieting spirit. But that is to be expected."

"And how does he intend to do that?" she demanded, her green eyes narrowing.

Oh, Lord. Why did I not watch my tongue? But it had to be said, and better the news came from me than from Edmund. I sank down on the sofa. "He wants you to leave Abbey House. There are to be no more séances."

Her face inflamed with color. "There! What did I tell you? He means to bury the truth, as he buried poor Lily Llewelyn."

"I cannot believe that. I will not."

"Foolish child. What kind of a husband do you think he will make you? A man who murdered his own mother."

"His stepmother."

It was an idiotic and pointless remark. But Mrs. Medcroft had magnified Lily's death into something resembling a Greek tragedy with Edmund in the role of the worst possible sort of villain. Unfortunately, my attempt to place her accusations in the proper perspective only made me look ridiculous—like a woman blindly determined to defend the man she loved, no matter what the crime.

Mrs. Medcroft merely looked at me, her eyes reflecting everything I was thinking, a what-did-I-tell-you smile on her face.

Stiff with displeasure, I rose from the sofa. "It's no good arguing. Whatever you may believe, we have no proof that Edmund did anything to harm Lily. As for me, I am convinced of his innocence and intend to marry him."

"Then why don't we hold another séance? Perhaps we will prove his innocence."

"Edmund would never agree."

"He might if *you* insisted."

"I would not ask it of him."

"Then I daresay you have earned your fate." With great dignity, she rose and pointed toward the door. "Go. Desert me as your mother deserted me. At least *she* found someone who, however undeserving of her, was both honest and dependable."

I stared at her, a quaking lavender column with a tear-streaked face. It was impossible to be indignant; she was too much to be pitied for the disappointment I had caused her. And her fears were in my behalf, I reminded myself, however little I wanted to consider what she feared.

I hesitated, reluctant to leave on this sad note. "I had hoped we could remain friends."

"Impossible. *He* will never allow it. You may tell him that Mr. Quarmby and I shall be gone from his house in the morning. He will have his victory despite my efforts."

She folded her arms across her chest and deliberately turned her back to me. It was pointless to linger. With a sigh, I bid her good-bye and left the suite. Perhaps time and a few letters would prove to her she was mistaken, both about Edmund and the possibility of continuing our friendship.

I met Chaitra in the corridor. In her arms she carried one of her mistress's dresses, a stylish black silk with layers of flounces and a swath of chiffon around the neck and sleeves. It had been freshly pressed and was, I assumed, the reason for her long absence.

She smiled upon seeing me, but it was a wan smile and there was a yellow cast to her skin. Her usual grace was also missing, replaced by a slow, awkward gait. Whatever I thought of Abbey House, it was not the place for Chaitra. Thank goodness she would be going back to London on tomorrow's train.

Laying a finger across my lips to warn her not to speak, I led her through my door. I thought it wise to tell her what she must expect upon reaching Mrs. Medcroft's suite. And we might not have another chance to say our farewells.

Chaitra paused just inside the room, a diminutive figure in a swath of sapphire blue cotton. She let me take the dress from her and lay it carefully across my bed, not once murmuring a protest, but her soft gaze caught my every move and she studied me as I had studied her. Even the same concern was visible in her dark eyes.

"Please come and sit down," I begged. "I will not keep you long but I have something to tell you."

"You will be staying," she said, not moving. "With him."

"Then someone has already told you."

"No one."

She stirred, coming to life at last. After glancing around her, like an exotic mouse preparing to cross an open field at night, she rushed toward me and took my hand in both of hers. They were like a child's hands, small with short, tapering fingers. But her grip was firm. Too firm even for someone who worked as she worked. I knew fear had given her that added strength. I could see its brightness in her eyes and smell its acrid odor.

"You must not be concerned for me," I said. "It is what I want for myself."

My words did nothing to lighten her mood or restore the smile to her face. Her hands tightened on mine. "It is dangerous. Have you forgotten my warning?"

"You said that if I did not leave soon, I might never leave. It appears you are right. But not in the manner you feared." And that was a relief.

But only to me. Chaitra shook her head, slowly and ominously. "It was not a marriage I saw. What I saw was nothing to be hoped for or desired. If I were you . . ."

A loud rapping on my door interrupted her. "Come in," I said reluctantly, expecting to see Mrs. Medcroft, recovered from her first defeat and poised to launch another assault.

But it was Ursula who stalked into the room, a thunderous expression on her face. Her gaze encompassed both of us, and she glared at Chaitra. "Will you excuse us, please?"

It was not a question, but an order. Chaitra hastily collected the dress, gave me a quick glance whose dark meaning I could not read, and slipped into the corridor. Ursula waited impatiently for her to leave and slammed the door after her.

"Apparently, you didn't listen to anything I told you," she said before the room had stopped reverberating.

"I gather Edmund has told you of our engagement."

"Engagement! It is a farce. You are no more fit to be his wife than Lily was fit to marry my father."

"I hardly think—"

"I should have known what you were about, mincing around the house in your demure black gowns. Pretending to dislike him. Challenging him at every turn. All to get his attention without letting him guess that was what you wanted. You are a sly piece, Miss

Carewe. Every bit as sly and dishonest as Fanny and her mother."

"You are mistaken. That was not at all what—"

"I don't doubt Sally was right. You did walk into that cave deliberately. Did you cling to him and thank him for saving your life? Did you pretend to be weak and tell him you loved him?" She noted the flush that spread across my face and, far from being pleased to discover how accurately she had perceived the situation, she became enraged. Her face turned bright purple and her eyes bulged.

"And to think I tried to help you. When all the time—"

She stepped toward me, and I gasped. Was she mad? Dangerously mad? Remembering how she had lunged at Fanny, I braced myself for her attack. Ursula was both taller and larger boned than I, and her fury gave her an added edge. I was not convinced I could defend myself against her if she tried to kill me.

As she had killed Lily?

I didn't know whether to be relieved at the thought—since that would mean Edmund was innocent—or frightened for my own life. Did she mean to throw me from the balcony, as Lily had been thrown from the church gallery? Ursula would have had the strength to succeed in both instances.

"For God's sake," I cried. "There is no reason for you to be upset. I love Edmund and he loves me. Can't you be happy for us?"

"What do you know about love?" she scoffed, and her upper lip curled back into a sneer that bared her teeth. "I have loved two men in my life. Kenneth and Edmund. The first was taken from me by a spoiled little chit who will make him regret his fickleness for the rest of his days. I will not let another like her steal my brother and my home."

"But Edmund will always be your brother," I protested. "And Abbey House will always be your home."

"Do you take me for a fool?"

Her short, menacing steps carried her to the edge of the bed where I was standing. Her eyes glittered and a wave of loss, unhappiness, and outrage struck me with the same force as the incoming tide at Durdle Door. Shaking with tension, her arms raised from their rigid position at her sides and her fingers tightened into a curve. Worst of all was the emptiness in her gray eyes, a look that said she had lost everything and had nothing more to lose.

I opened my mouth to scream.

She dropped her hands. "You would like that, wouldn't you? You want me to attack you. Then you have only to call for Edmund and let him rush to your defense. Naturally, he would not expect you to endure my presence after your marriage. Not if I had tried to murder you."

"Ursula, it is not my wish to see you leave Abbey House."

She laughed, a harsh, dead laughter that said she believed nothing I had to say. Without warning, she grabbed up a vase of roses that was sitting on my bedside table and hurled it across the room. It shattered against the wall. Shards of glass splintered and fell in every direction. The roses dropped to the carpet in a damp heap. And a pool of brown water splattered across the floral paper and dripped down the wainscoting.

Some of her rage vented, she turned to me. "You should have accepted Mr. Spensser's offer. This marriage will never happen. I shall see to it." She spun on her heel, silk skirts rustling furiously, and stormed from my room.

I gaped after her.

Had she threatened to murder me? Or did she have something else in mind? I was beginning to think I should take Chaitra's warning more seriously.

One thing was certain. I no longer questioned whether or not Ursula was capable of murdering her stepmother.

I was almost convinced of her guilt.

I collapsed on the bed, exhausted. What was I to think? And what would happen after I married Edmund? Could Ursula and I possibly live beneath the same roof with any kind of harmony? Would she slowly come to realize I didn't want to usurp her position in his household? Could I possibly bring myself to trust her again?

I didn't have any answers. Sighing, I rose and attempted to clean up the pieces of broken glass and wipe down the wall. Cleaning the wainscotting was a simple matter, but the floral paper would never be the same again. There was a faint discoloration that would be noticeable in direct sunlight, and it was possible to make out tiny brown dots between the pattern.

I opened the doors to the balcony to let the afternoon warmth dry out the moisture I could not remove. Beyond the French doors, the sunshine and the gardens beckoned to me. Thinking a stroll in the fresh air would help me rid myself of the unpleasant memory that remained fixed in my mind, I propped open the doors with a chair, took my mother's shawl from the dresser drawer, and wandered downstairs.

Unconsciously, I might have been hoping to

encounter Edmund. I was feeling the need for the comfort and strength I drew from being in his presence. But it was a short and solitary walk to the front doors, and there was no one on the stairs or in the foyer. If Edmund was nearby, I neither saw nor heard him.

My stroll was equally uneventful. I was left alone with nothing and no one to interrupt my thoughts. There was a great deal for me to consider. I knew I loved Edmund, but did he love me? My heart told me yes, but common sense told me to be careful. We had known each other only a short time, and much of that time had been spent in heated argument.

It was growing late when I returned to the house, and my mind was no more settled than it had been two hours earlier. I looked up at Abbey House and my gaze wandered to my balcony. I could see the chair propping open the doors and the chiffon curtains swaying in the breeze. Beyond them, I caught a flash of movement, a dark shadow reflecting on the white ceiling.

Then it was gone.

Was someone there?

I hurried through the tower doors and was met with a wave of antagonism. The evil that emanated through the house had become overpowering but, having remained inside since my accident, I hadn't realized how great the change. And that in only two days. Although I knew it was disloyal of me, I thanked God Mrs. Medcroft would be leaving. I stopped to catch my breath, then hurried on.

My walking shoes rapped across the marble tiles of the foyer, and my hands pulled nervously at the ends of my shawl. Fanny was sauntering down the stairs, a lace fan twirling in her hands, embroidered slippers poking from beneath her elegant silk and lace day dress.

"I have been looking for you," she said straightway, a pout on her cherubic lips and a hint of something worse than irritation in her violet eyes.

I hesitated, my hand on the bottom stairpost. "Were you just in my room?"

"I tapped on the door but had no answer. I assumed you were hiding from me."

Hiding? "Whatever for?" I demanded, forgetting my original question.

She shrugged, stirring the flounces at her sleeve into a shivery dance. "Isn't that obvious? You have let me down, severely. Nor can I bring myself to forgive you."

Her fan tapped impatiently against her wrist, and her lips pursed. I stared at her, trying to comprehend what had upset her. Save for that dark cloud behind her eyes, I would have thought she was merely irritated with me for some silly offense. But there was something more.

She was furious, I realized with a start. And desperately trying to conceal her anger. But that made no sense. I had done nothing to offend her and, if I had, it was unlike Fanny to hold her temper.

Or was it?

She glared at me and I realized she was waiting for me to respond.

"Forgive me for being obtuse. But you will have to explain."

There was a short sigh of exasperation, a quick toss of her ringlets. "Stuart drove out of his way to meet you, hired you on my recommendation, and then you turned him down."

"Is that all?"

"All? Isn't that enough? I felt like an absolute fool. Mellie and Stuart are two of my dearest friends. You might have told me you intended to marry Edmund."

Was that what was really upsetting her? That I hadn't told her of our engagement? "But I had no notion he meant to propose," I protested.

"Nonsense. I had only to look at Kenneth to know he would marry me if I encouraged him."

"Your brother is not at all like Kenneth. And nor am I as astute as you," I added, partly in an attempt to placate her, partly because I knew it was the truth. At least where gentlemen were concerned.

But Fanny was not prepared to be placated. "I don't believe a word. Sally was quite right about you. I should have listened. You're every bit as sly as Ursula."

I choked back my laughter. Two hours ago, I had been accused of being as sly as Fanny and her mother. The two of them were more alike than they realized. Unfortunately, they agreed in their dislike of me. Thank goodness I would not have to contend with both of them. Fanny would soon be marrying Kenneth and moving into Smedmore.

"I begin to wish you had drowned," she continued. "Although, at the time, I told Sally it was a nasty trick. Had I known—"

"A trick?" I queried, feeling horribly cold.

She slapped her fan against the railing. "Yes, a trick. Oh, don't tell me you couldn't guess. Sally put her hat on the driftwood deliberately. It was to make you and Edmund think we had gone inside the cave and go searching for us. Heavens, it wasn't as if she wanted to drown you. She only thought you'd be frightened and get a little wet, and Edmund wouldn't admire you if you were teary-eyed and your dress was ruined."

"And you let her?"

"I told her it wouldn't do a bit of good. Edmund knew I had more sense and he certainly wouldn't have let you go into the cave with him. It was only by chance he didn't see the hat and you did."

I stared at her incredulously. She was every bit as irresponsible as Edmund had claimed. And completely without conscience. I didn't know whether to be disgusted with her or grateful that she had shown me that Edmund wasn't hard-hearted and unforgiving, as I had once thought. He merely had a solid understanding of his sister. In an instant, my doubts about our engagement vanished.

"Do you intend to remain here until your marriage?" Fanny demanded, a faint scowl marring her pretty face.

I nodded.

The scowl deepened. "Then I will tell Kenneth I want him to marry me immediately. I will not remain beneath this roof if you are also to be here."

She flounced down the stairs, brushed past me, and disappeared into the drawing room. Only her irritation and the scent of her perfume lingered in the air. I was left to stare after her, my mouth open, my thoughts jumbled. Only one thing was clear to me.

Nobody wanted me to marry Edmund.

I hurried up to my room, anxious to find some privacy before someone else confronted me. In my haste, I was almost able to disregard the sour air and the icy drafts that blew from nowhere and curled around the back of my neck. Instead, I breathed a sigh of relief to find the corridor empty.

The sigh became a gasp. My door was ajar and the contents of my room had been completely overturned.

Had Fanny done this? But for what possible reason?

I picked my way through the heap of crumpled dresses and undergarments that sprawled across the carpet. My gaze fell on the open dresser drawer. It was empty. The two scrapbooks had been removed.

By whom?

And what would they do with them?

Fanny had warned me to say nothing of my mother's involvement with Mrs. Medcroft. Did that mean she intended to use them to ruin my hopes of marrying Edmund? But she had no need to search for them, and could have gone straight to their hiding place.

Ursula, then?

I sank onto the bed and stared at the disarray. She had threatened to stop the marriage. Perhaps she had found a way. How would Edmund react when he learned of my mother's history? Would he regard me as a slightly different version of Lily, or would he want nothing more to do with me?

With trembling fingers, I picked up my dresses and hung them back in the wardrobe. One by one, I folded up the corsets and the drawers, matched the stockings and rolled them together, and lay the handkerchiefs neatly atop each other. I had almost finished when I caught sight of a square of cardboard lying on the carpet, something written in flowery blue script on its surface.

I picked it up and discovered it was not cardboard, but a photo of Mrs. Medcroft, one of the more flattering shots. It must have fallen out of one of the scrapbooks. On the back, roughened circles marked where the paste had dried. In between were three lines of script.

> To Marion, my assistant and beloved friend.
> For her scrapbook.
> With love, Amelia.

The scrapbooks had belonged to my mother? It had been she who had carefully cut the articles from the papers and arranged them on the pages? I wondered why Mrs. Medcroft hadn't told me. And why had mother left them with her? As a gift, to remember their time together? Or because my father refused to let her take anything that might remind her of her past?

Both were possible, I supposed.

Another question occurred to me. What about the pages that had been cut from the end? Had my mother torn them out and taken them with her? There had been nothing in her personal papers except letters from my father and photographs of me as a child. It would be necessary to ask Mrs. Medcroft—if she was still talking to me.

Either way, she would have to be told about the theft of her books. Another unpleasant duty, since she was certain to raise questions that would have been better left unasked.

Mrs. Medcroft was taking her tea alone, with the weary Chaitra to wait on her. She stared over the painted china cup at me, hesitated, then beckoned for me to join her. She pushed the plate of tea cakes toward me. "I suppose you haven't reconsidered?" she asked hopefully.

I shook my head.

"Hmm. You don't seem particularly happy," she pointed out. "If Mr. Quarmby had proposed to me, I should be"—a light spasm trembled through her— "aglow."

And if she ever learned he had proposed to me, she would be a great deal more excited. I felt certain Mr. Quarmby would not advise her of his actions, and certainly the information would not come from me.

"Forgive my distraction," I said. "But something has upset me."

"I shouldn't wonder."

I ignored her thrust. "Someone has stolen the scrapbooks."

"What? My scrapbooks?" she asked incredulously and her black brows arched high above her eyes. "Whatever for? They had only to ask and I would have been glad to produce them."

I told her of Fanny's warning and also about Ursula's distress. "I suppose she has gone straight to Edmund with them."

"No, she would not do that." Mrs. Medcroft's eyes glinted. "That would put her in the wrong and he might refuse to look at them. She will expect us to go to her—privately, of course—and demand their return. Then she has only to deny having taken them and summon her brother. He, naturally, will want to know what has been taken. You, or rather your mother, will be exposed as my . . . let us say, accomplice, and the scrapbooks will turn up goodness knows where. Probably in Fanny's room, since that will give Ursula a chance to strike two birds with one stone. And Mr. Llewelyn would believe his younger sister capable of any misdeed."

I stared at her, amazed at how quickly her bewilderment had faded and she'd surmised Ursula's scheme. I hadn't begun to suspect the whole truth. If, indeed, Mrs. Medcroft was right—and her every word made sense to me.

"It seems I might be returning with you to London, regardless of my wishes," I admitted sadly. "Assuming you will forgive me."

Mrs. Medcroft said nothing but looked thoughtful. Her green eyes churned like storm-tossed waves. Impulsively, she reached out and patted me on the hand. "Don't you worry. We shall say nothing, and Ursula must either forget her plan or broach the subject herself. Whatever he thinks of your mother's history, Mr. Llewelyn will not approve his sister's methods. That may well work in your favor."

It was a gracious gesture, especially when I knew how badly she wanted me to stay with her. It made me feel awkward and grateful, both at the same time. And there was more than a twinge of guilt for having disappointed her.

She accepted my thanks with a broad smile. "Whatever happens, you will always be welcome in my home," she assured me. "But don't you worry. Mr. Llewelyn may never learn of our . . . little deceit."

17

Although he had already told—or fore-warned—his sisters, Edmund publicly announced our engagement that evening in the drawing room. He took me by the hand, interlaced his fingers with mine and led me to the enormous fireplace. After sending me a quick smile that made my stomach ache and my eyes film with tears, he surveyed the room and loudly cleared his throat. The chatter streamed on, unbroken, like a river that refused to turn or break its course.

No one, it seemed, wanted to hear his news. Only Sally Pritchard looked up, boldly ignoring Fanny's demands to pay attention, and her gaze slid from Edmund to me. "I hope we are not going to have an account of how Miss Carewe nearly lost her life," she said, her voice carrying across all the rest. "Too much has been made of her tiresome behavior."

"Good Lord, yes," Fanny agreed. "Do sit down, Edmund. You look ridiculous."

Edmund tensed, and I tried to conceal my irritation with both of them. The knowledge that Edmund and I might not have admitted to our feelings were it not for them helped me to overlook their perfidy. And I took an unkind pleasure in anticipating Sally Pritchard's disappointment—although it might be short-lived if Ursula found some way to outmaneuver Mrs. Medcroft.

"Can't this wait?" Ursula demanded. "It's eight o'clock and supper is ready to be served."

"It cannot," her brother replied with an equanimity that made me marvel. His tolerance for both his sisters was beyond my understanding.

"All right, Edmund." Winnie lifted his large head, winked at me from beneath a fall of tawny curls, then nodded to his friend. "Get on with it. The rest of us are hungry."

He cleared his throat again. "Miss Carewe has agreed to become my wife." He lifted my hand to his lips and brushed a kiss across the back of my palm. All the while, his gaze remained on my face and I flushed with pleasure. Only the fear of what might yet come mitigated my happiness.

There was a hush in the drawing room. Fanny pouted and Ursula turned her head, disdain etched into her face. Sally Pritchard appeared to be on the verge of tears, and both Mrs. Medcroft and Mr. Quarmby looked disgruntled. But after her kindness upstairs I knew she, at least, wished for my happiness.

Dr. Rhodes was the first to speak. "Congratulations, Edmund. It's about time. If you don't mind my saying so," he added, his voice dropping to a mumble.

Edmund threw back his head and laughed, and a

delightful shiver ran through me. "As it happens, I don't mind a bit. Indeed, I agree wholeheartedly."

Winnie glanced at Fanny and grinned mischievously. "The two of you might have a double wedding. Save time and money."

"We most certainly will not," Fanny retorted. "I don't intend to share my wedding day with anyone. Kenneth, you can't possibly agree."

"Have no fear," Edmund replied before her intended could speak. "I have no intention of waiting until you make up your mind to set a date. Hilary and I will be married as soon as something can be arranged." He turned hastily to me. "That is, if you don't object."

Edmund deferring to me? It was a novelty that would take some adjustment. I nodded, faintly bewildered, then hastily shook my head. "No, of course I don't mind."

"And I, for one, am glad to learn you will not be leaving Dorset," Winnie announced, oblivious or uncaring of the distress he caused his wife. "A very intelligent decision, Edmund. If I were single, I would have made the offer myself."

Eglantine turned varying shades of red and purple. I watched out of the corner of my eye with fascination and concern. She appeared on the verge of a having some kind of fit. Slowly, the color drained from her face and she mastered her emotions. No one, to look at her, would have supposed her more than mildly taken aback.

Surely she could not be concerned now that I was to marry Edmund? But marriage had not stopped Lily Llewelyn from having affairs, and one of those affairs might well have been with her charming—and nearest—neighbor. Why should she assume I would be any more resistant to her husband's charms? Save that Edmund was a young man—handsome, virile, intelligent, and charming. Lily had been married to an elderly man whose competence only extended to making money.

"If there is nothing else, then let us go into supper," Ursula said, with the air of someone dispensing with mild gossip. She was, I thought, entirely too comfortable. Save for that one look of disdain, she had handled his announcement with unexpected aplomb. Would she risk alienating her brother simply to destroy his marriage? I had a horrible feeling she would.

Edmund took my arm, prepared to escort me into dinner, but Eglantine rose and caught at my sleeve as we passed. "Do you mind?" she asked pleasantly. "There is something I would like to tell your young lady in private, Edmund. Something every young woman about to be married must know. We can join the rest of you in a minute."

His gray eyes scanned her and clouded with doubt. A slight frown creasing his brow, he glanced hesitantly at me.

"Please go on," I said. "I'm sure this won't take more than a minute."

Reluctantly, Edmund released me. I was equally sad to see him go. But whatever Eglantine wanted to say, it had better be said. And there was always the chance I could convince her I had no designs upon her husband. Edmund was all the man I would, or could ever, want.

The drawing room felt horribly empty with only the two of us standing there. Firmly, Eglantine pushed the door shut, and when she turned to me she was wearing a pleasant smile. But it was not a smile I liked or trusted.

"Shall we sit down?" she suggested. "We might as well be comfortable."

"As you like."

We settled on the sofa beneath the tall bay windows, and she spread out her dress with the care of child who had been invited to her first grown-up party. I watched, fascinated, until the last navy silk flounce had been laid flat, the wrinkles had been smoothed from her gloves, and her fan had been spread to its fullest.

Her smile still affixed to her face, she turned to me at last. "I am going to offer you a choice, my dear." She spoke in the same voice she might have used to offer someone a plate of tea cakes. "Either you can agree to leave Abbey House of your own accord, or I shall tell Edmund the truth."

Her words were completely inappropriate to her manner, and it took a second for me to absorb them. I gaped at her. Was it Eglantine who had stolen the scrapbooks?

She smiled. "I see we understand each other. You have had your fun with my husband, but now it is over."

"What?" I demanded, realizing she was referring to something entirely different. "You cannot be suggesting that Winnie and I are lovers?"

"Of course not." She wafted her fan lazily in the air. "I doubt that your friendship has progressed beyond a light flirtation. Anything more would be impossible while you are without a husband. But you have cleverly tricked Edmund into marrying you and—"

"I did no such thing."

"Nonsense, my dear. Do you think me a complete fool?"

"I begin to think you quite mad."

She laughed politely. "Hardly mad. Merely accustomed to my husband's penchant for younger women. You must know you aren't his first . . . shall we say, romance?"

"We shall say nothing of the sort. Indeed, we have—or rather you have—said entirely too much already. Your husband is of no interest to me and, although clearly you do not share my opinion, I suspect his admiration is nothing more than pretense."

I rose, stiffly conscious of my offended dignity, and swept to the door in a manner that Fanny could not have bested. But it took all my strength to walk at a reasonable pace instead of taking hurried steps, propelled forward on a wave of Eglantine's hatred.

The knowledge that both she and her husband had been present on the day of Lily's death did nothing to reassure me. Was Eglantine capable of murdering anyone who threatened or appeared to threaten her marriage? Physically, the answer had to be yes. But emotionally?

I couldn't tell myself with conviction that she was not.

My fingertips brushed the doorknob and I felt a surge of relief. Another second and I would be gone from there. And as soon as I was seated at the dining table, beneath Edmund's protective gaze, this would seem like nothing more than a bad dream.

But it was a dream from which I had yet to awaken.

"Don't think his odd absences have escaped my notice." Eglantine's strident voice carried across the silent room. "You will not succeed where others have failed. Nor is Winnie the man he appears to be. His true character might come as something of a disappointment."

Since I did not admire her husband, I doubted this was true. Nor did I much care. My heart thumping against my ribs, I opened the door and slipped gratefully into the corridor.

And immediately came upon Winnie.

His head was bent and he was searching his pockets with a theatrical flourish. Upon hearing me, he lifted his head and light glittered off the gold flecks in his eyes. "Are you all right, my dear? You look a little flustered."

"I'm fine, thank you."

"Silly of me," he continued. "I came back for my pipe tobacco, but it was in my pocket all the time." He pulled a leather pouch from the inside pocket of his coat and displayed it for me. "Are you sure you're all right? You look a little peaked. Not because of anything my wife said, I hope."

"Not at all," I lied.

He smiled knowingly. "She can be . . . difficult, on occasion. I hope you will be prudent when you find yourself in her company. In the past, she had behaved quite atrociously."

I could well imagine.

And Eglantine Winthrop had not much changed.

It was well after the barley soup had been served when she took her place at the table. From her demeanor, no one would have guessed that anything unusual had passed between us. Twice, she addressed some comment to me, once regarding the upcoming wedding and later in reference to my near misfortune on the beach. And if there was some darker meaning in her words, it would have been overlooked by anyone but me.

I had been seated next to Edmund, no doubt at his insistence, and throughout the meal he paused to glance across at me, his gaze warm. It was impossible to ignore the flow of energy between us, the flutter in my stomach he caused simply by glancing in my direction. Nor did I have any doubt he was aware of his effect on me. A smile curved at the corner of his lips, and there was nothing in the conversation to warrant his amusement.

Sally pouted at the bottom of the table, and she jabbed at her veal with her fork. Nor did she get much support from Fanny. She appeared to be over her lapse of temper, save for a brief resurgence that came when she learned of Mrs. Medcroft's imminent departure. But she quickly shrugged off her disappointment and turned her attention to flirting with Dr. Rhodes. Now and again, she glanced at her sister, surprised that her performance hadn't stirred the usual animosity.

But Ursula said nothing unless it was to answer a direct question. Her attention appeared to be for her guests' comfort and the series of courses that we ate over the next two hours. Yet I had the feeling that she was watching me, searching for signs of discomfiture. Again, I was convinced it was she who had taken the scrapbooks.

And if she failed to see my distress, it was not because I felt none.

My conviction that Mrs. Medcroft had surmised her plot correctly grew as the evening continued. After dinner, Ursula gave us every opportunity to catch her alone, and appeared vastly disappointed when neither Mrs. Medcroft nor I approached her. Her spirits dropped steadily with each passing hour and, when it came time to retire, she appeared completely deflated.

Upstairs, Mrs. Medcroft waved Mr. Quarmby

away, but lingered at my door to congratulate me. "What did I tell you?" she crowed. "You have nothing at all to fear. I doubt that Mr. Llewelyn will discover how we have deceived him until long after you have been wed. And then, naturally, it will be too late."

I stared at her. She was right. I was deceiving Edmund, although I had not thought of it in that fashion. My mother had done nothing that was either illegal nor immoral. Nor had her association with Mrs. Medcroft affected my character. But all of us knew he would reconsider his opinion of me if he knew the truth. And possibly retract his offer.

Certainly, *he* would regard my omission as nothing less than deceit.

And if he ever did discover the truth? What then? Would he think himself saddled with the very kind of woman he abhorred? Or would his love and respect for me persuade him to disregard my mother's past?

The time to discover the answer was before I became his wife. Not after.

I should have to tell him everything, of course.

Mrs. Medcroft stirred at my side, and she peered sharply at me. "Is something wrong, dear?"

"No, nothing. I am just a little tired."

"Why, that's to be expected. It's been an exhausting day for all of us." She kissed me on the cheek and smiled. "Go and get some rest. And don't forget. Mr. Quarmby and I will be leaving in the morning. I will expect you to see us off."

"I won't forget," I promised.

For all I knew, I might well be going with them.

I waited inside my room until I knew she would have reached her suite. Then I pulled my mother's shawl about my shoulders and hurried back downstairs. Everywhere in the house, I felt an energy that mocked me, not because of what I was about to lose, but for the honesty that drove me. Lily Llewelyn had been a liar and deceiver of the worst caliber. It shocked me to think I had nearly allowed myself to enter a marriage in the same fashion.

Had it not been for Mrs. Medcroft's unwitting choice of words, I might well have done exactly that.

As I had expected, Edmund had not yet retired. He was sitting at the desk in his study, the door ajar, scanning a small stack of papers. There was a faint frown on his face and, whatever he was reading, he did not seemed pleased by the content. His head jerked up at my knock and, upon catching sight of me, he swept the papers into his drawer.

"May I come in?" I asked, my voice little more than a whisper. "There is something I must tell you."

Eyes faintly bewildered, he nodded and rose.

Sitting at his desk, Edmund was formidable; standing, he overwhelmed me. The knowledge of what I was about to say and the response I could expect from him made me hesitate. I drew a long breath and took a last moment to contemplate what I was losing. The memory of his strong arms pulling me from the waves, clasping me to his chest, sent a tremor through me, but the ecstasy was mixed with fear.

Would I ever again enjoy his fierce embraces?

"Perhaps you should sit down," he suggested with growing concern.

I shook my head, needing to remain on my feet. If I did not speak immediately, I would not be able to force the words from my throat. "It is about my mother," I began. "Something you might not have known."

"And that is?"

"She used to work for Mrs. Medcroft as her assistant.

Fanny said you assumed she was nothing more than a client."

"You knew this?" he demanded, and his eyebrows drew together.

I nodded. "I learned of their involvement while in London."

"And why have you waited until now to tell me?"

"At first, I did not see that it was any of your concern. Nor was it. Until today," I added.

He folded his arms across his chest and regarded me severely. "Does it not occur to you that it was something I should have been told *before* I announced our engagement to my friends and family?"

I looked into his face and realized my error. Edmund would not back out of an engagement, any more than he would have backed out of a marriage. I remembered Ursula's comment on the stairs about Dr. Rhodes. "Too honorable to divorce Fanny when he discovered he'd made a bad marriage." Her brother was the same kind of man.

If he was to have his freedom, it was I who would have break off our engagement.

I tried to speak but could not bring myself to say what must be said. Dismayed, I turned and fled the room.

The foyer was dimly lit, but someone had already doused the gas lights above the stairs. I thought it strange, but was too distracted to pay much attention to the darkness that had settled upon the house. Nor did the gloom and the shadows inhibit my headlong rush. The foyer, the winding staircase, and the wide landing had become familiar to me. Too familiar. Abbey House was the only home I had known since leaving Bristol.

I was halfway up the stairs before my pace slowed.

An icy draft blew down from above and struck me in the face. There were always currents of cool air swirling through the corridors, but not like this. This had to have come from the depths of the abbey, with its frigid touch and odor of decay and mold.

Could it be the work of Lily Llewelyn? Each day she grew stronger, and it seemed she no longer needed to draw upon the energies raised by our séances. What would happen after Mrs. Medcroft . . . after *we* left? Would she fade back into the stones, or would she remain to wreak havoc on the living?

I took each step with caution, running my hand along the smooth mahogany banister and bending my head to shield my face from the cold gusts. The landing was like an icebox, but not as dark as I had first supposed. A yellow light flickered within the depths of the medieval fireplace.

And yet there were no flames.

It was a curious sight, and I was drawn forward to take a better look. To accomplish that end, I was forced to step inside the fireplace, but that was easily done. And with room to spare.

I ran my fingers down the rough stones where the yellow glow danced. From whence had it come? Not from above, for the chimney had been bricked shut. Nor from behind the stones, for they fitted together perfectly and their seams were no more than lines etched in what appeared to be a solid stone wall.

A blast of air hit the back of my neck and I turned.

And found the answer I sought.

There was an eighteen-inch opening between the side and back walls of the fireplace, an opening that was not usually there. Somehow a section of the stone interior had been slid sideways to reveal a narrow tunnel beyond. Within those depths a ball of light

burned, its glow reflecting on the opposite stones.
And it was from there, too, the drafts and the dank
odor emanated.

Slowly recalling Edmund's tales about tunnels that
led from the abbey into the hills beyond, I peered
inside. Something white flickered at the far end of the
tunnel and then disappeared. Had my eyes tricked
me? Seconds passed and I hovered there.

A trickle of laughter seeped from the distant blackness. Lily's laughter. The laughter that I had heard on
my first evening at Abbey House. Without thinking, I
squeezed through the narrow opening and stepped
into the tunnel.

Cobwebs brushed my cheeks, and the foul air
clogged my nostrils. Already I regretted my decision.
It was worse than the cave near Durdle Door.
Narrower and more confining. But Lily's laughter was
like a lure, beckoning to me and drawing me forward.

I crept toward the halo of light, but it eluded me. I
was drawn deeper and deeper into the depths of the
house. The tunnel wandered between the walls, never
varying in height or width. Here and there, iron fix-
tures had been set into the stones, but the torches
they'd held had long since rotted into nothingness.

Luckily the floors were smooth and there were no
steps, or I might have fallen. The bobbing glow in the
distance was enough to guide me, not light my path.
Several times, I saw a drift of white and there was
always that soft laughter, taunting me, compelling me
to follow.

My elbow scraped the stones. What rooms lay on
the other side of those walls? Had I traveled beyond
the family wing, into that part of the abbey that had
never been altered? Or had all sense of distance and
direction deserted me?

A low grating sound made me forget my questions and peer through the darkness. The tiny circle of light had ceased to dance and weave and hovered in the air. The drafts had grown stronger, but the air was fresher. Was I coming upon an exit? And what would I find when I got there?

The ghost of Lily Llewelyn?

The ball of light bounced forward again, and I hurried to catch up. Ten yards down the passage I came upon a second opening, wider than the first. Beyond lay a black chasm in which a single candle flickered.

So there was nothing otherworldly about what I had seen.

But what about the laughter?

I stepped over a stone sill and found myself standing on a bare wooden floor. Nor, in that one illuminated patch, could I see any furnishings. I hesitated and tried to discern my whereabouts. Most of the rooms at Abbey House were carpeted. Some had been tiled. And the older sections boasted the original stone flagging. I couldn't think of a single bare wood floor. Indeed, the only wooden structures I remembered were the posts in the drawing room, the oak beams and braces in the church—I gasped. And the gallery where Lily Llewelyn had plunged to her death.

That was where I stood.

But in whose company?

Most of the gallery remained cast in shadow—a pulsing, breathing nothingness in which something or someone lurked. There was a faint noise, the whisper of a soft foot against the boards, and a white figure crept to the outer ring of light.

"Fanny!" I exclaimed, and my legs trembled beneath the weight of my relief.

Her mouth curved into a teasing smile. "You thought I was my mother, didn't you?"

"Indeed I did. You play the oddest games."

"It's hardly a game," she protested. "Although it would have been if not for you."

"Whatever do you mean?"

"Mrs. Medcroft and her séances. They were meant to be amusing. She was a delightful old fraud." Her tone was mildly derogatory, filled with the amused contempt of a skilled performer for those less professional than she.

"But how can you say that after all that has happened?" I demanded. "And what has any of this to do with me?"

"You were the one who made Mama return. I knew the moment I saw the scrapbooks. The woman Sally took me to see was not the woman who conjured up Mama. Nor the woman the newspapers applauded. But your mother assisted her then. Just as you assisted her at Abbey House. What other conclusion could I draw?"

I gaped at her, wondering if she could possibly be right. Was that why Mrs. Medcroft desperately wanted me to remain with her? Why she had invited me to London? If Fanny was right, it explained a great many things. Such as why she had felt sadness where I had sensed evil. And why she had been peculiarly insensitive for someone of her calling.

My breath caught in my throat. It also explained why she had guessed Ursula's intentions. She had probably worked more than a few deceptions herself. Another thought occurred to me, and I gasped. Was that why she had persisted in referring to our "little deceit?" She must have known honesty would compel me to tell Edmund the truth. And by appearing to support me, she had succeeded in destroying our romance while still maintaining her guise of friendship.

And Mr. Quarmby. Had he also guessed the truth and seen the advantage of deserting Mrs. Medcroft and attaching himself to me? Likely, he had. If he had worked with her for many years, he would have known that the strange happenings at Abbey House were not typical of her efforts.

Fanny laughed softly at my dismay, reminding me that I was not alone.

"But why did you invite her here if you knew she was a fake?" I demanded. Nothing about Fanny's behavior made sense to me.

Her laughter harshened. "Do you really think I would wish to summon my mother? Good Lord, Hilary. It was Papa who loved me. Mama only loved herself. I was nothing more than a member of her audience . . . and that was before I pushed her from the gallery. I cannot believe her feelings for me were much improved upon her death."

"But you couldn't have," I said in a hoarse whisper. "You were only ten. A child."

"Mama was slight of build and I was very angry with her. I had only to catch her unawares."

Her face was sweet and earnest, like that of a child talking about a lesson she had learned that day. There was no guilt, no hint of remorse. No sign that she was troubled by her conscience. There was something inhuman about her, something lacking. Whatever Lily Llewelyn had been, her daughter was no better.

"Why were you angry?" I asked, determined to keep her talking until I could think of what I must do.

Fanny sighed. "She was going to have Winnie's baby. They used to meet in the church. Mama liked to conduct her affairs here. It . . . pleased her."

"And you knew about the baby?" I prodded.

Her head tilted to the side, and the present seemed to have vanished from her view. "Mama told me. She liked to provoke people. Even me, if there was no one else about. She said if it was a boy Papa would forget all about me." Her eyelids slid down over her eyes and her voice softened to a dreamy murmur. "He was the only one who really loved me. You see, I had no choice."

"Yes," I mumbled, becoming more and more aware of the danger in which I had placed myself. "I do see."

She blinked. Alert and watchful once again, she shot me a sharp look. "At first, I threatened to tell Papa it was not his child. But then she told me nor was I. And if I said anything, she would name my real father, and Papa would want nothing more to do with either of us."

"No wonder you hated her."

She nodded. "But I punished her. And I took Winnie from her, too." Carried away with her own thoughts, she ignored my gasp. "Do you think she knows? I tell her whenever I put flowers on her grave."

"You . . . and Winnie," I stammered, able to think of nothing else.

"You don't really think he was interested in you?" Lily's mocking laughter issued from her lips. "You were nothing more than a distraction for Eglantine."

A very effective distraction. Fanny's complete lack of scruples was amazing. But after what she had just told me, nothing should have surprised me. Nevertheless, it did.

"What about Dr. Rhodes?" I asked weakly. "He loves you deeply, more than Winnie ever could."

"Oh, good heavens. You don't really think I'm interested in him, do you? That ridiculous little man. I only wanted to punish Ursula for sending me to Switzerland." She smiled at me complacently. "Now you have had the whole story and you understand."

"Understand?"

"Why I must kill you. I have tried and tried and tried to make you leave Abbey House. I delayed the séances to keep Mama from telling my secret, as she would have done eventually. I even made Sally give up her favorite straw bonnet because I knew Mrs. Medcroft would do nothing if you had suffered an accident and weren't feeling well."

"But you said—"

She laughed at my näiveté. "Dear Hilary. I would have made a good actress, I think. Do you?" she asked, seriously seeking my opinion.

"Yes. Yes, I do," I agreed, edging backwards.

Fanny's right hand lifted from her side. She was holding a large knife. The candlelight flashed off the blade, sending streaks of light across the gallery and completely dazzling me.

"I shall leave you in the tunnel," she said matter-of-factly. "And if you like, I will bring you flowers, too. Edmund will think you left with Mrs. Medcroft and she will think you stayed here. They might never discover their error. And even if they do . . ." She shrugged. "They will never find you. Only Mama and I knew about the tunnels. She found them one day by accident when she was searching for a cash box Papa kept at the house." She raised the knife and took a step toward me.

A protective and familiar arm descended about my shoulders, and Edmund thrust me behind him. "It's no good, Fanny," he said gently. "I found the opening in the fireplace when I followed Hilary upstairs. You can't kill both of us."

"Then I shall kill you," she decided, immediately and comfortably adapting to the altered circumstances. "And blame Hilary. I can't imagine the authorities will take the word of someone associated with Mrs. Medcroft over mine. I never liked you, Edmund."

It was as though that was all the explanation or reason she needed to have or give. I glanced wildly around for some kind of weapon to use against her, but could see nothing. It should have been a simple matter for Edmund to disarm her, but I suspected it would not be. Fanny was strengthened with a dangerous kind a madness that would make her unpredictable. And her fragility was deceptive. He, however, would be hampered by a natural unwillingness to do her serious harm.

Edmund braced himself for her attack, and I stifled the scream that wanted to tear from me.

But that attack never came. A soft laughter slithered through the church and up the steps that led to the gallery. There was a menace in the sound, a determination and a need for vengeance. Fanny spun about, and the knife slipped from her hand and clattered to the floor.

The laughter grew louder, harder, and it swept toward Fanny in a rush. Like the tide pouring into the cave, I thought. Only there was greater force and a malignancy that the waves had not possessed. That had been the mindless force of nature. This was a directed and intelligent evil.

It seemed intent on destroying her, of draining her life and vitality to use for its own vicious purposes. Edmund and I stood on the edge of a whirlpool, able to feel the pull of the current without being sucked into its depths, but even that slight contact left me weak and disoriented. What, I wondered, was it doing to Fanny who struggled in the very heart of that vortex?

She screamed and, showing greater strength than I would have believed possible, backed away from the sound of her mother's voice. But there was no escape to be had. The farther she retreated, the nearer the sounds drew to her. Her pale and frightened face was captured in the candlelight, and her lavender eyes were wide and bright with terror.

Edmund and I stared, but neither of us moved. I strained to lift my feet, as he must have done to lift his, but they were fixed to the boards beneath my shoes. A heavy weight pressed down on my shoulders, making even the slightest movement impossible.

With no one to protect her, Fanny crawled to the far corner of the gallery. She curled into a ball and wrapped her arms about her knees in an attempt to shelter herself. But the laughter echoed around her head, battering at her, assaulting her senses and overwhelming her. At last, able to endure no more, all her energies exhausted or drained from her, Fanny keeled forward and sprawled across the floor.

The laughter shattered and died.

I gasped and the life returned to my limbs. Edmund sprang forward, reaching Fanny several strides ahead of me. He lifted her limp wrist and felt for her pulse.

"Is she . . . ?"

"Fainted, not dead."

Edmund nodded for me to fetch the candle, and lifted her in his arms. Together, we made the long and awkward trip back through the tunnel, the hot candle wax dripping from the holder and burning my fingers, the meager flame rapidly dwindling. Only seconds after we emerged into the foyer, it flickered and faded into a red glow. Another second and that, too, was gone.

Lily's ghost did not return to Abbey House. There was no need. Fanny never truly recovered. Her fear and need to escape had driven her inward, to a place only she could reach. And though she lived, it was not a life anyone would have envied her.

Not even Lily.

Two months later, Edmund and I were married. My confession had not been the startling announcement I had supposed. The detective he had hired, the stranger I had seen leaving the house, had given him a full accounting of Mrs. Medcroft's past.

He had been immersed in that accounting in the study that fateful evening and later shared with me the documents. They mentioned our hasty departure from London, prompted by Mrs. Broderick's accusations that the spiritualist had drained her of her meager inheritance then refused to countenance her client's continued presence in her home.

The documents included facts about my mother's past that explained a great deal. She, too, had been used by Mrs. Medcroft, but had not discovered the truth for five long years. It was my more experienced and less trusting father who had saved her. He had met her one evening and fallen in love. Thereafter, he had pursued her and slowly come to realize that any mystical powers that existed belonged to her.

Nineteen years ago, the scandal had rocked London. There were several newspaper articles describing the affair, and I wondered if Mother had pasted them into her scrapbook. Were those the pages that had been ripped out? I suspected they were.

Father had ruined himself by marrying her. Disowned by his family and scorned by his peers, he had retreated to Bristol and the quiet life we led. All for the woman he loved.

It restored my faith in him completely.

As for Edmund, it was not the truth that had upset him, only the thought that I had considered letting him remain in ignorance in order to become his wife. Given a few short minutes to deliberate, both on my confession and the short period I had been given to inform him, he had forgiven me and hurried to my room.

Instead, he had found me gone and the icy drafts had led him to the secret passage.

Neither Eglantine nor Winnie were invited to our small wedding. Only Dr. Rhodes and Ursula attended us, although she and I would never be as friendly as I might have hoped. It was difficult for both of us to forget the lies she had told me about Edmund, even though they had been prompted by her fear of losing her place in her brother's household.

Dr. Rhodes had been told only portions of the truth, but I think he surmised the rest. I fully expected the year would not close before he again proposed to Ursula.

This time, I didn't doubt that she would accept.

AVAILABLE NOW

THE COURT OF THREE SISTERS by Marianne Willman
An enthralling historical romance from the award-winning author of *Yesterday's Shadows* and *Silver Shadows*. The Court of Three Sisters was a hauntingly beautiful Italian villa where a prominent archaeologist took his three daughters: Thea, Summer, and Fanny. Into their circle came Col McCallum, who was determined to discover the real story behind the mysterious death of his mentor. Soon Col and Summer, in a race to unearth the fabulous ancient treasure that lay buried on the island, found the meaning of true love.

OUTRAGEOUS by Christina Dodd
The flamboyant Lady Marian Wenthaven, who cared nothing for the opinions of society, proudly claimed two-year-old Lionel as her illegitimate son. When she learned that Sir Griffith ap Powel, who came to visit her father's manor, was actually a spy sent by King Henry VII to watch her, she took Lionel and fled. But there was no escaping from Griffith and the powerful attraction between them.

CRAZY FOR LOVIN' YOU by Lisa G. Brown
The acclaimed author of *Billy Bob Walker Got Married* spins a tale of life and love in a small Tennessee town. After four years of exile, Terrill Carroll returns home when she learns of her mother's serious illness. Clashing with her stepfather, grieving over her mother, and trying to find a place in her family again, she turns to Jubal Kane, a man from the opposite side of the tracks who has a prison record, a bad reputation, and the face of a dark angel.

TAMING MARIAH by Lee Scofield
When Mariah kissed a stranger at the train station, everyone in the small town of Mead, Colorado, called her a hellion, but her grandfather knew she only needed to meet the right man. The black sheep son of a titled English family, Hank had come to the American West seeking adventure . . . until he kissed Mariah.

FLASH AND FIRE by Marie Ferrarella
Amanda Foster, who has learned the hard way how to make it on her own, finally lands the coveted anchor position on the five o'clock news. But when she falls for Pierce Alexander, the station's resident womanizer, is she ready to trust love again?

INDISCRETIONS by Penelope Thomas
The spellbinding story of a murder, a ghost, and a love that conquered all. During a visit to the home of enigmatic Edmund Llewelyn, Hilary Carewe uncovered a decade-old murder through rousing the spirit of Edmund's stepmother, Lily Llewelyn. As Edmund and Hilary were drawn together, the spirit grew stronger and more vindictive. No one was more affected by her presence than Hilary, whom Lily seemed determined to possess.

COMING NEXT MONTH

FOREVERMORE by Maura Seger
As the only surviving member of a family that had lived in the English village of Avebury for generations, Sarah Huxley was fated to protect the magical sanctuary of the tumbled stone circles and earthen mounds. But when a series of bizarre deaths at Avebury began to occur, Sarah met her match in William Devereux Faulkner, a level-headed Londoner, who had come to investigate. "Ms. Seger has a special magic touch with her lovers that makes her an enduring favorite with readers everywhere."—*Romantic Times*

PROMISES by Jeane Renick
From the award-winning author of *Trust Me* and *Always* comes a sizzling novel set in a small Ohio town, featuring a beautiful blind heroine, her greedy fiancé, two sisters in love with the same man, a mysterious undercover police officer, and a holographic will.

KISSING COUSINS by Carol Jerina
Texas rancher meets English beauty in this witty follow-up to *The Bridegroom*. When Prescott Trefarrow learned that it was he who was the true Earl of St. Keverne, and not his twin brother, he went to Cornwall to claim his title, his castle, and a multitude of responsibilities. Reluctantly, he became immersed in life at Ravens Lair Castle—and the lovely Lucinda Trefarrow.

HUNTER'S HEART by Christina Hamlett
A romantic suspense novel featuring a mysterious millionaire and a woman determined to figure him out. Many things about wealthy industrialist Hunter O'Hare intrigue Victoria Cameron. First of all, why did O'Hare have his ancestral castle moved to Virginia from Ireland, stone by stone? Secondly, why does everyone else in the castle act as if they have something to hide? And last, but not least, what does Hunter want from Victoria?

THE LAW AND MISS PENNY by Sharon Ihle
When U.S. Marshal Morgan Slater suffered a head injury and woke up with no memory, Mariah Penny conveniently supplied him with a fabricated story so that he wouldn't run her family's medicine show out of town. As he traveled through Colorado Territory with the Pennys, he and Mariah fell in love. Everything seemed idyllic until the day the lawman's memory returned.

PRIMROSE by Clara Wimberly
A passionate historical tale of forbidden romance between a wealthy city girl and a fiercely independent local man in the wilds of the Tennessee mountains. Rosalyn Hunte's heart was torn between loyalty to her family and the love of a man who wanted to claim her for himself.

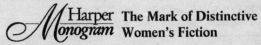 **Harper Monogram** The Mark of Distinctive Women's Fiction